Raves for Joe McKinney's
Dead City

"A rising star on the horror scene!"   —FearNet.com

"*Dead City* is much more than just another zombie novel.
It's got heart and humanity—a merciless, fast-paced, and
genuinely scary read that will leave you absolutely
breathless. Highly recommended!"

—Brian Keene

"Joe McKinney's *Dead City* is one of those rare books that
starts fast and never *ever* lets up. From page one to the
stunning climax, this book is a roller-coaster ride of action,
violence, and zombie horror. McKinney understands the
genre and relies on its strongest conventions while at the
same time adding new twists that make this book a
thoroughly enjoyable read."

—Jonathan Maberry, multiple Bram Stoker
Award–winning author of *Patient Zero*

"The pace never lets up as McKinney takes us through the
zombie apocalypse in real time—every second of terror is
explored in depth as the world goes to hell."

—David Wellington, author of *Monster Island*

d City is an absolute must-read for zombie lovers,
cKinney's excellent storytelling makes it a great
or anyone who loves the thrill of a gruesomely
ous page-turner."

—Fran Friel, Bram Stoker Award–nominated author
of *Mama's Boy* and *Other Dark Tales*

"*Dead City* is a zombie tour de force—the story moves along at breakneck speed and never lets up. Joe McKinney knows how to toy with readers' emotions, masterfully capturing the essence of humanity in the face of unspeakable horror."

—Amy Grech, author of *Apple of My Eye* and *Blanket of White*

"Joe McKinney's *Dead City* is a tense, thrill-a-page nightmare, written with great passion and authority. Surely one of the best zombie novels ever set down in blood."

—Lisa Morton, twotime Bram Stoker Award winner

"*Dead City* wastes no time jumping straight into mile-a-minute thrills and gruesome action. This seminal zombie novel culminates in a heart-wrenching finale, and I found that as the undead hordes multiplied, so too did my respect and admiration for author Joe McKinney. If you like your thrillers served with an extra helping of intensity, you're going to love *Dead City*!"

—Joel A. Sutherland, Bram Stoker Award–nominated author of *Frozen Blood*

"*Dead City* is an action-packed, pedal-to-the-metal zombie novel that never loses sight of its humanity. McKinney uses his background as a homicide detective to bring a level of realism to his vision of the apocalypse that is both urgent and frightening. A timely nightmare that you will not put down. I can't wait to see where this series leads."

—Gregory Lamberson, author of *Personal Demons* and *Johnny Gruesome*

FLESH EATERS

JOE MCKINNEY

PINNACLE BOOKS
Kensington Publishing Corp.
www.kensingtonbooks.com

PINNACLE BOOKS are published by

Kensington Publishing Corp.
119 West 40th Street
New York, NY 10018

All Kensington titles, imprints, and distributed lines are available at special quantity discounts for bulk purchases for sales promotions, premiums, fund-raising, educational, or institutional use. Special book excerpts or customized printings can also be created to fit specific needs. For details, write or phone the office of the Kensington special sales manager: Kensington Publishing Corp., 119 West 40th Street, New York, NY 10018, attn: Special Sales Department; phone 1-800-221-2647.

This book is a work of fiction. Names, characters, businesses, organizations, places, events, and incidents either are the product of the author's imagination or are used fictitiously. Any resemblance to actual persons, living or dead, events, or locales is entirely coincidental.

ISBN-13: 978-0-7860-2360-8
ISBN-10: 0-7860-2360-0

First printing: April 2011

10 9 8 7 6 5 4 3 2 1

Printed in the United States of America

Life is the new wealth.

—Max Brooks, "Closure, Limited"

CHAPTER 1

Eleanor Norton's earliest memories were of hurricanes. As a little girl, she had seen Rita and Ike and Jacob rip Houston apart, their winds shearing off her neighbors' rooftops and sending them sailing away like kites. She remembered her family huddling like frightened animals in the hall closet, her mother trying to be brave but still squeezing her so tightly she'd left bruises on Eleanor's skin. Then, in high school, she'd lived through Brendan and Louis, storms that carried shrimp boats ten miles inland and blanketed the city with ocean water that dappled like molten copper in the morning sun. She still carried memories of water moccasins gliding past the top of the swing set in her backyard and pickup trucks floating like rafts down her street and grown men on their rooftops, crying without shame for all that they had lost.

She never outgrew that fear of storms. Even now at thirty-five, a mother of a beautiful twelve-year-old girl, a wife to a wonderful man, a looming hurricane could still reduce her to jelly. The wind and the slashing rain and the overwhelming floodwaters touched some deep atavistic impulse inside her to run for shelter. Cataclysmic storms were a fear many Houstonians lived with, though most never talked about it. But now, as she stood in line at the Wal-Mart, she could sense her own terror mirrored in the scurrying anxiousness of nearly everyone around her. Like her, they just wanted to buy their water and batteries and cans of Sterno and get home to their families before the storm made landfall. Waiting in line like this was maddening.

Eleanor had been doing fine in the days leading up to Hurricane Hector. She was working in the Houston Police Department's Emergency Operations Command, attending all the briefings, and bringing home what she learned to her family, making sure they were ready. The ritual of getting prepared had helped to keep the fear at bay. But that morning, when she left for work, the sky had been a bloody red, and all the terror she'd felt as a child came back in a flood. She'd gone to work—and tried to work, she really did—but she was distracted and irritable. Captain Mark Shaw, her boss, had noticed. He noticed everything; and, in truth, it hadn't been hard to tell what was going on with her. She kept returning to the main window, the one that looked out over the green lawns of the University of Houston. Outside the sky was changing from a horror-movie red to a windy, sodden gray, and she couldn't take her eyes off it.

Captain Shaw, who, despite his reputation, was not without mercy, sent her home.

"You'll do more good with your family anyway," he told her. "We got this. Go on home."

"Really? You're okay with me leaving?" she asked.

"It's no big deal. Everything that can be done has already been done. Nothing else to do here but ride it out. You can do that at home just as easily."

"I really appreciate this, Captain."

He dismissed her with a wave of his hand.

"I'll see you in the morning," he said. "Worse comes to

worst, and we get some bad flooding, I'll send a boat by for you."

And so she'd gone to Wal-Mart for a few last-minute things, her fear mounting as the wind picked up and the sky grew darker. When she finally made it through the checkout line and walked outside to the parking lot, the gray sky above her was limned with an eerie chemical green. The air was dense as a wet towel against her skin. She swallowed nervously, ducked her head against a gusting breeze, and rushed to her car.

She hardly remembered the drive home.

But once she was home, she and Jim and their daughter Madison still had so much to do to get ready. She could hear Jim with his power drill out on the front porch putting up plywood over the glass, and, looking out the little window above the kitchen sink, she mouthed a silent plea for him to hurry.

It was getting really scary out there.

Part of Bays Bayou ran through the greenbelt behind their house, and Hector's storm surge had caused its waters to rise significantly. Already there was an inch or so of brackish water covering their lawn, and a sharp, howling wind sent lines of lacy silver waves through it.

They were surrounded by cottonwood and pines and giant oaks, and the same wind was tossing their branches back and forth, filling the air with leaves. Earlier that afternoon Hurricane Hector had been upgraded from a Category Three to a Category Five storm, meaning that it would blow inland with winds over one hundred fifty-five miles per hour; and though she tried to suppress the thought, she kept having visions of a sustained blast of wind breaking off tree limbs and shooting them like arrows through the sides of their home. It had happened before, during Rita and Ike, when she was a little girl.

She shook the memories of those storms from her mind and focused her attention out the window. From where she stood she could just see a corner of Ms. Hester's house across the street. The woman was eighty-four and struggling with what Eleanor suspected was incipient Alzheimer's disease; but she was a sweet old lady and, with both Jim and Eleanor's parents dead, had even filled in as the grandmother that Madison had never known. There had been several years, right around the time Madison was starting school and Eleanor was still slaving away as a detective in the Houston Police Department's Sex Crimes Unit and Jim was working at Gulfport Petrochemical, when they hadn't been able to afford child care. They were working all the time, but still miserably broke. Ms. Hester had come to their rescue. She took care of Madison during those years—cooked her dinners, taught her to paint, even picked her up from school on early-release days—and in so doing had earned a special place in Eleanor's heart. In all their hearts, actually.

And so it was with considerably more than neighborly concern that Eleanor watched the wind thrashing the pecan trees that surrounded Ms. Hester's little one-story white house. Madison had spent the last six summers collecting pecans from those trees, she and Ms. Hester shelling them and turning them into pecan pies and candied pralines. The trees were beautiful, even useful in their way, but they were notoriously ill-suited for bad weather. The wood was soft enough that the weight of the nuts alone could cause limbs to snap off in late summer. A strong Category Five hurricane wind would blast the trees to bits. How long would it take, she wondered, before one of those bits lanced through the roof, or a side wall, sending shards of glass through the house like bird shot from a twelve gauge?

"Mom, you okay?"

Eleanor half turned from the sink but said nothing.

"Uh, Mom, hello?"

This time Eleanor turned around. The thick note of sarcasm in Madison's voice was something new, something she'd picked up, Eleanor suspected, from Susie Tyler and Brandy Moore, two girls who had just recently become Madison's closest friends. The three girls spent nearly every day that summer running around together, sleeping over at each other's houses, learning how to be teenagers together. It was natural behavior, Eleanor knew, but that didn't mean she had to like it. Susie especially seemed like a bad influence, always so loud and disrespectful to the other girls' parents. She had an annoying habit of making everything a competition between her and Madison, never missing a chance to gloat over some small victory or rub in some awkward moment on Madison's part. And at twelve, Madison was having plenty of those.

Still, Eleanor backed off from actually telling Madison she couldn't hang out with Susie. Her own mother had been a shrew when it came to Eleanor's friends and had taken an almost sadistic delight in pointing out how much she disliked the girls Eleanor ran around with. It had made her afraid to have friends over, and Eleanor promised herself she wouldn't be the same way, even if it meant swallowing the urge to fire a broadside here and there.

"I think it's full, Mom," Madison said, nodding at the sink.

Eleanor glanced behind her and saw that the five-gallon plastic water jug she'd been filling at the sink was indeed running over. She turned off the tap, poured off a little, and then screwed down the cap.

She lifted it from the sink with a grunt and put it on the floor next to the other four jugs she'd just filled.

"That's the last of them anyway," she said.

Madison was sitting cross-legged on the linoleum floor, putting cans of soup into a cardboard box, but she paused long enough to study her mother.

"Mom, are you okay?"

"I'm fine, honey."

"You sure? You kinda zoned out there for a second."

Eleanor smiled, but didn't respond. There were times, certain moments when Madison had her head turned just the right way, when Eleanor could see how much her daughter really looked like Jim. It was in the profile, mainly. They had the same little upturn at the point of their nose, the same tapered chin, the same little tiny ears. Madison was the adolescent girl version of her father; but whereas those same features gave Jim an intelligent, studious aspect—especially when he wore his glasses—in Madison they became stunningly beautiful.

That girl is going to break a million hearts one day, Eleanor thought, and it was an idea that both terrified and delighted her.

"Why don't you take those upstairs, okay?" Eleanor said, nodding at the box of soup.

"I can't lift it."

"What? Sure you can."

"No, Mom," she said, the sarcasm oozing back into her voice, "I can't. It weighs, like, a whole ton."

"No, it doesn't. And don't say 'like.' You know I hate the way that sounds."

Madison sighed and made a dramatic show of rolling her eyes.

"Fine," Eleanor said. "We'll get your dad to do it. In the meantime, find something else you *can* carry. What's next on the family list?"

Madison huffed indignantly, then picked up a yellow, coil-bound notebook that Eleanor had prepared to guide the family during a hurricane. She called it their family disaster plan. It contained nearly everything they would need to know about the contents of their supply kits and evacuation routes, plus contingency plans for getting the family back together again after the storm, should they get separated. Each member of the family also had a backpack that contained an individual ninety-six-hour supply kit, a personal version of the yellow disaster plan notebook, family photos, important numbers, and a couple hundred dollars in cash. The backpacks were already upstairs. What Eleanor and Madison were doing now was checking off the family supply kit for sheltering in place and carting the contents upstairs, just in case the floodwaters swamped the first floor of their house.

Madison read from the list, pointing to items as she said their names. "Next up is sanitation. Toilet paper, soap, ladytime stuff"—Madison's eyebrows raised slightly at her mother's euphemism for feminine hygiene products—"disinfectant, bleach, garbage bags and ties. Why do you have those on here twice?"

"What?"

"Garbage bags and ties. You've got them here and in the Miscellaneous section."

"The sanitation section ones are for when you have to go to the bathroom. There should be a bucket with a tight-fitting lid there, too."

Madison's lips parted slightly, her nose crinkling in disgust. "A bucket? Mom, that's gross."

"No, that's survival, kiddo. You've never been through one of these storms. You don't know how bad it can get. I remember when I was a girl the water was off for two weeks after Hurricane Ike. What do you think happens when the toilets stop flushing?"

"Well, yeah, but . . ." Madison trailed off, her gaze shifting to the box of plastic trash bags as if she was suddenly too grossed out to touch them.

"You'll live," Eleanor said. "If it's all there, just take it upstairs."

The smile disappeared from Eleanor's face as she watched

her daughter cart yet another cardboard box of supplies up-stairs. There were rough times ahead, and the girl was in for one hell of an education on the fury of nature.

The thought sent Eleanor even deeper into her own head. She had talked with Jim an awful lot lately about how fast Madison was growing up. Her thirteenth birthday was only two months away, but the changes had already started. She and Madison had had the talk about the lady time, and it had been a lot harder, a lot more embarrassing, than Eleanor had expected it to be. But in a way that talk had prepared her to think of her daughter as a woman, something that Jim was having a much harder time doing. Perhaps it was Madison's smile, that giggly little smile of hers that so perfectly re-called the way she looked as a toddler. Or perhaps it was just Jim's stubborn streak. Eleanor wasn't sure. But whatever the reason, he seemed determined to avoid the issue. He still called Madison his little girl, and in fact had started using the phrase more and more in recent months, which indicated to Eleanor that he knew the truth, at least on some level, but was unwilling to face it.

She couldn't blame him. Not really. There were times—plenty of times, in fact—that she didn't want to face it, either.

Jim's electric drill had gone silent as he moved to a new window. The wind, too, quieted for a moment. And in that lull, Eleanor heard the sound of arguing from across the street. She craned her head out the window, and what she saw there made her chest tighten with both pity and rage.

Ms. Hester was standing in the front yard, looking smaller and even frailer than she had earlier that day, when Eleanor had passed her on her way into work. The wind was billow-ing her housedress out to one side, and her arms were crossed over her chest in a gesture that made her look com-pletely helpless. Rain rings formed chain-mail patterns in the water at her feet. Standing at the edge of her lawn, next to a beat-to-hell red pickup, was her grandson, Bobby,

When the guys at work mentioned meth heads, Bobby Hester was the image that flared up in Eleanor's mind. He was tall and lanky, so skinny his clothes fit him like a potato sack on a flagpole. He wore his filthy blond hair down to his shoulders, and there were tattoos all up and down his arms, where the veins stood out like electrical cords beneath his skin.

He was the one Eleanor had heard yelling, and as she watched he opened the passenger door of his truck and put Ms. Hester's TV inside.

That manipulative, thieving little bastard, she thought.

Though she couldn't hear what Ms. Hester was saying, she could figure it out without any real difficulty. Ms. Hester was scared. She wanted him to stay with her during the storm. She was probably begging him to stay.

But Bobby Hester would never agree to something like that.

He had miraculously reappeared in her life about two years ago, at the same time she started slipping a little from the Alzheimer's. To Eleanor it was no coincidence. He was a wolf sensing an easy meal, nothing more. Certainly not the long-lost grandson he no doubt claimed to be. Eleanor had tried to say as much, but Ms. Hester wouldn't listen to a word of it. She adamantly refused to see Bobby as bad news. She welcomed him into her home. And he repaid her kindness by robbing her blind.

Now he was telling her to stop her whining. That he'd be back. That he just wanted to take her electronic stuff someplace safe. She wasn't holding back, was she? There wasn't a TV someplace she hadn't told him about?

The fucking bastard is gonna pawn everything she owns so he can get cash for his meth, Eleanor thought, and suddenly the image of her putting a bullet in his brain was very strong, and more than a little satisfying.

A knock on the window made her jump. It was Jim, looking in on her, his knuckles still poised at the glass.

She undid the latch and opened the window.

"You're seeing this, right?" he said.

"Yeah." Her pistol was upstairs in her backpack, and she couldn't help but wonder if she'd be able to hit Bobby from here. One good head shot would be all it'd take. "That man's a slime ball."

"That's true," Jim said. "You want me to go over there and tell her to stay with us?"

"I tried that this morning. She kept saying Bobby was going to stay with her tonight. That's all she would say. 'Bobby's coming. I'll be okay, Bobby's comin' over.' "

"Yeah, well, I don't think that's gonna happen."

"Don't you think I know that?" she snapped, and then instantly wanted to pull the words back. "Sorry."

He nodded. "It makes me angry, too."

"Yeah."

He had a hand on the windowsill. He was filthy from putting up the plywood screens and cleaning up the stuff from the yard that might blow around during the storm and cause damage, but she didn't care. It was good to be home with him. She put her own hand on top of his and squeezed.

He looked past her to the kitchen. "Where's Maddie?"

"Upstairs. We're gonna need you to carry the food boxes."

"Sure."

In the distance, lightning flashed across the sky. A roll of thunder followed along close on its heels. The air smelled ominous, heavy with the scent of salt and sea.

"You can smell it, can't you?" he said. "The storm's getting close."

"Yeah."

Across the street, Bobby's pickup fired up with a loud snarl, and he sped off, leaving Ms. Hester standing in her front yard. Ms. Hester watched him go, obviously frightened, then slowly turned and went back inside her house.

"What do you want to do about that?" Jim asked.

"She's family. We'll take her in. As soon as we're done loading all this stuff upstairs I'll go over there and get her."

"And if she won't come? You can't make her leave if she doesn't want to."

"She's family, Jim. I won't let her ride this thing out alone."

"Okay," he said, and with that they closed the window and Jim dropped the last sheet of plywood into place over top of it.

The first heavy band of rain came about thirty minutes later. It slammed into the side of the Nortons' house in enormous wind-driven blasts, beating against the roof and the exterior walls, roaring like a passing freight train. It lasted less than two minutes, and then slackened off to a steady, needling patter.

They were in the game room upstairs. Madison's room was next door, but they had tacitly decided that the whole family would sleep here. Now father and daughter were rolling out sleeping bags, the two of them laughing over some stupid thing Jim had said. They seemed to be having a pretty good time of it, Eleanor noticed. She hadn't heard Madison laughing like this in a long while. Not even the wind and the rain outside seemed to bother her, at least not yet. She had her daddy with her, the two of them too absorbed in being goofy to be afraid of a little wind and rain. Jim was treating this like a big adventure, at least in front of Madison, and Eleanor was glad for that. It would help Madison to remain calm when things got really bad here in another few hours, and perhaps it would also help Jim to hold on to his little girl for a little while longer. A crisis like this, it would be terrible for the great wide world outside their house; but here, inside, the Norton family was in a good place.

Eleanor and Jim had met fourteen years before, back when she was a brand-new patrolwoman working every extra job she could find just to make the rent on a rattrap apartment on Houston's lower east side.

She was working security at a Flogging Molly concert the night he came into her life. He was with a group of his friends from his college days. He was cute, she thought. A little nerdy, maybe—certainly more of a nerd than the cops she was used to hanging out with—but cute. He kept coming up to her, using really weak excuses to strike up a conversation; and as much as her cop training told her to disengage so she could watch the crowd as she was being paid to do, there was a very human part of her that liked the attention.

During a break between songs he worked up the nerve to ask for her number.

"No way," she said. "Not while I'm working."

"Not while you're working? What does that mean?"

"It means I don't give out my number to strange men while I'm working."

"I'm not strange."

"You know what I mean," she said, smiling despite herself.

"You can trust me," he said. "I'm a good guy. Come on, I don't bite."

Her gaze shifted from the crowd back to him. He was leaning against a wall next to a dartboard, trying to look cool, but only managing a barely contained nervousness. He *was* cute, though. She couldn't deny that.

"I'll tell you what. How about you give me your number, and I'll think about it?"

His smile grew even wider. He hurriedly scribbled down

his number on the back of his business card and handed it to her.

"I usually get off around six," he said.

"I'll think about it," she answered.

And she had thought about it. For two days she thought about it. She hadn't realized it going into the job, but dating options for a female cop are few. She could date other cops, and a lot of girls did, but there wasn't a sewing circle anywhere that could gossip like a bunch of cops, and the girls who did date their fellow officers quickly developed reputations as sluts, or bitches, or psychos, or whatever, whether it was deserved or not.

The other option, dating a guy from outside the department, a civilian, was harder than it sounded. Most of the men she met came into her sphere because they were in the process of committing some kind of crime. And even if they weren't doing something illegal, finding time to go out with them around the demands of a rotating police schedule was nearly impossible. Plus (and this wasn't obvious, but it was something that nearly every female officer she knew had experienced) most men who weren't cops were intimidated by a girl who walked around with a gun in her purse . . . and who knew how to use it.

But Jim Norton wasn't that way. He didn't seem intimidated by her at all. He'd made her feel special from the first moment he'd tried his dorky lines on her, and in the end, she'd called and asked him out. They were married eight months later.

Memories of those early days together always made her smile, but unfortunately her reverie didn't last long, for just then the shutters started to rattle. Another blast of rain and wind swept over the house, carrying with it a train wreck sound and the horrible feeling that God's shadow was passing overhead.

"I need to go get her," Eleanor said.

Jim, who had rocked back on his haunches, a corner of Madison's sleeping bag still in his hand, nodded.

"Wait for this one to pass first," he said.

"Mom."

Eleanor looked at her daughter. The smile and the giggle were gone. For the first time there was fear in the girl's eyes. The knowledge that something big and angry had them in its sights was finally starting to sink in.

Eleanor crossed the room and put her arms around her.

"I'm gonna bring Ms. Hester here with us," Eleanor said.

"Mom, you can't go out in that."

"Sweetie, we can't leave her to face that alone. It'll stop in a second. I won't be gone long."

"Promise?"

Eleanor pulled her daughter close. "I promise."

Five days earlier, a Category Three hurricane named Gabriella had zeroed in on Matagorda Bay, just south down the coast from Houston. Houston was expected to get the dirty side of the storm, and all the newscasters prophesied a Katrina-like disaster. A massive evacuation was ordered. Nearly four million people fled the Houston area, turning the highways that led to San Antonio and Dallas into parking lots. For two days, the city of Houston turned into a ghost town.

But Gabriella didn't cooperate.

She fizzled to a weak tropical storm while still at sea, and when she made landfall, all she'd been able to muster was a good soaking for the grass and a couple of broken windows along the coastline.

Houstonians returned home, resentful of the ordered evacuation. It was why so many had ignored the current order to evacuate now that Hector was on the way.

In the back of her mind, Eleanor had hoped that Hector would blow itself out the same way Gabriella had, but when she stepped out her front door, all hope of that disappeared from her mind. Even the biggest trees were tossing wildly back and forth. Trash and leaves filled the air. Ocean-scented rain moved across the lawn in silvery, wind-blown curtains. A rainbow-colored canopy from a child's backyard swing set tumbled down her sidewalk.

On the other side of the street, the pecan trees that surrounded Ms. Hester's house were slamming against her kitchen wall, stray limbs raking across the roof, kicking up shingles and sending them airborne on the wind like playing cards.

"You stay here," Jim said. "I'll go get her."

"No," Eleanor said, barely aware that she was using the harsh, clipped tone of her cop's voice. "Let me. You stay with Madison."

He looked indecisive, as though he was torn between his male instincts to take the risk and his knowledge that she was the one trained for this kind of thing.

"I'll be okay," she assured him, but without softening her tone. It was best not to give him a chance to finish the debate, so that he wouldn't talk himself into doing something stupid. There was no time for that. "You stay with Madison. Keep her calm."

And with that she ducked her head and stepped off the porch and into the wind.

The rain needled at her skin. Standing upright was harder than she expected. She had to tense the muscles in her thighs just to keep her balance. The ground was spongy beneath her feet. An inch of water stood on the ground, and everywhere she looked she saw the crawfish that had washed up from Bays Bayou scurrying through the grass.

To the south was a bank of black clouds that stretched across the horizon like an angry, roiling cliff. Charleston

Street stretched a good half mile out in front of her before curving out of sight. Beyond the curve was the flat greenish-black surface of Bays Bayou, now flooding the areas adjacent to its banks, and beyond the water was an industrial park of concrete and glass buildings. From where she stood she could just see a line of those buildings disappearing beneath the bottom of the storm wall. To Eleanor, it looked like they were being eaten.

She was too stunned to move. She stood there, mouth open in awe, watching the approaching monster.

A loud crack to her right snapped her out of the moment and she turned just in time to see a large limb from one of Ms. Hester's pecan trees come crashing down on the corner of the house. It twisted in the wind, sagged, then scraped down the side of house, ripping the plywood covers Jim had put over her windows from their brackets. The glass behind the plywood exploded with a series of muffled pops.

But the tree didn't stop moving. Its dense cluster of leaves caught the wind like a sail and pulled it down the length of the house, tearing down a section of the wall as it tumbled away from the approaching storm.

"Oh my God," she said.

She couldn't believe what she was seeing. In a crazy, terrible, unreal way, it looked like the house was being zippered open by an old-style can opener, the pecan tree shredding the wooden siding with unbelievable speed.

"No!" she shouted.

The tree tore free of the house and sailed down the street as though it were being dragged behind an invisible truck.

Eleanor watched it go, then ran to the house.

She pounded on the front door, kicked it with everything she had, even threw her shoulder into it. "Ms. Hester! Betty Jo! Open the door. It's me, Eleanor."

Nothing.

She threw her shoulder at it one more time, then ran for a

damaged section of the wall, shielding her face from the wind with her arm as she searched for a way inside.

The gash left by the pecan tree had torn the kitchen wall in half. Shredded electrical wires extruded from the lath, their jagged ends reaching for her like dangerous fingers. The wind was roaring in her ears. The air around her smelled of musty insulation and ocean rain and crushed vegetation.

"Ms. Hester?" she called out. "Can you hear me?"

Nothing.

She was really scared now. Her face hurt from the pelting rain. *You gotta get inside right now*, she thought. *There's no time. Go, go, go!*

Eleanor climbed over the jagged fragment of kitchen wall. Inside, the house was a mess. Water was already pooling on the living room floor and dripping down the walls. Debris was strewn everywhere. A large recliner was upside down against the back wall of the living room, papers and pictures swirling around it.

Eleanor ran for the hall closet. Back in May, when all the literature about hurricanes had first started appearing in the papers, Eleanor had told Ms. Hester to take shelter there if she was trapped at her house during a hurricane. She threw open the door, but the closet was empty.

A sudden surge in the wind threw her against the wall, yanking the doorknob out of her hand.

"Ms. Hester?"

Her only answer was the wind ripping into the house, tearing the walls apart.

From somewhere behind her she heard a loud snap, followed by the sound of walls breaking apart.

No, she thought, shaking her head. *That is not possible.*

But it was happening. The house was buckling, the timber inside the walls snapping like bones as the floor shuddered beneath her feet.

Where are you, Betty Jo? Come on, damn it.

And then a memory surfaced in her mind. In the Academy they taught young police officers how to handle calls for missing toddlers. Abducted children, her instructors had told her, are rare outside of the movies. You get a call for a missing four-year-old, the first place you look is under the beds. The parents will tell you they've looked everywhere, but they're too scared to focus on the obvious. Chances are you'll find the kid there, under the parents' bed, playing, hiding, maybe even sleeping.

A small table along the hall wall began to sway and dance. All the pictures along the wall fell to the floor. A few blankets floated on the air, buoyed by the wind. Everything happened so fast all she could do was stand still and gawk at the destruction.

Then the floor shifted beneath her, and she ran for the back bedroom. The wind had blown debris into the doorway, but most of the room looked the same as it always did, neat and tidy. A flash of lightning filled the room, spilling light across the quilt at the foot of the bed. Eleanor got down on her hands and knees, lifted the bed skirt, and saw Ms. Hester curled into a fetal ball. She was trembling.

"Betty Jo, take my hand. I'm gonna get you out of here."

No response. The woman was in shock. Her eyes were open, glittering like coins caught by firelight, but they were unfocused and vague. Eleanor could hardly believe that the woman had made herself so small.

"Betty Jo, please. Take my hand. I have to get you out of here."

Eleanor tried to reach for her, but Ms. Hester had wedged herself deep under the bed, just out of reach.

"Please," Eleanor said. "There's no time."

Not gonna happen, Eleanor thought.

She stood up, grabbed the wooden bed frame, and tried to lift it. If she couldn't pull Betty Jo out, she'd throw the bed off her and scoop her up fireman-style. But it was a huge wooden sleigh bed, impossibly heavy. She strained against its weight with everything she had, but only managed to raise it a few inches off the floor.

Her fingers were slipping, the muscles in her arms and back and neck screaming at her to drop the weight.

"Come on," she said. "Please."

"Eleanor! Where are you?"

It was Jim's voice, coming from somewhere in the living room.

"In here," she answered. "Help me!"

The next moment he was by her side, his hands next to hers under the bed frame. She heard him grunting, felt his body tense next to hers, and the next instant the bed was rising, coming up above her head.

"Get her out of there," Jim said. "I'll hold it."

Eleanor dropped to her knees again and scrambled under the bed. Ms. Hester's body was curled so tightly into a ball Eleanor had trouble moving her.

"Hurry!" Jim said.

"Betty Jo, come on," Eleanor said. She slid an arm under the woman's trembling body and pulled her out from under the bed. "Clear!" she yelled to Jim.

He let the bed fall, then reached down and scooped Ms. Hester up from the floor.

"Find us a way out," he said. "I'll carry her."

The wind had blown a pile of crushed furniture and tree limbs and trash into the living room, and Eleanor had to climb over it to reach the front door. She kicked it once, twice, and it burst open as the wind caught it and ripped it from its hinges. In disbelief, Eleanor watched it slide across the yard and down the street.

But there was no time to wait. The roaring wind in the doorway created enough suction to pull her out, and she had to grab hold of the frame just to keep from getting carried away like the door.

Beyond the doorway, the sky had grown impenetrably dark. Rain was slashing sideways across her field of vision. She steadied herself against the wind, then reached in and took Ms. Hester from Jim.

"You got her?" he asked, yelling to be heard over the wind.

"Yeah, come on."

He scrambled out of the doorway after her and together, the two of them carried Betty Jo Hester across the street and into their house. Madison was waiting for them. She threw a towel over Ms. Hester and helped Eleanor clean her up.

Ms. Hester started to come around after they had her dry and wrapped in blankets.

She looked at Madison and tried to smile, but couldn't. Her gaze shifted to Eleanor, and the sadness in her eyes nearly took Eleanor's breath away.

"He didn't come back," she said. "Bobby didn't come back. He said he'd be right back for me. Why didn't he come back?"

Eleanor didn't know how to answer her. She leaned forward and kissed the old woman on the forehead. Only then did she realize how much she ached, how every muscle in her body was trembling. She looked around the room, taking in the sight of her family around her, and then she let out a heavy sigh.

They spent the next thirteen hours huddled in their game room like scared animals as the hand of God passed overhead.

The next morning they stepped out onto their front porch and gazed at the destruction.

Where before there had been a suburban neighborhood of well-paved roads and wide, green lawns, there was now only water. Every house was an island, every one of them missing shingles from the roofs. Eleanor stepped to the edge of her porch and looked down. She could barely see the grass down there, beneath a foot of brown water.

Out in the street it was deeper. She could see the roofs of cars poking up above the level of the water, which was flowing sluggishly to the south. She watched a large mattress float down the street. It hit the roof of a pickup and turned a slow pirouette before continuing on its way.

Somewhere off in the distance, a dog was howling. It was a lonely, frightened sound that sent a shiver across Eleanor's skin. She and Jim had debated about getting Madison a cat or a dog for the last several months, Eleanor saying no, absolutely not, and Jim, wishy-washy, as he always was when it came to saying no to their daughter, willing to give in to just about anything Madison wanted. She had hated being the bad guy when Madison asked, pleaded with them, for a pet. But now, listening to that terrified animal's howls, she was glad she'd stuck to her guns.

"Oh, wow!"

Eleanor looked back at Madison. The girl was wide-eyed, looking at all the water.

"It's something, isn't it, kiddo?"

"Yeah. Oh my God. Ms. Hester, look at your house."

Madison pointed across the street. A large pecan tree limb was jutting out of the house, the gash in the kitchen wall packed with green leaves and garbage.

"Did that happen while you guys were over there?"

"No," Eleanor said. "After."

She chanced a quick glance at Ms. Hester, who was staring at her house with an empty, shocked expression on her face. Eleanor put a hand on her daughter's shoulder and made a silent gesture for her not to say anything more about it.

To her credit, Madison picked up on the signals immediately, and the fascinated smile slipped from her face.

Good girl, Eleanor thought.

A motorboat came into view. The pilot eased back on the throttle and let it coast up to the curb in front of the Norton's house.

"Sergeant Norton," he said. "Good morning, ma'am."

"Good morning, Hank," Eleanor said.

The pilot's name was Hank Gleason. He was a member of SWAT Team 3, on loan to the EOC for as long as the city of Houston was in Phase III of the Disaster Mobilization Plan. Gleason was wearing green SWAT fatigues with a DayGlo green safety vest over top of his shirt. On his head was a floppy boonie cap, pushed far back, away from his sunglasses.

"How y'all doin'?" he called out. "Everybody all right?"

Eleanor couldn't help but smile. He had that effect on most women.

"We're doing fine, Hank. You come to pick me up?"

"Yes, ma'am," he said, tipping his hat to Ms. Hester and Madison. "Captain Shaw says if it ain't too much trouble he'd like you to come back to work."

Jim caught the bow of the bass boat and guided it up alongside the porch.

"Thank you, sir," Hank said.

He and Jim shook hands.

"How is it out there, Hank? It got pretty rough here last night."

For the first time that Eleanor could remember, the smile disappeared from Hank's face. His shoulders sagged and, in that moment, the unflappable SWAT veneer dropped away and he looked utterly exhausted.

And then, just as quickly, the smile was back again.

"Ma'am, I don't envy you folks over at the campus. You're gonna have your hands full."

"Why, what happened?"

"All the evacuees from Galveston, Texas City, Dickinson, those places," Hank said, "a lot of 'em were stranded on the freeway by the floodwaters. Captain Shaw decided to open the campus to as many people as it could hold. People've been coming in by the thousands since before sunup. The place looks like its own little city now."

Eleanor didn't know what to say. Captain Shaw was the incident commander for the entire region for the duration of the crises, but he didn't have the authority to throw open the doors of a university to a bunch of stranded motorists. Something like that would take an act of Congress or an order from the governor or something. What Hank was suggesting was . . . it was crazy. It was career suicide on Shaw's part.

"So, what, he just opened up all the dorms and let anybody who needed a place to stay come on in?"

"Yes, ma'am, that's about the size of it. The school's got restaurants, a hospital, its own power station. Captain Shaw opened it all up to the public."

"I can't believe that," she said. "That's . . . that's nuts."

"It's no joke, ma'am. I ain't never seen anything like it. Most of the folks they're taking in are the ones who aren't strong enough to continue on their own. Old people, families with young kids, sick people, you know? But they got folks everywhere, wandering around like they've just been dropped on the moon. Nobody knows what the hell's goin on."

Eleanor nodded, but she was still trying to imagine the scope of the gamble Captain Shaw was making.

"I can't believe this, Hank. Did the campus agree to let Shaw do this?"

"Ma'am, I don't know. Captain Shaw told me to come and get you, and here I am. All I can tell you is it's gonna be a mess when you get there."

"Yeah, sounds like it. Well, I guess we should get going."

"Yes, ma'am, I think so."

Eleanor turned and kissed Jim and Madison and climbed on to the bass boat.

It would be three more days before she made it back home.

CHAPTER 2

Captain Mark Shaw, head of the Houston Police Department's Emergency Operations Command, had slept in his uniform again. He'd been doing that a lot lately. Groaning, he sat up on the side of the bed and tried to stretch, but a sharp pain in his back made him flinch abruptly. He closed his eyes and waited for the pain to subside. Instead, an acid burn climbed up his throat. *Looks like it's gonna be aspirin and Rolaids for breakfast again*, he thought bitterly. He'd been doing that an awful lot lately, too. How in the hell had he let himself get to this point? He was only fifty-eight, for Christ's sake. It hadn't been that long ago when he could do a week's worth of twenty-hour shifts standing on his head.

But these days, there were too many headaches, too many backaches. Heartburn was getting to be a daily companion.

And he knew why, too. That part wasn't a mystery.

It was the job.

A police career wears down every cop who takes the oath. Good man or crooked, a hard worker or a slug, it just doesn't matter. Sooner or later, the job eats you up and shits you out its backside.

The thing was—and it hurt more than a little to finally

admit to himself that it was true—Shaw honestly thought it would never happen to him. Lesser men, sure. But he had somehow sold himself on the idea that he was made of iron.

Good God, he thought, *were you ever wrong*.

Rubbing the sleep from his eyes, he looked over at the clock.

Quarter past eight.

That meant he'd been asleep for just under two hours. Since Hurricane Hector seven days earlier he'd been working nonstop, managing only a catnap here and there . . . and there had been very few of those. Now, his exhaustion ran bone deep. With a heavy sigh he rose from the Red Cross cot he'd moved into this little storage closet off the main floor of the EOC's temporary headquarters, pulled on his gun belt, straightened his uniform, and walked onto the main floor.

Sergeant Eleanor Norton, his XO, was standing with a few other members of his staff, going over a map of the Houston Ship Channel. They made eye contact; then she excused herself from the huddle of officers and walked over to him.

"Anything new?" he asked.

"Yes, sir. A bunch. What do you want first, the bad news or the really bad news?"

He smiled tiredly. "Break me in easy."

"Okay. I got another call from the ATF just a little while ago. They're starting to get really uptight about the *Santa Fe*."

Shaw nodded. He'd seen that one coming. Seven days earlier Hurricane Hector had sent a sixteen-foot storm surge up the mouth of the Houston Ship Channel. That wave had wrecked countless offshore oil rigs and cargo freighters and homes and stripped massive amounts of trees from the landscape. It had also created a public safety nightmare. Every evacuation route out of the area was blocked. So too were most of the ways into the area. That left 2.5 million people homeless, screaming for help, with no power, no sanitation, no way out, and no way for rescue workers to get in.

Then, two days ago, while they were still trying to recover from Hector, they got hit by Kyle. Kyle made Hector look like a rainy day in the park. That storm had sent a thirty-four-foot storm surge right up the same course, almost as if it were on a set of rails, and this time, the waters came in to stay. Though Kyle was only two days in the past, the experts were already saying that the one-two punch of back-to-back storms had changed the shape of the Texas coastline forever, with most of the land between Galveston and Southwest Houston now permanently underwater.

And the storm surge had done something else, too, something the experts had never predicted. It had created a secondary wave that kicked up all the debris and floating chemicals and topsoil and dead animals and houses and sewage and leaking oil from the offshore drills and turned it all into a wall of liquid mud that pushed inland as far as the 610 Loop, nearly 45 miles. Everything that wall of mud touched was now buried in the muck and irredeemably polluted.

And that included a Venezuelan cargo freighter called the *Santa Fe*. According to the manifest her crew had forwarded to authorities at the Houston Ship Channel, she was loaded with some twelve hundred tons of ammonia gelatin dynamite, an underwater explosive used primarily by the oil companies to dismantle offshore oil drills. She was currently beached on a vast muddy plain near the suburban community of Deer Park, completely unsecured. An ATF special agent named Vernon Laidlaw had been crawling up Shaw's ass for the last two days trying to get the cargo secured.

"Did you tell him it's on our to-do list?" Shaw asked Eleanor.

"Yes, sir, I told him."

"And what did he say?

"Same thing as last time. He reminded us of the Homeland Security guidelines concerning unexploded ordnance. I've heard it enough I can quote the whole regulation chapter and verse, if you want to hear it."

"No thanks."

"Captain," Eleanor said, "I don't think he's gonna quit calling. He sounded pretty pissed off."

"Yeah, well, maybe he ought to come down here and lend us a fucking hand if he wants it done so bad."

"Actually, he *did* offer that."

Uh-oh, Shaw thought. "He did?"

"Yes, sir. He said he could send an FBI SWAT team down here to handle the demolition in situ if we couldn't do it."

Shaw barely heard her. "In situ?" he muttered.

"Yes, sir. It means where it sits."

He looked at her. "I know what it means, Eleanor. Were those his words, or something you came up with on your own?"

"That was him, sir."

"Thank God. I don't want any of my people to start talking like that." He shook his head. "Fucking feds. Give a cop a grad school education and you turn him into a dickhead without the common sense God gave to the ass end of a goat."

Shaw watched his staff working over the Ship Channel map and figured he couldn't wait any longer on the *Santa Fe* situation. He hadn't wanted to act on this now. They had a list of other problems so long they'd probably never get through them all. Plus they had another hurricane, Mardel this time, forming out in the Atlantic. And, considering the way things had been going, he was willing to bet Mardel would be coming their way, too.

No, he couldn't wait too much longer.

"Okay," he said. "This is what I want you to do. Call Laidlaw back and tell him we'll use our own people on the

Santa Fe. Last thing I want is the Federal Bureau of Ineptitude rooting around my backyard."

"Uh, Captain . . ."

"What?"

"Sir, with all due respect, I don't see how we're gonna be able to do that. We're buried under projects right now."

"We'll find a way to make it work."

"But sir, I mean, if they're offering help, shouldn't we . . . ?"

"I said no!" he snapped.

She drew back, her eyebrows going up in surprise. Out of the corner of his eye, Shaw could see some of the officers on his staff watching them.

"Look," he said, lowering his voice, "if the feds wanna help, let 'em keep their sorry asses north of the city handing out sandwiches or something. The last thing I want is a bunch of SEAL team wannabes blowing up cargo freighters while I'm trying to rescue civilians. Tell Laidlaw to keep his people out of my way, understand?"

"Yes, sir," she said.

Her tone was withdrawn, chastened, and he was sorry he'd snapped at her. She didn't deserve that. It was just that he was so damn tired. Really, really tired.

"Anything else?" he said.

"We had three more deaths this afternoon in the shelter over at the rec center."

"Damn," he said. "How many is that now, eighteen?"

"Yes, sir."

"What were these last three, the salmonella?"

"That's what Dr. Bailey thinks. He told me all about it. And then he went on a very long tirade about how bad conditions were down there. He reminded me, several times in fact, that you promised him something would be done about the Porta-Potties."

He scanned the room, watching his staff at their stations. Hector had done so much damage to southwest Houston they'd been forced to appropriate the campus as a forward dispatch point for relief efforts. They now occupied a large meeting room in the M.D. Anderson Library, the library's cozy armchairs and lamp fixtures hastily tossed aside to make room for laptops and maps and phones.

Originally, the university had given permission for Shaw and his staff to move in here for the duration of the disaster. But that was before Hector caught the 2.5 million people in the evacuation zones of Galveston and Harris County flat-footed. Within hours of the storm, Shaw found himself the only functioning police authority in the affected area. He had an empty campus—built to house thirty thousand students, equipped with its own hospital and sewage plant and dormitories and restaurants and even a grocery store—that was situated right next to the only major highway leading out of the disaster zone. He had tens of thousands of injured, sick, and starving people stuck on that same highway.

And so, acting far beyond his authority to do so, Shaw made the only decision his conscience would allow and opened the entire campus and all its facilities as a shelter for any of the evacuees who could get there. Within a day they had swollen the campus to a population of more than eighty thousand.

But what began as a decision made for mercy's sake quickly became a nightmare of filth and disease. They had, within a few days, run out of medicines and food and clean water and especially places for people to go to the bathroom. Staph and strep had already made an appearance. So too had salmon-ella. They had dialysis patients they couldn't care for. Broken bones they couldn't set. Cuts they couldn't keep clean. There was even ominous talk from the few doctors they had of an imminent cholera outbreak.

"I'll call Bailey back later," he said. "Maybe smooth a few ruffled feathers."

"Good luck," Eleanor said.

Shaw nodded.

Sheltering all these people here had been a bad idea. He could see that now. Never mind that it had been done for all the right reasons. Never mind that he would have been crucified in the national media, and probably in the history books, had he failed to do so. All that really mattered was that someone was going to have to answer for the mess it had become, and that person was going to be him.

"Thank you, Eleanor," he said. "Hey, by the way, how's your family, your daughter—uh, Margaret, right?"

She brightened. "Madison. She's doing good. I'm proud of her. We've got this older neighbor whose house got hit by a tree during Hector. . . . She's staying with us. But she's not doing so hot. Madison's been really strong, though. You know, helping out, taking care of her. I almost hate to say it, but I think this experience has been good for her."

"Well, times like these make us grow up fast."

"Yes, sir. They do indeed."

He excused himself and went over to his desk. In days gone by he had always kept a clean, orderly desk—once a Marine, always a Marine—but like the city outside his command post, his desk was now a wreck. He had to push reports and maps aside just to find his BlackBerry.

And because he hadn't had enough misery today he checked the missed calls screen and saw the number had climbed to three hundred twenty-four.

Fucking wonderful, he thought.

He dialed his youngest son's number and Anthony Shaw answered on the second ring.

"Hey, Dad, what's up?"

"I'm up to my ass in headaches. Where are you?"

"We're bringing the boat in now. It was rough out there tonight. There's a lot of bodies floating around. A lot of people in shock."

"Never mind that. I need to talk to you. How soon can you be here?"

"What, you mean at the EOC? I don't know. We got a lot of gear to offload. And these survivors we found, we need to get them to the infirmary. I guess I can be there in about an hour, maybe."

"That's not gonna work. I want to talk to you now. Let Brent and Jesse take care of the boat and the survivors. Get here in ten minutes." He paused for a moment, then added, "It's about the *Santa Fe*."

Anthony was silent for a long time.

Shaw could almost see his son's lips pinch together, his brow crease. The boy was the very picture of his mother when he concentrated on something.

"Ten minutes," Anthony said. "We finally gonna move on that?"

"Just get here, okay? I'll talk to you about it in person."

"Sure, Dad. On the way."

Shaw hung up, then fished into his shirt pocket for his pack of smokes. Like everything else, Marlboros were in short supply these days, but he had been smart and stocked up before Gabriella. He had three unopened cartons underneath his cot.

He went out the front door of the library, lit a smoke, and turned to the south to watch the oil rig fires burning along the horizon. They lit the sky a dusty shade of orange. In the heat of the day the smell of the burning oil was so strong it made his eyes water, but at night it wasn't so bad. He inhaled deeply and let the smoke out through his nose, savoring the cigarette and the slight head rush that came with his first bullet after waking up.

It was a good night, cool, no clouds, and a mild breeze out of the west was carrying the smell of the dead bodies away from him.

Thank God, he thought, *for small favors*.

* * *

When he came back inside his city-issued cell phone was ringing. He stood there, watching it, knowing exactly who was on the other end of the line.

Shaw looked up; Eleanor Norton was watching him, a half smile on her face.

"Evan Robinson?" she asked.

"Yep, I'm afraid so."

He let out a groan. *Trouble*, he thought, *is like a magnet. All it does is attract more trouble.*

He picked up the phone and hit TALK. "This is Shaw."

"Captain. This is Evan Robinson. I've been trying to reach you since last night."

"Yes, sir?"

"You don't return your phone calls?"

Shaw sighed. He pinched the bridge of his nose and tried to imagine how nice another cigarette would taste.

"Well?"

"Councilman Robinson, my cell phone has not stopped ringing for ten days now. I have no idea how many calls I've missed, but I'm sure it's a bunch. So tell me, what can I do for you?"

Robinson huffed indignantly. "Look, I'm sure you people are real busy down there. . . ."

"You have no idea," Shaw said.

"Yes, well, things are rough all over the city. Do you know what we're dealing with out here?"

Maids who can't make it to work, probably, Shaw thought, and smiled for the first time in ten days. Councilman Evan Robinson lived in the River Oaks subdivision, Texas's answer to Beverly Hills. It was, Shaw had heard, the wealthiest zip code in Texas, and the second wealthiest in the country. They had mansions there bigger than the elementary school where his wife Grace had taught for twenty-five years. Old Texas oil money at its most decadent.

River Oaks was built well beyond the flood zone. Shaw searched his memory for the last action reports he'd read on the area and couldn't come up with anything beyond the common nuisances that came with any bad weather incident.

"I guess you've got a few downed power lines, water service interrupted, roads closed, some property damage from airborne tree limbs. That about cover it?"

"As a matter of fact, no, Captain, that doesn't about cover it."

Shaw didn't have time for the other shoe to drop. "Okay?" he said.

Robinson huffed again, and Shaw had to smile at the mental image playing through his mind. Robinson was an effeminate man, delicately built, prissy, hardly what you'd expect from a family that grew out of Old West pioneers and wildcatter stock. Shaw could almost picture the man pushing the gold-rimmed glasses back up his nose while trying to hold on to his patience with both hands.

"Look here, Shaw, you know what a lift pump station is?"

"Yes, sir."

"So you know what happens when a lift pump station gets its electrical power knocked out."

"Yes, sir, I do."

The city of Houston had been dredged from a swamp back in the early 1800s. As it grew, it was forced to come up with sophisticated ways of disposing of its wastewater and sewage. Over the years a vast network of sewage lift pumps had sprung up around large developments. The lift pumps moved sewage out of the neighborhoods and into treatment plants owned and operated by a company called Center-Point.

When the power was off, the pumps couldn't work. Sewage backed up. Stinking brown water bubbled up from manhole covers. Backyards turned to rivers of filthy, muddy slime. The air thrummed with the collective murmuring of vast clouds of mosquitoes and flies. After Hurricane Ike back in 2008, the same problem had led to twelve reported cases of West Nile virus.

The answer, of course, was to get power back to the lift pumps; and to do that, relief workers had to physically climb into each station and connect it to a generator. They would then pump the station until it started yielding clean water again, and move on to the next station.

But it was a monumental task—maybe even an impossible one, under the present circumstances. CenterPoint had given him twenty-four generators, which was all they could find. Most of their equipment was still underwater, and probably would be for a very long time. And with those twenty-four generators and the twenty percent of their workforce they could locate, CenterPoint was setting out to do the impossible.

Of the city's three surface water treatment plants, two were currently underwater. The third was so badly damaged it would take months to bring it back online.

Of the seventy-five core ground water plants, all were currently offline. Of those, fifty-two would have to be completely rebuilt. Nothing was salvageable.

None of the city's six pressure-boosting/repump stations had survived.

And the list just kept getting longer with every new report coming across Shaw's desk.

Thinking about that lengthening list, Shaw almost missed what Robinson said next.

"I just got off the phone with Jason Weeks over at CenterPoint," Robinson said. "He tells me that you have appropriated every single one of their generators."

"Yes, sir. That's true."

"It is?"

"Yes, sir."

"And who, may I ask, gave you the authority to do that?"

"I'm not following you, sir."

"You're not?"

"No, sir. I'm not. What seems to be the problem?"

"The problem? The *problem*? Captain, are you trying to be obtuse? Is that what's going on here? Do you think this is funny?"

"Sir," Shaw said, his voice heavy with exhaustion, "last night I was on a bass boat touring the Lower Second Ward and I saw this dead little black baby caught in the branches of a pecan tree. Poor little guy wasn't wearing a stitch of clothes, his little arms just swaying back and forth in the floodwater. I could hear trapped people screaming for help in the attics of flooded houses. Everywhere you look you see the bloated bodies of people and animals floating on the current. So to answer your question, no, I don't think any of this is funny."

Robinson was quiet for a long moment.

"Look," he said, and his voice sounded more subdued now, the anger gone, "all I'm asking is for you to release one of those generators. I know what you're up against, and I—"

"You *know*? I'm sorry, sir, but did you say you *know* what I'm up against? You have no fucking clue what I'm up against, Councilman. I'm sitting on an eighty-thousand-person powder keg here. We're starving. Not hungry, mind you—starving. I've got people dying because they can't get fresh water. I've got people dying of diseases that aren't even supposed to happen in this hemisphere. I'm up to my fucking chin in major-league death here, and you've got the balls to try to take a generator away from me just because your twenty-million-dollar mansion smells like shit. Is that really what's going on here, Councilman?"

"Now hold on a second there, Captain Shaw. I understand that you are under a great deal of stress, but that does not give you the right to—"

"I'll tell you what it gives me the right to do, Councilman. It gives me the right to tell you to go fuck yourself."

Silence.

It went on so long Shaw almost hung up. But then Robinson answered, his voice seething with barely restrained hostility.

"My next phone call," Robinson said, "will be to Chief Harper. I have known your boss for the last fifteen years, and I guarantee you, Captain Shaw, that you have just cost yourself a job. You'll be replaced by the end of the day."

Shaw actually laughed.

"Seriously?" he said. "Is that a promise, Councilman? I'll tell you what. If you find somebody stupid enough to do my job, you send 'em down here and I will personally hand them the keys. But until then, do us both a favor. Next time you get a case of the ass, save your phone calls for somebody else. Got it?"

Shaw hit the END key and threw the phone down on his desk. He stood there looking at it, aware that his staff had gone silent. They were all watching him. He took a few slow breaths, forcing the anger back down where it couldn't be seen.

"That might have gone better," Eleanor said.

"Like hell." Shaw let out a long breath. "I shouldn't have baited him like that."

"Yeah, but it made you feel better, didn't it?"

He laughed. "A little, yeah."

"You don't think Harper will really listen to him, do you?"

"About relieving me? No. Or, rather, he will, eventually, but it won't be for a while. And he definitely wouldn't do it while we're still working this situation. Afterwards, yeah, he'll probably find some way to make all of this my fault."

"You don't sound too worried," she said.

"Fuck them," he said. "Let 'em bring it if they can."

He swept the room with an angry gaze.

"You know what? Fuck it. I'm going out for another smoke. Keep an eye on things for me."

"Okay," she said. "Oh, uh, what about Dr. Bailey?"

"Fuck Bailey. If he calls again, tell him I'm busy."

Shaw went out to the front steps of the library, lit up another cigarette, and listened to the sounds of dogs baying in the night. Their cries were lonely, frightened. Most were starving. Perhaps a few had even realized the fate waiting for them. To Shaw, it was the sound of loyalty betrayed.

It was a feeling he understood intimately. Six years back he was commanding the Special Operations Unit, a division comprising all five of the department's SWAT units, the negotiators, and the bomb squad, while waiting for his appointment to deputy chief to finally come through. He'd been on top of the world. With one son on the job already, another in the Academy, and his appointment to the command staff all but assured, he was creating a legacy. He was going to be a patriarch.

And then Grace got sick with breast cancer.

Shaw's world slipped off its rails.

He went from the hectic, high-powered world of city politics to the waiting rooms of doctors who were specialists in things he couldn't even pronounce, and for the first time in his adult life, Shaw found himself completely out of his depth. He took Grace to endless doctor's appointments. They did everything the doctors said to do. But in the end, the chemo and the drugs failed. They had caught the cancer late, and it moved through her hard and fast, relentless as an approaching winter.

Utterly baffled by fate, Shaw turned in the only direction he could.

He'd been brought up to believe the police department was a family. His fellow officers were his brothers and sis-

ters, the department their mother and father. Even if the rest
of the world was going to shit, an officer could always retreat
inside the family that cared for him and preserved him and
loved him. The fraternal brotherhood of police took care of
its own. It was the core belief that had sustained him through
thirty years of police service. It was the gospel he had
preached to his two sons. It was the solace he sought now.

And yet the brotherhood failed him in his time of need.
Faced with the demands of competing for the appointment
to deputy chief and taking the time off to be with Grace as
she slipped into the final stage of the disease, he'd done the
only thing his conscience would allow him to do. He had
friends on the command staff, and he tried to get them to go
to bat for him, but it didn't work. Everybody felt sorry for
him, sure, but if he wanted the appointment, they told him,
he would have to slug it out with younger captains, all of
them with graduate degrees and the willingness to snuggle
up in the embrace of the Houston political machine. That
meant going to parties, playing golf with councilmen on the
weekends, being seen. None of which he could do. He
watched, from Grace's hospital bed, as first one, and then another, younger captain moved into the command staff . . .
and soon his only friends and supporters were the dinosaurs,
all of them nearing the end of their careers, their stroke with
city council and the puppeteers in the political machine all
but dried up.

When Grace died, Shaw found himself a wreck in more
ways than one. The woman who had devoted her life to loving him and raising his sons was gone. She had been his rudder, and now he was floating without direction. In his youth
he had seen the department close ranks around officers in
times of grief like his, but to his dismay he found that times
had changed. The brotherhood was not what it had once
been, and in his floundering confusion, he was left feeling
bitter, disgruntled, openly antagonistic toward the adminis-

tration. They soon lost patience with him. Over the next year he was pushed farther and farther from the inner circle, until finally he was placed in the Emergency Operations Command. It was, perhaps, the cruelest blow imaginable, as it placed him under the direct command of the fire department's chief. It still rankled him, a cop working for a firefighter.

The family, Shaw realized, had kicked him to the curb. They wanted him gone.

Part of Shaw died with Grace. Not just his heart, not just his career, but his sense of worth, his sense of value. All of that was gone, and he was left standing in the wreckage, nursing his pride and too bull headed to admit he was beat.

And now, as he stood on the stairs of the M.D. Anderson Library, listening to dogs bay in the night, he looked at his hands and realized his cigarette had smoldered down to the filter. He dropped the butt to the concrete and rubbed it out with the toe of his boot. Then he took another from his pack and lit it.

Anthony showed up midway through his second cigarette.

"You got another one of those?" he asked.

Shaw handed him the pack and lit the cigarette for him.

"Thanks," Anthony said.

He was dressed in a green T-shirt tucked into battle dress uniform pants, a floppy boonie hat pushed high up on his forehead, the way all the younger officers wore it these days. His shirt was snug enough to reveal his well-muscled, wiry frame. He carried himself with the easy confidence of a veteran SWAT officer, full of the knowledge that on the male hierarchy, he owned the top rung of the ladder.

Back in his youth, Mark Shaw had been a founding member of Houston's SWAT Unit. He recognized the swagger, the confidence, in his son's body language, and it made him smile.

But the smile didn't last long.

He couldn't think of Anthony without thinking of his other son, Brent. Anthony had gotten his mother's small stature—he was only five-nine—and her striking good looks. Brent on the other hand, was the spitting image of Shaw, a big bear of a man, several inches over six feet, with a barrel chest and a round face and a deep, clear voice.

But that was where the similarities ceased. Anthony had gotten his father's drive, his mental toughness, his ability to make decisions under pressure. But not Brent. Brent, the older of the two, was a gentle giant. He rarely asserted himself, and lately had taken to drinking far too much. Shaw hadn't confronted him about the drinking, not yet anyway, but he had seen the signs of incipient alcoholism—the absences, the mood swings, the weak excuses for bad performance. Shaw knew it was yet another problem lurking in the wings, something he would have to confront as soon as all this other crap went away.

Shaw pointed east over Anthony's shoulder.

"Did you know your mother and I built our first house about a mile that way?"

Anthony glanced back at the darkness, but said nothing.

"It wasn't bad for a policeman's first house," he said. "Two bedrooms, a little yard with a garden. Your mom grew strawberries back then. I remember those things, not like you buy in the store." He sighed. "I saw it last night—the house, I mean. It's underwater mostly."

Anthony blew out twin streams of smoke through his nostrils.

"Nearly everything's underwater, Dad. This city's gone."

Shaw took a drag of his smoke and nodded. For Mark Shaw, those flooded ruins out there weren't just houses. They were homes. Lives had been lived there. Houston, for all its corruption and faults, was a place where men could raise their families. They could live quiet lives, not of desperation, but of honor, and integrity, and devotion to the ones they loved. And that was it. Family. Everything grew out of the family. That was the concept that defined a man, that ultimately decided if his life had value.

He wondered if Anthony understood that as well as he should.

"You okay, Dad?" Anthony asked.

"Yeah, I'm fine."

"You sure? You look tired."

"I am tired."

Shaw took a last drag on his smoke, jammed it out on the handrail, then dropped it in disgust. Sometimes he hated cigarettes, even though he knew he'd be lighting up again in ten minutes.

"You're not gonna have to worry about what's going on here in a few days," Anthony said. "We get that dynamite, and we're home free. I've already scouted out the bank. It's perfect. The whole building's underwater, just like Brent said. Once I get that dynamite, Jesse and I can be in and out of that vault in no time. Give me an hour and we'll all be seven million dollars richer."

"Yeah," Shaw said.

He looked east, into the darkened ruins, thinking about the house he and Grace had built all those years ago, Brent just a baby.

But so much had happened since then. His sons had grown up, and Grace had died. And now he was facing a murky future. Without Grace, without his rudder, he'd fallen back on the one pillar that had never failed him—duty. The father was the provider; that was his duty. His job was to carve out a future for his children, by force if necessary, but provide for them he must do. To fail was not an option. Even if it meant breaking his oath to the law.

The day before Hurricane Hector, he had been talking with Brent about Brent's extra job as a security officer at the

Republic of Texas Bank. Brent said that seven million dollars in cash was being stored in the bank's vault. Shaw had thought little of it until the day after Hurricane Hector, when he happened to read an action report that stated all of Southeast Houston's banks and jewelry stores and museums were now underwater.

The property loss, the report's author had written, *will total in the trillions. Maybe even the hundreds of trillions.*

Shaw had nodded in agreement. But the thought of seven million dollars waiting down there in the bowels of that flooded bank, already written off by the insurance companies, had started his mind working.

He had two sons, both of whom had joined the police department because he had led them to it with his talk of honor and brotherhood. It was a good job, he promised. No matter how bad the economy gets, you'll never get laid off.

But Shaw could read the writing on the wall. Houston would probably never recover from the twin scourge of Hector and Kyle, and if Hurricane Mardel hit them like the folks at the National Hurricane Center were saying, the city would be down and out for good.

All his promises of good jobs forever would turn out to be a lie.

And then, like a sign from heaven, the ATF delivered the Venezuelan freighter *Santa Fe* and its shipment of dynamite into his hands.

The decision made itself.

Shaw lit another cigarette, and it focused him back into the moment.

"Are you and Jesse ready to move on the *Santa Fe*?"

"Well, we can be. Not at this second, but we can be. We've still got a lot of planning to do."

"You have twenty-four hours."

"Twenty-four hours? Dad, holy shit. That's too soon."

"You have twenty-four hours, Anthony, or the operation's

a no-go. Got it? We wait any longer and the feds are gonna call in an FBI SWAT Team. We've got a narrow window of opportunity here. I want you and Anthony to get your gear together and move out tomorrow morning with first light. Can you make it happen?"

"Yeah," Anthony said, grinding his smoke out on the pavement. "Yeah, we can do it. But—"

"That's all I wanted to hear," he said. "Get it done, Anthony. Just get it done."

CHAPTER 3

The next morning, Brent Shaw sat behind the wheel of a small ski boat, watching the flooded houses in the distance, trying his best not to think about the dead bodies he kept running over. His dad and his younger brother had promised him this little excursion was going to be quick and easy. So far, it had been anything but.

"Okay, hold it up here," Anthony said.

"Why are we doing this?" Brent said. "Dad said for us to get this done fast."

"Just hold up. We'll get there." Anthony pumped his palm in Brent's face like an angry traffic cop. "Right here! Stop!"

The boat slowed and Anthony leaned over the gunwale.

"Oh, okay," he said. "No big deal. It's just a dummy."

"A what?"

"You know, like at the mall. A mannequin." Anthony reached into the water and scooped up a white arm with a limp plastic bag hanging from the wrist.

Anthony pointed it at Brent.

"See?"

Brent stared at his brother, not the arm.

"That's great, Anthony. Can we go now?"

Brent didn't do well around dead bodies. That was no secret. Though he'd been a cop for close to ten years now, the smell of decomposition could still make him vomit unexpectedly. And since riding out from their temporary HQ at the University of Houston's campus they'd seen hundreds of blackened corpses floating in the water. Brent was in hell.

But of course Anthony was loving it.

They'd run over several floaters already, and every time something thudded against the hull, Anthony would be ready with his one-liners. "Nice! Ten points." Or Anthony's personal favorite: "Hey, go back. I think you missed one."

Brent, meanwhile, would simply close his eyes and groan.

The dummy's arm that Anthony was now holding up so proudly was just one more excuse for his younger brother to needle him.

Anthony stuck the dripping arm around the side of the windscreen, the hand inching toward Brent's crotch. "You want me jack you off?" he said, speaking in a falsetto Vietnamese hooker voice. "Me got kung fu grip. Jack you off long time."

Brent swatted the hand away. "Jesus. Cut it out." He wiped the water from his pants. "Quit laughing, asshole. What are you, like six?" He sat down again, his big hands draped over the top of the wheel. He was trying his best to look tough and pissed, but only came across as rattled.

"You got problem with your wee-wee, big boy?" Anthony said, still in his hooker voice. "You no like me? Come on, you not too beaucoup for Rosie."

"I said cut it out."

"You sure? Rosie here's about as close as you're gonna get to a woman for a while."

"Throw it back in the water," Brent said. "Please."

"Fine," Anthony said, and threw the mannequin's arm away. "But you know, you need to learn to have fun every once in a while. Being with you is like having Eeyore for a brother."

Anthony got up and went to the back of the boat, where Jesse Numeroff was giving their dive gear a final once-over.

Brent watched him go, then hit the throttle and got them back on their way, trying his best not to think about the dull thuds he kept hearing against the bottom of the boat.

"Hey, Brent, what's that?"

They had just rounded a thick copse of trees. Ahead of them, a perfectly straight white line stretched across the floodwater.

Brent killed the throttle and scanned the water ahead. "Shit," he said.

"What is it?"

Jesse Numeroff was coming forward now. He looked left, then right, following the track of the white line.

"No way around it," Jesse said. "Looks like we're gonna have to swim from here."

Like Anthony, Jesse was short and slender and fast, built like an infielder. He and Anthony had been best friends since high school, where they'd played baseball together. Now he was a member of the Houston Fire Department's elite High-Water Rescue Unit. When they were planning this operation, Anthony had suggested bringing in Jesse because of his dive skills, and their father, who had always liked Jesse, agreed without hesitation. And just like that, the three of them had fallen into the old familiar pattern. Anthony and Jesse were the Wonder Twins, the ones in charge. Brent was the chauffeur, the guy who carried the heavy stuff, the butt of their jokes.

Anthony was standing beside Jesse now, looking at the white line in the water. "Okay, I give. What the hell is that?"

"That's the retaining wall for the Beltway," Brent said. "The top of it anyway. I can get you right up to it, but there's no way to get the boat over that without tearing up the hull."

"Just go around it?"

"It's too far," Brent said. "It'd take us an hour either way to get around it."

"Be quicker to swim it," Jesse said. "The *Santa Fe*'s about a mile that way, through those trees."

"I guess we don't have any other choice, do we?" Anthony said.

"Not really."

Brent turned the boat to their right and followed the retaining wall until they came to a purple charter bus up to its rearview mirrors in water.

"I can tie off here pretty easy," he said to Jesse. "Will this be a good landmark for you come back to?"

"Yeah," Jesse said, "this'll work fine."

Anthony and Jesse went to the back of the boat and donned their gear. As they climbed over the side, Brent said, "How long do you think this'll take?"

"Five to six hours, I'm guessing," Anthony said. "You gonna be okay hanging out here?"

Brent nodded.

"You sure?" Anthony said, smiling wickedly. "All these dead bodies. You're not gonna get too spooked?"

"Fuck you," Brent muttered.

He grabbed a pair of AR-15s and handed them to Anthony, who passed one to Jesse.

"Lighten up, big bro. I'm just funning with you. You shouldn't have any trouble. But just in case, like if a Coast Guard team shows up or something, have them call Dad at the EOC."

"I know what to do," Brent said. And then, almost below his breath: "I can take care of myself."

Anthony slid his goggles down over his eyes.

"I know you can. I'm just telling you because the old man told me to. Oh, and steer clear of the trees. Water moccasins like to get up in there during floods."

Brent glanced at the nearby oaks and swallowed. Anthony was still messing with his head, he knew that, but he couldn't help it. Snakes, like decomposing bodies, were one of his phobias.

He turned back to Anthony and tried his best to sound confident and in control, like their father.

"I got this, Anthony. You just do your part and I'll do mine."

Anthony laughed, gave him a thumbs-up, and then he and Jesse slid away from the boat, gliding silently through the murky water.

They dog-paddled most of the way to keep their legs out of the rubble that lurked just below the surface. Once they got out of earshot of the boat, Jesse said, "Hey, how did Brent's Internal Affairs case work out?"

"Which one?"

"There's another one?" Jesse asked. "I was talking about him being AWOL. Which one are you talking about?"

"He wrecked his police car again."

"No way, really? What is that, like three this year?"

"The crash review board gave him a fifteen-day suspension right before Gabriella, but my dad got it put on hold until we see what's gonna happen with Mardel."

"That was cool of your dad."

Anthony laughed. "He wasn't happy about it, that's for sure."

"No, I bet not."

They paddled on in silence. This close to the Ship Channel, they had a clear view of the damage Hurricane Kyle's storm surge had caused. Vast fields of garbage were strewn across the flooded landscape. Billboards were little more than skeletons with only a few scraps hanging from them. Telephone poles had been upended and tossed like driftwood against buildings that had every window blasted out. Nothing moved, and there was no sound but the splashing of their feet as they dog-paddled on and on.

They came to an eighteen-wheeler and Jesse climbed up on top of the cab and looked east.

"Not too much farther," he called down to Anthony. "There's a trailer park up ahead. Should be just on the other side of that."

He climbed down and dropped into the water next to Anthony.

"Hey," Jesse said, "listen, I gotta ask you something."

"Shoot," said Anthony.

"It's about Brent."

"Yeah?"

"Your dad's been covering for him a lot lately."

"Yeah, so? You've known my dad long enough to know he's not gonna let his kid down when he's going through a rough spot. That's not the kind of man he is."

"I know that. I wouldn't have agreed to get on board with this little operation if I didn't know that."

"So what are you trying to say, Jesse?"

"Well, it's just that it seems like Brent's been going through a little more than a rough spot. Seems like it's more serious than that."

Anthony didn't answer.

Though Jesse hadn't said the words out loud, they were back to Brent's drinking again. The subject had been coming up a lot lately, at work, at home, all the time. Brent had always been a heavy drinker, even back when they were in high school. But over the past year or so it had gotten way out of hand. From what Anthony had heard, Brent was calling in sick a lot, burning up his accrued leave bank. And there were other warning signs of bad things to come. Brent was obsessed with drinking. He talked about drinking all the time. He was irritable. They had grown apart since Anthony joined the SWAT Unit, but on the few occasions they'd hung out recently, Brent had gotten really blitzed, followed by blackouts the next day. It was troubling to watch him struggle, completely unwilling to talk about what was obviously going wrong in his world.

And Anthony didn't even want to think about the sudden rise in Brent's on-duty police car crashes. In the seven years he'd been a policeman, Anthony had known more than a few cops who pickled themselves in booze. It was a common enough thing, considering all the shit your average street cop sees in his career. But even though it was common, and tolerated to some degree because nobody wanted to cut a fellow cop out of his pension, it was never cool. Drunks were taken off the street, pushed into some meaningless job where they didn't interact with the public, where they couldn't fuck anything up. Cops like that, they became pariahs. The department's black sheep. They were snickered at behind their backs. Eventually, they were forgotten. Anthony bristled at the idea that his own brother was on the verge of becoming one of those kinds of cops. It stirred a vague sense of hostility somewhere down in his guts, coiling like a big snake.

"You think he's gonna be able to do his part in this?" Jesse said.

Anthony kept his eyes straight ahead.

"He'll be fine," he said.

"Hey, don't get upset, man. I'm just saying. I mean, I signed up for this because I trust you and your dad all the way. I respect you both. You're capable. But . . . your brother, I mean, let's face it, Anthony, he's a drunk. I like him and all, but I don't want him to—"

"It's not open for discussion, Jesse. He's in this with us. He's my brother, and I'm not gonna leave him out of the money."

"I don't begrudge him the money," Jesse said. "That's not what I'm driving at. He gets a share just like the rest of us. I'm cool with that. I'm just saying that, you know, he might not be able to do his part in the operation. That's all I'm saying."

"He'll do fine. Now drop it."

Jesse looked at him, then nodded slowly.

"Sure," he said. "Okay."

A short distance away they came upon the ruins of a trailer park. The destruction they had seen up to that point was incredible, though most of it was still underwater, only the tops of buildings and cars still visible. The worst of it was left up to the imagination. But here, in this trailer park, which was at a slightly higher elevation than most of the surrounding area, the water had for the most part receded, and what was left was far worse than either of them had imagined.

They rose to their feet as the water grew shallow, clipped their flippers to their belts between their legs, and walked through knee-high water, their heads on swivels as they scanned the wrecked trailer park. Several trailers were on their sides, tumbled together like a child's blocks. Some had been crushed by fallen trees. One was split nearly in half by a shrimp boat. Everywhere they looked they saw endless piles of lumber and roof shingles. There wasn't an unbroken window anywhere. Tree limbs and leaves and brown sea plants clung to everything.

And there were bodies. Lots of bodies.

Mud had poured into one of the trailers and set like a lava flow. Inside, Anthony saw a mother with her arms still wrapped around a child, partially buried in the muck that had invaded their living room.

Anthony looked upon the desolate scene, on the ruined

trailers, the toys and lawn chairs and the piles of gray, warped lumber, the broken windows so like eyes, the damp piles of leaves covering everything, and he felt a depression more complete than any he had previously thought possible. Those who knew him would never confuse Anthony for a deep thinker. Since boyhood, when he discovered that both baseball and girls came easily for him, little else occupied his thoughts. And so it surprised him to encounter such a complex web of feeling upon seeing this place. He was at once sickened and afraid. Turning his head slowly from one wrecked trailer to the next he wondered what it was that was making him feel such dread, such loneliness, but he couldn't quite grasp it. Whatever it was that rattled him so was just out of reach, an elusive thing, a half-resolved and ominous *it* lurking in the darkness, waiting to put a cold hand upon his shoulder.

With a tightness in his chest and the stench of rot and open sewage seeping into his mask, he continued on.

They saw a mangy black dog eating something that looked like a human leg.

Anthony didn't hesitate.

He raised his rifle and dropped the animal with a single shot. And after the sound of that shot died away, Anthony stood watching the animal. Despite all he had seen, this was the worst. That dog, eating on a human corpse, somehow brought everything into focus, and in that instant he realized that he was witnessing the end of the first half of his life. Just like that.

Abruptly, a strange memory surfaced in his mind. He remembered riding in his father's boat out on Clear Lake as a kid, the wind in his hair as he reached over the side, slapping the spray while his dad taught Brent to steer and work the throttle. They had passed a buoy, and Anthony, momentarily fascinated by it, had turned and asked his dad why it was there.

"It's the dividing line," his dad had said, "between the lake and Galveston Bay. From here on out, we're in deep water."

It was that last phrase that hung in Anthony's mind now.

Deep water, he thought. *Yeah, that was it. Deep water. That dog eating that corpse's leg, it was like a buoy, and everything from here on out is deep water. There's no coming back from this. The city of Houston is dying, even if it doesn't know it yet.*

He caught movement out of the corner of his eye and turned toward it.

"You see that?" he asked Jesse. He pointed to a trailer, the inside dark as a cave. "Over there."

Jesse scanned the trailer.

"No, what'd you see?"

"There's somebody in there. I don't see 'em now."

They were at a lower elevation now, the water up to their thighs. Jesse sank down into the water so that just his head was above water.

"If it's a survivor we'll pick 'em up on the way back," he said. "Come on. The ship should be just around those trees up there."

Anthony's gaze lingered on the trailer a moment longer; then he sank down into the water and followed after Jesse.

They rounded a copse of trees and there it was.

The *Santa Fe*.

It was an immense freighter, listing to one side, partially buried in mud and slag.

Anthony grew up in Houston. He was no stranger to the large freighters that frequented the Houston Ship Channel. But always, when he saw them on the nightly news or while driving down to Galveston for a day at the beach, they had been in the water, the vast majority of their bulk, like an iceberg, out of sight below the surface.

None of those memories prepared him for the *Santa Fe*.

The storm surge had pushed it at least a mile inland from the docks. Its huge bulk stood like a monument to destruction on a vast field of mud. Even from four hundred yards away, it caused the breath to hitch in his throat.

His chest felt tight once again. His eyes were dry and burning beneath his mask. His hands felt cold and an uncomfortable sweat popped from the skin on his arms. It was primitive fear, he realized with a sudden flush of humility, fear of this cathedral-like vastness rising from the mud, an endless jumbled plain of refinery wreckage.

"Damn," he whispered.

"Yeah, you ain't kidding."

"Are we gonna be able to find what we're looking for on that thing?" Anthony asked.

"We will if the blueprints the ATF gave your dad are right. Of course, the way that thing's listing, everything could have gotten tossed around in there."

They reached the ship and tossed their climbing ropes onto the deck. Both were experienced climbers and there was little discussion until they had the ropes securely fastened to deck.

It was then that Anthony happened to glance over his shoulder, back in the direction they'd come. There were people there, a small group, coming around the copse of trees. Anthony stared at them, and the vague, undefined sense of unease that had been nagging at him since they first entered the trailer park turned into a steady, blaring warning siren in his head.

"You ready?" Jesse said. There was a pause. "Anthony?"

"Huh?"

"I said are you ready?"

Anthony pointed back in the direction from which they'd come. "Look over there. You see them?"

The figures he was pointing at were too far away to make out any details, but even from where they stood Anthony could see that their clothes had been ripped to pieces by the wind and the rain, revealing emaciated arms and sticklike legs.

And there was something wrong with the way they moved.

They seemed stiff, their movements jerky, unnatural.

"What's wrong with them?" he said.

"Survivors, I guess," said Jesse. "If they've been out here since Kyle, they're probably starving. What do you want to do?"

Anthony forced down his unease. One thing he had inherited from his dad was the ability to focus when things started to unravel. Right or wrong, his father had always said, you make a decision and you go with it. The worst thing you can do is sit there with your thumb up your ass wondering what to do.

"We have to finish this," he said. "My dad said we only get one chance to handle this ourselves before the FBI sends in their people."

"Yeah, but what about them?" Jesse said with a nod toward the approaching survivors.

"We'll get 'em on our way out. Come on, let's go up."

They climbed the ropes quickly, Anthony reaching the deck first. He turned and extended a hand to Jesse. "Need some help?"

"From a SWAT puke?" Jesse said. "Not hardly."

Anthony waited for Jesse to climb over the railing; then the two of them, flat on their bellies, looked across the deck. Though Anthony knew little about large ships, he had read some Clive Cussler books, and that little bit of knowledge helped him feel like he was at least somewhat familiar with his surroundings. The boat was probably eight hundred feet long, her beam one hundred feet. There were seven derricks, all but one forward of the funnel and superstructure, leaning like terra-cotta warriors over the hold doors, waiting to unload cargo that would never again see the light of day. The deck itself was a wasteland of oil drums and tools and rusted equipment. The *Santa Fe*, evidently, had not been in very good shape even before getting beached by Hurricane Kyle's storm surge. Anthony could see patches of rust and flaking paint on the bulkheads and superstructure. Here and there he caught a glimpse of a porthole leering back at them like a cracked and yellowed eye.

"Where to?" Anthony said.

Jesse pointed to their left.

"The superstructure up there. We can get down into the hold from there."

Anthony nodded and fell in behind Jesse, and they worked their way to the superstructure.

They were dropped into darkness as soon as they stepped inside the bulkhead. Turning on their flashlights, they found the stairs and made the awkward downward descent, the deck below them tilted at a crazy angle so that they had to walk on the walls and on the railing.

Garbage had fallen down—or up, it was hard to tell—the stairs. It had piled up so high in places that they had get their shoulders behind a big piece of it and muscle it out of the way. The first time they did it a large metal cooler went tumbling down the stairs with all the subtlety of a fire truck trying to force its way through traffic. When at last the echoes of it died off in the darkness Jesse looked at Anthony and said, "Well, there goes stealth mode."

Anthony laughed, and they pushed on.

The cargo level, when at last they reached it, had five feet of water in it. The hold was pitch black, except where their flashlight beams lanced into the darkness. It was ungodly hot down here, and so humid Anthony could feel it in his throat. But the smell was the worst. Something was dead down here. He would have pulled his shirt up over his mouth if it too hadn't been soaking up the filth around them.

"This doesn't look good," he said.

"No," agreed Jesse. "Come on. I think we need to go that way."

Jesse pointed his flashlight into the bowels of the hold, revealing a length of metal railing and the ribs of the ship and a jumbled mess of crates and shattered pallets.

And then, in the light, something moved, followed by a heavy splash.

"Fuck, what was that?" Anthony said, simultaneously swinging his AR-15 into position. He hit the flashlight button below the barrel and a bluish-white LED lit up the section of railing where they had seen the movement.

"I lost it," Jesse said. "You see it?"

"No."

"What was that?"

"How the fuck should I know? Just stay ready. Cover right; I got left."

Jesse pulled up beside him, his own AR-15 now at the ready.

"Clear?" Anthony asked.

"Yeah, clear."

"Police officers," Anthony shouted into the darkness. "We are armed. Identify yourselves or you will be shot."

They waited, still scanning the darkness with the LED flashlights mounted on their rifles. Jesse's flashlight happened to catch the reflected glint of a pair of eyes, and both men swung their weapons toward it.

A rat, soaking wet and glistening from the sheen of oil on the water, glared malignantly at them from atop a wooden crate.

"Fucking rat," Jesse said.

"That was no rat," Anthony said. "Whatever that was, it was a whole lot bigger than a fucking rat."

Again, they scanned the darkness, listening for the sound of splashing, or anything else for that matter.

But whatever they had seen was gone now.

Anthony motioned for Jesse to lead on, and the two of them moved slowly forward, weapons at the ready as they searched for the crates from Tsing Si Chemical that held the ammonia gelatin.

They found them a short distance forward, half submerged.

"Is that gonna be a problem?" Anthony asked. "Being all wet like that?"

"It's an underwater explosive, you jackass. What do you think?"

Jesse reached into a pocket of his BDUs and pulled out a lock-blade knife, which he used to cut into the plastic sheet that covered the dynamite sticks. Anthony stared at the explosives, and his mouth went dry. He tried to swallow but couldn't force down the walnut that had suddenly formed in his throat. They were sitting on dynamite, for Christ's sake.

The next thing he knew Jesse had pulled from his pants pocket a device that looked like an old-fashioned transistor radio. He also had a small Ziploc baggie with a length of copper wire inside. As Anthony watched, Jesse connected the transistor radio–looking device to the wires, and then the wires into a few of the sticks of dynamite.

Then he pulled out five sticks and motioned for Anthony to turn around.

"What are you doing?" Anthony asked. But he knew even before he asked. He could feel Jesse tugging at the zipper to his backpack, working the flaps open to get the dynamite crammed down into the pouch.

"Relax," said Jesse. His voice was breezy. "These things won't explode without a detonator."

Jesse zipped the backpack closed again and went back to working on the rest of the dynamite still inside the crate.

"So what are you doing there?" Anthony asked.

"Attaching a detonator."

The walnut in Anthony's throat finally went down.

With a chuckle, Jesse finished the job and stood up. "Come on," he said. "Let's get moving."

"Just like that? That's it?"

"Yep, that's it. I'll activate the charges once we get to a safe distance."

"When you hit the detonator, there won't be any danger with the . . ." He trailed off there, but motioned with his thumb toward the dynamite in his backpack.

Jesse smiled.

"Stop being such a pussy," he said, slapping Anthony on the shoulder. "Come on, let's get moving."

They made their way back to their stairs and started up. Anthony was still tense, the smell of death strong in his nostrils, and he kept his AR-15 at the low ready. Up ahead of them, a hazy white daylight seeped down from the top of the stairs. Anthony kept his gaze moving, careful not to stare into the light too long so that his eyes wouldn't lose their low-light acuity. But the sweat was popping out all over his face and it was hard to tell if the flickering light above them was coming from his rapid blinking or something moving.

He stopped, and ducked into a crouch. Jesse continued a few steps up, then stopped as well.

"You hear something?" he whispered.

"Shh."

Anthony listened. He squeezed his eyes shut, then opened them again and slowly scanned the darkness. He had heard something. What was it? The faint clicking of fingernails on a table? Or was it simply the distant, muffled *plink* . . .

plink . . . plink of water dripping from a bulkhead somewhere down in the hold? It was hard to tell. The sound, if indeed it had been a sound at all, had seemed to come from above him and below him simultaneously.

But now, in the darkened stillness of the stairwell, all he could hear was the slow, measured sound of his own breathing.

"I don't hear anything," Jesse said, and stood up. "Come—"

In the low light, something moved fast behind Jesse. There was a crash, a sudden stuttering growl that sounded like a fast series of notes on a piano keyboard, and something that was all teeth flashed into the air, lunging for Jesse's head.

Anthony was ready, and fired, the stairwell turning orange from the muzzle flash, the *pop-pop-pop* of the rifle echoing off the walls.

A moment later, the after burn of the muzzle flash still sending white blobs of light sailing across his vision, Anthony lit up the crumpled form at their feet. It was a dog, its ribs visible down the flanks of its mangy coat, teeth still bared in a grimace of mad hunger.

Jesse, meanwhile, was leaning against the wall, staring down at the animal. He looked at Anthony, said nothing, then looked back down at the dog.

"You okay?" Anthony said.

"What is it with you and dogs?" Jesse answered. "Shit, man, I think I streaked my shorts."

Anthony shook his head. "Yeah, you and me both. Come on, let's go."

They climbed the stairs back to the deck and found their ropes. As Anthony was climbing over the side he happened to glance to the north and saw the five survivors they'd seen earlier. They were very close now, less than two hundred feet from the ship. Close enough that Anthony could hear them moaning.

"Jesse, over there," he said.

"Shit, they're way too close. Anthony, we have to get them out of here. They need to be at least a thousand yards from the blast point."

"Start down," Anthony said. Then he turned to the approaching figures, cupped his hands over his mouth to trumpet his voice, and yelled, "You there. Stop. The ship's not safe. Don't come any closer. We'll come to you."

He was about to yell again, for they didn't seem to hear him, but then he dropped his hands from his mouth.

Something was wrong.

They didn't move right. They didn't sound right. From where he stood, he could see their eyes, and it seemed to him that he had seen that same vacancy, that same profound emptiness, in the sightless, unblinking stare of the freshly dead.

The man out in front of the pack was nearly nude, his pants and shoes and most of his shirt and the left side of his underwear little more than tattered rags. He didn't walk. He shambled. His arms hung like limp ropes at his side. His lower jaw worked up and down but never completely closed. There was a clumsy, faltering stagger to his walk, but it was the man's eyes that held Anthony's attention. Those glassy, depthless eyes.

Three years earlier Anthony had been on a high-risk narcotics search warrant. He was the lead man into the house after Russell Marks smashed the door open with a battering ram. There, not eight feet from the door, sitting on a couch, were three grown men and a grubby-looking, half-naked junkie girl of about fourteen. "Down, down! Police! Search Warrant!" Anthony had screamed, and saw one of the men rise from the couch with a pistol in his hand. Instinct took over, and he fired a three-round burst. And sometimes, when he closed his eyes, he could still follow the track of the bullets as they left his gun and thudded into the man's chest and neck, knocking him back against the filthy gray wall behind him. The man had slid down to the couch and rolled over forward, landing faceup on the bare cement floor at Anthony's feet. Anthony looked down at the man, watching the life slip out of his frightened gaze, watching his face grow slack, horrified and even a little thrilled that he had just killed a man who was trying to kill him. The look Anthony had seen in that man's eyes as he died was the same look he was seeing now.

A loud, ululating moan rose up from the lead man in the group, and it snapped Anthony back into the moment. He grabbed onto the ropes and swung himself over the side, a small but insistent voice in his head urging him to go, go, go.

He and Jesse landed in the mud side by side. Jesse unhooked himself from the rope and started to walk toward the group, which was now almost upon them.

"Jesse, no!" Anthony said, and Jesse turned his head slightly back to Anthony as though startled by the urgency in his friend's voice.

"Back away!" Anthony shouted.

Jesse turned back to the approaching group just as the lead man raised his hands and tried to grab Jesse by the shoulders. The man's mouth came open, the moan still bleeding out, but changing now into something more like a wet, snapping sound.

Anthony was already running toward them. He had the butt of the AR-15 raised over his head, and as he closed the distance he slammed it down on the man's face.

The blow cracked the man's teeth off at the gum line and knocked him to the ground.

"He tried to bite me," Jesse said. His eyes were wide, his mouth slack with disbelief. "Did you see that? He was gonna take a bite out of me."

But Anthony wasn't listening to Jesse. He was watching the man on the ground. An injury like that should have had the guy rolling around, screaming his lungs out. But he was getting back up. And he wasn't making a sound. Blood was gushing from his mouth, his teeth little more than icicle-like stubs now, and he was getting up.

Anthony shook his head. *No*, he thought. *Not possible. Not fucking possible.*

"Move," he said, grabbing Jesse by the shirt and pushing him away from the people closing in on them. "Time to go."

They moved as fast as they could through the mud, their flippers swinging wildly between their legs as they ran.

Anthony glanced back over his shoulder. The survivors were turning slowly, stiffly, to follow them. But they didn't run. They didn't change their pace at all. They just kept shambling on.

"What the hell's wrong with those people?" Jesse asked.

"I don't know," Anthony answered. "Just keep moving. Don't stop."

And they didn't. Not until they rounded the copse of trees and came upon the edge of the trailer park. At that point Jesse reached into his pants pocket and pulled out the transistor radio–looking device and flipped it on.

"What do you want to do?" Jesse said. "Those people are too close. I hit this thing, they're gonna die."

Anthony nodded slowly. He knew that already. But his mind was replaying the things he'd just seen, the man getting up without saying a word, or showing even the slightest sign that he'd been hurt after having his teeth knocked down his throat, the dead vacancy in his eyes.

He heard a faint splashing to his right and turned. Anthony had just enough time to remind himself that the first dog he'd shot had landed over there, near that pile of gray, weathered lumber. But what he saw there now his mind refused to acknowledge. Three women, the clothes on their backs the same color as the mud on the sides of the trailers, were using their teeth and their fingernails to rip the dog's carcass to pieces. One woman turned her head slowly around, ropey lengths of muscle and fur hanging from her lips, and rose to her full height.

She started toward them.

"Oh shit, Anthony," said Jesse.

Anthony stared at the woman, transfixed by her, at the blood that had formed a wide, ghastly bib down the front of her tattered dress. For a long moment, he couldn't wrap his mind around her. It was all just too much, too much to take in. But then he saw her eyes, the same dead, vacant eyes he'd seen on the man back at the ship, and a low groan escaped his lips.

"Hit it, Jesse. Blow the charge. Do it."

"Yeah," Jesse muttered. And then, louder: "Get ready to drop."

Jesse hit the button on the detonator. Both men dropped to their knees, opened their mouths to equalize the pressure, and braced themselves for the blast.

The first explosion came a second later. It was a small blast, muffled by the hull of the ship. Anthony thought, *Is that it?* He was about to open his eyes when the next several blasts came, one after the other, so close together they might have seemed like a single blast if heard from a distance.

The blast wave washed over them a moment later. Anthony was facing toward the boat when it hit. He saw an enormous wall of fire rise up over the trees, huge curtainlike sheets of red, yellow, and orange rising into the sky. A low rumble moved through the ground, causing the trailers around them to jitter and dance. Disoriented and barely conscious he tried to rise to his feet and staggered dizzily to one side, landing on a knee in the shallow water. Something whistled above him and he looked up in time to see a huge piece of metal shaped like a bicycle wheel and trailing a tail of smoke and cables sail overhead like a mad comet.

"Get down!" Jesse screamed.

But Anthony couldn't hear him. He couldn't hear anything but a constantly ringing noise. Stunned, he watched the comet crash into the side of a trailer, splitting it in two and sending the smaller of the two halves tumbling end over end into another trailer.

Anthony watched it settle back into the water, the ripples moving out and away from it, and for a moment his mind was an absolute blank. When he turned around again a giant column of black smoke was rising into the air where he had seen the curtains of fire just seconds ago. The air seemed full of burning twine and the smell of oil and charred metal. His vision was hazy, his balance shot. Anthony turned to Jesse and couldn't focus on him. There seemed to be two of him crossing like ghosts into each other.

Jesse was yelling at him, but Anthony couldn't hear him.

Anthony shook his head in confusion, and Jesse grabbed him and half turned him toward the women they'd seen eating the dog's carcass.

The first woman was still coming toward them. She would take a few steps, list to one side, and pitch over into the water. But each time she fell, she got right back up, oblivious to the smoke seeping off her back.

". . . all wrong!" Jesse was screaming into Anthony's ear. "This is all wrong! We have to go."

Anthony nodded. The muscles in his neck seemed to have lost the ability to control his head. It tilted too far forward, too far back. He grabbed Jesse by the shoulder and tried to speak.

No sound came out. His voice was nothing more than a tickle in the back of his throat.

But it was enough to get his point across.

Jesse pulled Anthony's arm over his shoulder, and together they staggered back to where Brent waited with the boat.

CHAPTER 4

"Were you able to get ahold of your husband?"

Eleanor nodded. "I did, yes, sir." She handed the cell phone she'd just used to talk with Jim and Madison back to Shaw. "Thanks for letting me use that."

"My pleasure." He held the door to the conference room open for her. "After you."

"Thank you, sir."

Eleanor tried to smile as she walked into the meeting, but she was just too tired for pleasantries. Besides, it hadn't been a good conversation with Jim. He and Madison were holding up okay, but the stress of being stuck indoors for days on end, and of taking care of Ms. Hester, whose health had been steadily failing since Hurricane Hector, was starting to wear on them.

Eleanor could hear it in their voices.

They were quarrelsome, short-tempered, snapping at each other while she tried to explain why it was she couldn't come home just yet. This last call she'd hardly gotten a word in edgewise. Every time she opened her mouth, Jim interrupted her to yell at Madison, and by the end of the phone

call, she was left wondering why she'd even bothered calling
in the first place.

Part of her understood where they were coming from. It
had been two and a half days since she'd last been home, and
that was only to spend the night. Before that, she'd been
away for three days. But it hadn't been a cakewalk for her,
either. The last eleven days had been mind-numbing. In that
short time, her office had dealt with the fallout of two major
storms—three, if you counted Tropical Storm Gabriella—an
entire decade's worth of hurricane activity in the span of two
weeks. From her post at the EOC, Eleanor had watched
those storms change her city forever. She had been at the
switchboard of an endless stream of action reports and
emergency evacuations and interagency wrangling, so that
now, when she looked back over the past eleven days, she
found her memory a complete blur. She couldn't remember
what storm had done what. Like the city outside, her mind
was all a jumble.

But now that she was in the conference room, it was time
for business. In here, they dealt with the lives of the eighty
thousand people who had been crammed into the U of H
campus, and fights with her family were a distraction she
simply didn't need.

Eleanor settled into a chair just to the right of Captain
Shaw's. She'd sat there during their first meeting—which
had taken place the morning after Hurricane Hector, eight
days ago now—and it had become her regular place for
every meeting after that. Funny, she thought, how things like
that worked out. There was a sort of etiquette to it.

Captain Shaw of course occupied the head of the table.

Seated at the foot of the table was Shaw's counterpart in
the fire department, Assistant Fire Chief Frank Clay, who
also happened to be one of the handsomest men Eleanor had
ever seen outside a movie theater, like a real-life version of
Harrison Ford. These meetings had a way of going on way

too long, and there had been several times during the past week when Eleanor, tired and bored, had found herself staring at Frank Clay, daydreaming like a heroine from a Lisa Kleypas novel.

Occupying the middle seat to Eleanor's right was Joe Schwab, the head of public works, who, because he spent so much time helping his crews in the field, nearly always looked and smelled as if he had just got done mowing the yard.

Opposite him was Dr. Hugh Bailey.

Bailey had been one of the original refugees stranded by Hurricane Hector, but as the conditions worsened in the shelter, he had emerged as a leader, helping to organize their rapidly dwindling stores of food and medical supplies.

Among the five of them, they were overseeing a nightmare. When Captain Shaw opened up the University of Houston campus to any evacuee who could reach it, Eleanor had been in awe of the man's courage. He was acting way above his pay grade, and doing it without flinching. But as the days went on, and the federal aid they'd been promised still didn't come, Shaw's outpost of mercy turned into a death camp of plague and starvation.

These conference meetings had become increasingly tiresome, the news always worse than the day before, and she always felt exhausted and demoralized afterwards. But like it or not, she had to be here.

It was her job.

Shaw called them to order.

"I suppose you've all heard by now that Hurricane Mardel has been upgraded to a Category Five storm," he said. "According to the National Hurricane Center, it's a monster, nearly twice the size of Kyle. It's expected to make landfall in about six hours. That doesn't give us a lot of time. I want a quick status report from each of you. Major issues only. Don't bog me down with a bunch of bullshit. I just want to know what's wrong and what you're doing to take care of it. Doc, you want to start us off?"

Hugh Bailey nodded slowly. He had probably been a presentable, if undistinguished-looking man, before all this started, but for the past eight days he had been doing hard work in the trenches of the shelter with only two changes of clothes. Now the yellow polo shirt and jeans he wore were filthy and sweat-stained.

"Well," he said, "the salmonella drama continues. We've lost eighty people so far. A few infants, but most of them elderly. Right now we're storing the bodies in the freezers over in the restaurant management building, but we're running out of room, and, not to put too fine a point on it, those freezers haven't been working since all this started. They're cooler than anywhere else we've got to store them, but . . ."

He trailed off, then shrugged.

"But what?" Schwab asked.

The others were silent.

Bailey looked around the table, then finally settled his gaze on Schwab. "To be blunt, those bodies are starting to stink. I smelled them on the way over here. Pretty soon, and by that I mean pretty damn quick, we're going to have to figure out something to do with them. We can't leave them there. It's not healthy for the rest of us."

"But what can we do?" Schwab asked.

Again, Bailey looked around the room, and again, found no help from the others. "We're going to have to start thinking about burying the dead."

"What?" Schwab said. "We don't have the authority to do that. Not here on this campus."

"I don't see that we have any other options," Bailey countered. "Things aren't going to get any better anytime soon. We all know that, right? I've listened to the reports during these meetings, and I know for a fact that we're going to be stuck here for another two weeks at least. Maybe even longer.

That means more dead. And of course that doesn't take into consideration the additional problems Mardel is going to bring us. I'd be lying if I didn't tell you that things are going to get a whole lot worse before they got better."

He sighed.

"Which brings me to another matter. The electricity. Or rather, the lack of it. Without electricity, none of the water pumps work. Our water is filthy. Consider all those people out there in the shelter, eating food that none of us would have fed to a stray dog two weeks ago. We don't have any functioning toilets. We haven't had toilet paper in three days. And as if that wasn't bad enough, that storm surge from Hurricane Kyle overloaded the campus's sewage system. That's caused a backwash that has contaminated everything around us. We have eighty thousand people jammed into cramped quarters, many of them sick and injured. Some with really serious stuff too, like AIDS and hepatitis and TB. A lot of people who were stranded at the airport came here too. It's possible that some of them could be carrying really exotic stuff, frightening stuff. *Demon in the Freezer* stuff, for those of you who have read Richard Preston."

He looked around the table, then went on.

"The short answer is that a lot more people are going to be dying over the next few days and I don't have any way to help them. We can't store the bodies. It's hot as hell out there. Mosquitoes are everywhere. You put all that stuff together and you can expect a pretty huge die-off over the next few days. I say we start looking for a place to bury the dead. Temporarily maybe. The bodies can be moved to a proper cemetery later. But we need to find a grassy area now where we can dig some graves."

"I can't believe I'm hearing this," Schwab said. "How did this salmonella junk get started anyway?"

"I don't think that's really the issue we should be worrying about right now," said Shaw, holding up his hands in frustration. "Doc, we'll deal with the dead after we see what Mardel does to us. Right now, I just need the big picture. What else you got?"

Bailey nodded again.

"Okay. Big picture. Well, we're out of food. We need fresh water, too. A lot of it. The people who aren't busy shitting their guts out from the salmonella are starving and suffering from dehydration."

"Okay," Shaw said. "I'm supposed to be giving a press conference here in about thirty minutes. I'll mention it then, and hopefully it'll light a fire under Homeland Security's ass. Anything else?"

"Well, yes. While you're at it you might as well ask for a barge loaded down with antibiotics to be brought in here. On top of that I've got heart patients, diabetics, people with hypertension and about a hundred other chronic conditions. I don't have medicines. I don't have supplies. Even minor injuries are going to turn into something serious if I can't treat them correctly."

"I can't read all that on the news," Shaw said. "They'll just cut me off. Do me a favor and write out a list of medicines and supplies you need, and I'll see it gets forwarded. Anything else?"

"Yeah, I got a lot. You need to send those cameras into our shelters. If you want people to get motivated to help us, they need to see what's really going on in there. It's like walking through hell."

"I know, Doc," Shaw said tiredly. "Just put what you need on the list. I'll see it gets to the news. That goes for the rest of you, too. Give me your lists before I go live."

Shaw looked down at his notes and sighed.

"Okay, Joe, what have you got?"

"Um," Schwab said. He coughed to clear his throat and then squirmed in his chair until he was sitting up straight. Eleanor had the distinct impression that speaking out loud at these meetings was a real torture for him, that he was much more comfortable out in the field. "Okay. Um, well, first I guess I got a problem with feral hogs."

"What?" Eleanor said. "Did you say hogs?"

"Uh, yeah. I-I've had eight crews attacked so far."

"I don't understand," Eleanor said. "You mean pigs, right? You're men are being attacked by pigs. In the middle of the third-biggest city in the country?"

"Not exactly," Shaw said. "Feral hogs are different. They're pigs, but they've gone wild. Usually only takes a generation for it to happen. They grow as big as the pigs you've probably seen, but they've got tusks and they're about the meanest critters on the planet. I remember last year Sugarland had a bad problem with them. They invade a subdivision and tear up yards and eat trash, that kind of thing. They even kill dogs and cats. They'll eat anything they can catch. I imagine that includes your men."

"That's right," Schwab said. "The floodwaters are driving them out of the woods where they usually hide, and my men are running into them when they go to some of these pump stations. One of them gored a man last night. Luckily he had some other guys with him and they were able to beat the thing away with wrenches."

Schwab looked around the room, then settled his gaze on Shaw.

"Captain, I want some police protection for my men. The men would feel a whole lot better if they had somebody with a rifle going along with them."

Shaw shook his head.

"Joe, I can't spare an officer to go out with every crew. My people are stretched to the breaking point as it is. Tell you what, I'll ask for more rifles. What I get, I'll distribute to your people. I'm sure you've got some good country boys working for you who know how to shoot. How's that?"

"Yeah," Schwab said. "Yeah, that'd be okay."

"Good. Anything else?"

"Well, uh, I guess you know most of the problems I'm facing. None of that's changed. But there is one thing."

"Yeah?"

Schwab swallowed nervously. "Some of my guys have been telling me about survivors they've seen."

To Eleanor, Shaw seemed to suddenly stiffen in his chair.

"Yes?" Shaw said.

"Have you guys had any reports of people, you know, eating each other? Some of my men, they . . . they've heard from people they've pulled out of flooded houses that there are survivors out there eating each other. They break their way into homes and eat the people they find there. My men are scared."

Ah, there it is, Eleanor thought. *The genie's out of the bottle now.*

For several days, they'd been hearing the same reports. Survivors wandering through the flooded ruins of South Houston, in such a deep state of shock that they act like zombies. And there had been multiple reports of cannibalism. That part wasn't rumor. They'd confirmed that.

And though he wasn't in on the intelligence, Dr. Bailey had as much as predicted it during one of their previous meetings. Many of the survivors, he had said, will be dealing with stress levels far beyond their tolerance. Anxiety over the survival of family and friends, over their homes and pets and cars, would be driving even emotionally stable people to the breaking point. Post-traumatic stress disorder would be about as common in the flooded remains of the city as mosquitoes, and that would lead to some pretty odd behaviors.

"Listen to me," Shaw said. There was a hard note of warning in his voice. "That right there is gonna stop. We're not gonna go around spreading a lot of wild-ass rumors about cannibals, you understand me? Tell your men there are no cannibals out there. There are survivors who are starving, yes. A lot of them are probably in shock, too. But they are not cannibals. Got it?"

Eleanor looked at him, her mouth agape in surprise.

What was he saying?

The two of them had had conversations on this very subject. What he had just said was the exact opposite of reports he himself had confirmed two days earlier.

He caught her eye and gave her a barely perceptible shake of his head. But the message was clear: *Quiet. Don't say a word.*

"I-I got it," Schwab said. "I was just wondering . . ."

"There's nothing to those rumors," Shaw repeated. "Anything else?"

"No, sir."

"Good. Frank, how about the fire department?"

Eleanor was still looking at Shaw when Frank Clay started to speak.

"Big news for us is the nearly seven million 9-1-1 calls we've been unable to answer. By federal law, each one will have to be followed up on after Mardel. That'll mean some have been holding for nearly two weeks."

"Well, most of those will just have to wait, I guess," said Shaw.

"Yeah, but the time lag isn't the problem. The problem is what our men will encounter when they go into the areas where most of the calls are coming from. Rescue workers— that's your people and mine, Mark—are going to be dealing with a lot of unknown contaminants in the water. Chemical, biological, rotting dead bodies, sewage—you name it. The floodwaters are gonna be the nastiest soup you've ever seen. Every time our people enter a house they'll be dealing with mold and possible carbon monoxide poisoning. Buildings'll be collapsing. At this point, I have no idea how we're going to manage it. I guess we can hit up the military for some bio-hazard suits, but even then it'll be risky for our people. And of course we haven't even talked about what Hurricane Mardel is likely to do to us."

Shaw nodded slowly.

"That'll have to wait, Frank. Write me up a list of critical assets and we'll get some people to work securing them."

Shaw let out a sigh and stood up.

"All right," he said, "that's it for now. I want each of you to head back to your posts. Frank, send me anything you come up with to help us get ready for Mardel. The rest of you, batten down your hatches and pray for the best."

And, just like that, the meeting was over. The others filed out in silence, leaving Eleanor and Shaw alone. Shaw gathered up his papers and maps and jammed them into a canvas attaché case embossed with the HPD's logo on the side. He slid the strap over his shoulder and pulled out his pack of cigarettes.

They walked out of the room and down the library's front steps together. It was a little after 10:00 A.M. On a normal Houston September morning the sun would have been beating down on them, but the sky was dark and overcast and a steady breeze from the south carried with it the smell of the sea mingled with smoke and chemicals and, underneath all of it, the sickeningly sweet odor of mud and rot. The air had not yet turned the eerie chemical green that announced a coming hurricane, but the smell of the breeze left little doubt that it was on the way, and it was going to be a killer.

"Captain?" Eleanor said. "You mind if I ask you something?"

"Depends. You mind if I smoke?"

"No, I don't mind."

"Good. Then ask away."

She watched him shake a cigarette loose from the pack and light it with a brass-plated Zippo.

"You lied to Joe Schwab in there. Why?"

"You mean about the cannibalism?"

"That's right. You know as well as I do those reports are accurate. What if Schwab's crews end up dealing with those people? Don't they have a right to know what we know?"

He didn't answer her right away. He just stood there smoking, lost in thought.

Finally, he said, "Schwab's people are working primarily inside the Loop. All the reports we've gotten have been down around the Deer Park and LaPorte areas. Texas City, Dickinson, Webster, those places. We haven't seen any of that farther north."

"So why not tell him the truth?"

Again, he hesitated before answering.

"Look, Eleanor, I'm about to go on national TV and issue a plea for help. I do not want to have to explain that the survivors I'm asking America to help are cannibals. Do you have any idea what a story like that would do to the rescue efforts? Can you imagine what it would do to the morale of this city? I have to think about that. That is my responsibility. It's on my shoulders. It is my duty to make sure the people of this city get the help they need. I will not have them become pariahs."

Eleanor glanced across the trash-strewn lawn between the library and the back of Hoffman Hall, where the camera crews were already massing for the press conference.

"And what about them?" she asked. "What if they ask you about it point-blank? What will you say?"

"I will tell them we've had our fair share of looters. I'll say we've heard reports of people eating their pets. I'll tell them we've found plenty of shell-shocked survivors. But I'll deny any reports of cannibalism as unsubstantiated and just plain mean-spirited."

"Mean-spirited?"

"Racist, in other words," Shaw said. "Start calling the media racist and they'll knee-jerk so fast it'll make your head spin. Before you know it, they'll make this cannibalism mess a non-issue. They'll be afraid to mention it, and they'll condemn anybody who does."

Shaw finished his cigarette, dropped it to the sidewalk, and rubbed it out with the toe of his boot. Then he took his phone from his shirt pocket and checked it.

"Almost time," he said. "Listen, Eleanor, I want you to go home to your family."

"What? You mean right now?"

He nodded.

"Sir, I can't do that," she said. "Not with everything that's going on."

"Yes, you can. I'm telling you to."

"Captain, I can't just leave you like this. Not now. My duty is here."

"Eleanor, don't confuse your duty with what others expect you to do. We're both parents, okay? We have a clear set of obligations—family, country, job. In that order. Go home to your family. Be with them. When the storm's over, and they're safe, come back here."

"What about you, sir? What about your family? You've got two sons out there."

He smiled faintly. The last two weeks had really aged him, she realized. She'd read books in which people went through something awful, and it seemed to age them ten years in as many hours, but she always thought that was a writer's hyperbole. Real people didn't age like that.

But he had. She could see it in the slump of his shoulders and in the nests of lines that spread out from the corners of his eyes like river deltas.

"I've already taken care of my family's future," he said. "Don't worry about that. My sons will walk away from this with a future they can count on. Now it's time for me to move on to my other obligations."

She looked across the trash and mud-strewn yard, where

the reporters waited like a pack of hungry hounds, and an awful feeling stirred in her.

"What are you going to do?" she said.

"I'm going to go over there and become a scapegoat for every act of mismanagement this city has done up to this point. I'll take the blame so others can pick up the pieces when this is all done and lead the city forward. And when I'm done with that, I'm going to come right back here and see if I can't help some of the people in our shelters."

She started to object, but found she didn't really have the words for it. What he was saying was awful, but it did make sense. As soon as conditions in the shelter hit the front page of the newspapers and scrolled across the home pages of every Internet provider the world over, the public would demand to know why it had all gone wrong. If Shaw took the blame, it would give the city's leaders the public opinion mandate they would need to move Houston out of this crisis. If that was even possible.

"Go home, Eleanor," he said, and turned and walked off toward Hoffman Hall.

She watched him go, a little stunned, and filled once again with awe for the man's courage. The reporters closed on him, swarmed around him, and soon he was lost among the throng.

"Good luck," she muttered, and began the long walk down to the makeshift docks they'd built along Spur 5, where she'd left her canoe.

There was a cement loading dock behind the Student Service Center. Floodwater had come right up to the edge of the walkway that ran along the rear of the loading dock, and Eleanor and a few of the other police officers and firefighters who lived close by and who used canoes or small motorboats to get to work had taken to tying up their boats to an eighteen-wheeler that had been trapped in the flood. Somebody—Eleanor thought maybe it was Hank Gleason, but she wasn't sure—had spray-painted RESERVED PARKING FOR HPD ONLY along the side panel of the big rig that was nearest the dock. Along the other side of the rig, the side that was facing the floodwater and was therefore impossible to get to from the dock unless you were swimming, the same somebody had painted RESERVED PARKING FOR HFD HOSERS. It had been funny the first time she saw it, but it didn't seem so now. Now, the only thing on her mind was the approaching storm, and the disquieting notion that she was leaving her post at a critical moment. Why had Shaw insisted she go home? It didn't make any sense to her, not with so much going on.

She stood on the edge of the walkway, watching her canoe floating the water, tethered to the rig's rearview mirror, and tried to think it through.

But nothing came.

Shaw had always been a private man, never the kind to open up around those with whom he worked, especially when those people were younger than he was by a good twenty years and considerably below him in rank. But Eleanor had picked up a good many things over the two years she'd worked in the EOC, most of it by listening in on the edges of conversations, and she knew his talk of duty wasn't just a front. He really did think that way, as though the big concepts in life like duty and honor and justice were living things that could be fed and nurtured, the same way you would with children. And she knew the commitment he felt to those big ideas had made him unpopular with the department's current administration. They looked on him as an inflexible, hardheaded dinosaur, more a nuisance than an asset, somebody who needed to be put somewhere out of the way, where he could work out his remaining few years until retirement in relative isolation and then, they hoped, go away

quietly. She thought of him going into that horde of reporters, the camera crews looking as though they might
chew him to pieces, and smiled bitterly. Fate, it seemed, had
other plans for Captain Mark Shaw.

Still, the canoe waited. Her family waited. She thought of
Madison, who, at the beginning of this mess had helped her
move their household supplies upstairs with the bored air of
a teenager going through the motions, but who was now acting as a full-time nurse for Ms. Hester, carrying the weight
of responsibility like a grown-up, and Eleanor wondered if
Shaw hadn't had a point about the family being the prime
duty of a human being. Hadn't that been what attracted her
to working in the EOC in the first place? Didn't she feel a
sense of rightness when she prepared her family's disaster
plans? Maybe it made sense after all.

Eleanor untied the canoe and set out.

She paddled away from the Student Service Center,
through the ghosts of flooded buildings and over the roofs of
submerged cars. Occasionally she heard an antenna scraping
against the metallic bottom of the canoe.

Then she went under the freeway, and when she came out
on the other side she was in open water. In the distance she
could see I-45, a dark spine of concrete stretching across the
horizon. It took ten minutes of paddling to put the campus
well behind her. Home was another three miles to the south,
and she figured she'd be able to make the distance in plenty
of time to help Jim and Madison prep the house for the
storm.

In her mind she went through the lists of things he'd mentioned on the phone, small chores that had to get done, damage that had to be repaired before Mardel made landfall, and
soon she found herself drifting through a neighborhood.

She stopped paddling and looked around.

All the houses were dark, of course. That didn't surprise
her. Nor did the extraordinary amount of damage that had

been done. What did surprise her was the quiet. There were no cars, no planes in the sky, no screaming kids or lawn-mowers or ringing phones. A strange, eerie calm had settled over the houses, and the stillness that dropped over the city was both hypnotic and terrifying.

Off to her left, in the space between two houses, she saw a darkened figure wading toward her, chest deep in the flood water. She was pretty sure it was a man. He was moaning. Something about the sound chilled her nerves, and she took up her paddle and moved out again.

The man was far away, but even still, she nudged the AR-15 at her feet a little closer, just in case.

CHAPTER 5

The hammer came down on the back of his thumb, and for a moment, Jim Norton just stood there, his mouth hanging open in shock. He had just enough time to ask himself why in the hell he'd been so careless when the pain flooded in and his whole body convulsed.

A strangled cry of pain escaped his throat.

He dropped the hammer and squeezed his injured thumb in his right hand, his body jittering like a man who has never had to piss so badly in all his life but has to wait just a little while longer.

"Fuck!" he yelled.

And yelling made something click inside him. His eyes sprang open. The pain was still there, but the rude blunt shock of it had abruptly given way to anger. He was breathing very fast, panting really, purple blotches swimming at the corners of his vision.

"Goddamn holy fucking shit!" he yelled, and kicked the wall so hard a thin curtain of dirt sifted down from the window-sill.

He stood there, hurting. The hammer was at his feet and he gave it an angry kick.

"Piece of shit," he muttered.

Still clutching his injured thumb, he closed his eyes and focused on his breathing, trying to get it under control.

"Daddy?"

He opened his eyes. Madison was standing in the doorway, looking at him, her expression one of worry underscored by a note of fear.

"I hit my thumb with the hammer," he said.

She stepped out onto the porch. "Oh no." She reached for his hand. "Are you okay?"

What does it fucking look like? he nearly said, but caught the words before they had a chance to come out. That wouldn't do. Hurt as he was, it was hardly an excuse to lash out at her. God knows they'd done plenty of that over the last eleven days as it was.

With a great deal of effort he said, "No, sweetheart, I hit it pretty good. Do Daddy a favor, would you? Go get me a rag or something from inside."

She looked at his hurt thumb. A thin trickle of blood was seeping out between his fingers and running down the inside of his wrist. She nodded.

"Okay, Daddy."

Madison ran inside the house, and when she was gone, Jim took his right hand away and looked at the thumb. It was a mess. A small crescent-shaped cut had formed right below the web where the thumb met the hand, and within the curve of the crescent he could see the negative impression of the hammer's nicked head. The left side of the cut was deeper, and bright red blood was flowing freely from it.

Tentatively, he tried to move the thumb, and right away felt like somebody had jammed a live electrical cord into his wrist.

"Okay," he said. "Not gonna do that again."

Fuck, he thought, *probably broken. That's just great. We got a big-ass storm on the way and I go and break my fucking hand. Lot of fucking good I'm gonna be.*

He wiped the tears from his eyes with the back of his hand, and when he looked up again, Madison was running out the door with the tackle box they were using for their first-aid kit in her hands.

She put it on the porch next to his feet, then took his huge hand in her small ones.

"Easy," he said, wincing. "I think it's broken."

He tried to pull it back, but Madison held on firmly. She made a clucking noise and kept on examining his hand, turning it this way and that.

Jim Norton chewed his fingernails, always had and probably always would, no matter how much Eleanor complained about it. As a result, his fingernails always had a ragged, unkempt look. He wasn't especially self-conscious about it, no more than a smoker is about smoking, but it did make it difficult to pry open the tabs on Coke cans or pick coins off a counter. Eleanor would sometimes see him struggling and she'd make the same clucking noise Madison was making now. It was an impatient, *Here, let me do it* gesture, and as he stood, watching his daughter examine his injury, he realized how very much she was beginning to look like her mother.

"It's not broken." She said it flatly, like a pronouncement.

"Feels broken."

"It's not. Just cut real bad. If it was broken I wouldn't be able to move it like this."

"Huh," he said.

He looked at his injured thumb and frowned. Jim wasn't sure which surprised him more, the easy confidence in his daughter's voice or the fact that he was accepting as almost certainly accurate the medical diagnosis of a twelve-year-old.

"It is bleeding pretty bad, though. We'll need to clean it and bandage it."

She knelt down and examined the contents of the tackle box before finally settling on a roll of gauze and some hydrogen peroxide.

"This is gonna sting some," she said, and he had just enough time to muse how that too made her sound like her mother, before the liquid bit into his wound.

Jim closed his eyes and tried not to think of how the hydrogen peroxide would be foaming up upon contacting his blood and turning to little pink bubbles that ran greasily down his arm. He could, he knew, be an awfully big baby sometimes, and the thought brought on a wave of bitterness that was as palpable as half-chewed aspirin clinging to the back of his tongue.

Eleanor had once told him how thankful she was to have found him. They had been in the car at the time, coming home from an Astros game. Jim was driving and Eleanor was in the passenger seat, her legs curled up beneath her.

He glanced at her, a small, curious smile at the corner of his mouth, and said, "What brought that on?"

He knew she had dated some before they met. They never really talked about past loves. They both knew the other had had them, but there was never any reason to bring them up. Those were all in the past, and they hardly mattered, certainly no more than a batter's practice swings before stepping up to the plate for real, and what they had together was real. It was for keepsies, as she sometimes said.

So he was a little surprised when she started telling him about some of the guys she had dated before she met him.

"This was after I became a cop," she said. "Before that, you know, it was no big deal. Back in college, guys were just boys. No big deal. But after I became a cop, things just got weird. I learned to avoid telling guys what I did for a living, because once I did, they got all crazy on me."

"Crazy?" he said. "Like how?"

"Not anything mean. Nothing like that. They just sort of

drifted off, you know? Sometimes they'd become defensive. Sometimes they'd just stop calling. I used to think it was me, like maybe I was doing something wrong. I don't know. I wondered if I had a nasty case of halitosis or something."

She laughed, then put her hand on his arm.

"But then I was at the doctor's office one day, and I met this woman there. She was about fifty, I guess. Pretty, you know, but obviously older than me. She was a chemistry professor at Rice. Anyway, we got to talking, and I was kind of surprised at how much we had in common. We were both single, both struggling, both completely clueless about what we were doing wrong in the dating department. And then she told me something really strange. She said she never told guys what she did for a living. When they asked, she'd just say she worked at a college, let them think she was a secretary or something."

"Why would she do that?"

"Well, that's the thing. That's what I'm trying to tell you. You see, when guys found out she was a PhD, they ran the other way. They got intimidated, I guess. It was the same with me. Guys would find out I was a cop, and they would joke about it, but underneath it all, I could tell they were uncomfortable around me. I made them nervous. You can't build a relationship that way."

She paused then, and when he looked over at her, the smile gradually thinned from her face and became a look of utter gratitude.

"That's why you were different, Jim. That's why I fell for you. You weren't like all those other guys. I love whatever it is you see in me. It feels special, like only you can see it."

He hadn't really known what to say to that—he never did, in situations like that—and perhaps she hadn't expected him to say anything, for at that moment she put her cheek down on his shoulder and sighed, as if it was the best place in the world to be.

But looking back on that memory now, with his head swimming in pain, Jim Norton wondered if maybe she had misjudged him. Or maybe he was being unfair to her. He didn't know, but he suspected it amounted to the same thing, for he found that after all these years of marriage he was, after all, a little intimidated by his wife.

No, he thought, *maybe intimidated isn't the right word. Maybe you're resentful. Maybe that's a better word for it. You're resentful because here you are, the man of the house, the one who's supposed to be the rock, the provider, and instead you're standing here getting doctored by a twelve-year-old girl while your wife is putting on a uniform and saving the city. She's the one with the balls. Maybe you should just go ahead and hand her your dick, too. You're not gonna need it.*

He frowned bitterly at the thought. He didn't want to believe he was that shallow, but . . . was he? Did he really resent his wife for going out into that flooded mess of a world and doing her duty?

He was uncertain what he really felt, and that bothered him.

Madison was still busy wrapping gauze around his thumb. He gazed at the work she was doing and it occurred to him that she had actually done a really good job of it. The fit was snug, but not painful. He had experienced a moment of numbness in the thumb, but that was gone now, replaced by a dull, insistent throb of pain that he suspected would be with him for a couple of days at least.

"You did a good job on that," he said. "Thanks."

"You're welcome, Daddy."

Her voice was bubbly, as effervescent as always, and it brought a smile to his face. She had really done a wonderful job since all this began. His little girl was growing up.

The reason for that of course was Ms. Hester upstairs.

The poor thing was doing badly. After Eleanor had saved her (and he mentally hesitated over the memory, for yes, it had been Eleanor who did the saving), they brought her to their house, where she had slipped into a state of shock from which she couldn't seem to recover. They weren't equipped to care for her, at least not properly, not with the power out, and soon her shock took the form of a fevered sickness.

While Eleanor was at work, saving the city, and Jim was moving around the house, fixing this and that and occupying himself with any little task in a desperate attempt to ward off the restless boredom of cabin fever, Madison had calmly invested herself in the ceaseless effort to ease Ms. Hester's suffering. She was her nurse. She read to her. She held her hand and wiped her brow and fed her with a spoon and kept her hydrated and cleaned her when she went to the bathroom. Yes, he realized, she had played nurse, but she wasn't just playing at it. She was actually doing real work. She was recognizing a problem and confronting it head-on, like an adult.

Jim turned from his daughter's ministrations and glanced across the street, toward Ms. Hester's house. A light breeze carried the stench of mud and sewage across the patio. It made his nose wrinkle and his Adam's apple pump up and down in his throat. Ms. Hester's house was a shambles. Mud from Hurricane Kyle's storm surge had pushed through that side of the street and poured into the gaping hole on the kitchen side of her house. Water now filled the house up to a height of about two feet, not quite covering the top of the mud flow, and in the stillness the house, the tree that jutted through it had a skeletal eeriness that he didn't like. Not one little bit.

A figure was walking around the back corner of the house.

Jim watched the man carry something from the house

and put it into a small green boat and thought: *Is that really him? It can't be. That slime ball Bobby Hester is looting his own grandmother's house. Is that really what I'm seeing?*

But he was. Bobby Hester was carting a TV right out of his grandmother's house and putting it into the back of a boat that was almost certainly stolen as well.

What was next? he wondered. Her jewelry? Her collection of Spode china?

"Sweetheart," Jim said, pulling his hand away, "do Daddy a favor and go inside the house."

She followed his gaze across the flooded street to Ms. Hester's house.

"But, Daddy . . ."

"Don't argue with me, Madison. Go upstairs. Right now. Go on, move."

He gave her a gentle push toward the door. She resisted momentarily, then turned and ran inside. He followed her to the door and watched her run up the stairs.

"Stay put up there, you hear?" he said to her back.

She reached the landing and turned. "Daddy?"

"It's okay, sweetheart. Just stay up there, okay? Daddy's gonna go check something across the street."

"Daddy, no . . ."

"It's okay, Madison. Just hang tight up there. I'll be right back."

But part of him wondered if that would happen. It hadn't come across in his voice, at least he hoped it hadn't, but the truth of the matter was that he was very scared just now. He was pissed off at the idea that anyone would steal from an old woman, that much was true, but he was also out of his depth.

He watched Madison disappear into the game room upstairs, then turned back to Ms. Hester's house. What would he do if he actually got his hands on Bobby Hester anyway? Jim had picked up more than a few cop stories over the years of his marriage with Eleanor, and he thought he had a pretty good idea of what meth addicts were capable of doing. They tended to be violent and unpredictable, not the kind of people who listened to reason. If he were actually to catch Bobby in the act, what would he do?

He had a momentary vision of belting Bobby across the jaw with a hammer, his meth-addled body flying backwards, landing with a splash in the water and then going still as a small, thin groan escaped his lips. Jim would stand there, victorious, a suburban Conan the Barbarian, defender of all that was right and good.

As far as fantasies went, it felt like a good one. It appealed to his sense of justice.

But a nagging, insistent little voice in the back of his head kept repeating: *It'll never happen that way. He'll get the hammer from you and hit you with it again and again and before you know it it'll be you flying backwards, landing in the water, a pink cloud spreading out around your head. Only you won't go still, and he won't stop to gloat. You'll keep sliding under the surface of the water, unconscious, little silvery bubbles escaping from your nostrils as he drops the hammer and grabs your neck and holds you under until you're dead.*

He shook his head as though to shake off the voice and walked out the door. The hammer was where he had left it on the porch. He scooped it up, flexed his fingers over the handle, and stepped into his flooded yard.

Jim was halfway across the street, up to his chin in water, before he realized he hadn't planned his approach. For a moment he entertained using the downed pecan tree as a cover, but then he remembered all the water moccasins he'd seen gliding through the water over the past few days. They took shelter in the trees, he knew, and the idea of suddenly finding himself entwined in a bolus of writhing snakes was more than he wanted to deal with.

He sank a little lower in the water and dog-paddled around the bedroom side of the house and into the backyard, where he hoped to get the drop on Bobby Hester.

And, as he peered through the open back door and saw Bobby in the kitchen, struggling to remove a microwave oven from its alcove in the wall, it appeared his plan might actually work.

Staying low in the water, the hammer gripped tightly in his right hand, Jim glided through the living room.

He stopped at the edge of the couch and slowly rose from the water.

Bobby Hester was busy pulling at the microwave, grunting and cursing under his breath, but as Jim closed the distance between them, the situation abruptly changed for the worse.

Bobby took his hands down from the microwave. His back was still to Jim, but his head was turned just enough for Jim to see dark light in Bobby's left eye.

"You're in my house," Bobby said.

Jim froze. The distance between them was maybe eight feet. Even in hip-deep water Jim figured he could probably close that distance in the wink of an eye. But it wasn't going to happen. His fear had rooted him to the floor as surely as if hands had come up from the dark water and grabbed his ankles. A flood of adrenaline twisted his stomach into knots. He could feel his face and his scalp tingling with a heated electric flush.

Come on, Jim, he thought. *Do something. Don't just stand here. He'll know how scared you really are.*

"This isn't your house, Bobby."

At the mention of his name, a wicked smile lit the corner of Bobby Hester's mouth. One hand went into the dark recesses of the shelf in front of him and came out with an imposing ten-inch chef's knife. Jim saw a flash of light dapple across the blade as Bobby turned to face him.

"This is my grandmother's house," Bobby said. "Might as well be mine."

There was a maniacal light dancing in Bobby's eyes, not sane. Dark pockets, like bruises, filled the hollows of his cheeks, and when his burned and bloodless lips spread open, they revealed a mouth of broken and blackened teeth.

Jim thought: *That's a tweaker's face. The man is amped up as high as a body can go. Oh shit, what have I done?*

"You don't have her permission to be here," Jim said. He was trying as hard as he could to sound confident and strong, but no amount of trying could keep the tremors from his voice. He heard it, and he was pretty sure Bobby Hester heard it, too. "You need to get the hell out of here, Bobby. Just walk out that door over there."

Bobby glanced down at the knife in his hand. It was a deliberate gesture, full of implication. Then he looked at Jim, his eyebrows raised.

"I'll tell you what I need to do," Bobby said. "I need to get the rats out of my grandmother's house."

No sooner had the words left his mouth than he lunged forward, slashing the knife in the air between them. The thrust wasn't meant to cut Jim, only scare him, and that it did. Jim stumbled backwards, falling over something under the water (he wasn't sure what). He managed to keep from going all the way under, but the damage was done. Bobby threw his head back and let out a savage sound that was part laugh, part battle cry, and he charged again, jabbing the knife in front of him like a bayonet.

Jim scrambled away from the knife until his buttocks hit the submerged top of Ms. Hester's kitchen table. The next instant he was on top of the table and sliding backwards across it like a piece of wet ice over a tile floor. He caught himself at the back edge of the table and jumped to his feet, his jeans pulled halfway down his ass, full of water.

But he was on his feet. He looked down at the table, and then down at Bobby Hester, who was still closing on him, and it seemed impossible to Jim that only a moment before he had been down there in the water with that deranged, knife-wielding lunatic. He saw Bobby, his mouth a diseased O, staring up at him in surprise. *I did it,* Jim thought with a clear resounding sense of exaltation so intense that for a moment he wanted to laugh.

The laughter died inside him a split second later, though, for Bobby charged the table and grabbed it by the corners and started to shake it.

"Whoa-o-o," Jim said, as the table trembled below him. He could feel it tilting to one side, and as it reached the tipping point Jim's feet slid out from under him and the hammer went flying. For a horrible moment he tracked its flight, watched it tumble end over end until it plunked into the water and slipped into darkness.

But the table was still tipping, and Jim's balance was gone. His feet slid out from under him and he went down, landing on his ass just a few inches from the edge of the tabletop. He was lucky he hadn't landed squarely on it, for the table was heavy wood and slate and solid enough it might have broken his back had he hit a few inches farther to his right. As it was the force of his weight coming down on the table slammed it back down flat on the ground and Jim bounced, unhurt, into the water.

Bobby lunged for him again, screaming something that Jim couldn't exactly understand, though the murderous intent behind the sound was plain enough.

In that instant, a plan popped into his mind fully formed. Rather than try to get to his feet and run away, Jim went under the water, under the table, and kept on swimming back in the direction of the living room. The water was black. He didn't dare open his eyes, not with all the garbage and chemicals floating around in it. He just kicked wildly, his hands

groping blindly at the emptiness around him, hoping he was
going in the right direction.

When his hands hit the recliner he knew he was in the
right spot. He felt for the little side table Ms. Hester had always kept there. *Where are you? Come on,* he thought. *It's
here somewhere.* And then his right hand closed around a
small ceramic figure. Jim shot to the surface, drew a deep
breath, and spun around. Bobby Hester was still in the
kitchen, but was already charging toward him, the knife still
in his hand.

Jim had just a moment to examine the figure, an angelic
child dressed in a graduation cap and gown and holding a
small tightly rolled diploma, bought in honor of Madison's
promotion from elementary school to middle school, before
Bobby Hester shrieked at him.

"I'm gonna fucking kill you!"

But now, with the cold reassurance of some distance between them and still riding the excited high of his narrow escape over at the kitchen table, Jim Norton saw that he could
do this. He tossed the figurine an inch or two in the air, giving it a quarter turn, wrapped his index and middle finger
over the base like a pitcher about to throw his best heat, and
let it fly at Bobby Hester's head.

Bobby flinched away from the hurtling figurine. He threw
up one arm to block his face, but it was too little too late.
The figurine struck his forearm with the solid-sounding
clink of porcelain on bone and was immediately followed by
a howl of rage and pain from Bobby.

Jim reached under the water and came up with another
figurine. There was a whole army of the things down there,
and he was on fire. He threw the next figurine and caught
Bobby in the chin.

Bobby staggered back, stumbling over something in the
water. When he looked back up at Jim, there was an expression of utter surprise on his face.

Jim laughed at him. He reached into the water for another weapon, but when he came up, he found that Bobby was no longer looking at him. And the expression of surprise on his face was gone, replaced by a sour sneer of contempt.

Jim looked over his left shoulder, and saw Eleanor standing there, her pistol in her hand.

"That's far enough, Bobby. Put the knife down and leave."

"Fuck you, bitch. This is my hou—"

The word broke off mid-syllable, for at that moment Eleanor fired a single shot, the bullet smacking into the wall less than a foot from Bobby's ear.

"It's up to you," she said. "We can stay here and discuss it if you want to, or you can crawl your miserable hide right out that hole in the wall behind you. But just remember this: If you want to stay, I've got orders to shoot looters on sight, if necessary."

Jim shifted his gaze back to Bobby Hester. Bobby was a wasted life, his mind charred to cinders by all the meth he'd smoked, but nonetheless, Jim could see the logic working itself out in Bobby's mind. There was a look of savage contempt on his face, but he also seemed to know that Eleanor wouldn't miss on her next shot.

And that's a safe bet, you sorry sack of shit, Jim thought. *At this distance, she can shoot your remaining teeth out one by one.*

"You're gonna fucking pay for this," he said, pointing the knife at Eleanor. "I guarantee you, bitch. You're gonna fucking pay."

"Do whatever you're man enough to do, Bobby."

But he had already turned and slithered out the hole in the kitchen wall. Jim watched him go, caught somewhere between disbelief at the adventure he'd just had and the dawning realization that the only reason he'd survived it was because his wife had pulled his stones out of the fire.

Jim looked down and realized he was still holding the figurine, this one a little girl on a stone reading the Bible. He dropped it into the water. Outside the house, Bobby Hester was climbing into his boat. His movements looked hesitant, though, and Jim could see that he was holding his injured left arm where the first figurine had hit him.

"Are you okay?" Eleanor asked him.

Jim kept his gaze on Bobby. The motor fired up, and a moment later Bobby was speeding off between the houses, curving around a toolshed, and then slipping away out of sight.

"Jim?"

He turned around.

"Yeah," he said. "I'm good. Let's go home."

CHAPTER 6

"Okay, this is good," Anthony said. "Stop here."

Brent Shaw eased up on the throttle, but he wasn't fast enough. He could feel the boat gliding forward, past the mark he'd been shooting for, and it still wasn't stopping.

"Come on, come on," Brent pleaded with the boat. "Whoa-o-o!"

There was a downed tree just ahead of them, and he watched helplessly as the bow slid into the branches with a sickening crunch, burying itself deep in the foliage.

"Shit," he muttered.

He looked over his shoulder. Anthony and Jesse Numeroff were in the back of the boat, holding on to the railing, glaring at him.

"Sorry about that," Brent said.

He reversed the engine and the boat eased back, tree limbs snapping as they released their hold on the bow.

Out of the corner of his eye he could see Anthony and Jesse exchanging worried looks. Jesse said something under his breath to Anthony and nodded toward Brent. This wasn't good, and Brent knew it. The Wonder Twins had been riding his ass since they set out, and it was starting to really piss him off.

Anthony whispered something else to Jesse, then started walking forward.

"Shit," Brent muttered again.

Anthony put a hand on the windscreen above the steering wheel, the other on the seat back behind Brent's head. He was smaller than Brent, but that had never made any difference. Anthony was the one blessed with the looks and the speed and the self-confidence that opened every door. Brent got none of that. And when his younger brother loomed over him, as he was doing now, Brent, though physically huge compared to Anthony, felt small.

"What the fuck are you doing, Brent? We're trying to load dynamite back there, for Christ's sake."

"I'm sorry," Brent said without looking at him.

"You're sorry?" There was a pause, and when Anthony spoke again his voice was a savage whisper. "Holy shit. You've been drinking. You motherfucker, you've been drinking, haven't you?"

Anthony glanced back at Jesse in the rear of the boat, then turned back to Brent.

"What the fuck's wrong with you? You know how important this is."

"I'm sorry," Brent muttered.

"Don't tell me you're fucking sorry," Anthony said. "I don't give a rat's ass about sorry. I need you sharp. I need to know I can count on you."

Brent said nothing.

"Did you bring a bottle?" Anthony asked. A pause. "Answer me. Did you bring a bottle with you on this boat?"

"No," Brent said. It wasn't as much a lie as an equivocation. He had poured most of a pint of vodka into a thermos of grape juice that he'd been slowly nursing since before they'd left the EOC. The thermos was tucked out of sight, down by his feet, hidden by a life preserver.

"You better not have," Anthony said. "This is too important for you to fuck it all up."

"I'm not gonna fuck it up," Brent said.

Jesse looked up at them, frowning.

"Keep your voice down," Anthony said. His voice was an angry whisper.

"I'm not gonna fuck this up," Brent said, also whispering.

Though Anthony had always been the gifted one, the cool one, the one their dad thought of as a chip off the old block, it nonetheless rankled Brent to be accused of fucking up. He was doing his part, wasn't he? Maybe he wasn't going down into the vault with them. Maybe they wouldn't trust him to be within arm's length of the dynamite they carried. But damn it, he was doing his part. Sure, he'd had a couple pulls off the thermos, but he wasn't drunk. He had got them here, and he would get them back out again.

"I'm gonna do my part," he said.

Anthony eyed him coolly.

"Yeah," he said. "You do that. Come on back here with me. And don't you dare stumble. Don't you dare slur your words. You keep your shit together until we're all done, got it?"

Brent wanted to raise his chin and look his younger brother in the eye, but he couldn't.

"I got it," he muttered.

"All right. Let's go."

They walked back to where Jesse was packing the last of their gear. Jesse looked up at the two brothers and said, "Problems?"

"No problems," Anthony said, a little too harshly.

Jesse's doubtful gaze lingered on Brent for just a moment; then he handed one of the bags to Anthony. "That's the last of it."

Brent watched the two men readying their gear. They worked together seamlessly. Always had. Back in high school, while Brent was silently waiting out his senior year in a desperate attempt not to get noticed, Anthony and Jesse were building reputations as the best shortstop-and-second-baseman combination in Texas high school baseball. They were only sophomores at the time, but they were already local celebrities. One of the nightly news sportscasters had even called them the Wonder Twins.

At the time, Brent had been perfectly willing to step back and let his younger brother grab the limelight. At least no one was bothering him while they were worshipping his little brother. He had to swallow some pride, sure, but he knew his own limitations. He knew he wasn't in their league. He drank too much, for one thing. Even back in high school, he drank too much. And with the drinking came melancholic fits of depression and self-abuse, which made him a chore to be around. Underneath it all was an unpleasantness, a surliness that came from the realization that he was tolerated merely because of his proximity to Anthony and Jesse, the Wonder Twins. But only tolerated. Never welcomed. He knew that about himself, even then. Brent had hid the resentment back then, and he hid it now. He had grown used to it. He was good at it.

Jesse was explaining their schedule, but Brent found it hard to stay focused. He let his attention wander across his surroundings, across the murky water that covered the streets, the cars, nearly everything. They had stopped at the corner of Canal and Stiles, just north of Eastwood Park. It was past dusk, and their surroundings were lost in deepening shadows. As he watched, the night, like the floodwaters, seemed to rise all around him, filling the areas below trees and in the alleys between buildings first before spreading into the street and off to the horizon.

Looking down Canal Street toward Lockwood, Brent could

just see a long line of brick buildings, all of them with the windows busted out. Here and there the cabs of a few of the larger trucks were still visible. Black wooden telephone poles jutted out of the water at odd angles like the skeletal ruins of old docks. Everywhere he looked the city was still, the air charged with that restless electric murmur that proceeds a storm.

And somewhere out there, someone was moaning.

Brent frowned.

He looked back at Anthony and Brent. The Wonder Twins had their heads bent over a laminated map spread out on the white top of a red Igloo cooler. Apparently, neither of them had heard the sound.

He turned back to the flooded ruins and listened.

Nothing.

He strained his senses against the gathering darkness, trying to pick up the sound again.

And there it was. Yes, it was someone moaning. There for a moment he hadn't been sure—thought for a dreadful second that maybe he really had had too much to drink—but he was sure of what he'd heard now. The sound was coming from one of the buildings up on the left side of Canal Street. Past the Church's Chicken? He couldn't tell. Maybe the parking garage? Or that old white house over there? The noise was distant, muffled, but it was definitely there. Someone was moaning for help.

"Brent?" Jesse said. "Hey, Brent, you with us?"

"Huh?"

"Oh Jesus," Jesse said. He slapped the map and looked at Anthony. "Seriously? You said he was sober."

"He is," Anthony said. "Aren't you, Brent?"

Brent looked at them, his thumb hooked back over his shoulder in the direction of the noise. "You guys didn't hear that?"

"Hear what?" Jesse snapped. He listened. The night was

pulsing with the drone of mosquitoes and frogs. Jesse shrugged. "What, Brent? I don't hear shit."

"I thought I heard somebody moaning."

Anthony snapped his fingers at Brent's face.

"Hey," he said. "There's nobody out there. Pay attention to this right here." He tapped the map. "We don't have much time, and I need to make sure you know this. We won't get a second chance."

Brent hesitated a moment, his attention lingering on the ruins.

"Yeah," he said at last. He blinked at the map, trying to focus. "Yeah, I'm looking."

Brent watched the Wonder Twins slip into the water and go gliding over the sidewalk along Canal Street, dark shapes in the dark water. From the map and what little of the briefing he'd been able to follow, Brent knew they were going to swim up to the next intersection, where Canal met Lockwood, and enter the Texas Chemical Bank from the far side of the building, just around the corner, so that should someone official come along and question what Brent was doing there in the boat he would have some measure of plausible deniability. He didn't understand the rest of their plan and, truth be told, hadn't tried to. It seemed to involve an awful lot of math for just blowing something up.

And besides, from here on out, there were only two parts of the operation that mattered for him. The first was that he had about forty-five minutes to wait while the Wonder Twins blew the vault and surfaced with the cash. The second was to keep a weather eye on his surroundings. If he saw anybody that might give them trouble, he was to hit a button on a small black box Jesse had given him. The button would trigger a signal on a device Jesse wore around his wrist, warning them it wasn't safe topside.

That much he could do, and so Brent sat down behind the wheel and waited, listening to the wind in the trees and the gentle lapping of the water against the boat's hull.

The thermos with the grape juice and vodka was still down at his feet, and he took it out. He had about half the mixture in there, and that was just about right. He envisioned himself tilting it back, feeling the alcohol burn in his nostrils right before it hit his tongue and sizzled down his throat. There wasn't enough in there to get him wasted. He couldn't afford that. But it would tide him over until this "operation," as the Wonder Twins called it, was done and he could go somewhere quiet and start drinking seriously. And then he would drink and drink until everything went—

An unexpected sob in his throat made him pause. He put the thermos down and, for a moment, thought he might start crying. Sniffling, he rubbed at his eyes with the back of his hand. *Fucking pathetic*, he thought. *Weak and pathetic*. Here he was, a grown man, about to break down like a scolded child. He sat there for a long time, waiting on the tears, just on the verge of losing control, but to his surprise, they didn't come.

Brent was mad at himself for the weakness, but wasn't surprised by it. Like several other heavy drinkers he knew, Brent had spent a lot of time studying his addiction. Over the last few years, his life had taken up a sort of orbit around drinking. He couldn't deny that. He thought about it all the time. So yes, liquor was an addiction, an addiction that owned him, no matter how much he would have liked to believe otherwise. He knew this about himself. No sense in lying about it. Call a spade a spade, after all, as Daddy always said.

He went through periods where he needed liquor, where he hated it, where he couldn't remember what he'd done while drinking it. Other times, he'd stormed through his apartment pouring out every single bottle he'd hidden around the place. But love it, need it, or hate it, he always came back to it. Liquor had its own gravitational hold on him. Or, if he was in one of his more self-destructive moods, it was the hole at the bottom of the commode and he was the turd circling it. But regardless of his moods, regardless of the metaphor he used to describe his circumstances, its hold on him was real, and it was relentless.

He scooped up the thermos and took a long drink. It was warm and syrupy, harsh as homemade moonshine, and God did it ever feel good.

He'd been drunk pretty much continuously since Gabriella, and all the days and all the things he'd done since then seemed a blur. But not all his memories were gone. The really shameful ones . . . those he remembered with perfect clarity. Memories like being in Police Headquarters, appearing before the chief's Vehicle Accident Advisory Board. God, what a disaster that had been.

He set the thermos down on his knee and let the memory play out in his mind. He was powerless to stop it anyway. The board was a panel of seven officers, all of them clean-cut and serious, sober-looking, charged with hearing the facts of his latest crash and then making a decision on his punishment that they would then forward to the chief of police. The board's commander was Captain Ricky Macklin, one of his dad's partners from back in their days in Homicide.

Brent had been trying his hardest to crawl into a shell. His shoulders were stooped, his uniform a wrinkled mess, his mind a wrinkled mess, too. He felt as if his mouth was full of sand.

"Brent?" Macklin said. "We're waiting."

Brent had looked up at Macklin, at the other members of the board, all of them watching him expectantly, and said, "I . . . I—" and realized with a panic akin to drowning that there was nothing more. He had nothing. His mind was a blank slate. He looked at the young patrolman to his right, the man's uniform pressed and clean, his face freshly shaven, and sweat popped out all over Brent's body. His face felt hot, his skin damp. What was he doing here? What did they want from him? Couldn't they just leave him the fuck alone?

"Brent?" Macklin said. "The three hundred block of Irving? You sideswiped a parked car. . . ."

The utter bewilderment must have been obvious on his face. He couldn't remember any of it. He had no recollection of any accident. In his mind, there was only a long stretch of black, like an endless road with no scenery, where the memory should have been.

He hung his head, defeated.

Macklin had said something then that Brent didn't catch, but he must have dismissed the other members of the board, for they rose as a body and slowly exited the conference room. When Brent looked up, he and Macklin were the only two left in the room, sitting at opposite ends of a long oval table.

"Brent," Macklin said. "Your dad is one of my oldest friends. I remember driving him to the hospital the night your younger brother was born. I care about your family, son. So tell me, what the fuck is going on with you? How did you get like this?"

Brent had no answer. He'd sat there beneath an air-conditioning vent, sweating, ineffably miserable, embarrassed beyond—

He heard the moaning again.

Brent's pulse quickened. He stood up, scanned the dark and flooded buildings, and saw nothing. He heard nothing. Trees rustled in the wind, and the moon's reflection winked off the rippling floodwaters. But there was no movement.

And no other sounds.

Not even the frogs, he realized. The night had pulsed with

their noises earlier. Where were the frogs? The question hung in his mind and wouldn't let go. It unsettled him somehow. Had they left because of the approaching storm? Had they used that magical sixth sense that animals had that warned them of approaching natural disasters? Mardel was just hours away, after all. *That must be it,* he thought.

He lifted the thermos to his lips and was surprised to find it empty. He shook it. There was a little down there in the bottom, but just the dregs. Had he really drank it all? Strange. He didn't remember doing that.

The sound came again. Behind him this time.

Brent spun around. There was a car wash on the far side of Canal Street, one of those drive-into-the-stall-and-do-it-yourself places, and beyond that, a corner market and a Church's Chicken. On the opposite side of the street was a square-looking brown brick building, the windows dark and vacant and eyelike. A few trees, a few cars, poked up above the surface of the water in front of the building.

There was a figure moving around out there, crossing behind the brown brick building. Brent could only see the figure's head and shoulders, wasn't even sure if it was a man or a woman, but there was definitely a person out there.

"Hello?" Brent called out.

An answering shriek came from somewhere to his right. He spun around, his heart beating frantically in his chest. That familiar chewed-aspirin taste on the back of his tongue was back. He tried to swallow it down and couldn't. He spun around again, scanning for movement, and saw none. In that instant he realized how very alone he was, how very frightened. Really and truly frightened. He stood there in the boat, watching the ruined buildings and the floodwaters, and it seemed to him that the buildings were actually leaning toward him, as though they expected something. For a moment, he considered hitting the alert button Jesse had given him, but the thought of what Jesse and Anthony might say if they scrambled back to the boat and found that there was nothing wrong but a paranoid drunk screwing up their operation made him put the alert button down on the seat.

But was he just a paranoid drunk? In his heart, he didn't believe so. This wasn't, after all, the kind of fear that had followed him during his early days on patrol. That fear made sense. Fear that some abusive and jealous husband might charge out of a back room during a family disturbance with a shotgun and blast his brains all over the front door; fear that he might actually find that cottonmouth that had got into some lady's kitchen; fear that he might lose his job if he couldn't control his drinking—those were all real, solid fears. But this wasn't that kind of fear. It had a dreamlike quality to it, one that he hadn't felt since he was a child, stepping down a long staircase into a darkened basement, dead certain that some hideous thing with chitinous claws for hands and merciless yellow eyes and breath that smelled of the morgue was waiting for him down there in the dark. It was that kind of fear.

He tried shaking his head to loosen the fear's hold on his mind. It made no sense, after all. Why should he feel that every vacant window was an eye leering down at him? Why should the very wind itself smell of death and corruption? There were no ghosts out here. Certainly none but those made of alcohol.

Brent's hands were trembling badly, and it took him several tries to turn over the stopwatch Jesse had left for him.

Eight minutes left, provided everything was going according to schedule.

Jesus, he thought. *Hurry up, you guys.*

A splash behind him.

He spun around. Looking out across the flooded street he thought he saw people in the water. He blinked, leaned forward, squinted into the dark. Yes, there were people out there, wading down the flooded street. Four, six—no, ten of them.

At the same moment a Coast Guard helicopter, one of the big HH-60 Jayhawks, seemed to drop down out of the air above him, lighting him up with high-intensity spotlights. He threw up an arm to shield his eyes. Where had it come from? He hadn't heard anything. One minute, the sky above him had been clear, the wind whistling monotonously. The next, he could feel the thropping of the rotors reverberating off his chest. The noise was deafening. The downwash of air from the helicopter's rotors picked up trash from the boat and sent it flying around Brent's head. Still shielding his eyes and struggling to keep his balance, he hit the alert button.

"This is the United States Coast Guard," an amplified voice from the helicopter boomed at him. "You are in a restricted area. Identify yourself."

Oh shit, Brent thought. *Anthony, where are you?*

He went to the front of the boat and got the megaphone Anthony and Jesse had left for him, just in case somebody official came by asking questions. He pointed it up into the light and said, "This is the Houston Police Department. We're searching for survivors. I have divers in the water."

With his other hand he reached into his back pocket and took out his badge and held it up toward the helicopter. They wouldn't be able to tell if it was genuine or not, certainly not from way up there, but at least they would be able to see the light reflected off it and have an idea of what he was trying to show them.

"Roger that," the amplified voice from the helicopter said. "Do you need assistance? I have rescue divers standing by."

Out of the corner of his eye he saw the Wonder Twins emerge from the water less than twenty feet from the bow of the boat. They were stuffing several large black duffel bags into the backseat of a sunken car. As he watched, Anthony turned to him, a slight smile on his face. He gave Brent a thumbs-up sign, and Brent breathed a sigh of relief.

Hot damn, he thought. *Way to go, Wonder Twins.*

"Anthony, you guys hurry up," he said. "There are people in the water over here."

Anthony's smile slipped away. He said something, but Brent couldn't hear him over the noise from the helicopter.

"H.P.D., I repeat, do you need assistance? I have rescue divers standing by."

Fuck, Brent thought. He knew he had to do something, and he had to do it quickly. He glanced around the boat and saw a handheld spotlight. Pointing the megaphone up at the Coast Guard, he said, "I've got survivors in the water."

And then he turned on the spotlight and pointed it over the back of the boat.

And he froze.

There, in the water, less than twenty feet from the boat, were the people he had seen wading toward him. Or, rather, they had looked like people then, in the dark and far away. But now that they were close enough for him to make out their faces, Brent saw that they were, in fact, horrors.

He looked from one face to the other. Each one had a waxy, yellowish complexion, almost corpselike. Their mouths were bleeding. Some were badly wounded, almost as though they'd been attacked by dogs or wild hogs or been thrown face-first through plate-glass windows. They had blood and mud in their hair. But it was their eyes that made the goose bumps come up all over Brent's skin. Every single one of those people in the water, regardless of their injuries, stared back at him with white, vacant eyes that didn't blink in the glare of the spotlight. The amplified voice said something, but Brent didn't hear it. All he could do was stare.

A man with a nasty-looking gash down the side of his face put his hands up out of the water and reached toward

Brent, his fingers opening and closing as though he were begging for absolution. The man started to moan, and from somewhere down in his throat, Brent answered it with a moan of his own.

Two heavy ropes dropped into the water about fifteen feet from the back of the boat. Brent heard a loud noise, like someone tearing long strips of paper, and when he looked up, he saw two Coast Guard rescue divers rappelling down into the water.

"No!" he shouted. "No, don't!"

But they couldn't hear him. They plunged right into the water, one of them swimming toward the closest survivor, the other making broad, sweeping hand gestures to the crew above as they lowered a floating gurney.

Brent turned around and ran to the front of the boat. Anthony and Jesse were close now, almost within arm's reach.

"What the fuck's wrong with you?" Anthony said.

"Get in the boat," Brent said. "Right now. Both of you. Get in the boat!"

He looked over his shoulder and saw more people in the water, coming from around the far side of the building across the street.

"Hurry, Anthony. Jesus Christ, get in the fucking boat!"

He heard screaming coming from the stern. Looking back that way, he saw one of the Coast Guard rescue divers fighting with a small group of survivors. Brent couldn't look away. The Coast Guard diver was punching at the faces all around him. He was screaming in shocked anger and in pain. They were biting him. They were tearing at his clothes and at his face, raking his dive mask with their fingernails. And as Brent watched, the water around the man turned a murky green.

They had got to the other diver as well. He was waving furiously at the helicopter to raise him up, and at the same time trying to fight off a narrowing ring of attackers. Brent could hear the man screaming for help. In the flickering light from the helicopter's strobes he could see the man's face was twisted by panic and pain. And then, as the rope that led up to the helicopter went taut and an invisible pulley began to turn, Brent saw something that he couldn't believe. Two of the crazed survivors were clinging to the rope. One had his arms wrapped tightly around the rescue diver's shoulders, and he appeared to be tearing the man's ear off with his teeth. The other survivor was several feet above the rescue diver, entangled in the rope, flailing madly for the diver just out of reach below him. Brent watched the three of them rise up to the helicopter. He saw frantic movement at the Jay-hawk's open cabin door. And then the survivor who had been entangled by the rope pulled himself up and over the threshold and crawled inside.

"Oh my God," Brent said.

The helicopter held its position for just a moment. Brent thought he heard yelling from inside, but wasn't sure if that was real or just his mind filling in for the void the shock had left behind. He would never know the truth, though, for the next instant the helicopter rolled over onto its side and crashed into the side of a building.

Brent gaped at the scene. Somewhere in the back of his mind he thought there should be an explosion, but there wasn't. No gigantic fireball. Instead, the air abruptly filled with bits of brick and powdered mortar and needlelike splinters of wood that whistled past his head and pelted his bare arms like angry hornets. In shock, he watched the crumpled, insectlike wreckage of the helicopter tumble three stories down the side of the building and splash into the water. The wreckage was followed a moment later by a billowing gray cloud of dust and aerosolized brick that oozed down the face of the building and spread out in slow motion over the water like a gossamer curtain blown from an open window.

Brent was still watching the spreading gray cloud when

Anthony grabbed him by the collar and threw him down to the deck. He hit his mouth on something and rolled over, a hand clamped over a bleeding lip, to look at Anthony.

"What the hell . . ." he started to say, but never finished the sentence. Only a few feet from where Brent had been standing was one of the survivors, who had somehow climbed over the gunwale. He was staggering toward Anthony now, arms outstretched before him, hands clutching at the air, water dripping off his tattered clothes.

Anthony had a pistol in his hands, and it was pointed right at the survivor.

"Stop, police officer!" Anthony yelled. "Stop, sir!"

The man kept coming. He was moaning now, a horrible, half-drowned sound that seemed to echo from the other survivors still in the water.

"Goddamn it," Anthony said, and fired two shots.

Brent saw the shots hit the man center mass, right below the base of the sternum. The man convulsed like he was holding a live wire. But only for a moment. The next instant he was staggering forward again, arms outstretched. The same ululating moan filling up the night.

"What the fuck?" Anthony said.

He raised the pistol and fired a third shot, this one boring a hole right through the bridge of the man's nose and exiting out the backside in a pink spray of shattered bone and brains.

The man's body wilted to the floor.

Anthony turned to Brent. "Did you see that? I shot him twice in the chest, and he didn't stop. I did. I shot him. I know I did."

Brent said nothing. He couldn't speak.

"Brent, goddamn it!" Jesse yelled. He grabbed Brent by the arm and threw him into the driver's side. "Get us the fuck out of here. They're everywhere!"

Startled, Brent sat there watching Jesse, who had an AR-15 in his hands. There were survivors, their mangled hands clinging to the railing, trying to climb into the boat. Jesse shot three of them with the rifle, then turned back to Brent.

"Go, goddamn it!"

The night filled with the sounds of rifle fire. Brent hit the ignition, eased the throttle forward, and a moment later they were moving down the flooded street, skirting the wrecked Coast Guard helicopter.

And all the while Jesse kept on firing, screaming for him to "Go, go, go!"

CHAPTER 7

Once Bobby Hester was gone, they waded through the living room to the back porch, where Eleanor had tied up their canoe.

Jim held it steady for her as she climbed in.

"You mind if I ride up front?" she asked him. "My shoulder kinda hurts from all that rowing."

"Go ahead."

"You know," she said, giving him a flirty little smile, "later on I think I might need a backrub from the hubby. And maybe a margarita to help me work out the kinks."

Jim didn't return her smile.

"Go on," he said, nodding at the front end of the canoe. "I'll paddle."

They were both experienced with the canoe, and when he climbed in, it wobbled only a little. She felt raindrops on her arms and glanced up at the darkening sky. No doubt about it, they were in for a really bad one. Already the wind had picked up. It rippled the water that covered Ms. Hester's backyard and tossed the smaller trees back and forth. A hummingbird feeder hanging near the back was spinning wildly. *Yeah*, she thought, *this is going to be a crazy one.*

"Seems like I made it back just in time, huh?"

He mumbled something she didn't quite catch.

Eleanor sensed an unpleasant note in his voice. She turned around and looked at him as he used the paddle to push away from the house.

They floated out over the yard.

Jim glanced at her, then lowered his gaze to the water and started paddling.

"Jim, you okay?"

At first she thought maybe something had happened during his fight with Bobby Hester, like maybe he got hurt somewhere she couldn't see. But he wasn't acting hurt. He looked mad, pissed off.

"Are you mad at me?" she asked.

His only answer was a grunt.

The first thing she'd noticed when she made it home was how high the water had gotten. Eleanor had been at work for two days, and in that time, the water from Bays Bayou had come right up to the edge of their front porch. She could literally dive off her doorstep—that is, if she was willing to brave all the nasty stuff floating around in the water.

Their house was on the highest part of the street, and they'd been lucky in that regard. Most everybody else on the block already had three or four feet of water in their downstairs. So far, their house was still dry, but that was about to change. If the information she'd seen at work was accurate, and she figured it probably was, the storm surge they were about to get would completely swamp them. It would ride in on the standing floodwaters and sop everything in its tracks. By morning, they'd probably be able to go scuba diving through their living room, and that meant they had to hurry to get the last of their valuables upstairs.

They went up and down the stairs in a rush, lugging boxes

and pictures and the last of the food and fresh water from the pantry. Jim was still acting strangely distant, giving her the silent treatment, but she didn't have time to get it into with him. There was just too much to do and not enough time to do it in. It was the cop in her that allowed her to ignore his moods and push on with the job at hand, even though the woman in her wanted desperately to get him to say something, anything.

She was hauling the last of their family photo albums up the stairs when the shutters started to rattle. Eleanor put the albums down on the table in the upstairs hallway and listened. They were getting the first sustained winds. It wasn't gusting anymore, but coming on in a slow rumble, and she had the strangest feeling, as if she was standing in a passenger jet struggling to lift off the runway.

She went in to Madison's room.

Ms. Hester had never really managed to shake her fever, so they brought her into Madison's room and let her sleep on the bed in there. She was sleeping fitfully now, Madison sitting on a chair next to her, mopping her face with a wet towel.

"How's she doing?" Eleanor asked.

Madison frowned.

"Not so good, Mom. She's been asleep for the last few hours, but she keeps waking up. And I've heard her mumbling a few times. She says she's cold all the time."

Eleanor saw the battery-operated thermometer on the nightstand next to the bed. "What's her temp?"

"101.3, last time I took it. That was about ten minutes ago."

"It's been high for a while."

"Three days."

Not good, Eleanor thought.

"Okay, anything else?"

"I've been treating the fever with Motrin and Tylenol, alternating them every six hours like you told me to. She won't eat, but I've been able to get her to drink plenty of water, plenty of Gatorade, for the electrolytes. Dad went over to her house and got some of the Ensure from her kitchen and I've been giving her that, but it's not really a substitute for eating, you know?"

They hadn't realized it at the time, but when Eleanor pulled her out from beneath her bed, Ms. Hester had cut her left arm on the bed frame. The cut was deep, and Eleanor had been forced to use her first-aid kit to stitch it up. Madison had been a big help to her then, distracting Ms. Hester from the pain while simultaneously handing Eleanor the needed supplies, and together they had done a pretty good job. But the wound hadn't really healed since then. Despite their best efforts, it was almost certainly infected. Eleanor just hoped it wasn't something really bad, like staph.

"What about the cut?"

"No change. I've been giving her the antibiotics you got for her, but . . ."

Madison trailed off with a shrug.

"Is it still seeping?" Eleanor asked.

"Yeah. It doesn't smell very good, either. I've been keeping it clean like you showed me, but it's not healing. I'm kind of worried what'll happen when we run out of bandages. I don't know if I'll be able to keep it clean."

"We've got a ton of bandages," Eleanor said.

"Umm, not really," Madison answered.

"What do you mean? I had a whole case of them in the family disaster kit."

"Yeah, I know. But she goes through them really fast. She's been sweating so much lately. Every time I check the bandages they're filthy from all the sweat."

Ms. Hester groaned, and Madison turned to her. Eleanor watched as her daughter expertly mopped the older woman's forehead. When Madison was done she got a bottle of water from the nightstand and tilted it to Ms. Hester's lips.

When Eleanor had left for work eleven days ago, Madison had been a girl with posters of boy bands on her wall and stuffed animals in her bed. But now, here she was, the stuffed animals casually thrown to the floor, caring like a trained nurse for the woman who had been, in many ways, her grandmother. How did such a thing happen? How did it happen so quickly, and without Eleanor seeing any of it?

"Mom, you okay?"

Eleanor sniffled and tried to smile. "I'm fine."

"Are you sure? Why are you rubbing your eyes? Are you crying? Ms. Hester's gonna be okay. We just got to keep her hanging on until after this storm blows over."

Eleanor nodded.

"You're right, sweetie. You stay here with Ms. Hester, okay? I'm gonna go help Daddy get the last of our things upstairs."

"Okay."

Eleanor turned to go, but Madison stopped her as she reached the door.

"Mom, are we okay here?"

Eleanor turned her gaze to the top of the dresser next to the door. There was a little makeup mirror there. In it, she could see her reflection, and the face that looked back at her was dark with exhaustion.

"It's gonna be a bad storm," she said. "Maybe the worst one we've seen. But I think we're gonna be okay. The house may flood, but we'll be safe up here on the top floor."

"I know that, Mom. I was . . ."

Madison trailed off.

"What is it, sweetie?"

"The last couple nights, when I've been staying up with Ms. Hester, I've been hearing stuff."

"What kind of stuff?"

"I don't know. Stuff. Outside. People, I guess. I can hear them moaning. Sometimes it's so loud I get scared. It's a horrible sound. I . . . I can't really describe it. But it's like they're scared and angry and . . . I don't know. It doesn't sound natural. Are we okay up here, Mom? Nobody's gonna try to . . ."

"To what?"

"Well, get us. Are they?"

Outside, the rain was starting to come down hard. Eleanor listened to it whipping against the windows before she answered.

"Nobody's gonna get us, sweetie. Your Daddy and I, we're gonna be right here with you."

"But there is somebody out there. Bad people. I've heard it on your police radio. They say people are eating each other."

Eleanor tried to swallow, but couldn't quite manage it. She was having a nasty case of déjà vu, her mind turning back to the meeting at the EOC and Captain Shaw lying to Joe Schwab about the cannibalistic attacks they'd seen. Christ, what was she supposed to say? How do you answer your daughter's questions about people eating each other?

"We're gonna be okay here," Eleanor said. "I believe that."

Madison nodded.

Eleanor went to the game room. Jim wasn't there and Eleanor was relieved. Just a few minutes earlier she'd been looking for a chance to talk to him, but not now. Right now there was a nuclear bomb of a headache waiting to detonate just behind her eyes, and she needed a moment.

Lifting her shirt, she removed her Glock 22 from her waist and put it on the bumper pool table they'd pushed into the corner. It was her weapons table now, stacked with extra magazines for the Glock and for her Colt AR-15A3. There were boxes of ammunition, too. Leaning against the wall next to the table were the AR-15 and her Mossberg 500 twelve gauge. She looked from one to the other and finally settled on the twelve gauge. Then she took a box of 00 shot from the table and fed five shells into the Mossberg's magazine tube. The shotgun felt heavy, solid, reliable. She muttered a silent prayer that she wouldn't need it.

"I heard you in there," Jim said from behind her.

Eleanor sighed, then put the Mossberg on the table and turned around.

"Are you talking to me now?"

"I never stopped talking to you."

She huffed at him. *Seriously?* she thought. *Seriously?* She couldn't believe it. This was just like him, so damn passive-aggressive.

"Ever since I got home you've been acting like I've done something wrong. What is it? Why are you mad at me?"

"I'm not mad at you," he said.

"It sure seems like it. Jim, if there's something wrong . . ."

"I'm mad, okay. Yes, I'm mad. Just . . . not at you. It's not your fault. I'm mad at all this . . . this . . . goddamn it. I'm sick of being locked up in this house. I'm going out of my head here. Eleven days now. Every couple of hours I go to the door and I look out and all I see is fucking water. It's like I'm trapped on a goddamn island. At least you get to go out and see something besides the inside of our house."

"Jim, that's not fair. I have to work. I don't get—"

"I'm not upset at you, Eleanor. I know you have to work. I know you've been burning yourself up. I know that. Trust me, I get it. This isn't about you, okay? It's me. It's just me being stupid. I hear you talking to Madison about those attacks we've been hearing about on the radio, all those people eating each other, and I feel like I should be doing something. You know? I feel like I'm just wasting away, like I'm worthless."

"I know," she said, but even as she spoke Eleanor sensed that he was dealing with a level of frustration she couldn't really get her mind around.

Until recently, she'd enjoyed her canoe trips back and forth from the EOC. There had been a peacefulness that came from gliding through the flooded ruins of the city that had recharged her mental batteries. He hadn't had that opportunity, and it surprised her how willing her heart was to open up for him after only moments before lashing out at him for being a passive-aggressive boor.

"I'm sorry," she said. "Jim, I didn't even think about how isolated you and Madison would be here. Jesus, I should have thought of that. I spent weeks planning what we'd need in the family disaster kit, and it never even occurred to me that the worst part of it would be the isolation. I'm sorry."

He walked over to her and put his arms around her.

"We're gonna get through this," he said. "We're all right."

She pressed her face into his chest and then recoiled.

"What?" he said.

"You kinda stink," she said. "You need a bath."

"You and me both," he said, and hugged her tightly once more.

Later that night, during the worst part of the storm, Jim knelt on the floor of Madison's room with his wife and daughter. Ms. Hester was in the bed next to them, her groaning barely audible over the wind and rain. Outside the house the storm rumbled and howled, flashes of lightning coming through the gaps around the edges of the plywood boards that covered the windows and bathing the room in a purplish-white light. To Jim, it felt as if the wind were an avalanche coming down all around them . . . so constant, so powerful . . . it seemed to be trying to lift the house into the air.

They had decided not to move Ms. Hester. Her fever was still dangerously high and she was weak, and there seemed little point to removing her from Madison's bed when she was already about as comfortable as she was likely to get.

Still, he had terrible thoughts about her dying in Madison's bed.

He tried to reassure himself that she wasn't going to die, that he was only torturing himself with the usual cruel fates one can't seem to help envisioning for loved ones, but still, there was that voice in his head that just wouldn't leave the thought alone. He kept coming back to it, the way the tongue continually returns to an injured tooth. What would happen if she really did die in here with them? Would Madison ever be able to sleep in here again? Would he expect her to?

Something big hit the house.

Jim glanced at Eleanor, who was holding Madison's head against her chest. In the guttering candlelight, their faces had a yellowish tinge. They sat there for a long moment, stunned and frightened, watching each other and listening as the storm shook and battered their house.

The next instant they heard a prolonged ripping sound, like a wall being ripped away.

"Daddy," Madison said, "what was that?"

He shook his head. Whatever it was—a tree limb or something—had almost certainly done some damage to the far side of the house. He could hear the wind pounding unnaturally over there, as though it had succeeded in opening up the house.

He glanced at Eleanor once again. She was frightened, he could see that immediately, and a part of himself that he didn't like to own was thrilled by that fear. It gave him the chance to be the protector, for once.

"I'll go check it out."

"Jim, no!"

"It'll be okay." He stood up and gave her outstretched hand a squeeze. "I'll be right back."

He went down the hall and turned into the spare bedroom.

And there he froze.

The wind was very loud, like standing next to a jet engine. It had ripped a four-foot-long gash in the wall, and as he stood there in the doorway, he could feel it tugging on him, pulling him inside.

There were small tree limbs and leaves all over the floor, and the rain was swirling through the hole. Already it had puddled on the carpet. For years, they had been planning on turning this room into a craft room for Eleanor and Madison to share, and here and there soggy, colored pieces of Madison's artwork clung to the walls and swirled in circles on currents of air.

A flash of lightning turned the room purplish-white, and in the lingering brightness that followed, he looked through the gash in the wall and could see a long ways down the south side of the block. Many of the houses over there were gone, nothing left but a wall or a roof tilting down into the floodwaters.

As he watched, the Beales' house, two doors down from Ms. Hester's, began to shake. He could see the roof trembling atop the walls like the lid on a kettle of boiling water, and then, with one sudden, ferocious snapping sound he could hear even over the roaring wind, the roof finally came loose and sailed free. It tumbled up into the air and was lost in the darkness and silvery blasts of rain.

Jim gasped.

My God, he thought, *we were fools to stay. Our jobs be damned. They're not worth this. They're not worth gambling our lives on this. My God, preserve us please.*

The next moment he felt Eleanor at his side. He put an arm around her and felt her shaking. Another blast of lightning lit the night, and in the flash he could see the tears on her cheeks.

"It's all gone," she said. "Everything. Gone."

He pulled her close, only dimly aware that he was crying, too.

Later still, Eleanor opened her eyes, a little stunned that she could have fallen asleep while the storm was raging. Even now it echoed in her head.

Madison was sleeping in her lap. Her hair was damp with sweat and it had fallen in front of her face. Eleanor stroked her daughter's bangs back from her eyes, and when Eleanor looked up, Jim was awake and watching her.

"You okay?" he whispered.

She nodded.

From the bed behind her, Eleanor heard Ms. Hester calling for water. Eleanor eased Madison's head out of her lap and helped Ms. Hester drink from a plastic water bottle.

Ms. Hester was burning up and barely able to keep her eyes open, and she drifted back to sleep as Eleanor was sticking a baby thermometer into her ear.

"How is she?" Jim asked.

"Oh, Jesus," Eleanor said. "Jim, she needs a doctor."

"What is it?" he asked, nodding toward the thermometer.

"105.3."

He whistled. "Damn."

Eleanor put the thermometer back on the bedside table, wondering what she was supposed to do, if it was safe to move her.

From outside, she heard the sound of running water. She went down the hall to the craft room and looked out through the gash in the wall. The sky was a dirty white that made her think of dishwater. Still the sound of running water went on, even though there was no more rain, no wind. For a moment, she wondered if maybe a pipe had burst inside the walls. But she quickly dismissed that. The sound was bigger than a busted pipe, and anyway the water hadn't worked in two weeks. As she stood there in the doorway, her mind went back to a camping trip they had taken two years before on the Red River. She had stood on the bank one morning, watching the huge majesty of the moving water, and she realized that was the same sound she was hearing now, the slow, relentless force of a great quantity of moving water.

Holding her breath, she advanced to the wall and looked down. She saw a wide expanse of water. It stretched off as far as she could see, only the tops of nearby houses and the canopies of trees visible.

The water was flowing around their house, moving to the north. But this was not the dark green murky water of Bays Bayou. This water was a greenish-gray, flecked with white foam, Gulf of Mexico water.

And it was rising quickly.

Her mind reeled at the implications. There seemed little doubt as to what had happened. The man from the National Hurricane Center had warned them two days ago that this might happen. Storm surges from Hector and Kyle had obliterated most of the natural barriers that kept Galveston and South Houston from disappearing under the sea. With those barriers gone, there was nothing to stop Mardel from pulling the ocean along with it. They had talked about the possibility that these storms might permanently change the geography of the Texas Coast, and now, it looked like that had actually happened. Eleanor was looking at high tide.

"Wow," Jim said.

She looked back at him and managed to smile.

"Pretty incredible, isn't it?"

He nodded. "There'll be no coming back from this. That's the Gulf of Mexico out there."

"Well, you said you felt like you were stranded on a deserted island."

He smiled and shook his head.

Then Eleanor glanced past him. Madison was standing in the hallway, and she looked frightened.

"Mom?"

"What is it, pumpkin?"

"It's Ms. Hester. She's in a lot of pain."

"I know, baby. We need to get her to a doctor. I can't do anything for her with what I've got here."

Eleanor walked over to her and brushed the bangs out of her face again.

"I'm gonna try to raise somebody on my radio. You want to come with me?"

Jim and Madison followed Eleanor into the game room. Eleanor got her radio out of her gear bag and keyed it up. "Bravo eighty-three-fifty." She smiled at Madison. "It'll be okay, pumpkin." Eleanor checked the radio. It was nearly fully charged. She keyed the radio again. "Bravo eighty-three-fifty to EOC."

All she got was dead air.

"Why aren't they answering?" Jim asked.

"I don't know." She switched channels to the SWAT frequency. "Bravo eighty-three-fifty, anybody on this side monitoring?"

"Maybe the EOC got knocked out."

"That's possible," Eleanor said. "But that shouldn't do anything to the radios. They're on a multi-trunking system. Even if one tower goes out, another should be able to pick up the slack."

Out of habit, she checked the display on the front of the radio. She was on the right channel, and she had plenty of battery life. She was starting to get worried.

"So what does that mean?" Jim asked.

It means I'm sending signals, Eleanor thought, *there's just nobody on the other end to answer.*

Her gaze shifted from Jim to Madison.

"It'll be okay," Eleanor said to her. "I'll keep trying."

From somewhere downstairs, Eleanor heard the sound of splashing water. She looked up at Jim, and could tell by his expression he'd heard it, too. The sound continued and Eleanor had a chilling thought: *Someone's in the house!*

She picked up the Mossberg and racked a shell into the chamber.

"You two stay here," she said, and went to the head of the stairs. There was a man standing down there, his features lost in the shadows, water dripping from his tattered clothes.

She thought: *Not right. He is all wrong.*

Then the figure stepped forward and she saw it was Bobby Hester. He looked like a drowned man. His shirt was nothing but a rag matted to his bone-skinny, meth addict's body. His long hair was plastered to his face. There was an open wound on the right side of his chest that made him look as if somebody had tried to carve him open with a spoon.

Her first instinct was that he was dead.

Eleanor had seen many corpses during her time as a cop, and Bobby Hester—impossibly—looked exactly like a corpse. It was his eyes more than anything else that froze her there, unable to raise the shotgun. There was a dead vacancy in his eyes. The same vacancy she had seen looking up at her from traffic fatalities and murder victims.

Bobby raised his left hand and it thumped into the wall. He seemed unable to raise his right arm above his waist. A sickening moan welled up from within him and he started up the stairs toward her.

She thought: *This is not real. Not happening*. And then, in the same mental breath: *But it is. It is.*

"You need to leave, Bobby," she said.

But Bobby didn't stop.

He walked onward, his steps awkward, clumsy. He tripped and pitched forward, landing on his chin, then slowly pushed himself up and back onto his feet with his one good arm. Bobby was halfway up to her now.

"Bobby I'm gonna shoot you. Turn around and walk away."

He reached for her, and his fingertips were white as a fish's belly. *God help me*, she thought, and fired.

He was maybe eight feet from her. The shotgun blast hit the already-shredded flesh of his right shoulder and spun him backwards and around. He hit the wall and slid back down the stairs, smearing a long clotted trail of blood behind him.

She lowered the shotgun and put a hand over her mouth. Jesus, what had she done?

"Mommy!"

Madison's scream jolted her back to the moment. She ran back to the game room. Jim was holding Madison in his arms, but he let her go when Eleanor appeared in the doorway.

"Mommy!"

Madison grabbed her around the waist, and Eleanor, who was too stunned to respond, let the shotgun's muzzle dip to the floor.

"Eleanor?" Jim asked. "Are you okay? What happened?"

"Bobby Hester," she said. She glanced back toward the stairs. "I shot him."

"What?" He ran forward, took the shotgun from her, and guided her to a chair. She dropped down into it. "Jesus, Eleanor, are you okay? Did he hurt you?"

All she could do was shake her head no. "He didn't look . . . right."

"Did you kill him?"

She raised her gaze up to meet his and she thought: *No, he was already dead*. But instead she nodded slowly.

"I think so," she said.

But even as she spoke she saw movement out of the corner of her eye. Ms. Hester was at the door, walking stiffly toward the head of the stairs, her hands outstretched.

"Ms. Hester, no!" Jim said.

He jumped to his feet and ran after her, Eleanor following along right behind him.

When Eleanor rounded the doorway she stopped. Bobby Hester was already at the head of the stairs and walking toward his grandmother's outstretched arms as if he meant to fall into her embrace. *It's not possible,* she thought. But there he was, a walking corpse with his right arm hanging by a burned scrap of flesh, his eyes depthless and empty.

"Oh, Bobby," Ms. Hester said.

She stumbled, and in that moment he was on her. Eleanor saw Bobby lunge forward, his mouth opening to reveal black, bloodstained teeth. He grabbed her wrist with his left hand and at the same time clamped his mouth down on the side of her face. Ms. Hester collapsed beneath him, grunting, screaming, her fists pounding against his shoulders. Bobby Hester went down on top of her. And for a prolonged moment Eleanor could do nothing but stand there, mouth agape, watching as Bobby tore into his grandmother's face with his teeth, spraying blood everywhere.

It was the sound of flesh tearing that finally made her move. Bobby looked up at Eleanor and Jim and Madison with his dead-man eyes, and he had a great flap of bloody cheek skin hanging from his lips.

She didn't waste another second.

Eleanor raised the Mossberg high over her head and slammed it down butt-first into Bobby's forehead, knocking him to the ground.

"Get her out of here," Eleanor yelled at Jim.

Jim darted under the shotgun, grabbed Ms. Hester by the arm, and pulled her back into Madison's room.

Bobby had landed on his hurt right shoulder, but he never

cried out. He gave no sign at all that he felt any pain. He climbed to his knees, and then to his feet. When he looked at her, his face streaked with blood from the gash on his forehead and the torn flesh hanging from his teeth, his eyes registered nothing.

She thought: *He's nothing but a blank. He's empty inside.*

Eleanor pointed the shotgun at his chest, but he didn't seem to register it. He raised his one good arm and starting clutching the air between them, and right before she pulled the trigger he uttered a sound that was like air moving through old pipes.

The sound was cut off by the shotgun blast, and the next moment he was dead, large, sloppy bits of him oozing down the wall behind him. Eleanor stared at the mess, and only after her mind caught up with the magnitude of what had just happened did she feel the bile rise up into her throat.

At some point—she wasn't exactly sure when—Jim put his hands on her shoulders and helped her to stand up straight.

"You're okay," he said.

She wasn't sure if it was a question or a statement of fact, but the sound of his voice was calming. It helped to center her. She stood up straight and blinked as purple splotches swam at the corners of her eyes.

"Oh my God." She looked at the bloody mess that had been Bobby Hester and nearly vomited again. "Oh God."

"What in the hell was wrong with him?" Jim asked.

Eleanor just shook her head.

He took a step toward Bobby's corpse, almost as though he didn't believe the man was really dead. He said, "You saw that look in his eyes, right? What in the hell was wrong with him? Was he high?"

"I don't think so."

"What then? What was that?"

She was fighting for control, trying to stay on her feet.

"I don't know. Jim, it . . . it looked like he was dead."

"Yeah, he's dead all right."

"No," she said, surprised by the sudden violence, the absolute conviction, she heard in her voice. "No. Before. He looked like he was dead before I shot him."

"What?"

"Before I shot him. That look . . . Jim, I've seen that look. You know that look once you've seen it. It's the way a dead person's eyes seem to just stare off into nothing. There's nothing else like that look. Once you see it, you feel small, you know? You feel like you want to crawl into yourself. You feel so small, so . . ."

She trailed off helplessly. Whatever it was, she wasn't saying it right. She didn't have the words to tell him all the things that were wrong with the way Bobby Hester had stared at her, or the feeling of dread that had chilled her heart when he moaned at her.

"What do we need to do now?" he asked.

"What?"

He looked at Bobby's corpse, then down the stairs toward the water lapping against the walls of their entranceway.

"What do we do?" he said. "The water down there looks like it's about waist-high. We can't stay here, can we? I mean, we have to leave, right? We have to go somewhere. Anywhere else but here."

"We need to leave," she said. "We need to get Ms. Hester to a doctor. We need to report this shooting. We need to get the family somewhere with clean water and food and clean beds."

It was coming back to her now. Thinking about protocols gave her something for her mind to do.

"We need to leave here," she said. "We need to get our individual disaster kits together and get the family into the canoe. We can head toward the EOC and try to make contact with somebody with better information."

"Okay," Jim said. "Okay. Our disaster kits are in the game room. We've got about ten gallons of water left. We should take all that."

"Agreed."

Suddenly, Madison screamed.

Both Jim and Eleanor rushed to her door. Madison was up against the far wall of her room, her back pressed into the smiling faces of a boy-band poster. Crawling on the ground in front of her, pulling herself inch by inch toward Madison, was Ms. Hester.

"Mommy, help me!"

Eleanor ran inside, jumped over the bed, and landed next to Madison. She scooped up her daughter and tossed her onto the bed, where Jim caught her and pulled her back.

Then Eleanor looked down into Ms. Hester's face, and for a moment, she was so astounded by the snarling, dead-eyed thing staring back at her that she couldn't move. Ms. Hester uttered a thin, stuttering moan and raked the air between them with her fingernails. Her head was thrown back, the tendons in her neck standing out like cords beneath the skin, her mouth twisted into a lipless grimace.

How about now? a voice inside Eleanor's head shrieked. *How about now? You see those eyes. She's dead, and yet there she is, looking to drag you down with her. Do you believe it now?*

She nodded. "I believe."

Another moan escaped Ms. Hester's throat, and Eleanor backed away. The back of her legs hit the bedside table and she brought a hand back to steady herself. She felt a lamp back there and closed her fist around it. The next instant she pulled its cord from the wall and held the little pink lamp out in front of her like a talisman against Ms. Hester.

"Ms. Hester, please."

But the woman's expression never changed. There was no light behind those eyes. No emotion of any kind. She dug her fingers into the carpet and pulled herself forward. Eleanor could hear Ms. Hester's fingernails cracking, breaking, as she pulled inexorably closer, the wound on her face seeping blood onto the carpet in a continuous flow.

"Eleanor, come on!"

She looked up at Jim. He had Madison behind him, his hand outstretched over the bed to her.

"Come on."

She felt a light tapping against her leg and screamed, but it was only the lamp. She dropped it then and grabbed Jim's hand. He pulled her across the bed and the next instant they were running out into the hall, past the nearly decapitated body of Bobby Hester.

"Stop," she said. "Jim, wait."

"Eleanor, come on!"

"No," she said. "One second."

She ran into the game room and grabbed their backpacks and her Mossberg and her pistol. *No time for the water,* she thought. She threw the shotgun to Jim, swept as many boxes of shells as she could into her backpack, and together they ran down the stairs, where their canoe waited, tied to the front porch railing.

Eleanor didn't know it then, but she would never see the inside of their house again.

CHAPTER 8

A news helicopter crept slowly across the sky, endlessly circling, as though too stunned by the destruction to look away. Anthony Shaw expected to hear wailing cries for help from the hundreds of people wandering around campus, but not one of them made a sound, not one of them tried to wave the chopper down, and to him, that was even more chilling than the sight of all this water flowing through the buildings, blanketing the streets, drowning the cars. On the opposite side of the street, a black man with two orange cats in his arms and a little girl following along behind glanced up at the helicopter and then back at the little girl. She never even bothered to meet his gaze, just kept on walking.

The little girl held a white plastic shopping bag that might have contained some wet clothes, but they had no other possessions that Anthony could see. The looks on their faces said it all. Life as they had known it was gone. What was left was an alien world for which they had no frame of reference.

"These people look like they just stepped off a battle-field," Anthony said.

Beside him, Jesse grunted in acknowledgment. "That's

about the size of it. You know, your dad knew what he was doing when he set this job up for us. Don't think I don't realize that. These people . . . they don't have anything left."

"Yeah, the sorry bastards."

They were making their way from the UC down to the rec center, where the fire department had managed to scrounge together a mismatched assortment of motorboats from private homes and other city departments; but even getting across the campus had become a chore now. Water was everywhere. To Anthony, the really amazing thing, the thing that really shook him, were the objects that remained above water. The windshields of trucks poked up from the slowing moving flood like surfacing submarines. Elevated pedestrian skyways, the kind that connected one building to another, now looked like fishing piers. Everything had a washed-out, gray look, except for the red of the stop signs, which stood out like candy. Over by the UC, a statue seemed to be walking on the water. And a short distance beyond that, the white, covered arch of a colonnade snaked over an open lake between buildings. The water changed everything. The most ordinary, everyday things became mysterious, even sinister, as though the world was slowly lowering beneath the waves and a new, darker one was taking its place.

Also, there was a smell in the air he didn't like, a sea smell, but the sea mixed with mud and sickeningly sweet stench of raw sewage and mud and rotting bodies. He had thought that he'd grown used to it, that it had seeped into the background radiation of smells that was life in the city these days, but he was wrong. Today, with the heat of the sun beating down on them, the smell was worse than ever. It seemed thicker, and almost dangerous somehow.

Above him, the helicopter finally peeled off and headed north, and as it flew away, Anthony wondered if the rest of America wouldn't watch the images it had just captured and scoff that the networks were just showing them something they'd run through Photoshop to better their ratings. Surely this kind of destruction couldn't be real, not in America anyway.

"Where the fuck is your brother?" Jesse said.

Anthony let his gaze linger on the flooded ruins of the campus, ignoring his friend for the moment, choosing instead to marvel at just how thorough the storm had been. You had to look close at some of the buildings, but the damage was there. It hadn't left a single structure intact. And, really, as bad as all this destruction was, it was still easier to think about a flooded city than his drunken failure of a brother. He had been exercising some serious mental discipline to avoid thinking about what Brent was up to right about now, but it was an ultimately futile chore. A lot like trying to keep Brent sober, Anthony mused. He suspected it couldn't be done. In fact, Brent was probably passed out in one of these buildings somewhere, drunk out of his mind.

"You hear me?" Jesse said.

"Yeah, I hear you," Anthony said. "I don't know where he is. I told him to be here at thirteen hundred."

Jesse made an exaggerated show of looking at his watch. "Yeah, well, he's late."

"I know he's fucking late, Jesse. Give me a goddamn break, will you? He's my brother. He's my problem. You got that?"

Jesse sighed.

"And don't say a fucking word," Anthony said. "It'll only piss me off."

"I'm not saying anything."

"Yeah, well, you want to. I know that look. I know that sigh. Just don't, okay?"

Jesse held up his hands in mock surrender. "Whatever, man. Like you say, he's your brother."

Anthony spit into the water, and before Jesse could say more, before he could say what really needed to be said—

that family notwithstanding the longer they let Brent take an active role in things the higher the chances became that their plans would come completely undone—Anthony turned away.

They waded on in silence.

The small fleet of motorboats was massed in the student parking lot a short distance away. Most of the crowds had thinned out, so that now there were only a few people wandering around, and most of those were city employees working on the boats. The few shelter residents they saw looked lost, but everyone, even the city employees trying to clean up the mess from the previous night's storm, looked shell shocked. It was a look Anthony had seen a great deal of that afternoon.

"If he doesn't come, what are we going to do about the money?" Jesse asked.

Anthony had been thinking about that very thing. His father would expect him to include Brent in every step of the operation, not necessarily because he was needed, but because Brent needed it, and in his father's mind, that was the only factor that really mattered.

"I don't know," Anthony said. "It's safe, don't you think?"

"Yeah, it's safe, but . . ."

"But what?"

Jesse pushed a large floating tree limb out of his way. Now that they were closer to the highway, they were coming across a lot more debris. "It's safe for now. But you saw those people in the water last night. What do you think the military's gonna do when they get confirmed reports of cannibalistic survivors, especially ones that are attacking their people?"

"The same shit they always do. As little as possible. They'll help with evacuees, but they'll ignore the problem as long as they can, leave it to the local authorities."

"I don't think so, Anthony. This isn't like Katrina. This isn't a bunch of hard-luck cases stuck at the Superdome. You know what I think they're gonna do? They're gonna come in here with a shitload of National Guardsmen and they're gonna clamp down on order as fast as they fucking can. We're gonna see military everywhere. What do you think is gonna happen when they spot that wrecked Coast Guard helicopter? You think they're gonna leave that one be?"

Anthony kept on walking. He had been thinking about the same thing, the helicopter especially, and though he'd rather eat glass before showing how worried he was to Jesse, he was worried just the same.

"We need to get the cash tonight," he said.

"Now you're talking some sense," Jesse said. "At least you've got that part figured out."

"Hey," Anthony said, suddenly wheeling around on him. "You listen to me and you listen fucking good. I got this. You hear me? I got this. I know exactly what we need to do and when we need to do it. Don't make that mistake again, Jesse. You and I, we will get this done. Even if my brother fucks up, you and I will get this done. We will get it done, and then we will get the fuck out of this town. You see those people over there? I refuse to end up like them. You hear me? I fucking refuse."

Anthony stared at him, not blinking, waiting for Jesse's reaction to his words. Jesse was good. He was damn good. But he was a little bitch when it came to making sure he got his point across. Anthony didn't like that. He had this under control, and goddamn it, Jesse better fucking know it, too. If Anthony's dad had taught him anything, it was what it meant to be in control.

Jesse stared back at him, defiant at first from being talked down to, but he didn't have it in him to push the issue. They both knew that.

"Yeah," Jesse said at last. "Yeah, I hear loud and clear."

Anthony relaxed a little. He didn't like getting angry like that, especially at Jesse, but he was mastering it now.

"I'll talk to my dad," he said. "Even if Brent fucks up, we still need to include him. I know you know that. But you and I, we'll get it done."

Jesse nodded, but didn't say a word.

"Come on," Anthony said. "Let's get us a boat."

Like everything else about the city's response to these storms, the requisitioning of the motorboats was a hopeless mess. Nobody seemed to have any idea what was going on. Anthony was counting on that confusion so that he and Jesse and Brent could take one of the boats off to get the money.

There were a lot more people hanging around the parking lot area. One man, an older white guy with a sunburned face and white hair and a Hawaiian shirt open to reveal his prodigious belly, was arguing with the fleet master, a thirty-six-years-on-the-job sergeant named Frank Gibbs, an old friend of his dad's. Though he couldn't hear their conversation, Anthony could tell what they were talking about by their body language. Frank was going to confiscate the man's boat for the upcoming evacuation; the man didn't want to give it up. The man was animated, waving his hands around his head, stamping his feet on the padded seat cushions of his boat. Frank Gibbs stood on the roof of a sedan, a clipboard in his hands, nodding slowly, as though he completely understood. Anthony had once watched Gibbs handle a complaint from a couple whose car had been ticketed while they were parked under a sign that read NO PARKING ANYTIME. Gibbs had taken the couple out to their car and shown them the sign. Then he took out a pocket dictionary and read the definition of each word on the sign, and in the process utterly berated them without ever raising his voice or giving any indication that he was calling them dumb-asses to their faces. Anthony couldn't help but chuckle to himself. The poor guy in the Hawaiian shirt had lost the argument before he ever opened his mouth. He just didn't know it yet.

"Hey, Anthony," Jesse said, tapping him on the shoulder, "take a look at that dude over there."

Anthony turned to Jesse. "Where?"

"Over there. See him, in the green T-shirt, over by that staircase?"

The smile slipped away from Anthony's face. By now, he had seen literally thousands of survivors, people who had been pulled from upstairs windows or off rooftops, and he knew the look of one who has just been given a giant dose of humility from Mother Nature. He had also seen dead bodies that had been caught in the crotches of trees or in storm drains, the clothes shredded from their bodies by the wind and lashing rain. The man staggering down the grassy knoll from the staircase looked like a marriage of the two. What little clothes he had left hung from his body in strips. The look on his face was one of utter defeat at the hands of the storm. He could barely keep his balance, even though every step took him into deeper water. His shoulders were slumped forward, his head tilted grotesquely to one side. He had his hands out in front of him, his fingers opening and closing like he was begging for forgiveness from two firefighters who had their backs to him.

"What's his deal?" Jesse said. "He's acting like those guys last night, the ones from Canal Street. You don't think . . . ?"

Anthony took a few hurried steps forward.

"Hey!" he shouted.

One of the firefighters turned and looked over at him. So, too, did Gibbs and the fat man.

"Heads up behind you," Anthony said, and pointed at the man in the shredded green shirt.

The warning came too late. The two firefighters, confused at first by the urgency in Anthony's voice, were slow to turn around. When they did, the man in the shredded clothes lunged at them, knocking the closer of the two into the water and diving down on top of him. From where Anthony and

Jesse were standing it was difficult to see exactly what was going on, at least at first, though they could tell that the man in the water was flailing his arms about as though he was reaching for something to hold on to. He tried to scream, but the sound was cut off when his face went under the water.

The other firefighter just stood there, looking down at the stranger who had just climbed on top of his partner and was now tearing into his chest with his teeth and fingernails. The firefighter, who Anthony would learn later from Jesse was a fourteen-year veteran named Bo Moody, backed away for a moment, his face stricken with surprise and disgust, before rushing back to help his partner. Bo Moody threw an arm around the stranger's neck and yanked him off his partner. Moody was a strong man with huge biceps, a weightlifting junkie, and the stranger in the shredded clothes seemed to fly out of the water, turning almost a full backflip over Moody's shoulder in the process. He looked like a child's rag doll getting thrown about by the family dog.

The stranger hit the water stomach-first, but the belly flop didn't seem to stun him at all. He stumbled forward, draping his arms over Moody's shoulders like an exhausted runner crossing the finish line. Moody tried to get his hands under the man's chest to push him away but for some reason couldn't get enough leverage. He was off balance, staggering backward under the man's weight, and though the stranger's movements were clumsy and awkward, he nonetheless bent Bo Moody over backwards.

Both men went under.

Frank Gibbs was running that way, moving slowly through the waist-deep water. So too were Anthony Shaw and Jesse Numeroff, but they were farther off, and Frank Gibbs got there first.

"Gibbs, no!" Anthony shouted, already pulling his gun.

Gibbs closed on the Moody and the stranger and jumped into the fight. There were other groups of men standing around, checking the boats, and by now they too had advanced on the stranger. Seven or eight of them got to the stranger at the same time as Gibbs and pulled the stranger off Moody.

For a moment, Anthony couldn't see through the knot of bodies. Then he heard a scream and one of the men turned around, staggering away from the others, and as he fell into the water, still screaming, Anthony froze in his tracks. The ragged hole in the man's throat was gushing blood into the water. The injured man continued to thrash, churning up the water around him, turning it a cloudy reddish-green as his neck wound jetted his life out of his body with every heartbeat.

"Clear a hole!" Anthony shouted.

He was closing on the group of men now, less than forty feet away, but he didn't need to yell to clear the way. They were already falling back, separating, scrambling over each other to get out of the way of the madman in their midst.

To Anthony, the man seemed rabid. With his chest heaving, his hands gnarled as though with arthritis, thick, jelly-like ropes of blood and spit hanging from his mouth, he looked like something out of a Robert E. Howard story. And yet, for all the savageness of his countenance, the man's eyes were the same dark, expressionless pits Anthony had seen in the trailer park next to the *Santa Fe* and in the flooded darkness over at Canal Street. Those eyes were completely vacant. They were a dead man's eyes.

Holy shit, Anthony thought. *He's a zombie. He's a fucking zombie. But that's not possible. It can't be.* And then, after skipping a mental beat, he thought, *But it is possible. He's right there.*

Anthony raised his pistol and fired once, putting a bullet through the man's face, turning the spot where his nose had been to a dark slushy mess as the stranger sagged down into the water, rolled over onto his back, and went still.

The sound of the pistol shot echoed over the water like a loud clap, and then everything went quiet.

The men who, moments before, had been falling all over themselves to get away from the man now took a few tentative steps toward him. A few looked back at Anthony in shocked awe.

"Get away from him," Anthony said.

He walked up to the body and looked down on it. The man's eyes stared up at nothing, and looking into those eyes, those horrible, dead eyes, Anthony felt a shudder pass through him.

That is a zombie, Anthony thought, marveling at the ease with which his mind slipped into this new mental track. For once the mental leap was made, it made perfect sense. This man—with his crazy, drunken gait and gnarled hands; with the skin of his face cracked open and beaded with a pale yellow mucousy stuff; with his lips torn from his mouth, leaving a sneering rail of bloody teeth—this man was a zombie. *That's what you are,* the voice in Anthony's head insisted. *You can't be, but you are. Goddamn it, that's what you are. I don't know how or why, but you're a zombie.*

"What the hell's wrong with that boy?" somebody said.

Anthony glanced up to see who had spoken but couldn't tell. His gaze shifted from one face to the next to the next and saw the same stricken look of horror that he realized must be on his own face as well. It was the man's eyes, he thought. They hadn't changed. Despite everything that was wrong and impossible about the corpse floating faceup in the water between them, the real horror was the way the man's eyes had seemed dead even before Anthony shot him.

"He's a zombie," Anthony said.

He glanced at the others, almost daring them to challenge him, but nobody did. A few faces scrunched up in disgust, or perhaps in preparation for scoffing at him, but those expressions quickly melted away. He had touched on the word that none of their minds had let them speak, but now that it was out of the bag they all seemed to accept it as the only reasonable conclusion. This corpse was a zombie. There were zombies in the water with them. Anthony could feel a collective chill passing through them as the truth of it sank in.

In the confusion, Anthony had lost sight of Frank Gibbs and the two injured firefighters. But now, as he turned away from the dead zombie, he happened to catch sight of Gibbs, who was hanging on the side of a flooded pickup truck, breathing hard, a stunned look on his face. One of the other firefighters, the first one to encounter the zombie, was already dead. The other one, the big one who had just stood there in shocked surprise as the zombie munched on his partner (and Anthony could understand now why that had happened), was getting pulled onto the roof of a car. He was bleeding badly from one ear, rolling from side to side in near unconscious misery. The others tried to hold him still, but he was so big they were having trouble.

"You guys get him to the infirmary," Anthony said.

"That guy bit off one of his fingers," one of the men said.

It was true. Anthony could see a yellowed flake of living bone in the deep arterial blood running down the firefighter's arm.

"Well then, hurry it up," Anthony told them. "Get him to the infirmary before he bleeds out. And somebody help Sergeant Gibbs over there, too."

The others moved off with the injured men.

Anthony scanned his surroundings, looking for more zombies. He had absolutely no idea what was going on here. He had latched onto the term zombie because nothing else seemed to fit, and it had made sense at the moment. But now that he had some distance from that first initial shock he felt less certain. What did he really know about zombies anyway? Just what he had seen in George Romero horror movies, and he had been laughing at most of those, looking on zombies as nothing more than harlequins, the clowns of the horror world. But he wasn't laughing now. No sir, there was nothing funny at all about this. His whole world had just been turned upside down, and there was nothing funny at all about that.

"What are doing?" Jesse asked.

Anthony let his gaze wander over his flooded surroundings a moment longer, pausing wherever he saw someone wading through the water, watching them for signs of that drunken gait. He saw none, though. Everything had a washed-out, gray look to it. The only bright color belonged to the bone-white elevated portions of the highway in the distance. They looked like the skeletal humps of some enormous, snakelike sea monster frozen in time.

"Anthony?"

"I'm looking for more like him," Anthony said.

Jesse came up beside him and they both looked out toward the highway.

"What do we need to do about the money?" Jesse finally said. "This changes things, right? I mean, doesn't it?"

"No," Anthony said, shaking his head. "No. We still need to get the money. But we need to do it pretty damn quick."

CHAPTER 9

Captain Mark Shaw stepped through a set of double doors and emerged onto a small open-air balcony that had, until recently, served as a study nook for the University of Houston's film and technology students. But like everything else in Houston, it was a mess right now. The black wrought-iron furniture was tumbled in a heap along the railing to his right, and damp green leaves covered everything. They squished beneath his boots as he crossed the tiled deck. He went to the railing and looked out over the vast, shallow sea that now covered his city. The smell of mud and rot and ocean water rose up to assault his nostrils, and he grimaced.

From somewhere off to his right a radio was playing a Tejano song. He listened to its rolling polka beat and smiled. It had been, what, more than two weeks since he'd heard music on the radio? Strange that he should hear it now. He'd always thought of music as a sign of hope, a symbol of man's joy to be alive. He looked around and didn't see any signs of that hope now.

After a short while the song faded out and left silence in its wake. Perhaps someone had made the owner of the radio turn it off. That would figure. All things considered, it did seem somehow disrespectful.

Mark Shaw listened to the silence.

There were no birds. No one was yelling. And of course there were no cars. It seemed Hurricane Mardel had brought quiet as well as misery, and in the stillness of the moment he could hear his own breath wheezing in his ears.

He reached into the shirt pocket of his uniform, took out a rumpled pack of Marlboros and a BIC lighter, and fired up the last cigarette in the pack. The rush of nicotine calmed his jangling nerves a bit and he leaned on the railing, propped up by his elbows, smoking and thinking of his future.

Prospects were not good. In fact, they were downright crappy.

During the night, Mardel's storm surge—a forty-seven-foot-high monster—had swept over South Houston and completed the destruction her lesser siblings Hector and Kyle had begun. The campus was already damaged by winds, but the storm surge had been the real destroyer. It smothered everything, including his headquarters over at the library, and he'd been forced to relocate to the College of Film and Technology for his teleconference this morning with the head of Homeland Security.

One of his staff, a smart young officer named Mark Eckert, had set him up with a laptop and a webcam and showed him how to use a program called Skype. Shaw, who in his younger days had enjoyed the occasional science-fiction movie, had leaned forward and watched his own fish-eye image appear at the bottom of the screen with a strange sense of disappointment. His face skipped and flickered, not at all the crystal-clear perfection Hollywood had promised in Kubrick's *2001* and John Carpenter's *Dark Star*. Reality seemed cheap, almost ghetto, like the future promised in *Soylent Green*'s Malthusian nightmare.

Frowning, Shaw had watched the screen fill with the face

of George Dupree, director of Homeland Security. Dupree was a small, self-important man with prematurely gray hair that he slicked back with a handful of gel into a stiff-looking helmet. *Vegas hair*, Shaw had thought, with the flicker of a grin at the corner of his mouth. But Dupree's accent wasn't what Shaw had expected. He spoke with the slow, comfortable twang of Georgia or Arkansas, though the accent was stiffened by the aristocratic sophistication and aloofness of a Yale education. It was a strange combination, and Shaw had disliked it from the first.

"What exactly are ya'll doing down there?" Dupree had said.

Shaw bristled at that. *Well, sir*, he'd almost said, *we're dying down here and it would sure be nice if you lazy federal fucks could get off your asses and give us the help we need*.

But that dog wouldn't hunt and he knew it. Instead, Shaw had squared his shoulders to the screen and said, "We've surpassed our response capabilities by a considerable margin, sir. I have roughly two million people stranded and starving in the South Houston area and no resources with which to care for or evacuate them. I need some—"

"I'm aware of all that," Dupree said, and though the webcam cut most of the gesture off, Shaw could see his speech was being dismissed with a wave of the director's hand. "I'm talking about all these reports of people being attacked and eaten. What in the hell is that about?"

"Isolated instances, sir. These people are starving."

"Isolated my ass, Captain Shaw. Here, I want to read you something."

Dupree picked up a piece of paper and frowned at it as if it'd been smeared with something nasty.

"This is an e-mail you sent me four days ago. In it, you assure me that these reports of cannibals are, and I quote, 'Grossly exaggerated and mean-spirited attacks upon the people of Houston, many of whom have lost everything but their lives and their hope in the humanity and charity of others.' Okay, fair enough. But you go on to urge us to continue and even redouble our evacuation efforts. That we did, Captain."

He put the paper down, folded his hands on the desk in front of him, and stared directly at Shaw.

"In the past week, the United States Air Force has flown a continuous shuttle service of C-5 Galaxies from the Houston area to Lackland Air Force Base in San Antonio. They have evacuated nearly six hundred thousand people in that time. They have flown another seventy thousand to Dallas/Ft. Worth. It is the biggest civilian relocation in the history of the United States, and it was done on your assurance that these reports of pandemic infection and cannibalistic insanity are grossly exaggerated and mean-spirited attacks upon innocent people."

Shaw swallowed the lump that had formed in his throat, but waited stoically for what he knew was coming.

"You lied to me, Captain Shaw. You lied to the world. And do you know what has happened as a result of that lie, Captain?"

"No, sir, I don't."

"The city of San Antonio is in the middle of a war, Captain. They've had literally thousands of these cannibals of yours bust out of their shelters. Their hospitals are overrun. Their police department and fire department have been gutted. Do you understand me? I said gutted. The same thing, I understand, is happening in Dallas/Ft. Worth. But it is especially bad in San Antonio . . . and all because they opened their arms to your evacuation effort."

Dupree sifted through some papers on his desk. He found what he was looking for, but when he started speaking again, his tone had changed. Some of the anger was gone, replaced now with sadness and exhaustion.

"This is a report from a civilian doctor named William

Stiles at San Antonio's University Hospital. Dr. Stiles claims to have worked on several of these cannibals during the past few hours, and in this report he even identifies the specific disease responsible for their behavior. He calls it the necrosis filovirus, which he says is closely related to the family of viral hemorrhagic fevers. Are you familiar with a viral hemorrhagic fever, Captain Shaw?"

"No, sir, I'm not."

"Well, for your benefit then, let me just tell you that these are nasty fucking bugs. I mean, seriously nasty. Like you have to wear a spacesuit to handle them nasty. AIDS is a Level Two infectious disease. These things are Level Four. Ever heard of Crimean-Congo fever? Marburg?"

"No, sir."

"How about Ebola?"

"Yes, sir, I've heard of that."

"Oh, well, that's good, because you've just released Ebola's big brother on the world, Captain." Dupree looked over Dr. Stiles's report. "Let's see, what does he say here? Ah, yes. 'The major difference between the necrosis filovirus and other members of the viral hemorrhagic family is the incubation time from initial infection to full manifestation of the disease. A person who contracts Ebola or Marburg is likely to exhibit a headache, backache, and other flu-like symptoms within five to ten days. The necrosis filovirus on the other hand seems to amplify within the host in just a few hours. After that, an infected person experiences almost total depersonalization, essentially becoming a zombie. The illusion that these people are the walking dead is even more complete when you see the clouded pupils, the smell of necrotic tissue, and the almost complete lack of sensitivity to pain. We have handled several confirmed cases of victims who are still ambulatory even though they've been eviscerated or shot multiple times. So in many ways these victims are the walking dead.' "

Dupree paused there. He looked at Shaw, and despite the sketchy quality of the video feed, Shaw could still see the nests of wrinkles forming at the corners of Dupree's eyes and around his mouth. The man was nearly as exhausted as Shaw.

"Captain Shaw, do you have any idea what you have done to your fellow Americans? You heard what Stiles wrote in his report. These are the walking dead. They are zombies. You've damned us all."

Shaw bristled at that, but not because it wasn't true. He was thinking of Joe Schwab, the head of public works, who had said nearly the exact same thing when he limped back into the shelter earlier that day after losing most of his work crews to the zombies out in the ruins.

"You lied to me," Schwab had said. "You damned my men. You damned them all. You fucking bastard."

Shaw closed his eyes and bowed his head.

"I'm sorry," he said to Dupree. "There are nearly two million people left in this city who are not infected. I was only thinking of them. I thought there would be no way the government would evacuate them if they knew what we were dealing with."

Dupree just stared at him.

"You're no politician," he finally said.

"I've been told that," Shaw said.

"A politician would have found a way to pass this along. Are you really accepting full responsibility for this?"

"Yes, sir. I don't see what else I can do."

He had nearly added that he didn't cause the disease, that it was unfair to heap all this blame on him, but he stopped short of saying that because he wasn't entirely convinced it was true. Hadn't he ordered the campus opened up for all these evacuees? Hadn't this shelter, which had begun with such noble intentions, turned into a literal hell on earth?

That was his doing. All this mess, he had miscalculated. He had set the dominoes in motion.

Dupree sighed heavily.

"We will continue our evacuation efforts," he said. "But we're going to have to change the way we're doing things."

"In what way, sir?"

"Effective immediately all federal transportation out of the affected area will stop. We've already started setting up a staging area at the Sam Houston Race Park. You know where that is?"

Shaw nodded, and his mind was already leaping ahead, considering the logic of the military's choice. It made perfect sense. Located at the intersection of the North Beltway and the Tomball Parkway, both major expressways, it was easy to get to, especially seeing as most of the freeways were elevated and therefore above the water level. Also, the Tomball Parkway was wide, straight, and flat. The military could run planes, even the big C-5 Galaxies, out of there all day long. There were train tracks there, too, providing a second form of mass transit. And the race park itself was immense. It would make the perfect gathering point for the military to triage the crowds and cull out the infected, if any made it that far.

"We'll have National Guardsmen standing by," Dupree went on. "They will have a medical staff on scene who will examine every person looking to be evacuated."

Shaw nodded. But then he realized what Dupree had not said, the part he had left out. Dupree's people would handle the evacuation once Shaw got the survivors to the Race Park, but it would be up to Shaw to get them there. He would have to personally guide as many refugees as he could find across the flooded ruins of a city that was, geographically speaking, one of the biggest on the planet. And he would have to do it in the midst of a deadly plague. Suddenly things seemed a whole lot more complicated.

"Sir," he said, "can't you offer me any help at all? My men have scrounged every house, every marina, every boat shop in South Houston, and we have managed to come up with a little over three hundred usable boats. I simply don't have the resources to help these people. Can't you help me with anything? Helicopters, extra boats, anything?"

Dupree's face remained cold and impassive as he shook his head from side to side.

"I'm sorry, Captain," he said. "You're on your own."

"Yeah," Shaw said. "Yeah, I'm sorry, too."

And now, with the memory of that disastrous meeting still fresh in his mind, Mark Shaw smoked the last of his cigarette and flicked the butt out into the floodwaters. He looked up and scanned the gray sky. Then he closed his eyes and listened to the sound of his heart beating in his chest.

Footsteps on the tiled deck behind him brought him back to the moment.

"Sir?"

Shaw turned around. Mark Eckert, the same officer who had set up the Skype connection for him, was standing there in a uniform caked with mud.

"What is it, Mark?"

"I just came to see if you needed anything, sir?"

"You heard that, huh?"

Eckert smiled sheepishly. "Yes, sir, I'm sorry."

"Yeah, well," Shaw said, "there's a lot of that going around these days. Listen, I want you to do something for me."

"Yes, sir?"

"Make an announcement, spread the word, I want every policemen and firefighter down by the library in two hours. We're gonna be leaving this place real soon."

Eckert nodded and left without another word.

* * *

Twenty minutes later, Mark Shaw was inside the M.D. Anderson Library, headed towards the EOC's former office, wading through water that was up to his thighs. The entire first floor was flooded and the corridors were black. The only light came from the flashlight he carried. The smell of mud and rotten flesh was so powerful Shaw had to pull his shirt up over his nose, but even then he was constantly on the verge of gagging.

When he entered the EOC office, he saw why. Two of his officers were dead in here. But that wasn't all. A man was feeding off one of the dead officers, tearing shreds of flesh from the officer's upper arm. At first Shaw couldn't tell exactly what he was looking at. The man was doubled over the dead officer, his hair hanging down like a filthy curtain in front of his face. The officer's body was rising and falling with the zombie's exertions. Shaw thought to himself: *He's taking his pulse, right? Checking for a heartbeat.* But the next instant the zombie looked up at Shaw and a large piece of dark red flesh sagged from his mouth like raw liver.

"Oh Jesus," Shaw said.

The zombie rose to his full height, water pouring out of what was left of his clothes. In the flashlight beam he looked unnaturally white, the flesh hanging from his lips shiny and almost black. The zombie climbed over the dead officer, then over the computer console where the officer had been sitting when he died. He was moaning; a horrible, stuttering sound that Shaw could feel echoing in his chest.

"Stop where you're at," Shaw said.

He pulled his weapon and pointed it at the zombie without any real expectation that it would obey his command. Shaw could tell it wouldn't just by looking at the man's eyes. There was nothing behind those eyes. Nothing but hunger.

Shaw trained the flashlight beam on the zombie's face, and though it was one of the new LED lights, intensely bright, the zombie never blinked.

Shaw shot him then, one round that blew the man's scalp off and knocked him back into the water. He stared at the dead officer the zombie had been feeding on, half expecting him to get up and move. But the only movement came from the body gently rocking in the settling water.

"Goddamn this place," Shaw said.

He holstered his weapon and went into his ready room. The water had gotten in here, too, and floated his mattress up against the back wall. All the trash in the entire building had seemed to find its way in here. Papers, plastic cups, a lot of stuff that was so waterlogged he couldn't identify it—the trash was everywhere. He found his last three unopened packs of cigarettes in the wadded-up remnants of his bedding. A little condensation had formed inside the cellophane, but he figured the cigarettes themselves were probably still dry.

He was pocketing the smokes when he heard splashing out in the hallway.

Shaw let out a tired sigh as he drew his weapon and made his way out into the office. There was a figure over there in the darkness near the door, inspecting Shaw's handiwork on the zombie.

"What are you doing here, Anthony?"

The figure spun around suddenly, his gun raised. Shaw flicked his flashlight beam up just enough to illuminate his face, then brought it down again.

Anthony Shaw lowered his weapon. "You about scared the piss out of me, Dad."

"What do you expect? You come traipsing in here making as much noise as you are, you're bound to get surprised."

Anthony nodded. "What happened in here, Dad?"

"Don't know. That's Foster over there, and I'm pretty sure the one our friend here was munching on was Gene Murphy. I don't know how they died, though. Drowned, probably. Caught in here during the storm surge."

Shaw looked around the room once more. It was hard to

believe things had really gotten this bad. He caught Anthony looking at him.

"Where's your brother, Anthony?"

"I don't know. I came in here hoping you'd seen him." Anthony paused for a moment, then added, "Dad, you know he's probably passed out drunk somewhere."

Shaw looked at him sharply. His first instinct was to yell, to deny it. But he knew Anthony was probably right. Brent had probably crawled off into an unused building someplace with a bottle and drank himself into oblivion. The thought made him furious, but it was impossible for him to hold on to the anger very long. Brent was just too much like his mother. She too had fought her battle with the bottle, and for Mark Shaw, that was the hardest part of watching his oldest son slip deeper and deeper into alcoholism. He didn't want to experience the pain of watching a loved one go through that again.

"How about you, Dad? You okay?"

Mark Shaw shrugged. "Good as can be expected, considering the circumstances. How about you?"

"I had to shoot one of those things down by the boats."

"Just one?"

"Yeah. I see you got one, too."

"I suspect we'll be seeing a lot more of them here in the next few hours. The reports I've got so far, sounds like the water is pushing them farther and farther inland. Also, we've been taking in people from all over. Chances are pretty good the shelter's gonna have a few of them by now."

"You talked to the director of Homeland Security?"

"Sure did."

"And? That doesn't sound good. What happened? What did he say? They're sending in help, right?"

Shaw felt distracted. It was hard to focus. This place, the darkness, the smell, it was starting to get to him.

"No, it wasn't good," he said. "Dupree said we're on our own."

He told Anthony about San Antonio and Dallas/Ft. Worth, and about the necrosis filovirus and the zombies.

"That's nuts, Dad. What the hell do they expect us to do?"

"I don't think they have any expectations, Anthony, except for us to fail. My guess is he'll find some way to put this back on us in order to save his own ass. On me, rather. He's already said as much."

Anthony shook his head angrily. "This wasn't your fault, Dad. You did everything a man could be expected to do."

"The director of Homeland Security seems to disagree with you."

"Yeah? Well, fuck him. Dad, we have seven million dollars waiting for us just a couple of miles from here. Let him say whatever he wants. We'll be laughing all the way to the bank."

Mark Shaw opened his mouth to respond, then reconsidered and closed it again. He looked at his youngest son and a disturbing idea occurred to him. Since his boys were little, he'd known that Anthony was the pony to bet on. He loved both his children. There was never any question about that. But a lifetime spent as a cop had taught him a thing or two about human nature. Watching the two boys grow up, he'd seen that Anthony was more aggressive, more confident, the smarter child. He had talent. He could talk to people. He could lead people. Brent, on the other hand, was a turtle. Trouble would come, and Anthony would see it as an opportunity. Brent would simply duck his head into his shell and hide.

But now, looking at Anthony, he realized that maybe his pride in the young man's accomplishments had blinded him to his shortcomings. To Anthony, this was about the money, and nothing else. He didn't see that the money was just one small part of this thing Mark Shaw was trying to pass on to his children.

"Dad, did you hear me?"

"I heard you."

"Well, you agree, right? We get the money and we blow this place. Fuck this city and fuck the director of Homeland Security. We'll start over. The four of us, we'll take our money and we'll make new lives ourselves. That's what you always said, right? We did our part, now we take what's ours."

From somewhere out in the hallway, they heard splashing. And the sound of someone moaning.

"Dad, we don't have much time. We have to get that money and leave this city. Come with me. We'll get Brent and Jesse and get the money and get the hell out of Dodge."

"No," Mark Shaw said.

"What do you mean, no? Dad, this is what we planned for."

"Not quite. Listen to me, Anthony. You and Jesse, find your brother. Then the three of you go and get that money, and bring it back here."

"Here? Dad, why in the hell—"

"Because we have a charge to keep, Anthony. We have a responsibility."

"To who? Dad, our responsibility is to our family. That's what you always said. It's family above all else. In the end, nothing else matters."

"Honor matters, Anthony. Our family name matters. Outside those doors there are eighty thousand people that are here because they trusted in me to lead them. If I abandon them now they will all die."

Anthony was shaking his head as if he couldn't believe what he was hearing. "Dad, that's insane. You can't . . . you have less than three hundred boats out there. How do you think you're gonna transport all those people through a flood? There's no way in hell you can do that. It's crazy to try. You said yourself that Dupree doesn't expect you to succeed."

"Anthony, you have to understand why this matters. If I don't try to save those people, the name I'll pass on to you and your brother will be worthless. It'll be less than worthless. It will become a synonym for cowardice, and I will not allow my sons to wear that shame."

"Dad, I can change my fucking name."

Mark Shaw lunged forward, grabbed Anthony's shirt by the collar and slammed him down onto a computer console. For a moment, he was nearly blind with a rage he hadn't felt since he'd overheard Anthony calling his mother a drunk during his sophomore year in high school. The boy had been sixteen at the time, an athlete, and though small of frame compared to his father, every bit as strong. But when he'd heard what the boy had said, Mark Shaw stood up from his chair and slid the belt from around his waist and thrown Anthony facedown over the edge of the couch, at which point he'd begun to whip the boy's ass until his jeans were shredded.

Now, here they were, two grown men, and Mark Shaw was dangerously close to doing the same thing.

When he finally spoke, his voice was a brutal whisper.

"You will not change your name. Do you understand me?"

Still on his back, eyes wide with alarm, Anthony looked up at his father and said, "Yeah. Shit, Dad, I hear you."

Mark Shaw lifted his son off the computer console and then slammed him back down. "Say the fucking words, Anthony. Say you will not change your name."

"I won't. Christ, Dad, I won't change my name."

"You have a good name, Anthony. An honorable name."

"Yeah, an honorable name. Dad, I get it."

Out in the hallway, the moaning was getting louder. Mark Shaw looked up and listened. He thought he could hear two, maybe three of those zombies out there. Then he looked down at the terror on Anthony's face and for a moment was shocked and a little frightened with the violence he knew he carried around inside himself.

He let go of his son and backed away. Anthony slid off the console and stood staring at his father, his expression a mixture of resentment and fear that made him seem ten years younger, almost childlike.

"Listen to me, Anthony. I want you to go and get your brother. Go and get that money. When you have it, you come straight back here. You hear me? Live or die, I will do everything in my power to get these people out of danger. And I will make sure the name you and your brother carry out of this city is one you will never, ever think of changing. Is that clear?"

Anthony tugged his shirt down at the waist to straighten it.

"Yeah, that's clear."

"Good. Now go and find your brother."

The moaning was extremely close now. Both men could hear the zombies splashing out in the hallway.

"I'll take care of those first," Anthony said.

"No," Mark Shaw said, drawing his weapon. "We'll take care of it together."

CHAPTER 10

Eleanor stopped at her front door and stared at the water flowing through her dining room, her living room, out the broken windows along the back wall, momentarily stunned by it. The sight was completely insane, yet strangely beautiful.

"Eleanor, you okay?" Jim asked.

"Yeah," she said, mentally shaking herself loose. "I'm coming."

She followed Jim and Madison out the front door. She tossed her Mossberg into the canoe they'd tied to the front porch, then helped Jim with their backpacks. Next she reached down to help Madison up into the canoe, but when she tried to lift her, the girl shrugged her hands away.

"Madison?" Eleanor said.

Madison wouldn't look at her.

She turned away from Eleanor and held her hands up to Jim, the same way she'd done when she was three and begging Daddy to carry her off to bed.

Jim glanced from Madison to Eleanor, and she saw surprise there in his expression. Whatever was going on with Madison, it was news to him as well. He bent down and scooped her into the boat without saying a word to Madison, not even scolding her with a look, and Eleanor was thankful for that. Now was not the time.

"Go ahead," he said to Eleanor. He was nodding toward the boat, holding its sides to steady it for her.

She climbed in, then leaned forward and touched the back of Madison's shoulder.

"Madison, sweetheart?"

But Madison pulled her shoulder away again. "Don't," she said, without turning around, and scooted forward on the bench and hunched her shoulders forward. Eleanor could almost see her crawling into herself.

Eleanor glanced at Jim for some clue, some sort of help, but all he could do was shrug.

They moved away from the house, Jim and Eleanor paddling, Madison still silent and distant in the front of the canoe. The air was unbearably humid. A slight breeze blew from the south, but it wasn't enough to chase away the mosquitoes, and it wasn't enough to cool the heat on the backs of their necks. Eleanor was drenched in sweat, hot, and irritable and exhausted beyond measure.

She took it out on the mosquitoes. Just in the last few minutes they'd gotten terrible, practically swarming the canoe. She killed a big one on her arm, her face crinkling in disgust at its smashed body and the smear of blood in which it lay. Then she looked forward and saw Jim and Madison both swatting frantically at the bugs.

"I've got some bug repellant," she said.

"Thank God," Jim said. "Let me have some. These little bastards are eating me alive up here."

She pulled in her oar and got the combination bug repellant and sunscreen from her backpack. As far as getting her family prepared for this disaster, the backpacks had really been her crowning achievement. Making them was strangely satisfying, much like preparing Madison's nursery had been in the months before she was born. Eleanor had stockpiled water and food and supplies just like the guidebooks said to do, but all of that was lost back in their house. The backpacks, on the other hand, went wherever they were needed. Each one was basically a turtle shell, a house carried on the back. She had planned the contents of each, packed them, reconsidered, reorganized, and repacked them. Then she'd weighed each and repacked them a third time. Each containing a complete ninety-six-hour survival kit—everything the wearer would need to get by for at least four days. But Eleanor had gone beyond those basic needs, and that was what really made her proud. She'd had dog tags made for each of them. She'd included family photographs, in case they got separated. Cash for each of them. A three months' supply of Jim's Diovan, for his blood pressure. Even a carton of Marlboro cigarettes for each of them.

"You want me to start smoking?" Madison had said, holding up the cigarettes.

"Of course not, you goof," she'd said, stroking Madison's hair out of her face, secretly delighted with the look of disgust on her daughter's face. "They're for you to use as currency. Just in case, mind you. You never know what people will do if they want to smoke bad enough."

Madison scrunched up her nose in that uniquely teenager way of expressing complete revulsion with the world of grown-ups. "That's gross," she said, and tossed the Marlboros back in the front pocket of her pack.

But Jim's medicine had been her greatest coup. The city's insurance had given her hell about buying a three months' supply of Diovan, and she'd given it right back to them. "Why," she argued, "do you train me in disaster preparedness—a basic tenet of which makes it plain that you should have a long-term supply of prescription drugs on hand at all times—and then tell me that I can only buy thirty days at a time?"

In the end, it had been the pharmacy that finally gave in. "You want a three months' supply?" they'd said. "Fine. But you have to buy it on your own. Your insurance won't budge."

She'd paid the extra money, and at the time had been aware of how paranoid she must have seemed. But she certainly didn't feel silly about it right now. Glancing around at the submerged houses, the traffic lights dipping like low-hanging fruit toward the floodwaters, she was feeling anything but silly. As a matter of fact, she was basking in the righteous glow of vindication.

"Hey, Eleanor," Jim said, "you got that bug spray or what?"

His voice snapped her back into the moment. She had her hand jammed down into her backpack, and it occurred to her that she had no idea how long she'd been sitting there like that.

"Here it is," she said, and tossed it up to him. "Madison, you need to put some on, too, okay?"

Madison said nothing. She hadn't moved since they'd left the house, except to swat at a mosquito or two. Her shoulders were still sagging forward, her brown hair covering her face like a curtain. Eleanor watched the gentle rise and fall of her body under her shirt as she breathed, and she was pretty sure Madison was sobbing.

Jim put his hand on Madison's knee and gave it a gentle shake. "Hey, sweetheart, you okay?"

Madison suddenly lunged forward and buried her face in Jim's chest.

"Hey," he said, his eyes going wide with momentary surprise. "You're okay, sweetheart. We all are." He gave Eleanor a perplexed look, a *What am I supposed to do now?* look, and then finally put his arm around her and let her cry.

* * *

Over the past two weeks, Eleanor had made countless canoe trips between her house and the EOC. It usually took about three hours to make it one way.

But that was before cannibals started appearing in the ruins.

Now, as they paddled their way toward the EOC, they'd see dim figures moving through the endless piles of wrecked houses and jumbled piles of vehicles, stepping out from beneath the eaves of houses, staggering toward them. And always ceaselessly moaning.

There were only a few, at first. But as Eleanor and her family moved north, gliding through the debris fields, they saw more and more people staggering around aimlessly, stumbling after them whenever the canoe got too close.

The residential areas were the worst.

In some places, the moaning was so loud, so disconcerting, that Madison had screamed, her hands clapped over her ears, until she broke down sobbing.

Eleanor and Jim rarely spoke. A hush fell over them and it seemed dangerous somehow to speak. They watched the people who crashed out of doorways and stared at them as they floated by, and though it was impossible to know whether they were changed in the same way that Bobby Hester had been changed—that Ms. Hester, too, had been changed, Eleanor reminded herself—she'd hear them moan and the hairs would stand up on the back of her neck nonetheless.

And so Eleanor and her family kept moving east, off their intended course, away from the dead eyes staring back at them from the ruins. It still seemed ludicrous to her that she was being forced to avoid cannibalism that was, for all intents and purposes, contagious, but there it was.

And here they were, getting farther and farther off course.

* * *

Jim pushed the floating dead man away from the canoe, his paddle slipping off the man's shoulder and striking his skull right behind the ear with a wet thud.

"Eww," Madison groaned.

They had seen quite a few bodies in the last hour or so. They'd seen a lot of dead dogs and rats and cats and raccoons and even a big brown cow. Death, in fact, was all around them.

They were coming up through the Second Ward now, and a lot of the houses here had fared badly during Mardel's storm surge. In some places, they'd actually been uprooted from the ground and tossed together, one on top of another, like football players going for a fumble. In some of the houses, Eleanor could hear dogs howling out their hunger and their fear.

But the wailing of animals wasn't the only sound they heard. Here and there, amid the rubble, they could hear the voices of people, weak and muffled, but still insistent, as they cried out for rescue.

And there was another sound, too. A thin, solitary moaning that was not one of pain, or loneliness, or despair, but something else. Something that sent a bone-deep shudder through Eleanor's body and raised the gooseflesh on her arms.

Eleanor scanned the ruined houses and saw nothing but bodies floating facedown in the water, their backs matted with wet garbage.

"Why?" Madison said. Her voice was small and remote, almost a whisper.

"What did you say, baby?" Eleanor asked her.

Madison was quiet for so long that Eleanor thought her daughter would fall back into another of her spells, in which there was no reaching her.

But then Madison spoke, and when she did it was with such rage, such sudden violence, that Eleanor recoiled from her, much in the same way she had recoiled from the snarling wounded thing that Ms. Hester had become.

"Why did it have to happen to her? What purpose did that serve?"

Eleanor's eyes went wide. The little girl in front of her suddenly looked nothing like her daughter. Her lips were pulled back in anger, exposing large white teeth. Her cheeks puffed in and out, keeping time with the rise and fall of her tiny, nearly breastless chest. But it was the look of offended rage in the girl's eyes that caused Eleanor's throat to go hard as slate and her heart to skip its beat.

"Why, Mom? Why did that happen? Why did it happen to her?"

All Eleanor could do was shake her head.

"I don't know," she said miserably. "I'm sorry, baby. I just don't know."

And for the next twenty-four hours she'd be recalling her daughter's questions and still struggling for an answer that made any sense at all.

They came to a high white wall of painted cinder blocks that looked to run a couple hundred feet in either direction. Thick drifts of dead seaweed and trash and tree limbs were wedged up against the wall.

In the front of the canoe Jim sat looking at the wall, the oar across his lap. His shirt was soaked through with sweat, the back of his neck black with wet dirt.

He turned back to Eleanor and said, "Well, which way?"

Eleanor had a compass and a map in her backpack, but she hadn't needed it yet. Despite the fact that so much of the city was underwater now, there were still obvious landmarks to guide them. And besides, she'd been a beat cop for a good six years. She knew her way around the city, even as it was now.

"I don't see that it really matters," she said.

"Six of one, half dozen of the other."

"Exactly."

"Okay. Got a preference? Which feels lucky?"

He gave her a little wink with that last part, a private joke between them from back in the days when Madison was much younger and Jim and Eleanor could still make coded jokes about slipping off to the bedroom for a quickie, even while Madison sat in the living room watching cartoons.

She snorted at him.

"Neither one looks *lucky*," she said.

He pretended to look hurt.

"Go left," she said, and laughed at him quietly.

You know, she thought, as the laugh trailed off and became a smile, *he's still pretty cute. A little bit chubbier than when I married him, but then, so am I.*

She watched the muscles along his back move under his shirt as he used the oar to get them pointed in the right direction, his shoulders dipping powerfully, first one way, then the other as he plunged the oar into the water, and she was surprised by the warmth spreading over her skin.

Who knows? she thought. *Maybe the left would be lucky after all.*

Later.

"Do you think the EOC will still be functioning?" he asked, without looking back at her.

"I don't know," she said.

"But it's worth going there, right?"

"I think it is," she said. "Honestly, Jim, I don't know anywhere else to go."

"Okay," he said. He nodded gravely.

And they paddled on.

They'd gotten used to the sight of bodies floating in the water. By that afternoon, they'd seen literally hundreds of them. They were everywhere. And so, when Eleanor saw the body of the black man caught up in the limbs of a fallen tree, she paid him little mind. He was just another corpse, heavy-set, his clothes stripped from his body by high winds and water and debris, so that all that remained on his bloated frame was a filthy pair of briefs. He hung facedown from the tree limbs, his arms swinging lazily in the current. There were cuts and sores all over his arms and back, and he smelled of rotten meat. To Eleanor, he looked just like every other dead body she'd seen.

She looked away.

Off to her right was a wide, glassy sea of pewter-colored water, broken only by a line of trees and a white metal roof in the distance. The sky was a washed-out gray. Eleanor could see dark vertical streaks of rain beyond the white roof, but with the absence of a breeze, it was impossible to tell if the rain was coming their way or not. It looked depthless and utterly still over there, as if the rain was just hanging in the air.

There were structures to the left, and they seemed familiar. An AutoZone, a Mexican meat market, a CVS Pharmacy, all of them veering off at a forty-five-degree angle from Eleanor's position. Wooden power-line poles tilted at odd angles, their cables sagging near to the water, and from the ragged line they made, she thought she had a pretty good idea of where they were.

"We need to head down that road there," she said, and immediately realized how stupid she sounded. "That way, I mean. Where the road used to be."

But Jim didn't tease her. He just grunted and said, "Okay," and paddled on.

He must really be tired, Eleanor thought. *Poor guy hasn't gotten any—*

Eleanor wasn't aware the black man in the tree was moving until he was already on them. She heard a rustle of leaves, the snap of tree limbs, a splash as he hit the water and tried to scramble over the side of the canoe. Water hit her in the face and she flinched, turning away from it. When she looked back again, she was staring straight down into a corpse's face. The eyes were filmed over, a milky white. His skin had a gray, flabby appearance, as if it might slough right off the bone. His lips were cracked open, the teeth shattered and black with blood. And it really *was* a corpse's face. There was no getting around that. She had locked eyes with him for only a second, but that was enough. She was sure of what she had seen. And she had just enough time to realize that she had been sure about Bobby Hester, too.

And Ms. Hester.

They were all corpses.

The black man groaned as he shot out of the water and into the canoe, his hands going all over Madison, whose screams were so loud they felt like ice picks jammed into Eleanor's ears. Madison kicked him in the face, the heel of her tennis shoes smashing into the man's mouth. Eleanor could hear his teeth snapping. She could see blood spurting across his face. And yet the man made no attempt to block her kicks. He didn't seem to realize how badly his face was getting damaged. Instead, he just kept swiping at her, rocking the canoe wildly from side to side.

Eleanor tried to grab Madison and pull her back, but they were moving too much, pitching all over the place. She felt the boat rise beneath her, tilting, tilting, to one side, and she instinctively clamped a hand down on the gunwale to steady herself as the boat rolled over, tossing her headlong into the water.

She popped up immediately and looked around.

Jim was up by the bow, at the far end of the canoe from her. Eleanor saw him surface, swipe the water from his eyes, and spin around looking for her.

She couldn't see Madison anywhere.

The cannibal—for that was what he must be, Eleanor re-alized, one of those cannibals—was still on his feet, though, and he was looking right at her.

"Madison," Eleanor yelled. "Madison, where are you?"

She spun around wildly. She caught sight of Jim digging frantically at the water, but an impulse told her that he had no idea where Madison was, either.

"Madison? Madison?"

The cannibal growled.

The next instant, he was trying to climb over the capsized canoe in order to get at Eleanor, but the hull was slick with the oily floodwater and he slid off to one side. He tried again to scale over, and again he fell off. He was closer now to her end of the canoe, less than an arm's length really, and yet he tried a third time to climb over the capsized canoe.

Why doesn't he just go around? she thought. And some-where in the back of her mind something clicked. She had asked exactly the right question. Not *What in the hell's wrong with him?* but *Why doesn't he just go around?* One step to the side and he could be right there in front of her, and yet he didn't see it. He didn't see the obvious. Why?

But the next instant the question was moot, for the stern of the boat tilted under the water, pushed down by his weight, and when he slipped off this time he was right in front of her, nothing between them.

He charged her.

"Get Madison out of here!" Eleanor shouted at Jim as the cannibal fell on top of her. She could smell the putrescence on his breath. She could feel the rubbery give of the flesh on his arms as she wrestled with him, holding him at arm's length so he couldn't bite her.

He was a lot bigger than Eleanor, but he was clumsy, his movements uncoordinated, and she managed to toss him to one side.

As the man went under the water, Eleanor's muscle mem-

ory and training took over. At the police academy, the instructors preached the gunfighter's gospel: *Break contact,
create distance, get your front sight on the target.*

So she scrambled away from him, making sure not to lose
sight of him, and reached down to her hip for her gun.

But it wasn't there.

Where is it? The thought hung unanswered in her mind as
a panicky wave of nausea filled her gut. And then, with an
inward groan, she remembered. The gun had been digging
into her ribs as she paddled the canoe. Despite the threat of
cannibals, despite the tired but insistent voice in her head
that told her she was making a mistake, she had slid the
weapon from the waistband of her jeans and dropped it into
the front pocket of her backpack, along with all her extra
magazines.

Where it would be close, she thought bitterly, *just in case
I need it.*

Now the backpacks were floating away from the canoe,
carried by the sluggish current toward the line of bushes in
front of the CVS Pharmacy. There was no way she could
reach them now. The cannibal had his hands out in front of
him, clutching at the air. The growl was gone. The sound
crawling out of his throat now was an urgent, pitiful moan.
The first two fingers on his right hand were bent back, obviously and horribly broken. As his other fingers reached for
her, the two bent back ones hardly moved. All they could
manage was a feeble twitching.

She had been backing away from the man, cowering
really, but then her foot hit something hard under the water.
It was like a gunshot going off in her mind. Suddenly everything was clear. The cannibal lunged for her, almost diving.
She stepped nimbly to one side and the man found himself
facedown in the water. He seemed momentarily confused by
this, as though he was unable to process why his victim had
suddenly disappeared, and under different circumstances, the

way his face went slack and his mouth fell open would have been comical.

But for now, she was all business. Eleanor immediately jumped onto the man's back, got a knee planted firmly between his shoulder blades, grabbed his hair with both hands, and pushed his face under the water.

He began to thrash.

His arms splashed frantically, though clumsily, at the water, like a man who thinks he's a bird and might be able to fly away if he just flapped hard enough. She could feel his legs kicking against hers, his upper body convulsing as he gulped in water instead of air.

"Drown, you asshole," she growled.

Out of the corner of her eye she saw Jim looking at her. Without letting go of the cannibal, she met Jim's gaze. His face was a mask of horror and shock and helpless confusion. She couldn't help but wonder what it must be like to be in his shoes right now, watching his wife intentionally drown a man while she snarled at him like an animal.

The cannibal spasmed once, twice, and then he went slack beneath her. She slid her knee off the man's back, but didn't let go of his hair.

"Eleanor," Jim said. There was a curious sympathy in his voice.

She glanced at Jim again.

"He's dead," Jim said.

She looked down at the dark crown of hair just below the surface, saw the strands of it waving like seaweed between her fingers. Her knuckles were white. The muscles in her forearms were tensed so tightly they hurt, and she had to will herself to release her grip on the back of the man's head.

Madison, she thought, and that did it for her.

She pushed the cannibal's corpse away and said, "Where's Madison?"

Suddenly Jim was at her side, his arms around her. She

struggled against him, still screaming her daughter's name, when he finally grabbed her shoulders and spun her around to face him.

"She's here," he said, quietly, over and over again. "She's right here."

"Where?"

He stepped away from Eleanor and slapped the hull of the capsized canoe.

"It's okay, Madison. You can come out now."

Delicate fingers curled up and around the gunwale, and the next instant, Madison's head popped up from under the canoe.

A gasp leaked out of Eleanor's throat that was part laugh, part absolute relief and joy. "Oh my God," she managed to say, and then rushed for her daughter and wrapped her arms around her in a hug so tight it took both their breath away. "Oh my God," she said again. "Madison, I thought . . . I thought . . . oh thank God you're safe."

"Mom," Madison said. Her tone was full of protest, but she didn't make any attempt to pull away.

Eleanor released her grip and held Madison away at arm's length.

"Are you okay, sweetheart? He didn't hurt you, did he?"

Madison shook her head no. "I'm okay," she said.

"Oh, thank God."

Eleanor closed her eyes and let out a long sigh of relief. Her mind had been filled with such horrible thoughts of what that man might have done to her, and the fact that he'd had no time to do anything to her made little difference. *We invent such nasty fates for the ones we really love,* Eleanor thought. *Why is that? Why do we punish ourselves so much?*

The clatter of a metal fence brought her back to the moment.

She turned around and scanned the flooded ruins. About a hundred feet away a man was trying to pull his battered body over a chain-link fence, and Eleanor realized with a withering sort of horror that the man was a cannibal, like the one she'd just drowned.

He wore the remnants of a blue chambray shirt and khaki trousers that were flecked with green leaves and stained a reddish brown in places. It was blood, she realized coldly. And looking at his face she could see that he had fed recently. His chin and cheeks and hair were slathered with clotted blood. Even at a distance she could see that one eye had been gouged out. He poked his fingers through the diamond-shaped holes in the fence and started to climb. His movements were awkward and labored, but it only took him a few moments to reach the top, and when he did he let out a moan that sent shivers down Eleanor's back.

The sound carried over the water. There was a chilling rhythm to it, like the steady rise and fall of a large crowd heard from a distance. And then, from off to her right, she heard an answering moan.

She turned, and saw three more human train wrecks, up to their waists in water, shambling toward her. A short distance from them, the figure of a woman emerged from the broken windows of a storefront, her bruised face turning slowly until she zeroed in on Eleanor.

"There's more of them over here," Jim said.

Eleanor didn't have to ask where. They were surrounded. The late-afternoon air was filling up with an almost desperate chorus of moans, and Eleanor realized with deepening despair and fear that they were calling to each other.

They're ringing the dinner bell, she thought.

"We need to do something quick," Jim said.

"Into the boat," Eleanor answered him. "Everybody, into the canoe."

Hurriedly, they righted the canoe, and Madison and Eleanor climbed in. Jim grabbed the short rope they'd tied to the stem post on the bow and pulled them along. The oars had floated along with the current, headed in the same direction as the backpacks, and when Jim reached the first of them he scooped it up and tossed it back to Eleanor.

The moaning cannibals were all around them now, emerging from nearly every yawning doorway and from behind every building. Eleanor turned around on her seat, scanning the ruins in utter dismay. Where had they all come from? The area had been completely deserted just moments before, and now, they were everywhere. Had all this really stemmed from that one man moaning as he scaled the fence? Was such a thing possible?

Briefly, a memory surfaced in her mind. She'd been a young patrol officer at the time, working nights in Houston's Fifth Ward. One blisteringly hot summer night, while on routine patrol, she'd rounded a corner and seen a group of three teenagers arguing on the curb. Their voices were loud, but indistinct. She couldn't make out what was said, only the anger with which the words were yelled. Then, suddenly, one of the boys had taken two lurching stagger-steps backwards, his hands flying up in front of his face. As he turned away there was a flash and the sound of three gunshots. He stumbled into the street, bent over, and collapsed not twenty feet from her front bumper.

The two boys on the curb stared at her, their eyes huge in the glare of her patrol car's spotlights. One of them raised his pistol at her, but the other was already turning to run. He grabbed his friend by the shirt and pulled him after him.

By the time Eleanor got her car in park and scrambled out of it, the two were already gone.

And the third young man was dying.

She knelt down next to him and tried to talk to him, but all he could do was gulp air like a fish out of water. He died right there, on the pavement, as she was calling for EMS and backup.

But it was what happened afterwards that came to her

mind now, for when she'd looked up from the dead boy's blood-spattered face, she'd seen that the sidewalks on both sides of the street were filling with people. They watched her, their expressions impassive, unmoved by the tragedy in front of them, and as her gaze shifted from one to the next to the next, she thought: *It's the middle of the night. Where did all you folks come from? How did it happen? The street was deserted just a moment ago. Where did you all come from?*

There was, she guessed, a certain magnetic quality to violence. People flocked to it like moths to a bare electric bulb. They fed off it somehow, even as it drained some vital quality from their souls and dulled their senses.

Maybe that was what was happening here, she thought, as she watched the cannibals closing in on them.

"Jim, get in the boat. Hurry!"

The moaning crowd was getting ever closer. The man in the blue chambray shirt had made it over the chain-link fence and was less than thirty feet away now.

Close enough she could smell him.

"Hurry!" she said again.

But Jim had found the other oar and was already pulling himself into the canoe. He dropped down onto the seat and without another word he dug into the water with his oar, really stabbing at it.

Eleanor joined him, and they moved off at a snail's pace, following the current. Ahead of them was what had been a wide, four-lane road. It was full of people now, all of them splashing as fast as they were able toward the little canoe. Eleanor saw a new U-shaped building off to their right. It looked to be two stories high, glass all the way around, encircled by a wraparound balcony.

An office park, she thought. This part of town had been on the rebound before the storms, a lot of new development in the area.

"Take us over there to the right," Eleanor said.

"Where?" Jim asked, looking around at her.

"Over there."

"What are you thinking?" he asked her.

"Look at the light poles. The water looks deeper over there. They'll have to swim to follow us."

"Got it," he said.

They paddled toward the building, but they were going across the current now, and their progress was slower. The cannibal in the blue chambray shirt was nearly on them now. Another four or five steps and he'd be close enough to topple the boat.

"Mommy!" Madison screamed, and flinched away from the man.

Her movement set the canoe rocking wildly, and Eleanor had to grab her by her arm hard to settle the canoe. At the same time she raised her oar over her head and brought it down hard on the cannibal's outstretched hand. The oar connected with his knuckles with a crunch of bone, but the man never cried out. Instead, he turned slowly to Eleanor and tilted his bloody face to one side. Then, with his other hand, he reached out for her.

Eleanor raised the oar again, but before she could bring it down, the man's head burst open, and bits of bone and skin and lumps of his scalp splatted onto the water beside him.

Eleanor blinked at him.

For a second, her mind wouldn't wrap around what had just happened.

The cannibal, for his part, seemed unaware he'd just been killed. His face never changed expression. The bloody grimace that had turned his mouth into such an object of horror never relaxed. With no emotion of any kind, he slowly sank into the water, like a marionette whose strings had just been cut.

Confused, Eleanor looked at Jim, but he was clearly as confused as she was.

"What happened?" he said.

Her gaze went past him, fixing on a figure who was standing on the wraparound balcony of the office park. He was waving at them, a rifle in his hands.

"Is that . . . ?" Jim asked.

"Yeah," Eleanor said, a smile creeping across her face as she took in the wiry country boy with the boonie cap pushed high up on his forehead, away from his sunglasses. "That's Hank Gleason."

CHAPTER 11

The water was deeper around the building, which, Eleanor could see from a cream-colored granite wall near the entrance to the parking lot, was called the Meadowlakes Business Park. Eleanor looked down as they entered the lake that had once been the building's parking lot, and though the water was a dark gray and cloudy with silt and debris, she could still see the ghosts of cars down there.

She chanced a look behind her.

The crowd that had been closing in on them was struggling with the deeper water. Many were drowning as they tried to follow them. But there were many more gathering beyond the entrance, maybe a hundred total now, and their moans had become truly awful, rising to a deafening roar that seemed to echo off every building at once.

"Why won't they leave us alone?" Madison screamed. "Leave us alone!"

Eleanor turned back to her daughter and saw that Madison's face had turned an ashen white. Her eyes were wide, crazy looking, shiny and bloodshot. Beads of sweat had popped out all over her face, and the green T-shirt she wore was dark and wet at the neck and underarms. Her expression was one of utter despair and rage and exhaustion.

"Madison," Eleanor said. Her voice was firm, but not without compassion. "Baby, look at me."

Madison's gaze shifted from the drowning cannibals to Eleanor, and in that instant, Eleanor's heart broke.

"Mom, what's wrong with them? Why are they like that?"

Suddenly Eleanor felt very tired. Her eyes had gone dry and they hurt. It wasn't a needling pain, but the kind of soreness that came from too many hours of staying awake, heartsick with worry about life and family and the future. She pinched the bridge of her nose between her thumb and forefinger and let out a long, tired sigh.

"They're desperate," Eleanor said at last. "Desperate people do terrible things."

"Ms. Hester wasn't desperate," Madison countered.

She had that defensive, challenging tone that all teenagers seem to fall back on when the world of grown-ups stops making sense.

"She had *us*. We were family. We loved her. *I* loved her. Why did she change? Why did she turn into one of those crazy people?"

Eleanor opened her mouth to answer, but closed it again. She had nothing, no answer that would do her daughter's question justice, and she knew it. There were times, she thought, when she still got the teenager's point of view. It wasn't *that* long ago, for Christ's sake. But Madison was still looking at her with that look that was simultaneously defiant and wounded. And the truth was, Eleanor told herself, that she wasn't even sure she had been telling the truth when she called those cannibals over there desperate. Madison was right about that. Ms. Hester hadn't been desperate. She'd been attacked by her grandson, attacked so badly that, for a second, Eleanor thought he had killed her.

And then she became just like him.

Had something similar happened for each of those people at the edge of the parking lot? Did they have a Bobby Hester somewhere behind them, a crazed loved one who attacked them and changed them? She just didn't know, but the possibility terrified her. They could be sitting at ground zero of an epidemic.

Eleanor closed her eyes and tried to push the image of Ms. Hester crawling across the floor of Madison's room out of her mind.

But she couldn't.

She could still hear Ms. Hester's fingernails snapping as her clawlike hands gripped the carpet. She could still see the woman's face, bloodstained and twisted with an expression that wasn't quite rage, not quite pain, but something that was both of those things, and neither.

"Hey there, Sergeant Norton. How you doin'?"

Eleanor glanced up at the balcony. Hank Gleason was up there, smiling down at them with that cool, country-boy swagger of his, smoking a cigarette, and a momentary blush rose up in Eleanor's cheeks. A sixteen-year-old memory surfaced along with it. It had happened before Madison was born, even before Jim had entered her life. She had gone to see *The Twilight Saga: Eclipse* with two of her girlfriends from the department. They'd sat there in the darkened theater, feeling stupid, feeling like the only adults in a room full of teenyboppers, until the werewolf, Jacob Black, made his first appearance. Jacob was leaning against the trunk of a car, no shirt to hide the view, six-pack abs shiny with a thin sheen of sweat, and the entire audience, three hundred women in all, let out a collective, satisfied sigh.

Eleanor and her girlfriends held Hank Gleason in similar esteem. Like Taylor Lautner, who had played Jacob in *Eclipse*, Hank was pure eye candy. But whereas Taylor Lautner, a.k.a. Sharkboy, was really just a child growing into a man's body, Hank was the real deal. He was a man in a god's body. He was a six-foot-four monument to good genetics, for only perfect genes could account for a man who drank like an Irish poet and smoked like a barn on fire and yet still managed to look like an underwear model.

He'd been in the sun a lot these last two weeks, too. She could tell from the faint red glow of his skin, set off by the gold-rimmed aviator sunglasses and the OD green T-shirt he wore. The added color made him look even more delicious.

Eleanor cleared her throat.

"We're doing just great, Hank. Thanks for the help back there."

He took a last drag on his cigarette and crushed it out beneath the toe of his boot. "Always happy to help out a lady in need," he said, tipping his boonie cap jauntily at her. He looked over at Jim and said, "How about you, Mr. Norton? You doin' okay?"

"Just great, thanks. Call me Jim."

Hank's smile grew bigger, even warmer, if that was possible. He had lovely teeth. "You got it, Jim. Call me Hank. And you, little lady," he said to Madison, "how goes it?"

Madison tried to smile, but couldn't muster a very convincing one.

Hank's smile wavered a bit, but to his credit, he didn't push it. "Y'all had a rough ride, I guess," he said.

"Yeah," Eleanor agreed. "You could say that."

"Well, we got it pretty well covered up here. Water's deep enough they can't get to us, and even if they did, we got the only stairs blocked off."

He pointed down the length of the building, where a large metal staircase was completely buried in a tangle of pipes and cables and all sorts of heavy debris. On the balcony above the stairs Eleanor saw about ten metal-hulled canoes.

"I was watching when you guys first showed up," Hank went on. "I saw you flip over and lose your backpacks. They're still stuck over there along that line of shrubs. I can help you get 'em back tomorrow morning, if you want. In the meantime, we got a bunch of supplies up here if you guys want to spend the night."

"Who's we?" Eleanor asked.

"Me and about thirty old geezers from the Red Cross. Volunteers, you know? Good folks. They had a ton of supplies with 'em when I found 'em. Come on up."

Eleanor looked over at Jim.

"I don't see that we've got any other choice," he said.

"Yeah, I agree. Madison, this would be a good chance for you to get some rest. I know you had a really crappy day."

Madison nodded.

She looked up at Hank and was about to ask him how they were supposed to get up there, but he was already lowering a rope.

Hank pulled them up the rope one by one, and then helped them stow their canoe with the others. With the boat secured, he pointed them down the balcony. "We're this way. You guys hungry?"

"God yes," Jim said.

Jim was drenched in sweat, sunburned, exhausted. He had an arm around Madison's shoulder. His lips were cracked and pale, his face scruffy with a week's worth of whiskers. Eleanor looked at him, and then at Hank Gleason, who was walking next to him, resplendent in his testosterone-laden maleness, and there was no comparison. Jim was your standard American male, a little dopey looking, soft around the middle, full of flaws. But Hank, Hank was the ideal. He was tall and lean, with muscles so hard you could you bounce quarters off them.

And yet, now that she had the two of them before her, Eleanor realized why she had fallen in love in the first place. Hank just bled into the background. For her, it was all about

Jim. The sight of him hobbling along, sweaty, balding, kind of chubby, stiff from sitting in the canoe all day, but with his arm draped around their daughter, was enough to melt her inside. For her, that was real love.

"What?" Jim said. He was looking at her, a hint of a laugh in his voice.

"Nothing," she said. "I'm hungry, too."

Hank Gleason clapped his hands.

"Outstanding. After a day of dodging zombies I guess you guys are ready for some serious chow."

He spoke casually. There was even a breezy note of humor in what Hank had said. But it still sent a chill through Eleanor. They had been walking along the balcony, a long line of dark and empty office space to their left, and to their right a misty sort of rain falling on the flooded city. The air had a briny, ocean smell. Eleanor, who was beginning to sense the mother bitch of all headaches coming on, had been trailing along behind, trying to relax. But her mind rebelled to the idea of zombies, and she stopped in her tracks.

"What did you say?"

The others walked on a few steps, unaware she that she was no longer following. Hank looked back at her over his shoulder and stopped walking too. He was still smiling, but the expression had lost some of its easy charm. He looked like a man just beginning to realize he'd said something wrong.

"I . . . I'm sorry, ma'am?"

"You called those people zombies. Those cannibals."

"Uh, yeah?"

"Zombies? Like in the horror movies? The walking dead."

"Well . . ." He trailed off, and abruptly he looked very un-comfortable. He glanced over at Jim, maybe for support, and Eleanor could see the Adam's apple working up and down in his throat. "Well, I mean," he went on, "they're not exactly . . .

you know, dead. But . . . yeah, I mean, they're zombies. I mean, that's what . . . isn't that what you guys saw?"

Of course not, you idiot, Eleanor thought. Adonis though he may be, she'd never held any delusions about Hank Gleason's good genetics extending all the way up to his brain. *Zombies? Seriously? People are eating each other out there, people are dying, Ms. Hester is dying, and you're making jokes about zombies? This shit is for real.*

But doesn't that one word make a lot of sense? asked a tentative voice in her head.

Eleanor thought back to the horror movies she'd seen when she still watched garbage like that. Jim of course loved his horror movies, always had. But Eleanor, who had seen real monsters, who, during her tour of duty in Sex Crimes, had seen more murdered children than any normal person should have to see, was unimpressed by Hollywood's trivial attempts at fear-making. Their monsters paled in comparison to the real-life horrors that walked the streets of every city in America and hunted its children like trophies. In her mind, zombies were nothing but harlequins, clowns in shabby makeup. They staggered around, pantomiming death, while cheesy music played on the soundtrack and bare-breasted bimbos titillated the teenage boys in the audience. From her youth she remembered the movie version of Max Brooks's *World War Z* and the TV series based on Robert Kirkman's *The Walking Dead,* and she remembered those grossing her out, but never scaring her. They were ridiculous. They were slow and stupid and little more than an excuse for a whole generation of angry-minded, disaffected youth to safely and sanely fantasize about killing loads of people. Zombies were wish fulfillment, nothing more.

But doesn't that one word make a lot of sense? repeated the faint, tentative voice in her head. Only now it was less tentative, gaining strength. *Doesn't it?*

Eleanor glanced out across the water. A misting rain was still falling. The water coursed slowly as it pushed, finger-like, into the low places between the buildings. And here and there, dark shapes moved at the edges of the parking lot, their moans echoing across the flood.

She turned back to Hank.

He was looking at her, that uncertain grin still on his face. Beside him, a head shorter and looking utterly bedraggled, Jim was also watching her. She stared back at Jim and wondered if his mind was having the same trouble linking up what they had seen with the word "zombie" and all it implied. It didn't seem so. He, and Madison beside him, looked unruffled by the use of the word. It had no power over them. Not in the same way it did over her.

"But they're alive," she said. "Out there, when I . . ." She was about to say, *When I drowned that man out there*, but the words wouldn't come. The memory of her own anger, and the look of disgust and worry and fear she had seen on Jim's face afterward, crowded into her mind. "They're not dead," she said.

"No," Hank said slowly. "No, they're alive all right."

"So how can they be zombies?"

"Well, I don't mean zombies like in *Night of the Living Dead* and stuff like that. You're right about them being alive. Those aren't corpses. But the rest of it fits, doesn't it?"

Again he looked at Jim, who nodded readily enough.

He does believe it, Eleanor thought. *He, and Madison, too, they're both buying this.*

"You've seen the way they stagger around. The way they moan. You can't reason with them. They don't even seem to hear you. They don't seem to feel any pain. I watched one of them walking around with his intestines hangin' out of his belly. And, I mean, they're . . . you know, eating each other. What else could they be?"

Yeah, she thought, remembering the look she had seen in

Bobby Hester's eyes and all that had come after that, *what else could they be?*

"I don't know," she said at last. "I just don't know."

Hank took them inside, where the Red Cross volunteers had set up a temporary shelter. There was no electrical power, of course, and the room was poorly lit by a single candle burning on a makeshift desk against the wall to the left of the door. Almost as soon as she entered Eleanor recoiled, not only from the smell of thirty people who had been living together in close quarters without air-conditioning, without bathing, without washing their clothes in days, but from the way their eyes had seemed to glow with a pale reflected light when they all turned as one to look at the new arrivals.

"It's all right," Hank said. "We don't bite."

She gave him a caustic look, but the poor man was too dumb to realize he'd made a poor choice of words. Jim and Madison didn't hesitate, though. They followed Hank inside and smiled and muttered thank you as he introduced them around.

Eventually, Eleanor followed, too.

The glowing eyes she'd seen upon entering the room were gone now. They'd been replaced with worn, exhausted, but kind and smiling, faces. Hank had been right out there on the balcony when he referred to these folks as geezers, Eleanor thought. Not a single one of the volunteers looked to be under sixty-five. She spotted several older women playing bridge on an old Army cot. The women smiled at her, and especially at Madison, and Eleanor pushed down renewed thoughts of the thing that Ms. Hester had turned into.

But, she realized, Ms. Hester was another point in favor of Hank's theory that the cannibals out there were zombies. Their bites are contagious, just like in the movies.

She shook the thought away and instead turned to Hank.

"How did you find these people?" she asked.

He beamed at her.

"I just got lucky, I guess. Captain Shaw sent me out night before last to find anybody I could and bring 'em back to the EOC. These folks here, they was set up in the gym over at the Elgin T. Baker Elementary School. They had the place all ready for refugees. Food, medical supplies, bunk beds, board games, you name it. They were ready."

"Well," said Eleanor, glancing around, "where are the refugees?"

"Nobody ever showed," he said, and shrugged like it was no big deal. "Who knows why? It's a shame, too, with all the supplies they had. I guess it's just another one of those screw-ups that always seem to happen during times like this. You know?"

"Yeah," she said.

Just another one of those screw-ups, she thought bitterly. It made her wonder, when this was all said and done, just how much of the city's disaster mitigation efforts would be summed up by those words. They were living through the greatest natural disaster since the 1906 San Francisco earthquake, and yet, despite all their training, all their drills and FEMA classes and grant money, they were bumbling around like idiots, humbled by the reality of nature.

Hey, but it's all right, that voice inside her head said. Only now the voice was anything but tentative. It was full-on sarcastic, laced with meanness. *It's just another one of those screw-ups, ain't that right?*

Yeah, she thought. *That's right*.

"Sarge?" Hank said. "You okay?"

"Huh?" Eleanor asked. "Oh, yeah, I'm fine. I was just thinking. Go on, you were saying?"

"Um, yeah, well . . . so when I get to the school, the area around it is pretty much hip-deep in water. The neighborhood, I mean, all the houses and stuff. I'm motoring down this street in a ski boat and at the end of it I see a playground and soccer goals. But the school itself is up on this hill, dry as a bone."

"How'd you find out there were people inside?" Eleanor asked.

"I knew something was up. I could smell those zombies, you know? You know the way those zombies stink?"

"You could smell them? You didn't hear them moaning?"

"Not at first. I heard 'em later, but the first thing I noticed was the smell. It's that set-in dead-guy smell, like a really bad decomp. You've smelled that before. You know what I mean."

Eleanor nodded.

"You ever smelled a body that's been rotting inside an apartment with no air-conditioning in the middle of summer for three weeks?" Hank asked Jim.

Jim shook his head.

He looked amused by Hank's easy manner, even as his nose wrinkled at the thought of a rotting corpse, and Eleanor realized that this was why Hank was so popular at work. Everybody loved him because he made them feel as if they were the center of the world.

"I remember this one time," Hank went on, "a bunch of years ago, I got this call for a suicide. I could smell it from the street when I pulled up, and I knew what I was gonna find even before I got out of the car. You just get that feeling that it's gonna be a bad one, you know? So my partner and I went up to the house and got inside and there was this big fat dude hanging from his bedroom ceiling. He'd been there long enough for the rope to stretch his neck out like one of those African tribes in the *National Geographic*, you know the ones?"

Jim nodded.

"The guy was so fat the contract body-removal guys had to hold him by the legs while the firefighters cut the rope up near the ceiling. Of course he was bare-assed nekkid, too. Man, you should have seen it. When the body dropped, it sagged over the shoulder of one of the body removal guys like a bag of flour, and when that happened, all that decomp gas and the guy's rotten guts shot straight out his ass. It sprayed the wall behind him and, oh man, did it smell. You should have seen us. Grown men—veteran cops and fire-fighters and morgue employees—we all went running out into the front yard. And of course it was a slow news night. Channel 13 was right there with a camera crew. They got a great shot of us puking our guts out."

Jim looked as if he couldn't make up his mind to laugh or vomit. Hank, of course, was laughing at his own story, his face turning red. His laughter was contagious, though, and Eleanor, despite everything on her mind, found herself laughing along with him. *Cop humor*, she thought. *God, we are a screwed-up bunch of folks.*

"Anyway," Hank said, after the laughter had died down, "I thought that was about the worst stink I'd ever smell in my life. Until I ran into the zombies around that school, that is."

"They stank that bad, even outside?" Eleanor asked.

"Yes, ma'am. There was a lot of 'em."

"How many?"

"I'm not sure, ma'am. Two hundred, maybe more. I cir-cled around the corner of the building, and that's when I heard them moaning. I'd already dealt with a few of them, but I hadn't seen a group that big. They were beating on the walls outside the school's gym. Really goin' at it. I bet they'd been at it for a while, too. A lot of their hands had started to bleed from beating on the walls."

"So what'd you do?" Jim asked.

"Well, I had my AR-15. I went up to the front of the boat and laid out a mess of magazines and then I started yellin' to get their attention. One by one they turned around and came at me. After that, I just took it one shot at a time."

"And you said there were two hundred or more of them?" Eleanor asked, horrified by the implications.

"Yes, ma'am. There were bodies everywhere by the time I was done."

"What did you do then?"

"Well, I figured those zombies were after something inside that school. So I went inside and found these folks. We waited out the storm, and then this morning, when I couldn't get the EOC on the radio, I figured we needed to take matters into our own hands. These folks here already had those canoes you saw out there, and together we made our way here."

"What happened to your boat?" Jim asked.

"Lost during the storm."

"Where were you guys gonna go?" Eleanor asked.

"Well, that's the thing, ma'am, I don't rightly know. I was kind of hopin' you guys had heard something different. Maybe had some idea of what was goin' on."

Eleanor shook her head.

"No, I'm afraid not. I guess maybe we could double back to the EOC and see what's going on there."

"I still don't understand why that's a good idea," Jim said. "If you can't reach them on the radio, doesn't that mean they're in as much trouble as we are?"

"They probably are in trouble," Eleanor said. "But it doesn't mean they aren't the best place to go for help. It just means their communications are offline. There could be any number of reasons for that. Plus, if there's going to be any sort of organized evacuation effort, it's going to be focused there. I think we'd be taking too big of a chance going anywhere else."

Jim didn't look as if he was convinced, but he didn't say anything more on the subject. He just frowned, then nodded reluctantly.

Hank turned to face the rest of the room.

The place smelled of unwashed bodies and filthy clothes, but the Red Cross volunteers had nonetheless done an adequate job of keeping the place neat. There were plenty of cots against the far wall, and the ones that weren't being used were smartly made. Off to the right they'd set up a long folding card table with a selection of MREs and cookies and bags of chips and bottled drinks. Madison was over there, Eleanor saw with a sense of relief, helping herself to some cookies. With everything else that had happened in the last twenty-four hours, at least her appetite was intact.

"Hey everybody," Hank said to the room, and waited as the others quieted down and faced him. "Looks like we're gonna be heading out in the morning. We're gonna try to get to the EOC over at the University of Houston campus. From there, hopefully we'll hook up with some folks who can get us evacuated."

This was greeted with a murmuring of relieved voices from around the room. Eleanor could see several of the volunteers actually letting out deep sighs and clapping each other on the back.

"But we need to head out early," Hank went on. "So get your stuff together tonight. I wanna leave at first light."

Eleanor turned from Madison to Jim. He was staring back at her. That look of wearied exhaustion was back again.

"Are you sure this is what we need to do?" he asked.

"I really don't see that we have any other choice."

"What if we just get in the canoe and head north? We're bound to reach safety sooner or later."

"But Jim, you've seen those cannibals out there . . . those zombies. Whatever it is that's causing them to be the way they are, it's contagious. That means their numbers are going to be growing. You heard Hank. He faced down at least two hundred of them. There are probably at least that many out there, waiting for us. We'd never survive on our own. We need to group together if we're going to get through this.

And that means going to the EOC. I don't see any other way."

Before he had a chance to answer, Hank put a hand on both their shoulders.

"I promised you guys some chow. What do you say? You hungry?"

Eleanor took an MRE from the table and a plastic gallon jug of water and looked around the room for Madison. She found her sitting on the edge of a cot with no sheets, preparing her own MRE.

"You mind if I join you?" Eleanor asked.

Madison looked up at her with forced nonchalance and shrugged. "It's a free country."

Damn it, Eleanor thought, feeling the heat rising in her cheeks. *Why is this always so hard?* Times like this she didn't feel like other moms. She'd watched other women handle their kids' attitudes in public with patience and self-control, even though it was obvious they were burning up inside. Eleanor figured she missed that part of the deal when they were handing out mothering skills because at times like this, when she made an honest effort and Madison just tossed it back in her face, all she could think to do was get mean. It infuriated her, both because her daughter was being a little shit and because she wasn't being enough of a grown-up to deal with it. *Jesus*, she thought, *why did parenting have to be so damn hard?*

But this had to be done. They had to talk. It couldn't go on like this. Eleanor knew that, and she suspected that Madison did, too.

So she sat down next to Madison and unpacked her MRE. The entree was beef enchilada in sauce, which wasn't great, but at least it wasn't chicken fettuccine. God, that stuff was awful.

Beside her, Madison was filling her meal pouch bag with water. Eleanor watched appreciatively as her daughter activated the chemical heater and dropped it into the water, then folded over the top of the pouch and stuffed it into the entree carton. That done, she leaned the carton against the leg of the cot to keep the assembly properly inclined, then opened up her package of peanut butter and spread it on some crackers.

"You know your way around an MRE," Eleanor said, genuinely impressed.

"I've eaten a bunch over the last two weeks."

Eleanor opened her mouth to tell Madison not to take that tone with her, but closed it again. That wasn't going to work here. It would just drive Madison further away.

She separated out her own MRE, prepared her own meal pouch assembly, and then tucked the instant coffee into the back pocket of her jeans. Her clothes were still wet, but there wasn't anything she could do about that.

"Hey," she said to Madison, "what'd you get for dessert?"

"Chocolate pudding."

"Ah, you got the good one. I got banana pudding."

"I don't like the banana pudding."

"No, me, either. I guess you won't switch with me then, huh?"

Madison tossed her dessert pouch into Eleanor's lap. "Here, you can have mine. I'm not all that hungry anyway."

"Baby, I was—"

"Don't call me baby, Mom, I hate that."

"Oh," Eleanor said. "Oh, okay. I . . . I'm sorry, Madison. What would you rather I call you?"

"I don't care. Anything but baby. I'm not a kid."

"Madison, come on, you're not even thirteen."

As soon as she said it Eleanor knew it was wrong. But she didn't get a chance to head off Madison's reaction, for in that moment, her daughter's face twisted out of shape as if she'd suddenly smelled something nasty.

"I don't want to be reminded I'm a kid!" Madison nearly screamed at her.

An older woman who had been sitting on a nearby cot reading a David McCullough book looked up at them, caught Eleanor's eye, and quickly looked away again.

Eleanor turned back to Madison, who was on her feet now, and said, "Madison, please. I'm sorry. That was a stupid thing for me say." She patted a spot on the cot beside her. "Would you sit back down, please?"

"Why?"

"Please, Madison. I just want to talk."

"About what?"

Once again, Eleanor felt a hot rage flash across her skin. She was very close to losing it. The urge to grab Madison by the front of her blouse and pull her down onto the cot was almost overpowering. But instead of giving into it, she closed her eyes and pushed the anger away.

After a few deep breaths, she opened her eyes again. Madison was looking at her, her hands on her hips, a twitch at the corner of her mouth that somehow knew better than to develop into the mocking sneer it had the potential to be.

Eleanor almost asked her to sit down again, but told herself she had to pick her battles.

"You're upset about what happened to Ms. Hester, I know. I am, too." Eleanor patted the cot next to her. "Will you tell me how you're feeling? I'd like to know what's on your mind."

For just the thinnest of moments, the hard veneer of resistance on Madison's expression wavered, giving Eleanor a glimpse of the wounded child underneath. Her heart filled with tenderness for her daughter then, and she thought: *Most of the time I don't understand her. Not anymore. She's grown*

*into somebody who'd rather push me away than open up.
There's a cold, whispering emptiness between us now. But
right there, that's the little girl who used to sit with me on the
couch and laugh when I tickled her and shiver with delight
when I read her the Harry Potter books.*

But the thought was clipped off right there, for Madison's
face suddenly hardened, and the old obstinacy flooded back
in.

"Jesus Christ, Mom, what do you think this is? You act
like we're living in some kind of sitcom. You think you're
gonna come over here and have a three-minute little heart-
to-heart with me, and that's gonna be enough to make everything all better again. Well, it's not, Mom. This is real life. It
sucks here. It fucking sucks."

And with that Madison spun on her heel and stormed off.

Eleanor watched her go, dimly aware that most of the
others had heard the outburst and were watching her out of
the corner of their eyes. But Eleanor didn't care about that.
The most important thing in the world to her was walking
away, her hands balled into fists, her cheeks wet with tears.

Eleanor felt as if a pit had opened up beneath her. The
voice in her head that had spoken to her out on the balcony
came back. *Go after her*, it said. *Do something. Do some
real parenting for a change.*

But all Eleanor could do was sit there, stricken, unaware
of the tears falling down her own cheeks.

Later, after the sun went down, Eleanor made the instant
coffee from her back pocket and took it out to the balcony to
watch the water and try to think about everything that had
happened. The coffee was good and hot. She drank it black.
The misting rain from earlier was gone now, and looking up,
she could see stars through the tattered remnants of gray

clouds. Far off in the distance—to the south, she guessed—she could see a pale orange smear of a large fire burning just over the horizon. To the east, she could hear the hollow clap of rifle fire echoing off the floodwater. And all of this she took in absently, not really seeing any of it.

Things were really, really bad. There was no denying that. The full weight of just how bad weighed heavily on her mind. Not only was the world as she knew it collapsing around her, not only did her daughter hate her guts for some mysterious reason that continued to elude her, not only were there zombies out there trying to eat them . . . as if all that wasn't enough, she was about to lead the only part of her life that still mattered into an uncertain future. She was gambling with her family's lives, and that made her heartsick.

There were, in fact, so many problems pressing in upon her that she couldn't number them all. She couldn't pick them apart and deal with them individually, which was her usual way of attacking a difficult situation, for all those problems were interconnected, like a web.

She closed her eyes and listened to the sound of the water lapping against the sides of the building, trying to impose a sense of peace on a mind that would have none of it, and that's when she heard the splashing.

Her eyes flew open.

All at once her body was tense, hairs standing up on end. She looked straight down over the edge of the balcony and saw a zombie moving along the ground-floor wall, trying to find a way inside. The water was up to his chest, and she thought: *That can't be. They were drowning before.*

And then she saw why. Off in the distance, beyond the edge of the parking lot, the water was down. Cars that before had been up to their windows in water now appeared to be standing in shallow puddles. The water barely covered the bottom of the tires.

More splashing off to her right caused her to turn around. She could see a large crowd of zombies wading through the parking lot toward the building.

The glass doors slid open behind her and she spun around, startled.

Jim was standing there.

"She's sleeping now," he said. "I think she cried herself to sleep. Maybe tomorrow she'll—"

"Jim, we have to get out of here. Now!"

"What?"

"There's no time, Jim. We have to go. Look!" She pointed toward the approaching zombie horde.

"Oh my God," he said. "What happened? How did they . . ."

"Low tide," Eleanor said. "It's low tide."

CHAPTER 12

Mark Eckert slammed the door behind him and stepped out onto a small concrete patio. Before the storm the university's art students must have used it as a smokers' station. There was a battered metal chair to his right and next to that a low, cylindrical ash can. Here and there he saw a few soggy cigarette butts wedged into the cracks in the concrete. He grabbed the chair and slid its back under the door handle, the way he'd seen done in the movies. He had no idea if it would actually work or not, but then, he only needed a second or two head start.

From the other side of the metal door he could hear moaning. The zombies had caught up to him already.

So much for his head start.

Gingerly, he touched the burning gash on his right shoulder where one of them had bit him. It was hurting bad, already starting to smell like rot, and as he touched the edges of the pus-filled wound and tried to press a dangling flap of skin back over the missing chunk of his arm, he felt the first pangs of nausea. His head was a soupy mess, and it was hard to focus. What had he been trying to do again? Why couldn't he remember? It was like his brain kept slipping into neutral.

A body slammed into the other side of the door with an explosive crack, knocking the chair out from under the door handle and sending it skidding across the concrete. Mark Eckert jumped, jarred out of his confusion.

He stepped back to the edge of the concrete patio, his heels hanging over the side, just as the door exploded open and the first zombies staggered through it. Mark couldn't move his right arm. It hung limp as an empty sack from his shoulder, and that meant he had to shoot left-handed. It was a skill they drilled on constantly when he was a cadet in the Houston Police Department's Training Academy, but even under the controlled conditions found at the gun range, he'd never been very good with his left hand.

But now, with a horde of zombies closing in on him and his head swimming and his body burning itself up with fever as it fought the virus waging war in his veins, conditions were anything but perfect.

Pretty damn crappy would be more accurate, he thought, and a thin, weak laugh crawled out of his throat.

Still, he had enough presence of mind to fire off a round as the lead zombie crashed into him, knocking the wind from his lungs and sending him sprawling off the back of the patio. But as his body tumbled backwards he caught a glimpse of scalp and blood and bone exploding out behind the zombie's head, and in the moment before he crash-landed, he let out a half-formed cry of victory.

Got you, you fucking bastard!

He landed with a splash, and for a moment, nearly blacked out. He had to struggle to hold on to consciousness. There was something inside him that seemed to be pulling him down, the way sleep can pull your head back to the pillow after a restless night of broken sleep. Only the pain in his shoulder kept him going. Mark shook the fog from his mind. His butt and lower back were underwater. Only his knees and his head and shoulders remained above it, making him look like a man trying to sit up in the bathtub. The water wasn't deep, not nearly as deep as it had been earlier that afternoon, and, absurdly, the thought *Maybe it's all going away and we'll be okay!* played in his mind . . . except that it wasn't going to be okay, not with the rest of those zombies tumbling down off the side of the patio like penguins off an iceberg. They were still coming for him, and nothing was ever going to be okay again.

Painfully, uncertainly, he pulled himself to his feet.

He was exhausted.

The downward pull toward unconsciousness was almost irresistible. But he hadn't lost his will to live. Not yet.

He turned and limped off toward the EOC.

Mark made his way as fast as he could around the corner of Farish Hall and continued on through the courtyard, past the Cullen Performance Hall and then onto University Drive. The library was up ahead on his right. Glancing around, he saw about forty zombies following him. Some were starting to fall back, but more than a few were keeping pace. A few were even gaining on him. He could probably make it all the way to the parking lot where Captain Shaw was trying to assemble the refugees and put them onto boats, but somehow he doubted it. The entire campus was overrun with zombies. The captain was surrounded the last Mark had heard, and that had been about two hours ago. He'd be doing his impression of Custer at the Little Bighorn by now. And besides, Mark thought bitterly, the way his body was rebelling against him, he'd probably collapse before he made it halfway. And that would mean letting those things tear him apart with their teeth and fingernails. That wasn't going to happen.

So Mark Eckert ran.

But not wildly. As a kid he'd played with his dog in the surf down at Galveston and he knew how tired you could get running through shallow water if you didn't pump your knees like pistons when you ran. Up ahead there was a ten-foot-high

chain-link fence with a large white sign with red letters—
KEEP BACK FIFTY FEET AUTHORIZED PERSONNEL ONLY—posted
near the gate. All he had to do was get through that gate and
lock it. From there, the main office of the EOC was only a
short distance away.

The gate was hanging open a few inches. His heart was
pounding when he reached it. Every breath made it feel as if
he were getting stabbed in the ribs with a pointed stick.

But for as bad as he felt, he stopped and took a quick look
back at his pursuers.

The original group of forty or so that had cornered him in
the lobby of the art building had thinned out to a long staggered line now.

The nearest zombie was a big white guy in mud-soaked
jeans and a T-shirt that hung in bloody rags from his shoulders. Through the tattered shirt Mark could see the man's
white belly glistening. Water drops splashed up around him
like white sparks as he charged the fence.

Behind him, maybe ten paces at the most, was another
man who was missing one side of his face. The rest were
coming up behind them. He could hear them, but he couldn't
see them in the darkness.

He jumped through the gate, spun around, and pulled it
closed. Someone had left the padlock dangling from one of
the diamond holes in the fence—even when the EOC was in
everyday use, they'd been sloppy about locking it. Mark and
his fellow officers had joked about the piss-poor security
around here more than once, but he was thankful for it now.
He fumbled with the padlock, trying to pull it out, but his
fingers felt fat and numb. And trying to hurry only made it
worse.

The lead zombie was closing on him now, close enough
that Mark was getting splashed by the zombie's awkward
movements through the water.

"Come on, come on," he pleaded with himself. "Come on, damn it."

And then he had it. The padlock slid off the fence and Mark held it up triumphantly in front of him. He glanced at the zombie, and a chill went through him. The man's eyes were clouded over, nearly completely white, as though with cataracts. They seemed utterly empty . . . even as the man's lips drew back, revealing blood-soaked teeth and shredded gums.

Mark swallowed the lump in his throat and then jammed the arm of the padlock down through the latch and locked it.

A moment later the zombie crashed into the gate. He was followed by two more, then a third. Within seconds there were seven, then nine, twelve. And more were appearing at the fence with each passing moment.

Mark backed away from the fence, his head swimming, his vision blurry. He was wincing with every breath. He looked down the row of ruined faces leering vacantly back at him through the fence and he suddenly felt more scared than he had ever been before. At that moment, listening the almost musical clink of fists against the chain-link fence, it suddenly dawned on him just how much trouble he was in.

Earlier in the day, just before sunset, he'd been with a detachment of officers assigned to quell a fight at the field hospital. The four of them had waded into a confused mass of screaming refugees and seen a handful of what looked like drunks taking bites out of one of the nurses. Mark, who was wearing only a paper surgical mask and latex gloves for protection, had thought little of wading into the fight. He pulled the man off the gutted body of the nurse and tried to cuff him. He'd gotten the bite on his shoulder for his trouble. Only then had he realized he and his squad were surrounded by people with ruined faces and bloody mouths and vacant, empty eyes.

He'd managed to fight his way to the lobby of the art building across the quad from the field hospital before they finally pinned him down. Mark had drawn his pistol and screamed commands at the crowd closing in around him, but he hadn't fired until he saw the gutted nurse from the hospital among their number.

After that, his night had turned into one long rolling gunfight.

But one thought had nagged at him since he was first bitten. At first, while he was still running and shooting, it had been only a feeling, sensed, but not articulated. But the thought was clear as a bell on country Sunday morning now.

Mark Eckert, you are going to die.

"No," he said aloud. "No, I won't."

His fear had fed his denial, keeping the thought of death at arm's length. But now, as the necrosis filovirus waged war within his veins, he felt a sort of reluctant acceptance pour over him, and his fear slipped away. And with that acceptance came a moment of clarity. In it, he saw clearly what had happened to him, and what would come. The fog in his brain was only the beginning. Soon, maybe in a few minutes, maybe a few hours, he would become like those people out there. His face would look like theirs, the expression vacant but somehow sinister, lips shredded like confetti, ropes of bloody drool hanging from his chin. He would become like them, one of them.

Mark Eckert, you are going to die.

And all at once a memory opened up and he was standing in his parents' kitchen. His father was off by the refrigerator, hands stuffed deep into the pockets of his pants, his eyes pointed down at his shoes, while Mark's mother turned her back on him and dried her hands on a dish towel over by the sink. He could hear her sniffling back a tear.

"You're going to get yourself killed," she said quietly. She hated the idea of her only child becoming a policeman, especially a Houston policeman, and now that he was standing here in her kitchen with his acceptance letter to the academy in his hand, her anger and fear and hurt were causing her to lash out with tears.

"Mom, it's a good job," he said. "No matter how bad the economy gets, the job will still be there for me. And cops make good money these days."

"You have a master's degree, Mark," she snapped back. There was a look on her face as if he had just tracked across her kitchen floor with something nasty on his shoes. "You can get a *real* job. One that doesn't involve getting shot at by drug dealers and"—and here her face puckered so that it looked as if she was spitting out the next words—"wife beaters."

"Mom, with a degree I can promote fast. I could go as high as I want to. I could even use this to go into politics."

"You could get shot," she said, and turned to her husband, who had been conspicuously silent since Mark broke the news. "Say something, James. For God's sake, he's going to get himself shot."

James Eckert was a pediatric dentist who had told his son on more than one occasion that the federal government had fucked up health care so badly that he would not wish a career in medicine on his worst enemy. And Mark wasn't sure about this, but he had a sneaking suspicion that his father was secretly thrilled about his son becoming a cop. It was a chance to live a life of action and adventure vicariously through his son. Mark would later get confirmation of this, for when he got out of the academy and was working the evening shift in Houston's gang-addled Second Ward, his father made him call him every night, regardless of the time he got home, and regale him with stories of fights and car chases and crazy calls.

But for now, the problem was his mother.

"Well," she said. "Tell him."

"Listen, Gina," he'd said in that slow, measured way he had of talking when he knew he was about to piss his wife off, "I'm not really sure it's such a bad idea. He's a tough kid. He's a smart—"

"Oh, for Christ's sake!" she'd screamed. Then she'd thrown her dish towel on the counter and stormed out.

Mark looked at his father and waited.

The next words out of his father's mouth weren't entirely unexpected. "You've thought this through, I suppose?"

"Yes."

"And it's what you want to do. You know it'll break her heart."

"Dad . . ."

"No," his father had said, "hold up for a second. I want to tell you some good news and some bad."

A pause.

"Okay," Mark had finally said.

"The bad news first. Somewhere right around forty, you get tired. Your hair gets gray, your belly gets fat, your muscles soft. Work is hard. It grinds you down. Some days, all you want to do is say fuck it all and take a nap. That's when your will, your drive, call it whatever you want, takes over. That's when you decide when you're going to be a success or a failure. The success stories . . . those are the ones with the will to work beyond the body's exhaustion."

"Okay," Mark said hesitantly. None of that made sense, but okay. "So what's the good news?"

"Well, the good news is that you've got today. You've got your health and strength and your looks and your flat belly. Revel in it, Mark. Seize the day. If you want be a cop, son, that's fine. . . . Just promise me that you'll be a damn good one."

"I will, Dad."

"Good. Your mom's going to be pissed as an old wet hen for a good long while, but she'll get over it. Just make sure you remember she loves you more than her own life. That's why she's so mad."

Mark nodded soberly.

"And son?"

"Yeah, Dad?"

"Do me a favor and try not to get shot."

The memory faded slowly. It was easy, he found, to shut off his conscious mind and let himself float. Too easy. But even as he tried to focus, he found that his body didn't want to comply. Everything ached now. He'd had the flu two years before, shortly after getting assigned to Captain Shaw's team at the EOC, and the way he was feeling now was a lot like the worst part of the fever back then.

It was seeing the zombie falling off the top of the fence to his right that finally got him moving again. A large tree had fallen across the fence there and bent it back and a few of the zombies had already found a way to crawl up and over the chain-link slope. Two more fell off the top of the fence. More were climbing over.

"Shit," he said. "Gotta go."

He turned and pulled himself slowly toward the library.

The water was two feet deep inside the library. The only light came from the mini LED flashlight he kept on his gun belt, and that light bounced constantly around the darkened hallways as he struggled to control his movements. Even through the haze in his brain he was aware of the sickeningly sweet odor of open sewage and rotting bodies.

He found four of them in the main ops room.

Two were policeman he couldn't recognize because they'd been partially eaten and because decomposition had set in. The other two were civilians with bullet holes in their faces.

Mark Eckert pulled one of the dead policemen aside and sat down at the laptop where the man had died. Miraculously, the thing still worked. Briefly, it occurred to him that he had expected it to work. He had no Plan B. He fired it up, activated the video feed feature he had set up for Captain Shaw earlier in the day, and started talking.

"My name is Mark Eckert. I'm a Houston police officer assigned to the Emergency Operations Command. My direct supervisor is Sergeant Eleanor Norton and above her Captain Mark Shaw. I don't know if either of them are still alive so . . . oh God, it's hard to think."

Mark swallowed with obvious difficulty and then took a deep breath and went on.

"I don't know who's still alive and who's dead. A lot of people are dead. I think I'll be dead here pretty soon. But I guess . . . hell, I don't know, seeing as I'm not dead yet and they probably are I guess that makes me the one in charge. Wahoo!" He raised a not-quite-clenched fist into the air. "Hear that, Mom? I made it to the top after all. Go me."

Here, on the video, Mark can be seen to sag visibly into himself. He tries to laugh, but then he begins to cough. The coughs are violent and painful-sounding. They go on for thirty-seven seconds. Several large flecks of black blood are hacked up onto the screen.

But Mark is a strong kid, as his dad once told him, and eventually he pulls himself together and focuses on the screen once again.

"Let's see . . . oh, yeah . . . we've got zombies here. How do you like that? It's pretty screwed up, actually. It's not anything like the movies we all saw."

He leans forward, smiling, sort of, as only one side of his mouth manages to curl upward. The other sags like the curiously limp arm at his side. In the short few sentences he's spoken his voice has taken on a whiskey roughness.

"They're dead," *he says in a mock stage whisper.* "You can shoot 'em, burn 'em, cut 'em . . . you name it. If it'll kill you, it'll kill them. The only thing is, they don't know it. You can see 'em walking around with their guts hanging out of their belly and gunshot wounds to the face, and they don't know they're supposed to lie down and die. But hey, whatcha gonna do?"

He falls back in his chair, still staring at the screen (and later, several commentators would note that he never blinked, not once) and gives the audience that half-formed smile again.

"Don't come and rescue us," *he says.* "It would be suicide for you. Let us die and make this city our tomb. Hell, we're already dead. We just don't know it yet. Sorry about that, Mom and Dad. I guess I went and got myself dead after all."

He laughs suddenly, a demented sound accompanied by another round of hacking coughs.

"Wow, I really messed that promise up, I guess."

He leans forward and wipes a spot of blood from screen. Then he looks at it on the tip of his finger and his nose wrinkles in disgust.

"Okay," *he says, and he's obviously giving it everything he's got just to rally up the strength for this last part of his warning,* "here's the deal. We got overrun by . . . wait. We got . . . okay, I'm . . . Mom, I love you. Dad, I love you, too. Please don't be mad. I didn't want this. I didn't . . ."

And there's no more on the audio track.

But there is more video.

Mark's head falls back against the chair, and he remains motionless for twelve seconds. Then he raises his head, and when he does, his eyes have glazed over with a white, cloudy film. His mouth is slack. His face has taken on an emptiness that a few conspiracy theorists attempt to blame on withdrawal from heroin.

But Mark Eckert is no junkie.

He rises from his chair and slowly turns around. And as he walks off into the darkness, he has no idea if his message reached anyone. He has no idea that his video, though ini-

tially denied and dismissed as a hoax by the White House, has in fact been posted to the Internet and gone viral like nothing before it. He has no idea that within twenty-four hours his video will be watched more than half a billion times.

He has no idea that he is the first zombie rock star.

And he has no idea that his simple and poignant farewell to his mom and dad will become the clincher that will eventually cause his government to seal more than six million people behind a quarantine wall that stretches from Gulfport, Mississippi, to Brownsville, Texas.

Some people get their fifteen minutes and never know it.

CHAPTER 13

As it turned out, Brent Shaw *had* crawled off and gotten drunk, just as Anthony suspected. Anthony finally found him curled up on a couch in the lobby of the Cullen Performance Hall, a bottle of vodka cradled to his chest like a child's favorite toy. He was sobbing in his sleep.

Anthony called his name and shook him, gently at first, and then, when he still wouldn't wake up, more brutally, finally kicking him out of frustration.

"Get up, Brent. We got work to do."

Brent sat up groggily and only looked at him for a moment. He blinked, and Anthony could see that behind the screen of drunkenness, his older brother was terrified.

"What's wrong with you, Brent? Jesus Christ, we got work to do."

Brent sniffled. He had tried to meet his little brother's gaze, but quickly turned away. He seemed uncertain, still frightened. Fumbling drunkenly, he'd tried to unscrew the cap on his bottle of vodka.

Anthony watched the display with mounting disgust.

"Gimme that," he finally said, and snatched the bottle from his brother's hands. He threw it against the wall and it exploded with a muffled pop, the liquid spreading down over a poster advertising a student-run production of Harold Pinter's *The Homecoming* that was fated now to never see the stage.

Brent had watched the bottle fly, his hands still outstretched, with a strangled cry eking from his throat.

"Why did you . . . ?" he managed to say.

"Shut up!" Anthony screamed. "You drunken shit. Get up. Come on, get up!"

But Brent could only manage an inarticulate groan.

The sight of his brother sitting there, stupefied by vodka, unable to speak, was like a red haze dropping over Anthony's mind. The anger rose up in him so suddenly, so powerfully, so like his father, that he was hardly aware of when he started slapping Brent's face. He was only aware of the anger coursing through him. He was grinding his teeth in rage, grunting with every ferocious slap he raked across Brent's cheek.

In the end it was the sound of his voice, his growling, that stopped the blows. "Why do you gotta be like her?" he'd heard himself screaming. "You saw what drinking did to her. Why you gotta be like Mom? Got off the fucking floor, you goddamn disgusting fucking drunk."

Anthony stood there, looking down at Brent, a cowering, dumb giant who was bleeding from his lips and nose, and then he looked at his own right hand, the hand that only seconds before had been a relentless, merciless weapon. Brent's blood was on Anthony's palm. But it wasn't the blood that Anthony saw. His gaze was turned inward, and backward, over the years. In his mind he saw his mother, who, like Brent, had drunk her way into a useless oblivion, and Anthony found himself wondering if, in his mind at least, it had been his mother that he was slapping.

Yes, it had been.

He couldn't deny that, not now that he had spoken the words. That was where the rage was. Not here. It wasn't focused on what Brent had become, but on the example that had set him up for self-destruction. He felt the truth wrap around his heart like a cold, wet fog, and he was ashamed of it.

"I'm sorry," he said to Brent.

But Brent still wouldn't look directly at him. *I hurt him bad*, Anthony thought. *Oh Jesus, I hurt him and I didn't want to. I didn't mean to. It just happened. Oh Jesus, please help me.*

He extended his bloody hand to Brent, and in Anthony's mind, Brent wouldn't take it because he was scared. They were acting out the roles their parents had played growing up, one the drunk, the other relentlessly violent, and then just as relentlessly repentant. *Brent sees that*, Anthony thought, *realizes the drama they're repeating, and it terrifies him.*

But Anthony was wrong.

Perhaps on some subconscious level those things were playing out in Brent's mind, moving like slow currents beneath a frozen lake, but the real demon that had locked him up and driven him down into the bottle was in fact nothing more complex than a drunkard's shame and self-loathing. Anthony did not know it at the time, and would only learn the vaguest details of it later that night, but while Anthony and his father were shooting the zombies in the EOC, Brent had been looking for a place to hide. He'd already seen a few of the infected and made the mental leap that enabled him to acknowledge them as zombies.

Trembling with fear, he'd wandered through the uninhabited parts of the campus, looking for a place to hide and drink. He'd rounded a corner, and almost walked smack dab into the middle of four zombies who were wrestling a young girl of perhaps ten or eleven down to the ground. That part of the campus had, for the most part, stayed above the water level, and Brent had been lost in the squishing his boots made in the spongy grass when he heard the girl cry out.

He'd looked up, and there she'd been, one hand outstretched as the four tore at her clothes with their teeth and nails.

"Please!" she'd screamed at him. "Please, mister, help me!"

And Brent had just stood there, unable to make himself move.

"Please!" the girl screamed again.

Brent did move that time. He took a few steps back. His breath was whistling in his ears now, his heart beating painfully against the walls of his chest. His mind was screaming at him to turn and run. The little girl seemed to realize at the same time as Brent that he would be doing nothing to help her, and for just a moment, all her terror left her, and the look on her face changed to one of shocked abandonment and disbelief.

"Please!" she screamed again.

But if she said anything after that it was lost as the zombies huddled over her. Her pleas degenerated into inarticulate grunts and screams. None of the zombies noticed Brent. He was still backing away, shaking his head, slapping his hands over his ears as he tried to block out the sound of the girl's pain and the wet, tearing noises the zombies made as they ripped her open and fed.

And, improbably, at that moment, the one clear thought that Brent could muster was not of the horrible tragedy playing out before him, or even of his own impotent response, but of that day he'd appeared before the chief's Accident Advisory Board and Captain Macklin had asked him, "What the fuck's going on with you? How'd you get like this?"

That memory and the shame it dredged up had been behind the look on Brent's face as Anthony stood above him, his hand outstretched, trying to offer compassion. In the end Anthony had been forced to scoop his older brother up and half walk, half carry him out the door. They'd met up with Jesse Numeroff down by the loading docks, and Jesse had taken one look at Brent and said, "No. No fucking way. He's so drunk he can't even . . ."

But Jesse had trailed off.

He'd taken one look at the emotional weather brewing in Anthony's eyes and he'd quickly realized the wisdom of keeping silent on the matter. He'd taken a step back and watched as Anthony dropped Brent down into the front of their bass boat. And when Anthony looked up at him and said, "Well, you coming?" he had only nodded.

Several hours later, while Mark Eckert was fighting his way into the EOC so he could say his farewells to his parents and, unwittingly, become an Internet sensation, the quick little errand that Anthony and Brent and Jesse Numeroff had started out on soon turned into a rolling firefight through a flooded version of hell.

The trouble started as they entered what appeared to be a deserted housing project. The project's cinder-block walls, though scrawled with graffiti, had survived the storms. Only the doors and windows were gone. Water coursed through them, so that as they glided by, they could see straight through many of the buildings.

"Do you hear that?" Brent said.

He was sitting in the bow of the boat, where Anthony had put him before they left. The city around them had grown eerily quiet almost as soon as they pulled away from the campus, and when that happened, Brent had become jumpy, taking on the frightened wariness of a small animal

Jesse had gone to the back of the boat because he was disgusted by him, but even with the length of the boat between them, he could barely disguise his contempt.

"Dude, would you shut up?" he said. "Christ, you make me sick."

"But I heard something," Brent repeated. His voice was small, uncertain.

Anthony was driving the boat and Jesse nudged him with the toe of his boot. "Can you make him shut the fuck up, please?" There was anger in his voice now, above and beyond the contempt.

Anthony stared back at Jesse without speaking.

Then he looked forward to where Brent huddled against the bow. Brent looked as if he were trying to make himself invisible.

Anthony fetched up a deep sigh, and had someone told him that the gesture was an uncanny duplication of his father when confronted with matters he thought beneath his consideration, he would not have been surprised.

"Just give it a rest, Jesse," he finally said.

"But—"

"I said, give it a rest. You're not helping."

The argument stopped there, for at that moment, as they glided past the end of one of the tenements and into the area that had been a parking lot just a few days earlier, they saw a nearly naked woman kneeling in the bed of a pickup. She looked up at them, and there was blood all over her filthy face. Her hair was matted with it. In her right hand she held what remained of a small black dog's back leg.

Slowly, she rose to her feet and dropped the leg.

The remnants of the light-colored dress she'd worn were hanging from her hips in tatters. Her breasts, small and streaked with sooty grime, rose slightly as she raised her arms in the familiar clutching gesture of the infected. Despite the gore that covered her, and the knowledge of what she was, Anthony found himself glancing at her erect nipples.

Behind her, coming up quickly through the flooded parking lot, was a man whose right arm had been eaten away. His face bore a look of shock and empty horror unlike any Anthony had ever seen. A deep cut across his forehead appeared to have been opened with a swiping motion, as though someone had been trying to scratch his way into his skull with their fingernails. But it was the arm that drew Anthony's attention. It had been chewed off below the elbow and the bones inside shattered. A momentary image of some zombie greedily sucking the marrow from the ruined, severed part of the arm forced Anthony to close his eyes and mentally recollect himself.

From the front of the boat Brent let out a pitiful groan, and that was enough to connect a circuit inside Anthony's mind.

When he opened his eyes, he was all business.

He pulled his pistol and shot the woman in the head, dropping her to the bed of the pickup even as a chunk of her scalp flew away behind her.

Then he centered his front sight on the chest of the one-armed zombie and fired. The man let out a gasp of air, as though he'd been punched in the gut, but he didn't go down.

"No," Brent groaned. He was holding his ears, his body curled into a fetal posture. "No, no, no."

Anthony took a breath, then resighted his weapon on the man's bleeding forehead.

His next shot made the zombie's head snap back, and he sagged into the water.

Anthony scanned his surroundings, checking for more threats. The noise of gunfire had attracted a few others, and they were moaning, the sounds echoing off the cinder-block walls of the tenement, but they were out of pistol range and so Anthony holstered his weapon.

In the bow of the boat, Brent was now rocking back and forth, muttering to himself. He would be almost useless from here on out, Anthony realized. Best to just leave him where he was, where he couldn't do any damage.

He turned back to Jesse, who had pulled out their AR-15 guns while Anthony was shooting the two zombies.

"I can get those zombies over there by the gas station, no problem," Jesse said.

"Yeah, and then what?" Anthony asked.

He looked up at the sky.

It was getting dark fast, but even in the low light he could see more and more of the infected emerging from the surrounding buildings.

"Hold your fire. I want to try to stay mobile as long as we can. But keep those rifles handy. I'm pretty sure we're gonna need 'em."

Eleanor ran back inside the building, Jim right on her heels, and started looking for Madison. The room was lit only by a few guttering candles, throwing most of the room into shadows. She could make out about two dozen figures dozing on cots, none of them with sheets because it was hot and damp inside here.

"Where is she?" Eleanor demanded.

"Over there," Jim said, and pointed toward the far wall.

"Madison!" Eleanor shouted. "Madison, get up."

Most of the Red Cross volunteers had been trying to sleep, but now they were sitting up on their cots, blinking at her. More than a few of them were grumbling at being rousted.

In the dim gloom Eleanor made out her daughter's face. She was blinking sleepily, and as Eleanor closed the distance between them, she could see the bloodshot haze of recent tears in her daughter's eyes, her puffy cheeks, her red nose.

"Mom?"

Eleanor knelt down next to Madison and pushed the sweat-matted bangs from her face.

"I need you to come with us, right now? We're not safe here."

"Why? What is it? Did something happen?"

"Yes, sweetheart. We're in trouble. There are more of those people outside."

Madison got up from the cot so quickly she nearly knocked Eleanor over. She was wearing a baggy T-shirt she'd borrowed from one of the Red Cross folks, but they hadn't been able to replace her jeans. Those were still soaking wet.

"You mean those . . . zombies?" she asked. She too could barely bring herself to say the word.

Eleanor nodded. "Come on, Madison. We gotta go."

Hank was standing there when they turned around. Behind him, most of the Red Cross volunteers were looking on, their faces reflecting confusion and irritation.

"Ma'am, what's going on?" he asked.

"Hank, the water out there. It's getting to be low tide. It's down to about six feet right outside the building."

She saw his face harden at once.

"How many did you see?"

"I don't know. It's dark out there. I saw thirty or forty, but . . ."

"Yeah, there's probably more."

He turned to the Red Cross volunteers, all of whom were watching him fixedly now, waiting for instructions.

"All right, listen up, people. We may have some bad company here real soon. I hope you packed your gear when I told you to, 'cause we may have to cut out here real fast."

He pointed to two of the volunteers.

"Frank, you and Jason check the south point over there. Try to get me an accurate count. The rest of you just hang tight."

He turned then and moved for the door.

"Where are you going?" Eleanor asked.

"I'm gonna check the east side of the building over here. Try to see what we're dealing with."

"Hank, we have to leave here. Right now."

"Sergeant Norton, with all due respect, ma'am, there's only one stairwell leading up to this level, and I blocked that off with so much furniture those zombies'll need blasting gear to get through it. We're safe for right now."

"Like hell," she said. "Hank, that junk on the stairs will stop one or two of them as long as they're over their heads in water, but there's a whole mess of 'em out there now."

And at that moment a low moan rose up from the night outside.

They heard a crash from the other side of the building.

Hank glanced that way; then he scooped up his AR-15 that was leaning next to the front door.

"Everybody hang tight," he said. "I'll check it out."

Jim came up next to Eleanor and touched her hand as Hank disappeared out the door. "What do you want to do?" he asked.

"We'll let him scout it out. When he gets back, we'll figure out what to do."

"So, you trust this guy? He knows what he's doing?"

"Yeah." She turned then and looked at her husband. He was nervous. She could hear his breath whistling through his nostrils, but he had his other arm around Madison's shoulder, and if she had doubts of their chances before, the sight of the two of them together gave her all the reassurance she needed. They were going to get through this. "Hank's got it under control. He's dumb as a bag of rocks in most things, but when the bullets start flying, he's the best there is."

"That's good to hear," Jim said. "Because I think we're gonna need all the help we can get."

* * *

The sky was ribbed with lightning, and thunder echoed over the desolate ruins. Behind the wheel of the bass boat, Anthony Shaw stared into a drizzling rain, into the dark, and was worried. The rain would cover the noise of splashes, which the zombies couldn't seem to avoid making, and it cut visibility down to almost nothing. They were moving through uncertain waters now, surrounded by countless ruined buildings, weighed down by the knowledge they were being watched from every busted window, every darkened doorway.

Anthony had slowed the boat to a crawl. There was no sense in blindly racing around a corner and finding themselves in the middle of a crowd of zombies, something that had come dangerously close to happening twice already. But with the money so close, it took every bit of self-control he could muster. He fought down the urge to dig into the throttle and instead coasted forward through the rain, tense and watchful. Soon all this would be behind them.

He glanced forward to where Brent was sitting. He was no longer rocking back and forth in that oddly disturbing way that made him look like an autistic child in the middle of a meltdown, and from the dull light in his eyes Anthony guessed that some of the shine was wearing off his drink, but he still seemed too scared and too fragile for a man his size.

Behind Anthony, Jesse was quietly watching the ruins on either side of the boat, ready to fire if needed. It had been on Anthony's mind a lot lately about what would happen to the three of them after this was all over, and while he was worried about Brent, he had no doubt that Jesse would come out on top. Jesse was a cat. He'd land on his feet no matter what.

Anthony was still contemplating their future when, a few minutes later, a boat resolved itself out of the rainy gloom ahead. Instantly, the hairs went up on the back of Anthony's neck. The boat was floating silently on the current, drifting towards them, while a figure staggered around by the controls.

Anthony resisted the urge to hail him. They'd seen far too many of the infected in these buildings, and with the tide at its lowest, those zombies could conceivably wade out to them and climb into the boat.

As the other boat drew closer Anthony saw that his instincts had been correct. The man on board was a zombie. Had to be. Anthony didn't need to see the blood oozing from where the man's left ear had been to see that. The vacant, yet insatiably hungry, look in the man's eyes told him all he needed to know.

The zombie saw them at the same time Anthony spotted him, and for a moment, the zombie seemed uncertain of what to do. Then he climbed over the seats, stood as far up in the bow as he could get, and extended his hands outward as he began to moan.

The sound carried quickly, and as Anthony sat there behind the wheel, he could see heads popping up in the windows all around them. Soon moan was answering unto moan as the cries echoed back and forth.

"Shit," Jesse said, "they're calling each other out."

"Yeah," Anthony said, turning around slowly. He could see about twenty of the infected making their way into the flooded street, and what had been nothing but empty ruins moments before did not feel so empty anymore.

"We got to shut him up," Jesse said, and before Anthony could stop him, Jesse raised his AR-15 and fired a single round at the zombie on the boat. The shot hit the man square in the forehead and threw him back against the pilot's windscreen, his head falling back over his shoulders in a posture that made him look like an exhausted man finally at rest.

"What the fuck are you doing?" Anthony said, wheeling around on Jesse and pulling the gun from his hand.

"He was calling to them," Jesse said.

"So you thought you'd fire a shot?" Anthony shook his head in dismay. "What the fuck, man?"

From the front of the boat, Brent let out another groan.

"Will you *please* be quiet?" Anthony said. "Jesus."

But when Anthony looked back at Jesse, he froze. Jesse's eyes had gone wide, and his gaze was focused on the distance over Anthony's left shoulder.

Slowly, Anthony turned around.

The flooded street ahead of them was filling with zombies. They were pouring out of the buildings on either side of the street. Anthony watched them, mouth agape, and as he wondered where in the hell they were all coming from, the dead zombie's boat glided by to port.

Anthony turned to watch the dead man floating past, and as he did, saw even more of the infected coming down a side street.

He and Jesse both turned and scanned their surroundings.

"Oh shit," Jesse said. "They're everywhere."

"Yeah."

"Hey, Anthony?"

"Yeah?"

"Can I have my gun back, please?"

"Yeah," Anthony said, and pushed the AR-15 into Jesse's hand. "I'd better get mine, too."

Anthony's AR was leaning against the pilot's seat. He scooped it up, ejected the magazine, checked it, and then jammed it back into the receiver.

"What do we do?" Jesse said.

"Get the ammo cans."

"Okay, sure."

"Better get all three."

Anthony watched the zombies getting closer while Jesse removed three large ammo canisters from underneath a waterproof tarp. He put them on the center seat and flipped open the lids. Inside each can were twenty fully loaded magazines of thirty rounds each. In addition to that, both men wore tactical vests with twelve thirty-round magazines mounted to their chest. As Anthony scanned the crowds of zombies closing in on them, silently estimating the number of rounds this was going to take, he figured it was going to be close.

"One shot, one kill," Anthony said to Jesse. "Make 'em count."

Jesse only nodded.

"Set up in the stern there. I'll take the bow. Holler out if you need help."

Anthony met Jesse's gaze.

His friend looked ill. His Adam's apple was working up and down in his throat like a piston.

"You okay?" Anthony asked.

Jesse closed his eyes and took a deep breath. When he opened them, he met Anthony's gaze and nodded.

"Good. Let's go to work."

Eleanor waited with Jim and Madison and the Red Cross volunteers just inside the doorway. Nobody spoke, nobody moved. The distant sound of thunder shook something inside Eleanor's chest, and the occasional flashes of lightning lit the doorway with a bluish-white light.

More rain, Eleanor thought darkly. *Just what we need*.

Her nose wrinkled at the stale, lived-in smell of a roomful of unwashed bodies and filthy clothes. Somebody coughed. And then, moving very quietly, Madison squeezed her way between Jim and Eleanor and took Eleanor's hand in hers.

Eleanor looked down in surprise.

"I'm sorry, Mom," Madison said. "What I said earlier, that was mean."

Eleanor put an arm around her and pulled her close, aware that Madison was trembling. She felt so small, so scared in that oversized T-shirt.

"Oh, baby," Eleanor whispered, her chest swelling with emotion. "I love you, Madison. I'm gonna get us through this. I promise."

But if Madison answered, her voice was lost in the commotion that followed. From outside on the balcony they heard Hank shouting. The next instant there was another loud, rolling crash—not lightning this time, but the heavy clanking sound of metal falling down a staircase—followed by at least ten rifle shots. Eleanor pulled her pistol and held it at the low ready, her eyes on the doorway.

"Sergeant Norton!" Hank shouted.

Eleanor glanced at Jim, and then at Madison. "I'll be right back," she said, and ran out the door.

"Mommy!"

"It'll be all right, Madison. Stay with Daddy."

She sprinted outside, but came to abrupt stop just outside the doorway.

A drizzling rain fell on her face and her arms.

Below her, the water had gone down considerably, and in the flash of a lightning bolt, she saw that it had exposed a number of cars in the parking lot. They looked like hippos in an African river, only the humps of their backs cresting the surface. A huge crowd of zombies was filtering between the cars, moving as quickly as their ruined bodies would allow.

Glancing down the balcony, she saw that a small group of them had managed to pull down the barricade of furniture that Hank had assembled across the staircase. All but two of the zombies were dead now, their bodies draped over the furniture and the staircase railing like marionettes with their strings cut. But the two of them that were still alive thrashed around in the water, churning it into a oily foam. Hank leaned over the railing and shot both, and the rifle's report made Eleanor jump.

"Get everybody out of there," Hank said, "then get down here and help me throw these canoes over the side. Hurry!"

He didn't wait for a response. She outranked him by a considerable margin, but this was combat, and it was his game. He was trained for battle; she wasn't. Eleanor's job was support. Stay out of his way and do as she was told.

As Hank fired out the remaining rounds in his magazine Eleanor ran inside the building and ordered everyone out.

"Down the stairs," she yelled. "Come on, everybody. Hustle!"

The Red Cross volunteers formed a ragged line and started toward the stairs. Eleanor, who had to yell at the top of her voice to be heard over the moaning of the zombies and the nearly constant bark of Hank's AR-15, reassured when she could, pushed when she had to, but eventually got them moving down the stairs.

Jim and Madison remained at the top of the staircase, waiting on her.

"Go," she said to Jim. "I've got to help him get the boats in the water."

Then Jim put an arm around her waist and kissed her. Eleanor was so shocked she could barely respond. He broke contact and, with Madison's hand in his, sprinted down the stairs.

"I love you," she muttered, watching him go down to the water level.

Eleanor had just enough time to scan the crowd of zombies that was closing in around them when the first canoe went over the side, hitting the water with a dull *thwack*.

"Sergeant Norton, I sure could use a hand, ma'am."

"Coming," she said, and helped him toss the rest of the boats over the side.

The others were already climbing into the canoes when Eleanor and Hank jumped into the water.

Jim paddled the boat over to her and helped pull her in.

Then he turned the boat around and pointed them to the north.

All the others were doing the same except for Hank. He was all by himself and paddling hard, his canoe pointed straight for the thickest part of the approaching zombie crowd.

"What are you doing?" Eleanor asked.

"Getting your backpacks, ma'am. And maybe thinning out this herd a bit. You get up front and help get these people going. I'll be right there with you."

Before Eleanor could protest Hank dropped his paddle into the canoe and came up with his rifle. He started firing at a frightening speed. Eleanor, who was a pretty good shot with an AR-15, though certainly not a pro, wondered how he even had time to aim. But aiming he most certainly was, for he was dropping zombies one after the other, every shot landing on target. It was a sickening, but almost beautiful display of fighting prowess, and Eleanor watched it in rapt fascination before that voice in her head ordered her to get moving.

"Let's go," she said to Jim, and the two of them started paddling.

Lightning flashed overhead, and in that moment Eleanor could see the other canoes moving out ahead of her in a crooked line between battered buildings and ruined cars, a bluish-white glow on the water, almost like moonlight.

And then the drizzle turned to rain.

* * *

They saw the wreckage of the Coast Guard helicopter first. In the darkness it resembled the busted exoskeleton of some enormous insect, a praying mantis maybe, that had slid down the face of the building and was now trying to crawl back up. Anthony stared at it, unaware he was holding his breath. While he'd seen this before, during the crash and after, things had happened so fast he never had a chance to absorb the sight of it. But now, all that twisted wreckage, the half-eaten body of one of the pilots hanging out the starboard-side window, the enormity of it caught up with him. When helicopters started dropping from the sky, the shit was really bad.

His fingers were shaking, but not badly. Jesse wouldn't see it. Brent certainly wouldn't see it, not in his present condition. But they were shaking, and that had him worried.

He was not in this to save Private Ryan.

He was in this for the money.

Anthony curled his fingers into a fist and focused on their surroundings, scanning constantly, the way he'd been taught in tactics training. Beyond the helicopter was the Church's Chicken and the parking garage and farther on still the Texas Chemical Bank, which had been so kind to them as of late. Nothing seemed to be moving, and that was good. That was very good.

Gradually, the anxiety he had felt upon seeing the wrecked helicopter faded, and he was able to focus on the money. Thinking about it changed his mood considerably, and he was surprised to feel his mouth starting to water. Seven million dollars were only a few feet away now. *Gonna leave this town*, he thought, and in his head the words were almost a song. *Gonna leave this town with a sack full of loot. A new truck, a new house, a new life. And all I have to do is take it.*

"Come to papa," he muttered.

The car—it was an old Volkswagen; he could see that now—was up to the top of its doors in water. Anthony hit it with a spotlight. He could see the two duffel bags through the rear windshield. He wasn't sure if the water was subsiding for good, or if this was just low tide, but whatever the reason they'd been lucky to find the money still here. Had someone come along, they could have reached inside pretty as you please and come up with more money than any honest man would know what to do with.

Lucky for all of them that hadn't happened.

Anthony let his gaze slide over to where Brent was sitting. He was rocking back and forth again with a steady metronome-like motion, muttering constantly. Anthony couldn't tell what he was saying, but he knew he didn't like it. That was gonna be a problem right there. And it would have to be dealt with sooner rather than later.

Let Dad take care of it, he told himself. *Just get the money.*

He turned around to Jesse as he took off his tactical vest. "Here," he said, "take the wheel for a sec. I'm gonna go get us started on our retirement plan."

Jesse beamed a huge smile.

"Now you're talking," he said.

The boat was turning in a slow pirouette as it came out of the rain. At the sight of it, everyone went quiet. The low murmurs that had marked most of their journey through the flooded landscape disappeared and all eyes turned forward. One by one, they drew their paddles up into their laps, almost as if they were working off the same mental circuit, and stared as the gruesome spectacle drifted past.

Eleanor thought it was cutting across their line when she first saw the boat. The gray, foglike rain distorted her senses that way, made depth perception almost impossible. But she saw the truth a moment later. The boat was a derelict, floating aimlessly on the current.

And inside the boat was a man, seated against the pilot's windscreen, his face tilted up toward the sky, his dead, unblinking eyes filling with rain. There was a bullet in his forehead, and when he came up even with her, Eleanor closed her eyes and turned away.

"You ready?" Jim asked her.

Earlier, Hank had managed to retrieve their backpacks, and Eleanor had slipped into a yellow raincoat and an Astros baseball cap. The rain sizzled on her hood and drained in curtains from the cap's bill. Peering through the rain she saw Madison and Jim huddled beneath a blue plastic tarp, looking back at her.

"Eleanor? You ready?"

"Yeah," she said. "Let's go."

They were the eighth canoe back from the front, placing them roughly in the middle of the pack. Hank was out in front with his AR-15, taking the point position. Nobody had argued. Two of the Red Cross volunteers near the back had shotguns. Hank said the scatterguns would work best covering their rear, especially as one of the Red Cross volunteers was a retired Marine who had fought in Afghanistan during the war. The volunteer's name was Frank. He was in his sixties, she guessed, white-haired, but his belly was still flat as a board, and he spoke with an accent that sounded as if he was from Maine or Massachusetts or one of those states up east. Having spent her entire life in Texas, Eleanor really didn't know and didn't care about the difference in New England accents. They were all just Yankees as far as she was concerned, and they all sounded like Kennedys to her. Still, she'd seen Frank kill three of those zombies with his shotgun shortly after they fled the Meadowlakes Business Park, and Yankee or not, the man knew how to carry himself in a fight. She felt good with him back there, watching their tail.

She was watching the empty windows on the building to their right when Hank whistled. It was a quick, short sound, like one hunter might use to call to another in thick brush. Eleanor turned forward, and at the same time heard the old ladies in the canoes between her and Hank start to gasp.

There were dead bodies in the water. Lots and lots of them.

They looked like driftwood floating in the current. One corpse bumped against the front of their canoe and rolled over onto his back.

Madison uttered a high, piercing scream.

"Madison," Jim said, and pulled her close, hiding her face in his chest.

Eleanor nodded her thanks to him, and then looked down at the dead man. He was Hispanic, probably in his late thirties, a little overweight, with scabbed-over scars all over his arms and neck, as if he had thrashed his way out of a tangle of barbed wire.

But there was no question what had killed him.

A large-caliber round had entered his head just above the line of his eyebrows. The exit wound had blown the top of his head open. Three large sections of his skull clung to his scalp like continents trying to break apart. It gave his head an impossibly stretched and distorted look, like something glimpsed in a funhouse mirror, and Eleanor had just enough time to process that all the gooey inner matter had seeped out of the skull cavity before she turned away, her stomach in her throat.

But there was nowhere to look that didn't show her more of the same. The bodies were everywhere. There were literally hundreds of them.

Hank had turned around and was now paddling up beside them.

"You ever watch them shows on the History Channel about the Civil War?" Hank asked Jim.

Jim, who looked as ill as Eleanor felt and still held Madison against his chest, shook his head.

"I like watching them shows," Hank went on, apparently oblivious to Jim's discomfort. "I saw this one about the Battle of Chickamauga. . . . They said ten thousand soldiers died there in one day . . . most of 'em while fighting hand to hand in the Chickamauga River. The water was supposed to have turned red by the end of the day's fighting. Kind of looks like what we got here, don't it?"

He laughed to himself, but there was no insanity behind it. It wasn't that kind of laugh. It was, rather, the sound a man makes when he thinks he's seen enough, been asked to do too much, and then is forced to do a little more. He laughed like a man who had been worn down to the nub, but who refused to quit.

"Sergeant Norton," he said, turning to Eleanor, "whatchu wanna do, ma'am?"

Eleanor opened her mouth to answer, but then closed it again. There was something moving up ahead, at the far end of the street near the Church's Chicken sign.

"Hold on a sec," she said, and reached into her backpack and took out her binoculars.

"What is it?" Hank asked.

The first thing she saw was the wrecked Coast Guard helicopter, and it made her gasp. It had evidently crashed into the side of the building and tumbled down it. She could see first one, then two more dead bodies inside the helicopter, all of them still wearing their flight gear.

Then she focused the binoculars on a small dark-colored bass boat that was about fifty feet in front of the helicopter. A handsome younger man she didn't recognize was behind the wheel. Another man, who looked disturbingly like a younger version of her boss, Captain Mark Shaw, was sitting in the front of the boat, rocking back and forth as if he was shell-shocked, an emotion that, at the moment, she felt she understood quite well. A third man was in the water, trying to force open the door of a flooded car.

As she watched, the man finally got the door open and reached inside. He came up with a large black duffel bag and handed it to the good-looking man behind the wheel, who took it and tossed it absently into the back of the boat.

The man in the water was wearing a mask, but even with that covering his eyes and nose, Eleanor could tell right away who it was.

"What is it?" Hank said again.

"That's Anthony Shaw," she said, handing him the binoculars. "And I'm pretty sure that guy in the front of the boat is his brother."

"Are you sure?"

He put the binoculars up to his eyes and brought them into focus.

Yeah, I'm sure, she thought.

Anthony Shaw she knew well . . . or, rather, she knew quite a bit about him. She'd seen his pictures up on her captain's desk. Anthony Shaw had evidently been some kind of stud on the baseball field, and had translated those glory days into success with the ladies as an officer on the department.

Shortly after she'd moved to the Travelers Unit Eleanor had befriended a pretty young patrolwoman named Megan Weber, who was temporarily on assignment to Sex Crimes. Once she'd grown out the little-boy haircut they make female cadets wear while at the academy, Megan had turned into a knockout with a little waist and big boobs and a smile that made every man in the room forget what he'd been talking about. But she was nice, too—good people, as Eleanor's dad used to say—and Eleanor had taken an instant liking to her, even though she was ten years younger. But Megan, like several other female officers her age, had fallen hook, line, and sinker for Anthony Shaw, who of course wasted no time getting into her pants.

Eleanor warned her about hanging out with SWAT guys.

"They're cute, they're built like gods, but they're just man whores," she'd said to the starstruck girl, and even as she said it she knew Megan wasn't listening, not really.

Well, Megan hadn't gotten pregnant and she hadn't gone all *Fatal Attraction* on him and gotten herself kicked out of the department. Nothing as melodramatic as that.

But she had gotten her heart broken.

Anthony Shaw asked her to get a friend they could, in his words, "throw into the mix." She'd told him she didn't want anything like that in their relationship, and he'd simply said, "What relationship? We're just fucking here."

And that was that. Cops gossip worse than grocery-store magazines, and soon word got around that Anthony had kicked her to curb. As was always the way with working in the boys' club that was the HPD, Megan had been branded an easy lay and Anthony went on about his business, able to proudly boast: "Yeah, I tapped that."

It made Eleanor sick sometimes, thinking about it.

"Yeah, that's him all right," Hank said. "The guy in the front of the boat is his older brother, Brent. He's a drunk. I don't know the other guy, but I don't think he's PD."

"What are they doing? I saw them pulling duffel bags out of that car."

He handed her the binoculars back.

"Don't know," he said.

Something was happening behind them.

Eleanor heard voices, several of them at once, and then someone shouting. She and Hank both turned around at the same time, and they saw Frank, the retired Marine, leveling his shotgun at a clumsy figure approaching them in the water.

Frank yelled for the man to stop.

He didn't.

And the next instant, before either Eleanor or Hank could say anything, Frank fired and nearly took the zombie's head off.

"Form up!" Hank yelled. "Everybody come forward."

Hank turned his canoe and paddled furiously toward the shooting.

Eleanor raised her binoculars, and saw Anthony Shaw staring back at her with binoculars of his own.

And then he lowered his.

The man behind him hit the throttle and the bass boat took off.

Eleanor continued to watch Anthony Shaw's face as he slipped away into the rain-streaked night. His expression was difficult to read, almost inscrutable, but she could tell he wasn't happy.

CHAPTER 14

With his pistol in one hand and a bullhorn in the other, Captain Mark Shaw pushed his way through the fringes of the terrified crowd and into the enclosed shallow lake in the front of the Engineering Building.

"Keep moving," he shouted. "You've got to keep moving."

To his left and behind him the campus was on fire, the orange glow from the flames reflecting on the water, making it look like molten rock. Black smoke turned the sky to a filthy, choking haze. And everywhere he turned, the screams of the frightened refugees and the moans of the dying and the undead threatened to fray his nerves to pieces.

Off to his right a SWAT officer was knocked down by three of the infected. The man raised his hand to push them away and got two of his fingers bitten off. At the same time the officer managed to get his pistol under the chin of one of the zombies and fire.

Both men went down.

Shaw was already pushing his way through the waist-deep water to help the officer. He put down the remaining two attackers, emptying one of his few remaining magazines in the process.

Shaw ejected the empty magazine and jammed it into the officer's injured hand.

"Hold this," Shaw said. "Just keep your hand up and hold it. Keep it elevated."

The officer, who was already looking pale, his eyes strangely unfocused, tried to comply. He held the stump of his injured hand in the air while he swayed drunkenly. Shaw had to catch him once to keep him from tilting over sideways.

The man was a goner, Shaw knew that. He'd seen the infection spread from one injured person to the next all night, and he knew this man had maybe thirty minutes before he too changed into one of those things . . . that was, if he didn't bleed to death first. Either alternative looked likely.

Briefly, Shaw glanced around.

They didn't seem to be getting any closer to the boatyard, no matter how hard he pushed and how loud he shouted. The infected were still everywhere. His own people were mostly dead now, and of the eighty thousand refugees he'd tried to evacuate, there looked to be fewer than four thousand. Most of them were so scared and unorganized they were beyond help. In the dark, it had become nearly impossible to tell who was a refugee and who was a zombie.

Shaw reloaded his weapon, holstered it, and then took the SWAT officer's AR-15 and pistol from him.

"I'm sorry, son," Shaw said.

For a moment, the man seemed to understand what was about to happen, and was thankful for it, but the clarity soon slipped away. Sweat was popping out all over his face, and his eyes were clouding over.

"You fought well," Shaw said.

Then he shot the officer in the head.

Now Shaw was down to just a few officers to help him.

They were spread out around the fraying edges of the refugee crowd, equipped, like Shaw, with bullhorns to keep the crowd together. But with so many of them dead, and so many of the infected swarming the area, even Shaw was beginning to doubt if they would survive.

Turning on the crowd, he raised his bullhorn and urged them on.

"Keep moving forward! Everybody move to the sound of my voice!"

He had been yelling all night long, and his throat was raw, his voice hoarse, but he kept on. All they had to do was get through the gap between Melcher Hall and the engineering building, and they'd be at the boatyard. If they could just make it this last short distance, they might escape.

"Keep moving, everybody. Officers, keep your edges tight. Watch your flanks!"

The north side of the engineering building was on fire. Through the smoke and flames he saw a man stumbling toward him in tattered clothes. He had what looked to be grass in his hair. He was dragging something, a piece of sheet metal maybe, possibly a board.

But he wasn't moving right. He seemed to stagger and lurch.

Shaw raised the AR-15 to his shoulder but didn't fire. Perhaps the man was another refugee, only injured, not infected. But then more shapes resolved out of the swirling smoke behind the man and Shaw knew. They were in trouble.

He circled around in front of the refugees from the shelter and yelled for them to hurry, waving his arms in a huge circular motion like an enraged traffic cop.

"Come on, people, let's move it along! Come on, move it. Keep going!"

Exhausted men and women and children slogged through

the water, shuffling past him at an aggravatingly slow speed. He wanted to grab them, throw them where he wanted them to be, but he could tell from their slackened expressions that they'd all been pushed past their breaking point. Most of them were only a few steps from falling over and quitting.

"Keep moving!" he said again, but without the anger this time.

From behind him, the zombies started to moan.

He turned and saw the zombie who had been dragging the sheet metal emerging from the flames. His back was on fire, and yet he seemed completely unaware of the pain.

Shaw raised his AR-15 and emptied the magazine into the approaching zombie crowd. Then he slung the rifle over his shoulder, got his bullhorn, and yelled, "Get some more officers up here! I need somebody to hold this gap."

The water was up to his armpits here in this part of the courtyard, and he glanced up. Daylight was an hour away at least, but as the dawn approached, so did high tide. The water *was* getting deeper. Slowly but surely, it was getting deeper.

That'll make moving difficult, he thought, *but it'll make it hard for those zombies, too. And it'll make getting out of here in the boats easier, too. If we can ever get there.*

But that was the thing. Getting out.

It had seemed like such an easy thing yesterday afternoon. After his video conference with Homeland Security Director George Dupree, and then his chance meeting with Anthony in the EOC office, Shaw had gone back to his temporary command post at the film and communications building and collected all the available officers he could find. From there, he'd gone to the main part of the shelter, issued weapons and bullhorns to his men, and told them start moving everybody out.

"We are evacuating immediately," he said to the crowd,

most of whom hadn't slept in two days, or eaten in longer than that, and so could barely lift their heads to hear him. "Take only what you can carry."

He'd gone from bunk to bunk then, rousting people, pleading with them to hurry, but everywhere he went he passed the sick and the disabled, and they couldn't move, no matter how much he pleaded. A few had family, and they were the lucky ones. There would be somebody to carry them, care for them.

Most, he knew, would be left behind.

The first attack came while he was still trying to get people out of their bunks. He had two of his SWAT snipers posted along the east wall of the building, and they sent up the hue and cry that they had a large group of zombies gathering just outside.

Unable to take his preferred route straight down Wheeler Street, Shaw ordered the building evacuated. He and his officers directed the refugees out the west doors, but it couldn't happen fast enough. Zombies overran the SWAT officers along the east wall of the building and poured into the building. A blind panic took over then, with refugees pouring out windows and knotting together in doorways, crushing each other even as the screams and moans grew louder at their backs.

Shaw had no idea how many thousands must have died in that first onslaught. He'd run out of the building with everyone else, shouting and pushing and kicking to keep people from running back into the path of the zombies, but once the refugees hit the water, their panic reached a fever pitch. Clothes and backpacks and blankets and endless drifts of trash filled the water, which was churning with bodies now. The trampling continued outside, and many who had barely been able to fight their way free of the exits found themselves hitting the water with no idea of where to go. They froze in place, only to be drowned by the crowd pushing its way free of the building.

Looking around, Shaw saw other panicked people flooding out of other buildings. They were screaming, pleading for someone to save them.

Off in another part of the campus, buildings were burning, turning the dark sky a sooty orange.

Here in the core of buildings that had served as the main shelter, thousands of people were trapped, unable to escape the zombie crowd pouring in from the east. Shaw could hear their screams as they were torn to pieces.

More still were caught in the upper floors, unable to get down, and here and there Shaw saw bodies dropping from windows three and four stories up.

He had to restore order, he knew that. For a horrible, gut-churning moment he saw the whole thing slipping through his hands, the situation on the verge of complete failure, but then he looked across the parking lot to his right, and he saw his chance.

A low concrete retaining wall had been run across the western edge of the lot just before Hurricane Kyle to help keep order while they were passing out food. A good two feet of the wall was sticking up above the water, and would serve as a natural defensive line. He called for every officer with a rifle to set up behind the wall while he ran up and down the lines of panicked survivors, telling them where to go.

Once the officers behind the wall started shooting, the sound of gunfire became almost continuous. Shaw had to yell at top volume to make himself heard, even with the bullhorn, but it worked.

He managed to get the disorganized crowd to push south through the campus.

He himself brought up the rear.

In the hellfire glow of the burning buildings he looked back and was about to raise the order for his men to fall back when they were overrun. Zombies in tattered clothes, their faces vacant and yet somehow wild, too, clawed their way over the HPD's best fighting men. Men Shaw knew personally were torn to pieces before his very eyes, and all he could do was watch with a mounting sense of stunned horror.

But he didn't quit. He pushed on, pleading with the survivors to move along. He fought the tightening ring of zombies pouring into the campus and rising up from the ranks of fallen.

Until daybreak. High tide was coming in. And still he hadn't been able to get his charges to the boats.

Had he really come this far to fail now?

He refused to believe that. They were close, he told himself, and he allowed a spark of hope to fire inside his chest. Just around this building. That's as far as these people had to go. They get there, and they just might live through this.

In fact, many of the remaining survivors were already around the last corner. A few of his officers were there already, too, using their bullhorns to coax people forward into the waiting boats. He could hear their shouted orders even now.

"Keep moving, everybody!" he yelled. "You're almost there. Keep moving."

Screams erupted from the back of the line.

Shaw ran that way and saw the zombies had overtaken a few of the more exhausted survivors.

He threw his bullhorn down, got a pistol in each hand, and started shooting as he backed up, yelling over his shoulder for the crowd to keep on moving.

Then he rounded the corner and entered the boatyard, and his heart sank. The scene was complete bedlam. They had collected hundreds of ski boats and fishing boats and everything else they could find that floated, but the yard master had been unable to position the waiting craft in any sort of orderly way. They were spread out at random over what had been the student parking lot along Calhoun Road, clustered together like a redneck yacht club at anchor, and the ragtag survivors were pouring over them in waves, crowding onto the boats closest at hand, capsizing several in the process, while the others farther off went unoccupied. His few remaining officers were desperately trying to maintain order, to keep the people moving forward, but there were just too many panicked refugees and not enough officers. Once again, Shaw saw it all slipping through his fingers, all control lost.

A noise, like a low rumble coming up from beneath the screams of the panicked survivors, made him turn his head to the east. The sun was coming up now, spreading a smoldering orange and copper-colored glow across the water and the windowless buildings. The water looked as if it were on fire, and through that molten sea flowed hundreds upon hundreds of the infected.

And when their moans reached Shaw, a sound that was part laugh and part groan escaped up his throat.

Anthony, Brent, and Jesse had seen the fires from a long ways off.

At first glance, the campus had looked like a mad streak of flame and soot across the sky. But from close up, it was a different sight entirely. Anthony Shaw cut the engines and simply stared, open-mouthed, at the destruction that lay before him.

The campus had been changed considerably by the storm damage and by the occupation of eighty thousand refugees, but that alone did not account for this. As a kid, Anthony had seen plenty of movies about the apocalypse, *The Postman*, all the Mad Max films, *12 Monkeys*, George Romero's zombie films, and countless others, and what he was looking at now, the ruined skyline of the campus backlit by flames and the rising sun, was so much like that. The destruction was so complete, so indiscriminately savage, that it simply boggled his mind.

"Anthony, this isn't good," Jesse said.

"Is Dad okay?" Brent said.

Both Anthony and Jesse looked at him. It was the first time he'd spoken since earlier that night.

"I don't know," Anthony said.

"What's your plan?" Jesse asked.

Anthony thought about that. In the distance, he heard what sounded like screaming and possibly gunfire. When he closed his eyes it almost reminded him of the sound of a Friday-night football game heard from a long ways off. That was probably where they'd find his father, who would no doubt be trying to get all the survivors down to the boatyard. That had been the plan before they left, and it didn't seem likely that his father would have given up on it. Not the great Captain Mark Shaw. He never gave up on anything, once he set his mind to it.

"I want to head east down I-45 over to Spur 5. From there we'll head south and come up along the boatyard."

"And then?" Jesse asked.

"I don't know, Jesse. I really don't know."

The land between the Interstate and the northern edge of the campus was flat and relatively empty. The only building in the area was the General Services Building, which marked the northernmost point of the campus, and once they rounded that they were faced with open water.

But Anthony resisted the urge to give the boat full throttle.

With the water only now starting to rise again, there were still numerous hazards, such as submerged walls and the roofs of cars and trucks, lurking only inches below the surface. Every now and then he could feel the hull glancing off something out of sight or scraping over the roof of a car, and the last thing he wanted was to rip the hull off the boat because he was in too big a hurry.

It took fifteen minutes to cover the distance down to the boatyard, but they knew they were headed into trouble even before that. They could hear the screams and see the panicked rush of bodies clambering onto the boats.

"Oh my God," Jesse said.

For a long moment, neither of the others spoke. Brent was watching the crowd, his head slowly shaking back and forth as though he couldn't believe it; and when he turned back to Anthony, his face was pale, his eyes overly bright, as though he was about to cry.

"Where's Dad?" he asked.

Anthony looked at his older brother, and then raised his binoculars and scanned the crowd. He recognized several officers on the edges of the crowd. They were doing everything they could to get people to move forward into the unoccupied boats, but they were fighting a losing battle.

He kept the binoculars moving over the crowd, but when he reached the southernmost edge of it, he froze.

"I see him," he said.

Then he put the binoculars down, told the others to hold on tight, and gave the little bass boat all the throttle it had.

Captain Shaw stared at the approaching crowd of zombies and considered his options . . . and there weren't many.

He was wearing an olive drab T-shirt and green BDU-style pants. He reached into the pockets on his thighs and came up with five fully loaded magazines for the Glocks and a sixth magazine that only had eight rounds in it. From the number of zombies he saw coming down into the boatyard, he could tell he didn't have anywhere close to enough ammunition for a stand-up fight. He could get most of the ones out in front, maybe, if he made every shot count, but there were bunches more pouring in from the residential area south of the campus. Probably fleeing the rising tide, he thought. And that meant far more than he was equipped to deal with. Staying put was going to be suicide.

But, really, what other option did he have?

A quick look over his shoulder answered that.

Less than a quarter of the people he'd managed to lead this far had found their way into the boats. Some of the boats, he saw with mounting anger, were trying to leave, even though they were only half full. Some, he saw, had only one or two people in them.

"Fill the boats up front first!" he yelled at the crowd.

Barely twenty feet away, a man with a little girl on his shoulders turned to stare at him. His eyes were lit with a fevered intensity, like something inside his mind had let go. Thick cords stood out in the man's neck. His lips were drawn back, exposing teeth clenched so tightly Shaw wondered why they didn't shatter.

The man made some kind of inarticulate reply, and Shaw made to rush him, to grab him by the shoulder and spin him around and push him toward the front of the boatyard, but then he saw the look on the little girl's face. It wasn't fear. She looked dazed, her mouth slack. Her eyes had a glazed vapidity to them that made him slow, then stop, his head shaking from side to side very slowly.

"Go on," he said, not yelling anymore.

Then he turned back to the advancing zombie crowd. The wind shifted as he did, and he caught the sickly sweet stench of open sewage mixed with gasoline and mud and rotting flesh. Hurricane Mardel had pushed immense piles of debris up against the southeastern edge of the campus, like snow-drifts against a prairie barn. The zombies wouldn't be able to get through and come around on his right flank. They'd be forced by the walls of trash to veer more and more to the east, toward the highway, where the ground sloped away so much that, in places, the water was forty feet deep. Maybe, he thought, he wouldn't need to kill them all to have a chance. If he could set up on a point along that wall of trash he could direct fire into the crowd and maybe force the zombies into deep water, where they'd drown.

It was as good a plan as any, he decided, and loaded fresh magazines into both pistols. He waded back toward the trash wall, right into the middle of the first few zombies to make it down to the boatyard, shooting them as he went.

He had made it most of the way to the wall when he heard the whine of a boat motor at full throttle coming up on his left. Shaw turned, and at first he thought he was looking at one of the refugees who had managed to get one of the boats running and was now tearing off in a blind panic.

The damn fool's headed the wrong way, he thought. And then stopped. *That's Anthony driving that boat. Holy shit, that's my boy!*

The zombies were closing in on him, but even as he shot two of them, a wide smile spread across his face.

He let out a wild rebel yell, watching the boat as it swung toward him.

"That's my boy!" he shouted.

He was delirious with excitement now. All the exhaustion of the preceding night seemed to slip away from him, and at that moment, he felt like his lungs had finally started to work again. Great waves of air rushed into his chest, filling him.

Yes!

But then the smile faded. They were slowing down. Shaw watched, dumbstruck, as Anthony slowed the boat to a stop. They were less than thirty feet from the nearest zombies, and they were stopping.

"What the . . . ?"

And then Anthony was forcing Brent over the side of the boat.

"What are you guys doing?" he yelled. "Jesus, what are you doing?"

Brent was trying to claw his way back into the boat, but Anthony was pushing him away with a rifle. Brent looked as wild eyed as the man who had been carting the little zombie girl around on his shoulders, maybe even worse.

And then Shaw realized: No, Anthony wasn't pushing Brent away with the rifle. He was trying to give it to Brent, to make him take it. And a small black duffel bag, too.

"Get back in the boat!" Shaw called out to him. "Get back in the boat now!"

But Anthony was already pushing away. His eyes were fixed on Brent, but he was motioning wildly toward Shaw, and Shaw could hear his younger son yelling, "Get him that rifle! Help him!"

The next instant Anthony was behind the controls again, the throttle buried as the boat sped into the middle of the zombie crowd, plowing over bodies with reckless speed.

Brent turned around, holding the AR-15 across his chest like a young girl does her schoolbooks, visibly trembling in the waist-deep water. He looked around at the zombies shambling toward him, and a sickening cry escaped his throat.

"No," Shaw said, and ran that way.

"Holy fucking shit, Anthony!" Jesse said, looking over his shoulder as Anthony steered the boat away from his father and brother. "What in the hell are you doing? You just left him back there."

Anthony turned the boat hard to the left, making a wide swath through another crowd of zombies. Their bodies folded under the boat with a series of loud, wet thuds, and when Anthony turned back to see what he had done the water was thick with twisted, deformed corpses.

He turned the boat yet again, this time back toward the boatyard, and backed off the throttle.

"What are we doing here, Anthony? What about your brother?"

"He'll be all right," Anthony said, and for a moment the image of his brother's terrified face as Anthony forced him over the side both angered and worried him.

But he shook the doubt away.

He'd told Brent to get the rifle and the ammo to their father. Brent had understood what to do. Anthony was sure of that.

"Get those gas cans," he said to Jesse. "We're gonna make another pass through that crowd. You just make sure you get that stuff poured out into the water."

"You're not gonna—"

But Anthony wasn't listening. He was already laying into the throttle, rocketing the boat forward.

"Oh shit," Jesse muttered, and moved to the back of the boat where they kept the extra fuel. Holding on to the gunwale with one hand, he put the first of the plastic gas cans between his knees and unscrewed the cap.

"You ready?" Anthony said.

"Yeah, go."

Anthony turned the boat again and accelerated into the main body of the approaching zombies. He started to turn the wheel sharply back and forth, kicking up a huge wake that knocked many of the zombies off their feet.

"Do it!" he yelled at Jesse. "Dump it all."

When they had emptied all five gas cans, Anthony sped down to the eastern corner of the rec center, slowed to a stop, and turned to face the zombies. There were hundreds of them now. Their moaning had become so loud it drowned out the shouts and gunfire from the boatyard.

"Hand me that flare gun," he said to Jesse.

Jesse got the gun out of the storage compartment under his seat and handed it to Anthony.

"You think this'll work?" he asked.

"Only one way to find out."

But Anthony was pretty sure of himself. Between the oil and the chemicals that were already in the water from the refineries down south and all the gas that had been spilled when the yard masters were getting the shelter's impromptu fleet ready to go and the gas they had just put down, the water might as well have been a field full of kindling.

He raised the flare gun and fired a skipping shot over the water, igniting a trail of fire like a torch dragged through dry grass. But the flames dimmed, and then seemed to die out completely. Anthony watched it with a sinking feeling in his chest, and then he hung his head and let out the breath he'd been holding.

He glanced back at Jesse, expecting to see his own dark sense of failure staring back at him. But Jesse was watching the water, not blinking, his mouth hanging open slightly in expectation.

Anthony followed Jesse's gaze, and as he did, the water erupted with a *whoosh* so forceful he felt it against his chest like a hard shove. The next moment, a blast of searing heat swept over his face, and he turned away, shielding himself with an upturned palm.

The flames burned intensely bright for perhaps twenty seconds, and then died down, leaving the air oily and black with smoke and thick with the smell of burning bodies and chemicals.

The smoke hung on the water like a fog, and for a long moment, everything was quiet.

Here and there Anthony could make out the sound of someone moaning. A few zombies, their hands blackened, the skin peeling away in charcoal-like clumps, reached for the boat as it glided silently by, but most didn't move. They floated on the garbage-choked water, burned and dead, in such numbers that it left Anthony speechless.

"You did it, man!" Jesse said. "Holy shit. I can't believe that worked."

Anthony only looked at him. He wanted to smile, but he couldn't. He was too stunned by his own success. Slowly, his gaze turned back to the water.

Cheers rang out from the boatyard.

He wasn't sure how he picked his father's voice out of all that yelling, but gradually he became aware of his dad yelling Brent's name.

They had drifted back toward the campus, close to the spot where he had dumped Brent over the side and told him to get the AR and the extra ammo to their father, and now, through the screen of oily smoke he could see that Brent hadn't moved. He was still standing right where Anthony had left him, looking small and scared and very much alone amid a tightening cluster of zombies. He still held the gun across his chest as if it was an armful of chopped wood.

Another thirty or forty yards beyond Brent, Anthony saw their father, his face twisted with rage and fear, running toward Brent. He was yelling his son's name, screaming for him to fight.

"Why won't he move?" Jesse said.

"Brent!" Anthony shouted. *"Shoot them, dammit! Shoot them!"*

Brent lifted his head, as though he had heard the sound of someone speaking to him, but not caught the sense of it, and that was when one of the zombies fell on his back and pushed him down onto his knees. Brent let out a shriek and popped up again, but without the AR.

"Brent!" Anthony cried, and jumped out of the boat.

He ran toward his brother.

Anthony pulled his pistol and fired into the crowd of zombies swarming around Brent.

The zombie's touch had turned something on in Brent's mind, for as soon as he got back on his feet, he started running. He was moving more quickly than Anthony had ever seen him move, and he was headed straight for the deep water near the base of the freeway.

"Yes," Anthony said to himself. "That's good. Keep going." Then, more loudly: "Keep going, Brent! Run!"

But he didn't make it far.

As Brent was running, one of the zombies managed to grab on to the back of his pants and hold on. Brent punched and slapped at the zombie, twisting one way and then other, but he couldn't break the hold, and the next instant the zombie was on him.

Two others closed in.

Anthony fired and hit one of the zombies in the shoulder, but didn't stop it. And that had been his last round. The slide was locked back in the empty position, the gun useless. Anthony holstered it and sprinted that way, and as he neared them he could hear thudding blows and the sound of his brother screaming.

Brent Shaw, who was a full six inches taller and eighty pounds heavier than any of his attackers, was getting pushed and pulled between the zombies like a kitten caught in a three-way dogfight. The zombies snarled and snapped, slashing at him with their teeth and nails. Brent's body jerked and flopped without any sort of control. It took Anthony less than ten seconds to close the distance, but in that time, the zombies shredded Brent's clothes and laced his bare skin with cuts and bites. Huge runners of blood ran down his chest and over the swell of his white belly, and all the while, his face grew ever paler.

"Brent, no!" Anthony shrieked. *"No! No! Brent, hold on!"*

Anthony grabbed one of the zombies and threw it off his brother. One of the other two reached for him, but Anthony was able to bat the zombie's hand away and push it down into the water. The third never took its dead stare off Brent. It continued to slash and tear at him even as Anthony punched it in the back of the head.

He finally managed to pull the filthy thing off Brent and toss it away.

When he turned back to check on his brother he saw their father was already picking him up in a fireman's carry and taking him away.

"Dad, is he . . . ?" But Anthony said no more. His father stopped, turned, his eyes bloodshot and shining with threatening tears, and then walked away.

Anthony heard the crack of gunfire and looked around.

He felt disconnected, lost, mentally numb, and he barely registered that Jesse was leaning over the gunwale of their boat with his pistol, shooting the few remaining zombies before they could reach the spot where Anthony was standing. To Anthony, the sounds of the shooting and the moaning and the noise of the refugees trying to climb into the boats had taken on a strange, muffled quality, and it occurred to him that he had grown used to it.

What a strange thing to think at a time like this, he thought, *with your brother dying over there. That's your fault, you know. Yours and yours alone.*

"No," he said aloud. "No, all he had to do was fight. Or get to Dad and let him do the fighting. That's all he had to do."

But he wasn't made for that, the voice inside his head insisted. *You knew that, and you let you go anyway. You let him down. And you let Dad down.*

"It wasn't my fault," Anthony said. But the words tasted rotten in his mouth.

He saw his father and his brother then.

Mark Shaw had put Brent on top of a white brick wall, and even from a distance, Anthony could see his brother's chest covered in blood. It was rising and falling rapidly as he fought for air. He was turning his head from side to side like a man trying to ward off a fever dream.

Mark Shaw was sitting in a boat just a few feet away. His chin was resting on his chest, his mighty shoulders drooped with exhaustion and grief. He had his elbows on his knees and a pistol in his hand. He hardly moved.

When the time comes, Anthony thought, *he'll have to be the one to put Brent down. Despite all his grief, despite the weight of everything pressing down upon him, he'll be the only one strong enough to do it. I could never . . . never.*

"I'm sorry," he said. "Brent, I'm so sorry."

CHAPTER 15

Just before dawn broke over the flooded ruins of Houston, a small flotilla of canoes lay anchored in the shelter of a park pavilion, waiting for daylight. A light rain was falling on the metal roof above them, and for the moment, the world seemed peaceful. Eleanor, Jim, and Madison shared a breakfast of MRE cheesy mac and reconstituted eggs and smoky franks, though only Eleanor appeared to actually enjoy the meal.

Eleanor had been able to vary her diet during the past few weeks. At least a little. She'd had some federal rations brought in by the Red Cross and the FEMA people, so the MREs were still a once-in-a-while thing for her. If not a treat exactly, they were at least rare enough to still seem like a novelty. The little bottles of Tabasco sauce, for example, were just plain cute. But of course Jim and Madison were sick of them. For the two of them, opening an MRE meant dragging themselves back to the trough. It meant drudgery. It meant sameness. It meant morale-sucking boredom. And so, when Madison had referred to the MREs as "meals rejected by Ethiopians," Eleanor had nearly choked on the Welsh rarebit she was eating.

"Don't be nasty," she said. "What a horrible thing to say."

But then she saw the wry smile on her husband's face, and the way he nodded in agreement with their daughter's complaint, and she realized that they had bonded, that they belonged together. *They have a special power when they're together*, she thought, and she was momentarily confused by the conflicting envy and joy the thought brought her. *The two of them are crazy and wonderful and a little frightening sometimes, yet together, they are powerful.*

And they were hers. That felt good.

The rain stopped shortly after daybreak, and they got going. The air was dense and humid, and though it wasn't hot yet, by midmorning the heat would be oppressive. Already the air hummed with insects, mosquitoes mostly, and the volunteers and the Nortons and Hank Gleason grumbled as they swatted at the pests.

They paddled down flooded streets between ruined buildings, marveling at how much damage the storms had done. Nothing had escaped the storms' destructive power. Every billboard they passed had sections hanging loose from the frame, or blown out entirely. And so many buildings had burned. This, Eleanor remembered from her many briefings at the EOC, was an inevitable consequence of people forgetting to turn off the gas before the storm, despite the numerous warnings on the news and on the radio. It looked to Eleanor that some of those buildings must have blown sky high, judging from the burned bits of lumber floating down the street. There were plastic toys everywhere because they, too, floated. A shutter banged open and closed in the breezeway created by a roofless house. Somewhere, a dog howled. In the distance they could see a swarm of seagulls feeding on something, but they were too far away to see exactly what, and Eleanor didn't really want to know anyway.

The water was full of debris and dead animals and some-times even dead people. But there were living people wan-dering around, too. That alarmed Eleanor at first because she was still rattled by the zombies they'd seen at the Meadow-lakes Business Park, but the people who were out now were clearly not zombies, even though they moved like people did in her nightmares. They seemed lost, disconnected from each other and their own fates. They were shiny with sweat, their faces traumatized, their clothes torn to rags. The city, and the people who haunted it, seemed to her to have taken on an otherworldly appearance that Eleanor found more and more claustrophobic as the day wore on.

They passed a man seated on some kind of large board he'd put between the hoods of two pickups. As they drew closer a hush fell over the flotilla of canoes. Now, passing di-rectly in front of the man, Eleanor could see the board was the front door of the house behind him. He was holding the drowned body of a child, a boy not much older than Madi-son. The man's eyes were very white against the filth that covered his face.

Hank pulled his canoe up to the man and spoke so quietly to him that Eleanor couldn't hear what was said.

The man made no attempt to answer.

Hank turned back to the group and caught Eleanor's gaze. He shook his head as though to say the man was lost to the world.

They saw looters who didn't even try to disguise what they were doing. Water moccasins moved like ribbons in the wind as they glided out from fallen trees. Eleanor saw dead bodies floating like driftwood, while not five feet away two men and a woman ate from a jar of mayonnaise they'd found somewhere. A helicopter passed overhead, and though they tried to flag it down, it never even slowed.

"Don't do any good to flag them down," Hank said, gliding up next to their canoe. "That was the National Guard. They don't stop anymore."

"Why not?" Jim asked.

"Too many looters. Too many people shooting at the looters. I've talked to their pilots. They don't want to fly into a situation and get shot by the people they're trying to save. I can't really blame them, I guess."

"So what good do they do? Why the flyovers?"

"I guess so they can report what they see."

"To who? If they're not gonna help, who is?"

Hank shrugged. "Don't know."

They all grew quiet.

"What's wrong, Hank?" Eleanor asked suddenly.

He looked at her, surprised. "Ma'am?"

"You've been acting down since we saw that man with the dead boy. Are you okay?"

A wan smile danced at the corners of his mouth, and in that instant, Eleanor saw the stunning good looks that made all the women in the department sigh whenever Hank walked by. He really was a heartbreaker.

"Just wondering what's going to happen to us," he said, gesturing at the destruction around them with a vague wave of his hand, "after all this is over."

"We'll get through it. We'll start over."

"No, ma'am," he said after a long, thoughtful silence. "No, ma'am, I don't think that'll happen."

"Why the change in attitude, Hank? Last night, and yesterday, you didn't seem to have doubts at all."

He smiled. "Yeah, funny how that'll happen to a guy."

He paddled on, occasionally glancing back at the rest of the volunteers, making sure they were all still together. He was silent for so long that Eleanor thought that was all he was going to say, but when he spoke again, it was as though he hadn't paused at all.

"It's just . . . all this stuff is gone now. Houston, I mean. I lived my whole life here. I don't know how to begin starting over, you know?"

"Yeah," Eleanor said. "Yeah, I know."

When she was seventeen, Eleanor lost her grandmother. Or, rather, her grandmother had simply died. Eleanor didn't really lose anyone, as her mother hadn't spoken with her parents in a dozen years or more. She had only the vaguest of memories of her maternal grandparents, and at the time she'd had absolutely no clue as to why they'd dropped out of her parents' life, and not enough sense to ask.

But Eleanor was eager to meet her grandfather, even under the sad circumstances. Unfortunately, the man she ended up meeting was a broken one. If he had been a bad father to Eleanor's mother, he had evidently been a loving husband to her grandmother, and over the course of the week they spent together, Eleanor watched the man fall apart. He barely spoke to any of them, but he had said something to Eleanor that had mystified her at the time.

"Our lives," he said, "are like a junkyard tumbling down the stairs. We have no control over what happens. There's no master plan. We just exist until, eventually, it all comes crashing down."

Now, many years later, Eleanor understood the awful power of that nihilistic urge. She saw how strongly it called to the weary and the destitute, as though it had its own gravity. And if it could absorb Hank, who was blessed with so much and treated life with such simple, boyish joy, none of them were immune.

And then, almost as if he were responding to a movie director's cue, a man floated around the corner on a rickety pool chair singing "Bye, bye, Miss American Pie, drove my Chevy to the levy, but the levy was dry." The man was bare-chested and righteously drunk. He had an Igloo cooler tied to the back of the chair and the two remaining beers of a six-pack hanging from the chair's headrest.

One of the Red Cross volunteers began to chuckle, and Eleanor did, too.

Someone called out to him, asking him if he wanted a ride.

He looked at the long row of canoes as though startled, breaking off his song mid-verse. Then his smile grew large again and he raised his beer high and began to sing, his voice loud and off-key and not at all sane. "Them good ol' boys were drinking whiskey and rye, singing 'This'll be the day that I die.' "

Eleanor and the others stopped paddling and turned to watch him float by, the chair keeping a surprisingly straight course through the current.

He raised his beer to them one last time and sang, "This'll be the day that I die."

Jim shook his head. "I think he's right."

"Zombies'll get him before nightfall," Hank agreed. He looked around at the others. "Anybody need to stop for a rest?"

Nobody did.

"All right then, let's keep going."

Later that afternoon, they arrived at the I-45 junction with Spur 5, on the northeast corner of the University of Houston's campus. Eleanor, looking at a sea of burned and mutilated bodies, tried not to gag.

Others weren't so strong. She could hear them vomiting over the sides of their canoes, then muttering apologies to those around them.

As they drifted closer to what had been the EOC's boat-yard, they began to hear moans coming from some of the bodies, and Madison clapped her hands over her ears to keep the sounds away.

"What happened here?" Eleanor asked Hank.

He scanned the campus and the floating field of burned bodies and he said, "I don't know. You can see where a lot of these buildings have burned, but I don't think that's what did this to these people."

"Do you think these were people from the shelters?"

"Ma'am, I ain't got the foggiest idea. It's quiet now, though. Either everybody left or . . ."

"Or they're all dead," Madison said sharply.

He looked at her, not unkindly, then nodded.

"Yeah, I'm afraid so."

"What are we going to do?" Madison said, looking from one adult to the next.

"Well, if they're not here, one of two things must have happened," Hank said. "One, they got evacuated, which doesn't seem real likely, or two, they went somewhere else to get evacuated. We need to figure out where."

"Okay, great. How are we going to do that?" Eleanor asked. "I went to every EOC meeting for the last five weeks and they never mentioned going anywhere specific to get evacuated. They threw out some suggestions, but nothing was ever decided on."

He shrugged.

"I think I know where they went to," Jim said.

They all turned and stared at him.

"Look there," he said, and pointed at the wall of the rec center. "See it, just above the waterline."

Eleanor followed the line of his finger, and when she saw what he was pointing at, she laughed. "Yeah," she said. "I see it."

Written in black paint that had started to run like the print on a horror movie poster were the words: ORDER TO EVACU-ATE: PROCEED TO SAM HOUSTON RACE PARK.

"Huh," Hank said. "Well, I guess that answers that."

"Oh man," Jim said. "You cops are something else. It's a wonder you ever solve any crimes at all."

"Cute," Eleanor said. "Thanks for the support there, hubby."

"My pleasure," he said, smiling at her.

And then Hank rapped his knuckles against the side of their canoe.

"Ma'am, check that out over there. See him, on top of that wall there?"

He was pointing at a dead man in tattered green BDU pants. His chest was laced with cuts and deeper wounds, like teeth marks. Someone had made an effort to cover him with a blanket, but the wind had blown that away so that now it hung from the spot where it was still tucked under his legs. The man was big, heavyset, and there was a bullet hole in his forehead. For a second, Eleanor thought it was Captain Shaw, but the man was too young, his hair still black.

"Is that . . . ?" she asked.

"Yeah, I think so."

"But we just saw them last night. He was with Anthony and that other guy."

"Yep," Hank said. "Funny how things work out, ain't it?"

CHAPTER 16

What Mark Shaw had wanted most after shooting his son was to dig a grave. Overcome with grief and rage, he'd wanted to slice the earth open with a shovel, tear into it, perform some violent, destructive act that would absorb all his fury.

But he had wanted the *work* of digging, too.

In a strange way that he didn't completely comprehend, the digging would be both a destructive act and at the same time a creative one. It was the destruction he wanted, but it was the creative act he knew he needed. He needed to sweat. He needed to feel the muscles in his arms and his back burn with exertion. He needed to feel the blisters form and burst on his palms, because these things would honor his son. Self-flagellation would be the last act of love he could ever do for the boy.

But in a world covered by water, graves were impossible, and he had been forced to leave Brent on top of the wall where he died, covered by a yellow tarp. He had carefully tucked the corners under the body and then sat back in a small boat that he had claimed for his own. And while the rest of the refugees filed out of the boatyard, Mark Shaw watched the tarp flutter in the breeze and thought of Brent, not as he had been there at the end, perpetually drunk and scared, but as the four-year-old boy who would sometimes come downstairs in the middle of the night to crawl into bed between his parents.

It was funny, he thought, how memory grabbed on to the littlest moments, the ones that simply *are*, the ones without a beginning or an end. Like the feeling of letting go the day he taught Brent to ride a bike, watching as he wobbled slowly down the sidewalk. Or driving him to school in the morning, that little-boy smile of his, no front teeth and full of radiant joy. Or watching football with him on the couch on Sunday afternoons. Or teaching him to shoot.

But he remembered these things, too.

The chemical stench of the floodwaters.

Burning buildings glowing against a nighttime sky.

Brent standing in the smoke-covered water, holding the AR-15 across his chest, trembling, unable to speak, unable to move.

The city, drowned and quiet and every bit as desolate as the Jerusalem of Jeremiah's visions, shimmering in the light of the rising sun.

The faces of refugees, shocked and exhausted, as the boats carried them away.

Zombies.

His son, so much like him, dying on top of a wall.

Anthony saying, "Dad, he was supposed to run straight to you. He would have been safe if he'd just done it like I told him."

Anthony saying, "Dad?"

Anthony saying, "Dad, say something, please."

Later, Mark Shaw sat in the same little metal boat he'd been in when he said good-bye to Brent, bringing up the rear of the ragtag fleet of refugee boats. He was exhausted from fighting all night long. He was emotionally drained by his grief and his rage. The droning of the little 25 Johnson Outboard was trying to put him to sleep. The only thing keeping him awake now was willpower.

From his position at the back he had a clear view of the rest of the fleet, some four hundred–plus boats of every make and degree of seaworthiness. His best guess was that they had gotten away with fewer than three thousand of the original eighty thousand who had grouped together at the campus. Those few survivors were jammed into the boats now. Some boats were so overloaded that people were forced to hang over the sides, making them look, to Shaw, like those trains in India and Bangladesh with the natives spilling out like candy from a piñata.

From somewhere up ahead he heard people yelling and a woman crying. Shaw looked around for one of his officers, but none of them were close by. After the battle at the campus, he had only six left, and all of them were busy sprinting up and down the line, shepherding the fleet.

Shaw fed the engine a little more throttle and sped up to the disturbance.

The yelling was coming from a white Maxum Runabout with an open bow and yellow trim on the stern. Several younger men were trying to heave the body of a dead man over the side of the boat, while a wild-eyed woman tried desperately to stop them.

One of the men pushed the woman down, but she got right back up and wrapped an arm around the dead man's neck.

"Let go of him!" she screamed. "You fucking bastards, don't you touch him."

"Hey," Shaw said.

They didn't hear him. Another of the men tried to pull the

woman's arm loose, and when that didn't work, he balled his fist and made to punch her in the face.

"Hey!" Shaw said.

The man hesitated, his fist hovering above the woman's wildly rolling eyes and terrified grimace. He and the rest of the men looked over the side, and into the barrel of Shaw's Glock.

"You hit her, son, and I'll put a bullet in your head."

One of the other men reached for a shotgun, but only got it halfway up before Shaw covered him with the pistol.

"Don't be stupid," he said. "Go on, put it down. That's it. Okay, everybody, hands where I can see 'em. Just like that. Perfect. Now how about one of you guys tell me what's going on here?"

They all yelled at him at once, and Shaw held up a palm to silence them. He felt tired and, in a crazy sort of way, bored.

"One at a time," he said, and pointed at the man who'd been trying to pick up the shotgun. "You. What are you guys doing?"

The man looked to be barely twenty years old. He was thin and rough-looking, like a South Houston redneck meth head, tattoo sleeves that curled up to his neck.

"This dude just died," he said. His tone suggested that that was all there was to say on the matter, and the others seemed to agree, for they were nodding in agreement.

"Okay," Shaw said. "What did he die of?"

"How the fuck should I know? I look like a doctor to you?"

Shaw laughed. "No, son, you definitely don't look like a doctor to me."

"He's gonna turn into one of them zombies. I don't want no fucking zombies on this boat."

The others all started talking at once, but Shaw didn't try to silence them this time. What was happening here was pretty plain now. He could tell them that the zombies were diseased *living* people, not the walking dead like in the movies, but what was the point? None of them would listen, or understand if they did; and besides, there was an easier solution to the problem.

"Hand him down to me."

That silenced them. They looked at Shaw, and then at each other.

"Come on. We're wasting daylight. Hand him down."

The woman, whose panic had flared again, said, "No! He's not gonna change into one of them. He's not infected."

"Ma'am," Shaw said, patiently. "Ma'am." The woman looked at him, her chest heaving. "I know that. I'm gonna put him in this boat. I got room for both of you. You can tend to your husband while I steer."

"He's my brother," she said.

"Okay, your brother. The two of you can ride with me."

The wild fear cooled in her eyes. She looked at the men in the boat with her, and then down at the corpse. She swallowed hard and began to cry.

"Hurry it up," Shaw said to the men. "Hand him down to me."

They did as he asked, moving the body and helping the woman down to him in silence.

"You okay?" he said to the woman.

She was sitting against the gunwale, her brother's head in her lap. She shook her head, but said nothing.

"Hold on to something."

And with that he turned the boat away from the men aboard the Maxum and resumed his place at the fleet's rear.

For the third time in an hour, Mark Shaw saw a Coast Guard helicopter fly overhead. They were crisscrossing back and forth over Northwest Houston, and probably elsewhere too, announcing the military-run evacuation point at the Sam Houston Race Park. Shaw stood up in the boat and looked around for landmarks he recognized. In the distance he could see the elevated sprawl of the Beltway, which meant they were almost there.

"Shouldn't be too much longer," he said to the woman, who still cradled her dead brother's head in her lap. She stared at him, her eyes hollow and miserable-looking behind the stringy curtain of her hair. He had taken her aboard three hours earlier, and though he had tried to ask her name several times, she'd refused to say anything to him. She was, he feared, shutting down mentally. Many of the refugees were.

A few minutes later he saw Anthony's boat speeding back to him. Anthony was behind the wheel, while Jesse rode in the front with an AR-15. Shaw had assigned the two of them to ride point for the fleet, and if they were coming back to the rear now it meant something was happening.

Shaw slowed his boat to a stop. "What's going on?" he said.

Anthony looked at the woman and the dead man curiously, as though he wanted to ask where they came from, but decided better of it. He turned to his father, and then quickly looked down at his own hands on the wheel. He was too ashamed to meet his father's gaze, that much was obvious, and Shaw thought that was probably just as well. If he got too close to Anthony right now he might punch his lights out. The anger was still fresh, still very raw.

Anthony said, "There's some activity on the other side of the Beltway. Hand him the binoculars, Jesse."

Jesse reached into one of the storage bins and handed the binoculars over to Shaw, who took them without comment.

"Where?" he asked.

"Over there," Anthony said, and pointed past the Beltway. "It's all around over there. Look anywhere."

To the naked eye, it was just a long shimmering line against the water. Shaw hadn't thought twice about it when he first noticed it, thinking that maybe it was just a trick of the light on the water. But now that he was looking at it through the binoculars, he could see what it was.

A chain-link fence.

An enormous chain-link fence that stretched for miles.

"I've seen soldiers patrolling outside it," Anthony said. "They've also put up some barriers at the base of the fence and wrapped everything in barbed wire."

Shaw lowered the binoculars.

"Those crazy bastards. They're building a wall around the city."

He shook his head in disbelief.

"What do you want to do, Dad?"

"The plan hasn't changed. Get us to the Beltway. I want to find the on-ramp closest to the military's evacuation point and get us up there. Once you find the on-ramp, start forming these people up and working them through."

Anthony nodded.

"Go on," Shaw said.

"Yes, sir."

Anthony turned his boat around and glided off so as not to create a wake around his father's much smaller craft.

When he was gone, Shaw raised the binoculars again and studied the fence.

"Those crazy bastards," he muttered.

They reached the Beltway a little before one o'clock that afternoon. Shaw sped up and down the line of the fleet, watching as his officers helped civilians up the freeway on-ramp. He offered encouragement wherever he could, and for the first time in quite a while, he saw smiles and an appearance of collective relief on the faces of the refugees he passed. They were here. They were finally getting out of this hellhole.

He coasted over to the on-ramp and looked over the side. He could see the street below and he guessed the water was about four feet deep.

"Come on," he said to the woman.

He climbed over the side, dropping into water that was up to his chest.

"Where are we going?" she asked.

The sound of her voice surprised him. He looked back at her.

"Ma'am, we have to leave here. There's a military checkpoint up at the top of this ramp. From there, to be honest, I don't know what will happen. But I do know that we have to leave now."

"What about my brother?"

He sighed. He'd known this moment was coming, but he hadn't wanted to think about it.

"They won't let you bring a dead body through the checkpoint. I'm sorry."

"You're sorry? You fucking asshole. This is my brother. I can't leave him here. I can't. I won't do that."

"Ma'am," he said, not unkindly, "I've brought you here to the way out. I can't make you go through it. That's gonna have to be your choice and yours alone. I know how hard this is. I understand."

"You understand? Bullshit. Don't patronize me. You don't understand shit."

His control almost broke. He could feel his anger rising. He could feel his mouth starting to tremble, the tears threatening. Shaw hadn't wanted to cry, not yet, and certainly not in public. He knew he would, eventually, but it would be on his own terms.

"I lost my son back at the shelter," he said.

That stopped her.

She sucked in a ragged-sounding breath and stared at him.

"It happened right before we got on the boats. He was bit by one of those zombies." Shaw made a vague gesture toward the holstered pistol on his hip. "I had to . . . it was really hard."

His hands were shaking. He closed his eyes and balled his hands into fists. When he looked back at the woman, there were tears streaking down her cheeks.

"You can go without him, or stay with him. I won't tell you which is best. To be honest, I don't know which is best. But I have a job to do, and right now, that's all I've got. Good luck to you."

And with that, he walked toward the ramp.

"Dad."

Shaw stopped. Anthony and Jesse were standing in the bow of their boat about twenty feet away. Both looked worried.

"I told you two to help get people through the checkpoint."

"I know, Dad. That's what I wanted to talk to you about. Can we talk?"

It was an intensely hot day. The air had taken on an almost tropical steaminess, and Shaw, who could feel the sun burning the back of his neck, was feeling irritable and tired.

"Make this quick," he said.

Anthony glanced at Jesse, who quickly looked away, then at his father. "We just came from up top. Dad, you should see it up there. It's crazy. All those people. And the military's only letting them through one at time. There's no order."

"Anthony," Shaw said, cutting him off, "say whatever it is you need to say, but don't stand there fucking jerking my chain. Speak plainly."

"Okay. All right, Dad. As crazy as it is up there, we think

this is our best chance to get out of here with the money. They're checking everybody over, making sure nobody's been infected, you know . . . but being who we are, we could get through there. With all that confusion up there, we could slip away and be five hundred miles from here by nightfall. What do you say, Dad? You give the word, we'll be out of here in no time."

Shaw looked down at his hands. They were still trembling.

Then he looked to the south, across hundreds of flooded homes. In the distance, he could see people coming. Not zombies, but people. Refugees, like the ones he had risked everything to bring to this spot. He saw them carrying the remnants of their lives on their backs, whole families made transient.

He listened. Above him, thousands of scared people were growing restless. A helicopter's rotors thrummed off into the distance.

He mopped a hand across his face, wiping the sweat from his eyes.

He found it difficult to put into words exactly what he was feeling. Right after his wife's funeral, after he was done with the etiquette of death, the inane process the living put themselves through to say good-bye to a life, he had gotten in his truck and driven north, eventually ending up on the shores of Lake Livingston. He had gone midway to Dallas for Christ's sake, with no idea what he was doing or why he was doing it.

So he'd stopped at the lake and gone down to the water's edge and looked out over a drab, November day. The horizon had been a watercolor smear of rain clouds, laced with threads of blue lightning.

He'd been thinking of Grace, and of duty. He'd hated her for dying, for abandoning her family, and he had hated himself because he knew how unfair he was being.

It was that same illogical hate that he was feeling now for

Anthony. It wasn't the boy's fault, and he knew it. To Anthony, who was so perfect in so many ways, these storms, these zombies, this horrible messed-up clusterfuck of a world, were just bumps in the road. He wasn't connected to anything, certainly not to the same sense of duty that governed Shaw's life, and for him, life would go on. There were no wounds to heal because nothing cut him very deeply. How could it, without a sense of duty?

"Anthony," Shaw said, "I want you to take those duffel bags and stash them somewhere safe. After that, you are to go topside and help get those people through the gate."

"But Dad—"

"Do not talk back to me!" Shaw exploded. "Don't you fucking dare. You hear me, Anthony? Don't you fucking talk back to me. Boy, I don't think you have the first fucking clue about what's important in life. Maybe I've failed you. Maybe I assumed that you were so talented you would know those things without me teaching them to you. If so, that's my fault. But I'm gonna rectify that right now."

He turned to Jesse.

"Jesse, I have no control over what you do. You're not mine. If you want to take your chances, if you want to abandon these people, go on. Take your share and get the fuck out."

Jesse swallowed hard.

"No, sir," he said. "I'll stay."

"Yeah, well, okay then," Shaw said. "Good. At least one of you has got some sense of what's important."

"Dad, come on. I—"

"No," Shaw said. "No. You shut the fuck up. I don't want to hear you speak right now. You will listen. You will keep your mouth closed. No son of mine is gonna creep away into the night like a thief. You got that? Your name is Shaw, and you will wear it proudly, for I worked hard to make it worth something. You hear me?"

"Yes, sir."

"Good. Now take those bags and stash them. Once you've done that, you get your ass topside and you do your duty. You have taken an oath, and you will live up to it. You will keep the charge that you have asked for."

He stared at them both, dared them to speak.

Neither one did.

"Better and better," he said. "Now get the fuck out of my sight."

Anthony waded over to a red Toyota pickup. He remembered what had happened back at Canal Street when the water receded from the Volkswagen in which they'd originally stashed the money, leaving it in plain sight.

He didn't want to take a chance like that again.

This pickup was hidden between a school bus and an overturned eighteen-wheeler. No one would find it unless they were looking for it, so he figured it was safe.

He popped the hood and put the duffel bags in with the engine. Then he waded back to the boat, and he and Jesse went to do their duty.

Captain Shaw walked up the freeway on-ramp and emerged onto the elevated deck of the Sam Houston Tollway. The noise and the stench of filthy people was almost too much. There were refugees as far as he could see. The road was packed with them. There were babies screaming. Injured people hobbling down the road as best they could. A few who couldn't walk moaned and begged for someone to help them, older people mostly. Others just stared off into the unknown distance, their faces drawn, their eyes wide and vacant. One man was muttering madly as he swatted at invisible bees around his head. "This is the end," he said.

"Gonna get us all. I know it. I know it." Children cried and clutched at their parents when they saw him. One father threatened to toss the lunatic over the side, and a few others grumbled in approval.

Shaw saw families with everything they owned stuffed into backpacks or wheelbarrows, or resting on top of doors they carried between them like stretchers. He was momentarily amazed at the number of little red wagons he saw. He didn't know they still made them. Anthony and Brent had one just like that when they were kids. He remembered pulling them around in it when they visited SeaWorld in San Antonio, and Brent . . . God, the kid had been crazy, wheeling down hills, his head thrown back while he screamed with delight. "Daddy, look at me! Weeeee!" The memory brought a smile, but it quickly faded.

He turned and looked out over the flooded city. He counted at least thirty towering columns of black smoke in the distance. Sunlight dappled on the water, making it look like liquid silver. And there was a smell, too. He hadn't really noticed it when he was down in the boats, but up here, the chemical stench and sewer smell of mud were overpowering.

In the near distance, he could see more refugees approaching the freeway. Few of them had boats, and the others were forced to swim, for the water was a good fifteen feet deep out there. He thought about sending some of his men out there with boats to pick them up, but he knew that wouldn't work. One of his officers, an older black patrolman named Garrity, was nearby, trying to help a woman with three crying kids find her missing son. Looking up and down the line of refugees, he could see his other officers were all trying to put out similar fires. They were every bit as exhausted as the people they were trying to help, and yet not one of them had quit. Not one of them had abandoned their post. Shaw was proud of his people. No one would be able to say that his men had shirked their duties.

A black kid of about sixteen waved Shaw down. "Hey man, how much longer they gonna make us wait? I'm fucking sick of standing in line."

"I have no idea how long you'll have to wait," Shaw told him.

"Yeah, well, you the fucking law, ain't you? Why don't you get up there and find out?"

Shaw just stared at the kid. He didn't even have the desire to go over and slap his face, which was what the kid needed. It was what his whole generation needed. It didn't matter if they were black or white or Mexican, they all grew up with a sense of entitlement that was sickening. Everybody owed them something. They assumed they could talk to the law the same way they talked to their friends because the world had gone soft and they knew it. Everything was tolerated because nobody was at fault.

And to think, this was the generation that was going to inherit a world full of zombies.

Humanity is gonna go extinct in less than twenty years, he thought bitterly. *With little pieces of shit like that kid at the helm, we're doomed.*

But like it or not, the kid had a point. The line didn't seem to be moving at all. People had dropped their backpacks and they were sitting on them, shading themselves from the midday sun with whatever they had available. They looked tired and irritable and supremely bored.

Shaw walked down the line, toward the gateway.

What he saw there was incredible. People were being led one by one into a sort of holding tank between two large chain-link fences that ran from one side of the road to the other. Soldiers in white plastic biohazard suits and gas masks pointed rifles at each refugee as they were led inside the holding area, stripped of every scrap of clothing they wore, and inspected from head to toe. If they refused to undress, they were turned away. There were no second chances, and no explanations were given. You either did as you were told the first time, without complaint, or you were turned away.

Shaw saw it happen twice.

One woman, whether out of vanity or her own sense of entitlement, refused. She demanded to speak to the officer in charge. The soldiers pushed her back through the gate, and when she turned to scream at them, they raised their weapons at her face and ordered her to back away. Stunned and speechless, she just stood there, crying.

Another woman was led inside. She had a dazed, drunken look about her. She was limping and coughing, shielding her eyes against the sunlight.

"Stop there," Shaw heard one of the soldiers say.

The woman did as she was told.

"Take off your clothes."

The woman hesitated, and Shaw heard a soldier give the order to push her back through the gate.

"No," she said, raising her palms at them in a gesture of surrender. "Okay."

She began to undress. She untucked her blouse and started to fumble with the buttons. She seemed to be having a great deal of difficulty. From the stiffness of her movements, Shaw guessed she'd been badly hurt, and recently too.

The woman wasn't making much progress on the buttons. She had to stop every few seconds to cough, and from the way she was swaying on her feet, Shaw thought she might fall over at any moment.

One of the soldiers gave an order Shaw couldn't hear, and another soldier came up behind her and yanked her blouse off. She wasn't wearing a bra, and she stood there, trembling, looking scared and small and helpless. Her back was laced with cuts and there was a large, festering wound between her shoulder blades that looked to Shaw to be a bite mark. The soldier who had pulled off her blouse turned her around to show the injury to his superior, and it was then that Shaw got a look at the woman's face. Her eyes had turned bloodshot and were lost in the black shadows that spread up from her cheeks. Her lips were cracked and pale, and when she coughed, he could see black bits of bloody phlegm fly out of her mouth.

The woman was changing right in front of him, becoming one of those zombies. Her hand had been across her breasts, but it was slipping away now. She shook her head, as though there were no-see-ums biting at her cheeks, but it was a dreamy sort of gesture and one she evidently couldn't control. She staggered once, righted herself, and began to moan. Slowly, laboriously, she turned toward the soldiers and raised her hands, clutching at them.

"Do it," Shaw heard one of the soldiers say, and the next instant, the woman's body was bouncing and jittering as the bullets slammed into her chest.

She landed on her butt, her shoulders sagging, arms limp at her side, her legs out in front of her like a child sitting on the grass. Her face was flecked with blood. Her mouth tried to move, but at that instant, the soldiers fired again and she was laid flat under a hail of automatic weapons fire.

At the same time, the sound of gunfire sent a wave of panic through the assembled refugees. People were screaming, running away from the gate, creating a backwards surge that collided with the others farther back in line, who were pushing forward to see what the commotion was all about.

Shaw watched people trample each other.

A man was thrown off the side of the highway.

Still others, in the drive to escape, were throwing punches at those who blocked them.

The soldiers, too, were on edge, for many of them spun around to face the crowd, their weapons up and ready.

"Cease fire!" Shaw screamed at the soldiers. "Stop it!"

He pulled his badge from his belt and held it up high as he advanced on the chain-link fence.

"Don't you dare shoot!" he said. "Lower your weapons. Put them down."

The soldiers didn't move. They were nervous. Even behind their gas masks, Shaw could tell they were green troops, not veterans. One of the soldiers pointed a trembling M-16 at him. Shaw slapped the chain-link fence and made the man jump.

"Lower your weapon. Now!"

The solder lowered his rifle a little, and looked around for someone to tell him what to do.

"You," Shaw said to the soldier. "Get your commanding officer up here right now. I need to talk to him. Move!"

The man took a few steps back and yelled, "Colonel Adams!"

A man on the far side of the second fence came forward.

"Sir," the soldier said, "I need you up here, Colonel."

Shaw waited as the man approached. Shaw's presence in front of the soldiers had eased the tension somewhat. No longer were refugees screaming in retreat. Many were keeping their distance, but all were turned his way, watching nervously. A few brave individuals even walked toward the gate, but the sight of the dead woman, her skull ruptured and her brains splattered across the pavement, kept them quiet.

Only the soldiers remained on edge. They kept their weapons trained on Shaw and on the crowd behind him.

The ranking officer stepped forward, suited and gas-masked like the others, and stood on the other side of the fence from Shaw.

"You the man in charge?" Shaw asked.

"That's right. I'm Dr. Robert Adams, U.S. Army Medical Research Institute of Infectious Diseases."

Shaw thought: *Active-duty man. That's good.*

But he also noticed the man referred to himself as doctor, and not colonel. Military doctors were like that. They didn't think of themselves as soldiers first and foremost, but as doctors who had to wear a uniform every once in a while.

He said, "Dr. Adams, this is not working."

"Who are you?" Adams said.

"My name is Mark Shaw. I'm the director of the Houston Police Department's Emergency Operations Command and the overall incident commander for the police department. I brought these refugees here so that—"

"Mr. Shaw, I appreciate—"

"No," Shaw said. "No, I don't want to hear your platitudes, Doctor. I'm telling you that we have to find a better way to get these people through. The water's deep out there right now, but when it gets dark, and the tide ebbs, we're going to get the infected swarming this area in droves. These people will be sitting ducks up here."

Adams crossed his arms over his chest, his plastic suit crinkling audibly.

"I have my orders, Mr. Shaw. This is the way my commanders have told me to get this thing done. We cannot allow any infected persons out of the city. The risk is too great."

"I'm not asking you to let any of the infected through," Shaw said, forcing himself to remain calm. A vision of Brent getting torn apart by those zombies flared up in his mind, but he forced that away, too. "I know how dangerous the infected are, Dr. Adams. We've been fighting them continuously for the last two days. All I'm asking you to do is help me find a way to help these people."

"That's what I'm trying to do," Adams said.

"Have you talked to them? Have you sent your men out of these gates to explain to them what's going on, what they'll be expected to do when they get up here?"

Adams hesitated, then said, "No, I haven't. But I'm not

going to send my men out there. I have orders about that, too."

"Okay," Shaw said. "I have officers out here. Let them do it."

"We can do that," Adams said. "Sure, we can allow that."

"Good. I'll bring several of my men up here. Can you get one of your officers to brief them? Once they know what to say, I'll send them down the line here."

"Absolutely."

"And Dr. Adams . . ."

"Yes."

"It would help these people a lot if you could feed them. Do you have any rations I could pass out?"

"Yes, we'll do that too. Is there anything else?"

"Yeah. When nightfall comes, things are gonna get ugly back there." He pointed over his shoulder, to the south. "Most of my men are out of ammunition. We need rifles and bullets."

"Oh, I don't know about that," Adams said. "My orders are—"

"Doctor, please. I'm begging you. At least help me give these people a fighting chance. I need rifles, ammunition, binoculars if you've got them, flashlights."

"I don't . . . It'll be just for your men, right? Not regular civilians."

"That's right."

Adams let out a long sigh. "Okay," he said, with the air of a man who is about to get himself fired. "I'll see what I can do."

"Thank you," Shaw said. "At this point, every little bit counts."

CHAPTER 17

Eleanor and her family didn't really get to know any of the Red Cross volunteers with whom they were traveling. There were passing comments made back and forth, the usual pleasantries between amicable strangers, and several of the women even complimented Eleanor on having such a beautiful daughter. But there was never more than that. They just never gelled. Eleanor and her family felt tacked on to the group, and not really part of it. She and Jim dealt mainly with Hank. He became the bridge between the two groups, and everybody seemed fine with that arrangement. There was a general understanding, after all, that they were together only until they got out of the city.

Still, Hank's relationship with the volunteers wasn't all that perfect either.

One of the volunteers, the ex-marine named Frank Miller who had been so helpful while they were escaping the Meadowlakes Business Park, seemed to rankle at Hank taking the leadership role. There were never any harsh words spoken between them, but Eleanor was a good judge of body language, and she could tell there was tension between the two men.

And judging from the fact that both were professional soldiers, trained to be leaders during combat situations, it wasn't hard to gauge the weather between them.

After they left the EOC Eleanor became acutely aware of the strained, tightly wound bearing the men had when in close company, the stiff, almost ritualistic civility between them.

Jim picked up on it, too.

Someone on the outside looking in, he said, would probably think them the best of buddies. Hank made it a point to solicit Frank's opinion on which way to go. Frank carried one of Hank's pistols, and sometimes, when zombies would emerge from the houses they passed, Hank would give the shot to Frank. They were like a talented first lieutenant and his grizzled, veteran platoon sergeant, trying desperately for the sake of their charges to make it look like everything was fine. Frank Miller, especially, tried to maintain a dignified air, but the resentment was there, the elephant in the room that nobody wanted to acknowledge.

Something had to give, and, around midday, it did.

Hank stopped the group for lunch. Frank approached him, and the two men paddled a short ways off, stopping their canoes under the covered drive-through awning of a Jack in the Box, arguing in hushed tones.

Afterwards, Hank didn't speak. He seemed to almost shrink up within himself. He spent a good thirty minutes watching the wilderness that the city had become. The vast expanse of the floodwaters seemed to hold him enthralled, and the deeply thoughtful bearing he assumed made him seem, to Eleanor at least, as darkly handsome as any man outside a movie had a right to look.

But by the time they resumed their course after lunch, Frank Miller and a few of the others were gone.

Eleanor thought Hank would lose it. Maybe, in his anger, he would yell at those who remained with him, demand to know if any of the others wanted to strike out on their own too.

But he didn't.

He remained oddly calm, almost stoic. And when it came time to move out, outwardly at least, he seemed the same old solidly reliable Hank Gleason, SWAT officer extraordinaire.

But when Eleanor tried to find out what happened, all he would say is: "They've gone."

Nothing more.

She never learned exactly what they'd argued about. And she never saw Frank Miller or any of the ones who left with him again.

They just disappeared into the flooded city, and it became one of the many unresolved questions that the Houston disaster created.

It was nearly eight o'clock when they made it to the Beltway. Dusk was settling over the city, throwing whole streets and the spaces between buildings into dangerous shadow. The water was receding, too, leaving behind the stink of chemicals and mud and rotted bodies. It wouldn't be long, Eleanor figured, before the vast sea that surrounded them would be shallow enough to allow the zombies easy movement. There would be trouble later.

But for now, there was work to do.

From the water, they could see the huge line of refugees waiting to pass through the military checkpoint. They could see boats of every description clustered around the on-ramps to the freeway. And, in the distance, they could see the wall the military was building around the city.

"What do you suppose they're doing?" Jim asked.

They were coasting up to the on-ramp now, looking for a way up.

"Medical screening, I guess," Eleanor answered.

"Because of the zombies."

"Well, yeah," she said.

"You think they have a cure or something?"

"I don't think they have a cure," she said.

She pointed over to the far side of the Beltway. There were several bodies, perhaps six or seven in all, together in a heap. Even from a distance she could tell they'd been shot multiple times.

"Oh," he said. "Wow."

"Yeah, I know. I just can't believe it's come to this."

The group slid up to the freeway on-ramp and climbed out of their canoes. Eleanor helped Madison into her backpack and then turned around so Jim could help her with hers. It was the last real intimate family moment they had, for at that moment Hank came up to her and asked her what she wanted to do. She understood right then that he was relinquishing his role as leader. He had got them this far, shepherded them through the war zone, and now it was her turn to lead. She was a police supervisor again.

The group of volunteers gathered around them. Eleanor watched their faces, and she could tell they were waiting for her to tell them what to do.

"Well, this is it," she said. "Once we get up top we're going to have to fit in to whatever plan the military has got in place. I don't know what that's gonna be, but I'm pretty sure they're going to need some help on this side of the checkpoint. I can't make you guys do anything, though. You don't work for me. If you want to get in line with everyone else, I understand."

"We came down here to help," one of the men said.

Several of the others spoke up in agreement. Nobody, as far as Eleanor could tell, was ready to quit.

"If there's something for us to do up there," another man said. "We'll do it. We're in it for keeps."

"Excellent," she said, and sincerely meant it. They were

quite a crew, these Red Cross volunteers, and at that moment she regretted not taking the time to get to know them better. These people had backbone. "Okay, then, if you guys are ready."

They nodded back at her, and she put an arm around Madison's shoulder and together they walked up the on-ramp.

But when they reached the top of the ramp and saw the line of refugees and the barely restrained bedlam of wailing babies and sick, scared people and the occasional fighting, Eleanor's confidence wavered.

"Oh my God," one of the volunteers said.

Eleanor saw an older black officer she recognized from the EOC and asked him to bring her up to speed. He explained that Captain Shaw was up front, where the military was feeding people through the medical checkpoint one at a time. The remaining officers from the EOC—and Eleanor gasped when he told her there were only six of them left— were working up and down the line, trying to keep order, finding lost kids, answering questions.

"They want us looking for people who might be infected, too," he said, and gestured uneasily toward his rifle.

"Please tell me you're joking," she said. "They expect you to . . ."

"It's already happened a couple of times. Not in my section, but it's happened. I've got my eye on about twenty different folks in my area. Hopefully, they're okay, but I got my doubts."

"This is insane," Eleanor said.

"Yes, ma'am," the officer agreed. "It is at that."

"Where'd you say Captain Shaw was again?"

The officer gestured toward the checkpoint.

"Okay," she said. "I appreciate it."

"Uh, ma'am . . ."

"Yes?"

He pointed toward Jim and Madison.

"Ma'am, if you don't mind me saying, you should probably get your family set up somewhere over here in my section. I can get them worked in without creating too much of a hassle."

Eleanor smiled.

"I appreciate that officer, but I can't do that. It wouldn't be fair."

"Ma'am," he said. "You don't understand. It's taking them about twenty minutes per person to get these folks through that checkpoint up there, and as you can see . . ." He gestured toward the back of the line. It stretched at least a mile down the length of the elevated roadway. There were literally thousands of people waiting back there. "With the sun going down and low tide coming, those zombies are gonna be storming our location. And I don't how long we can hold 'em off. Most of those people back there, they're probably not gonna live to see the morning."

Eleanor looked back at Jim and Madison, her gaze lingering on her daughter. The girl was dripping wet. It made her seem too skinny, too small, too fragile.

"Ma'am," the officer said, "this ain't no time to be playing fair."

Eleanor nodded.

"Thank you," she said. "I'm sorry, I'm terrible with names."

"Garrity," he said. His smile was kind—exhausted, but kind.

"Thank you, Garrity. I mean it, thank you." Eleanor turned to Jim and Madison. "I want you guys to go with him. He's gonna set you up with a place here."

"Mommy, no!"

"Where are you gonna be?" Jim asked her.

"It's okay," Eleanor said to Madison. "I'm gonna be right here in this area. I'll come by as often as I can and check in. You just go with Daddy, okay?"

"But Mommy, I don't want to get separated."

"We won't be," Eleanor said. "I promise. I'll be right here. No matter what happens, I'll be here with you. I love you, Madison. We will not get separated. Okay?"

She kissed Madison on the forehead and hugged her. Then she kissed Jim and handed him her backpack and watched as Garrity led them over to the line.

Jim turned to wave, then put his arm around Madison and sat her down on top of their backpacks.

Eleanor went up to the front of the line.

Captain Shaw was standing near the gate with a bullhorn in his hand. Eleanor saw armed soldiers in space suits hosing down a naked man inside a chain-link cage while other space-suited soldiers—doctors, she figured—circled around him, discussing him like they would a show pony up for auction.

Suddenly, nothing felt real. It was too weird, too alien, like some kind of science-fiction movie.

"Sergeant Norton," Shaw said, and gestured her over to him. "I'm glad to see you made it."

"Thank you, sir. You too." She hesitated, unsure of exactly how much to say. Finally, she said, "We went by the EOC. I saw Brent, sir. I'm sorry."

He didn't even miss a beat. He dismissed her condolences with a casual wave of his hand and said, "We've all lost somebody. But right now, we got a job to do."

"Yes, sir," she said.

"There's an Army doctor over there named Captain Miguel Hernandez. He's the one supervising the physicals. He'll give you a briefing about how this is working and what you need to tell these people. Once you get your briefing, get a rifle and a flashlight, and start walking up and down the Beltway here. Just make sure our people are doing okay. If they've got any problems, do what you can for them."

"I talked to Garrity back there. He said that they're supposed to shoot any of the refugees who might be infected."

"That's right. If they see anybody who's been infected

they're supposed to offer that person a chance to leave, but none of them do. They try to argue. No one wants to be left behind."

"And so we're shooting them?"

"If it comes to that."

"What if we're wrong? What if they're not infected?"

He looked at her, and in that moment she was stunned by how much he'd aged. He seemed to have hardened. That was the only word to describe it. It had been little more than two days since she'd seen him last, but in that time, he'd grown cold and distant. He was, she knew, bearing a huge burden, but she'd had no idea just how heavy that cross really was until just now. Captain Mark Shaw was a changed man.

"If we're wrong, we're wrong," he said. His eyes were nested in webs of deep wrinkles and full of exhaustion. "Our job is to make a decision," he said. "Right or wrong, you make a decision. If it turns out to be the wrong one, so be it. But I would rather you be wrong than stand there looking lost and indecisive. Now go on. It's getting dark."

"Captain?"

"What is it, Sergeant?"

"Sir, I have about two dozen Red Cross volunteers with me. Do you mind if I use them to relieve some of our officers?"

"No, I don't want that. Let them back up the officers if they want to, but the officers themselves stay on duty. I need men I can trust with their weapons ready." He put a hand on her shoulder, and for just a second, the tough veneer mellowed a bit. "Now, go on, Eleanor. Help me out, okay?"

She carried out her orders. The Army briefed her, gave her an M-16 and a flashlight, and sent her on her way.

She left the checkpoint feeling stunned and overwhelmed. Her head was pounding, her heart going a mile a minute in her chest. So many questions swirled in her head. So much had happened, and there were so many answers yet to find.

She felt disconnected, uncertain about the future, and she wandered over to the edge of the freeway and looked out across the city. The light was failing fast. Already the distance was lost in darkness. Closer in, the glare from the lights illuminating the military's checkpoint spilled over onto the wrecked cars and buildings nearest the roadway, casting them in a bluish haze.

A figure was moving out there.

Eleanor leaned forward, and squinted into the darkness. At first she wasn't sure, but then the man turned slightly, as if he was checking to see if anyone was following him, and at that point she was certain.

"Anthony Shaw," she muttered. "What the hell are you doing?"

He was supposed to be up here with the rest of the officers, helping out. What did he think he was doing? And why did he look so paranoid?

As she watched, he picked his way through the obstacles in the water until he reached a pickup between two larger vehicles. Eleanor heard yelling behind her, and made a quick backwards glance. More fighting, she saw. When she looked back toward the water, she thought she'd lost Anthony, but he reappeared at the front of the pickup the next instant and was raising the hood.

Really curious now, Eleanor leaned forward some more. Most of the pickup was obscured behind the body of a school bus, but she could see just enough to realize he was pulling two duffel bags out of the engine compartment.

"What the . . . ?"

He opened one of the duffel bags and looked inside. Eleanor couldn't see what he was looking at, but evidently Anthony was satisfied with what he saw, for he zipped the duffel bag closed again and put it back in the engine compartment of the pickup.

She wondered if they were the same duffel bags she'd

seen him pull out of that Volkswagen the previous night, and
it seemed like they probably were.

"I wonder . . ." she said.

Eleanor walked down the on-ramp and stopped at the
water's edge. She hadn't, she realized, thought this through.
She couldn't exactly take a boat over there. A motorboat
would make too much noise. Even a canoe would attract
undue attention. And besides, what if she was getting all curious over nothing? She had a backpack for herself, after all.
Every member of her family had one. What if Anthony Shaw
was using the duffel bags to stash his MREs and first-aid kit,
same as her? What if he had old family photo albums in
there?

"Yeah, right," she said aloud. There was no way. If it
looks suspicious, that's because it is suspicious. "You're up
to something, Anthony Shaw."

There was no more hesitation. She walked into the water,
which had receded to the point where it was a few inches
below her hips now, and waded through floating trash and
driftwood toward the cluster of vehicles where Anthony
Shaw had been doing his thing.

The halogen lights from the military checkpoint threw a
blue circle of light onto the water, and she skirted around it.
No sense in giving her position away if she didn't have to.

And that was probably what saved her life, for at that moment she heard the pickup's hood snap shut.

She froze, looked around.

There was no where to hide. She could hear him splashing as he moved around the front of the big rig between
them, and she had nowhere to go. Another second and they'd
be face-to-face.

For a second she considered playing it off. She had seen
something from the freeway but wasn't sure what. She came

down to investigate. And what exactly are you doing out
here, Patrolman Shaw? Did you see something, too?

But in the same instant she knew that wouldn't work.
He'd never buy it.

And if he is up to something, she thought, *he'll kill me.*

The splashing was getting louder, and so she did the only
thing she could. She dropped down into the water and held
her breath and prayed he hadn't seen or heard her. This had
been a grassy field before the flood. She gripped a handful
of St. Augustine and held on, uncertain how long she could
do this. Certainly not long enough to wait for him to pass by.

Gotta get behind him, she thought.

She swam toward the big rig. Maybe, if she was lucky
enough, she'd come up close enough to the rig that she could
use it as concealment. It had been, what, about sixty feet
from her when she went under? She could do that.

Except that she didn't dare open her eyes under this
water. With all the chemicals and trash and oil and God
knew what else floating around in it, she didn't dare. She
was probably taking twenty years off her life just by swimming in it.

That is, if Anthony Shaw didn't get her first.

Luckily, she didn't swim headfirst into anything. She'd
felt the grass give way to asphalt beneath her, which meant
she was lucky. She could have hit a guardrail or a drainage
pipe or anything. She could have cut herself up pretty bad.
But luckily that didn't happen.

She swam until it felt like her lungs were going to burst,
and then she slowly rose from the water, wiped it from her
eyes, and opened them.

She was about ten feet from the rig.

Anthony Shaw was just a dim shape receding into the
night. He, too, was skirting the blue circle of lamp light, and
that little observation convinced her she'd been right to be
cautious. He was up to something.

And this was her chance to find out what.

She slid back under the cover of the big rig and watched him go up the on-ramp. Concealed in darkness, she waited until he got to the top of the ramp. He glanced back, scanning the area around the trucks, just as she knew he would, and then went back to his duties on the elevated part of the Beltway.

When he was gone, she went over to the pickup, reached through the busted-out driver's side window, and popped the hood.

The two black duffel bags were jammed into the narrow space between the fan belts and the radiator. She had difficulty pulling them loose, because he had really wedged them down in there, but eventually they came. She rested one on top of the engine and zippered it open.

It took her a moment to process exactly what she was looking at.

It took her a moment to process exactly *how much* cash she was looking at.

"Jesus," she said. "Oh Jesus."

Nervously, she glanced back toward the freeway, scanning the retaining wall as if it was the guard tower of a prison and she an escaping con.

"Holy crap," she muttered.

Again she wondered how much money she was looking at. There were bundles of what appeared to be twenties and fifties and hundreds wrapped up in tightly sealed bricks. She'd seen heroin shipped like this, layer upon layer of cellophane strapped down with duct tape. The bags were wet, but the money looked dry as a bone. Whoever wrapped this money up, she realized, knew it would have to sit in the water for a few days.

And then she remembered when she had first seen Anthony Shaw with these duffel bags. She tried to play back in her mind the buildings around them. The Texas Chemical

Bank was right there on the corner of Canal and Lockwood, less than half a block away. Anthony Shaw had been there with his brother, Brent, and some other guy that she hadn't recognized.

And now Brent Shaw was dead.

She looked back at the retaining wall at the edge of the freeway.

"What exactly are you up to?" she said.

Thinking of the possibilities made her angry.

When she first came to Sex Crimes as a brand-new detective, Eleanor's lieutenant had called her into his office to welcome her aboard the good ship Perversion, as her fellow detectives not-so-lovingly referred to the unit.

Entering the office she'd seen little porcelain birds all over the walls and on his desk. And not realistic ones, either, but cutesy ones painted in pastel colors, soft pinks and greens and blues, adorable little smiles on their cartoon faces.

"I collect them," he said proudly. "Been doing it since I was in high school."

"Wow," she'd said, "that's kind of gay."

The words were out before she quite knew what she was saying. She regretted them instantly. But they couldn't be called back.

And so had begun her awkward stay in Sex Crimes.

But the incident was typical for Eleanor Norton, who had a way of saying and doing things before she truly thought them through.

She was doing that now.

She had both duffel bags in her hands. They weren't that heavy, which had surprised her at the time, but the thought slipped away and was forgotten as she walked up the on-ramp, looking for Anthony Shaw.

Eleanor found him standing near a broken-down Ford Econoline van, watching the line of refugees, many of whom were sleeping or playing cards or just sitting on their stuff, looking off into the distance at something only they could see.

"Officer Shaw, I need a word with you."

He turned around. He had an expression on his face as if all of this was putting him out, as if it was a big giant waste of his time. But then he saw the duffel bags in her hands and his eyes went wide.

"What is this?" she demanded.

He was nervous, she could tell that. He was scared, in fact. But he moved quickly, too quickly for Eleanor to react.

He crossed the roadway saying, "Ma'am, I can explain that. It's not what you think. That stuff is from my house. It's our life savings."

He put his hands on her shoulders and guided her around to the back of the Ford van. She was out of sight of the other refugees and the Red Cross volunteers before she quite realized what was happening. Just like that, he had taken her out of view of everyone, and now here she was, alone with him.

"Let me go," she said.

She backed up.

He took a few steps toward her, his hands still reaching for her.

"You stole this money," she said. "You're nothing but a common looter."

"No!" he said, sharply. He stepped closer. "That's not true. That money is my family's life savings."

She read his body language. He was like a cat about to pounce. He had that same predatory look in his eyes. Eleanor turned, suddenly terrified, and was about to run when she felt his hands on the back of her blouse, clutching at her.

"Let me go!" she screamed.

He yanked back on her blouse, slinging her up against the side of the van with a loud crash of dented metal. The impact knocked the air from her lungs and made her vision turn momentarily purple. When it cleared, he had his hand clasped around her throat, squeezing.

"Drop the bags," he snarled. "Right now."

He was constricting her air flow. She could feel her throat threatening to collapse under his grip, but before that happened she managed to gasp out, "You're a thief." She brought her knee up, aiming for his groin, but he was too quick for her, and she only managed to graze his knee.

He shoved her back against the side of the van and threw three hard punches to her gut. She doubled over onto her hands and knees, unable to breathe, and had just enough time to realize he was moving around to the side of her before he grabbed her by her hair and turned her face toward him.

He punched her twice in the mouth and she collapsed onto the pavement.

Then he straddled her chest and punched her twice more in the face.

But the next instant he was off her.

What had just happened? Why did he stop? She could barely see. It felt as if he'd knocked her head out of whack. She couldn't think. She couldn't control her hands. Using her elbows she managed to push herself up. All she saw were blurry shapes.

But the voice she recognized.

It was Jim, calling her name.

"No," she murmured.

It was the only sound she could get out. Her lips felt like they'd been smashed. Dimly, she became aware of a long rope of bloody spit hanging from her mouth.

But the next instant, she was looking up at Anthony Shaw's back. Jim was right in front of him, trying to pull Anthony out from behind the van. He was no match for Anthony, though, who came in hard and fast and threw three powerful jabs right into Jim's mouth. Anthony followed the jabs with two big upper cuts to Jim's solar plexus, and that dropped Jim down to his knees.

Eleanor felt as if she were moving through a dream. No matter how hard she tried to stand, her body just wouldn't obey. She watched Anthony move in, so that he was standing over Jim. She saw Jim look up at Anthony and try futilely to block as Anthony slammed an elbow down on the bridge of his nose.

Jim collapsed into a heap.

Anthony took a step back, reached into his pocket, and pulled out a big black tactical knife.

Eleanor heard it click as he unfolded it to its full length. The knife was curved, at least five inches long, with wicked serrations down the length and an edge that gleamed, even in the dark.

She shook her head.

Her pistol, she thought. She had to reach her pistol.

But at that moment a shrieking scream pierced the night. Anthony Shaw folded the knife over, hiding behind his wrist. Eleanor looked past him, and to her horror, saw Madison standing in the middle of the road, about twenty feet away, screaming for someone to help her parents.

"No," Eleanor groaned. "Don't hurt her. Run, Madison. Run!"

Her voice was barely a whisper. Her vision was hazy, blurred. She wasn't sure what exactly she heard or saw, but she thought she heard people yelling and shots fired. It was hard to tell, because the blood was roaring in her ears. She felt like she was going to faint, and the last thing she remembered was the sight of Madison screaming for someone to help her parents as Anthony ran . . .

* * *

. . . out from behind the van, holding both duffel bags in his fists. The fucking little girl was still screaming at him, but he didn't have time for that right now. He didn't have time for Sergeant Norton and her husband, either. There was no time, because in the two minutes he'd been behind that van, the refugee line had erupted into a full-blown riot.

Looking to his left, Anthony saw Garrity down on his knees, wrestling with a man and a woman. The next instant, the woman lunged at Garrity, knocked him onto his back, and took an enormous bite out of his throat.

Anthony's eyes went wide.

He took a step that way, but stopped. There was no time for that, either. It was down to the wire now. He had to find his father, find Jesse, and get the fuck out of this god-forsaken city.

But people were running everywhere, screaming, fighting with each other. There were others staggering slowly through the crowd, and Anthony could tell at a glance that they were infected. He counted six, nine, fourteen of them. Then more to his right.

"What in the hell just happened?" he muttered.

He pulled his pistol and started moving forward, looking for his dad.

He found Jesse instead.

Jesse was fighting with two zombies near the checkpoint. As Anthony approached, he saw Jesse break away from them, take a few steps back, and open fire with his M-16, dropping them instantly.

"Jesse!"

"Holy shit! Where have you been?" Jesse shouted at him. "Dude, your dad's been looking everywhere for you." Then Jesse noticed the duffel bags. "What are you doing with those?"

"We got to get out of here," Anthony said. "Where'd my dad go?"

"He got some night-vision goggles from the Army. He was looking out over the city over there and saw a shitload of those zombies coming this way. That's when he started yelling for you. Dude, where were you?"

"Getting these. Where is he now?"

"All hell broke loose back there," Jesse said, pointing down the length of the refugee line. "He went that way."

Anthony looked down the Beltway. From where he stood, he could see three on-ramps along its length. There were zombies coming up each of them, driving the refugees into a high panic. They were stuck, nowhere to run. The few officers posted along the line were laying down a steady stream of gunfire, their muzzle flashes like torches in the night, but Anthony knew they were doomed.

"My God," he said. Then he turned to Jesse. "Okay, dude, we gotta go right now."

"What about your dad?"

"He knows how to take care of himself."

"Seriously? You're gonna leave him here. He wouldn't leave you."

"Bullshit. The whole reason for doing this was to be able to start over once we get out of here. We can't do that without the money. Now come on. Let's get the fuck out of here."

Jesse looked around uncertainly.

"Okay. Where are we gonna go?"

He pointed back to the nearest on-ramp.

"We can't go that way."

"Through the checkpoint."

Before Jesse could object, Anthony took off running toward the checkpoint. Behind them, the riot had risen to a horrendous din of screams and moans and gunfire. Ahead of them, the refugees were surging forward, pressing up against the chain-link fence separating them from freedom. Through the huddle of bodies, Anthony saw the space-suited soldiers backing up, raising their rifles to their shoulders.

"No!" he screamed, but even as he yelled the bullets started flying. Those closest to the fence were nearly sawed in half. Those behind turned and ran, screaming even as they were shot in the back.

Anthony and Jesse were caught up among them, Anthony using his M-16 as a battle hatchet, swinging it back and forth to knock the panicked crowd out of his path. And then, suddenly, there was nothing between his position and the soldiers behind the fence but open ground and quite a few dead bodies.

Anthony saw three soldiers lower their weapons slightly.

"I'm a police officer," he yelled at them. "We're not infected. Open the gate!"

Another space-suited figure stepped forward and Anthony heard him give the order to fire.

"No!" Anthony shouted.

The soldiers raised their rifles again and opened fire. Anthony hit the ground and rolled over by a dead man who had come to rest on his side. He could feel the dead man's body jittering as the bullets smacked into him. He kept down, yelling for Jesse to do the same. But when he rolled over onto his side to look for Jesse, he saw his friend facedown on the pavement, eyes and mouth open, with a puddle of blood spreading out from beneath his chest.

"No," Anthony said. "No!"

But Jesse didn't move. His sightless eyes just stared at Anthony, like a blank accusation.

"No, Jesse. Oh shit, man. No."

Anger flared up in him and he rolled over onto his belly, the barrel of the M-16 resting on the dead man's thighs. He flipped the selector switch to automatic and opened fire on the soldiers. Two of them went down. A third dived onto his belly. Two of the men who had been doing the medical inspections ran for the back gate. Anthony sighted in on their backs and fired, dropping them both.

He glanced over the dead man's legs and saw more soldiers coming up fast from the far side. *Shit*, he thought. *Gotta move.*

He looked back toward the city and saw a crowd of the infected coming toward him. He was caught in the middle with nowhere to run.

"My ass," he said.

Slowly, he inched his way over to the duffel bags and wrapped the straps around his fist. He took a few quick breaths, jumped to his feet, and started firing at the soldiers as he ran for the retaining wall at the edge of the roadway.

The next instant he was the over the edge and falling feet-first into the blackness of the water below.

"Mom."

Eleanor groaned.

"Mom, please wake up."

Eleanor groaned again: *Stop it. Hurts.*

Madison shook her even harder.

"Mom, please get up!"

"Madison?" Eleanor blinked. Her vision was blurry and her head felt as if it were about to collapse in on itself. What in the hell had Anthony Shaw done to her? "Madison, stop shaking me."

"Mom, please, we have to go right now. Those things, they're everywhere."

Eleanor groaned. With Madison's help she managed to sit up, but everything hurt. The right side of her face was sizzling with pain, as if she'd pressed it to a hot skillet. Jim was rolling on his side a few feet away. His face looked bad, his shirt soaked in blood, his eyes black and swollen. Eleanor's mind was floating free, unable to focus, and looking at her husband she had a crazy, almost hilarious flash of Rocky Balboa in his corner, a battered man staring across the ring.

"Eleanor . . ." he said, reaching a trembling hand toward her.

"Mom, please, I need you to get up. There are zombies—"

But the words were clipped away by an ear-piercing scream. Madison was on her feet now, pointing at the blurry figure who had stumbled around the front bumper of the van.

Eleanor blinked at it, and an apparition from a horror show came into focus. The man was blood-streaked. His clothes were filthy and hanging off him in strips. His hair was dark with blood, one of his eyes gouged out and oozing gore. Part of his lips had been torn away. The one remaining eye leered at them with a bloodshot combination of murderous hate and numb emptiness, rolling in its socket as he raised his shredded hands and clutched at them.

"Mom, get your gun!" Madison screamed.

Eleanor rolled over, groping at the pavement around her. There was no gun. She tried to tell Madison that, but the girl wouldn't stop yelling. Then Madison was pushing Eleanor over on her side, up against the retaining wall.

"Hey, what are you . . ."

"Get up, Mom!"

Eleanor felt something slide underneath her. She looked down, and in her disconnected haze she saw Madison standing up with a rifle in her hands.

"No . . ." Eleanor said.

But Madison was already firing, the gun jumping in her hands. A three-round burst erupted from the barrel, and Madison fell backwards against the van, the gun still pointed at where the zombie had been.

The rattle of gunfire cleared Eleanor's head. She looked at the zombie, dead now, flat on his back, the top of his head blown off, and then back at her daughter. Madison was breathing hard, the air coming in big, heaving gulps. Her eyes were wide, staring at the dead man, her mouth open in terror that was slowly giving way to triumph.

"Mom, did you see that?

She turned to Eleanor, inadvertently pointing the M-16's barrel at her.

"Whoa, whoa, whoa!" Eleanor said, and grabbed the barrel and pointed it in a safe direction. "Yeah, baby, I saw it. Good job. Here let me have that."

Eleanor took the M-16 and turned its selector switch to single fire. Rising painfully to her feet she turned and fired at the four zombies who had stumbled around the back of the van. Then she turned back to the front and fired twice more. But she might as well have tried to stop a cattle stampede with a police whistle. There were zombies coming around both sides of the van now, and the three of them were trapped. Eleanor looked to the top of the van, but knew that wouldn't work for long. And that only meant one thing.

"Jim," she said, "can you go over the side?"

Long ropes of blood hung from his nose and chin. One ear had a nasty case of road rash where Anthony Shaw had dragged him over the pavement. But through the swollen bruises, his eyes were clear and bright.

He stood up and leaned over the side. "The water's not that deep," he said, "but it's only about a twenty-foot drop."

"Go," she said.

Without saying another word, he put his chest on the top of the retaining wall and rolled over.

Eleanor heard him splash.

"Jim?"

"I'm okay," he said. "Send Madison down."

"Go, baby. Hurry!"

To her credit, Madison didn't hesitate. She put her hands on the wall and was about to hurdle it when she stopped, scooped up her backpack, and jumped.

"I got her," Jim called up. "We're okay. Hurry, Eleanor!"

The zombies were closing in on both sides of her now, less than five feet away. Their moaning had reached a frenzied, urgent pitch. Their hands reached for her. She turned to face the retaining wall, and looked down. It seemed like a million miles.

"God help us," she said, and took a breath and jumped.

CHAPTER 18

Right before she let go from the retaining wall, Eleanor saw the water below writhing with bodies. She hit the water hard and went under. The next instant there were hands all over her and she screamed, slapping them away. She spun around, teeth clenched, fists raised, and barely recognizing the faces of her battered husband and her daughter as they grabbed at her.

"Behind you, Mom!"

Eleanor turned.

The water was full of zombies. Four of them were already wading toward her, less than ten feet away. She let Jim and Madison pull her back as she scrambled to get the shoulder strap of her M-16 off her arm.

"Come on, Mom! Hurry!"

The screams of the dying filtered down from above them. People were running, leaning over the retaining wall, yelling for help. The rattle of gunfire was nearly constant. A military helicopter raced overhead, a dim shape, like a dark, gigantic bird against a black sky. And sounding above it all were the zombies in the water, moaning with a fevered intensity that was deafening. Eleanor looked around and realized there were hundreds of zombies closing in on the refugees who had fallen from the Beltway, and the thought occurred to her that this must be what it felt like to be caught in the middle of a swarm of sharks in a feeding frenzy.

She heard an ear-piercing scream.

She turned and saw a woman get the flesh stripped from her body by a huddling mass of the infected.

For a second, all Eleanor could do was stand there and gawk at the sight of that woman wailing in pain and fear, and she was hardly aware of Jim putting his hands under her shoulders and lifting her from the water until she was most of the way into the boat he had found.

Eleanor dropped down into a cushioned bench seat, still staring at the woman. Madison was shaking her shoulders, pleading with her to snap out of it.

"I'm okay," Eleanor said. She grabbed Madison's forearms and steadied herself. "Really, I'm okay."

Jim was already kneeling over the outboard, getting it started.

The motor roared to life.

"Hold on to something," he said, and fed the throttle and turned them away from the thickest part of the zombie crowd.

"Where are we going?" Eleanor asked him.

He pointed underneath the Beltway. In the distance, Eleanor could see forty or fifty boats heading toward the military's chain-link fence. Several of the smaller boats were already approaching the tangled rolls of concertina wire and large metal crosses in front of the fence, and it looked to Eleanor as if they were going to ram the fence and punch their way through.

Eleanor held her breath, waiting to see what would happen.

But she was unprepared for the sudden, blinding light that filled the night from the other side of the fence. Power-

ful spotlights hit the water and turned the boats and their oc-
cupants to silhouettes. Beyond the lights, Eleanor could see
the outlines of several Coast Guard vessels spaced along the
fence line. She heard harsh voices amplified through bullhorns, ordering the refugee boats to turn back.

None of them did.

She knew exactly what was going to come next, but the
fierce mechanical surge of .50-caliber machine-gun fire still
took her by surprise.

In the glare of the spotlights she saw the first volley turn
four of the lead vessels into airborne splinters.

There was a momentary pause, and then the orders came
again.

"Fire! All boats, fire, fire, fire!"

Soon the gunners were firing at will, tearing up the boats
and survivors and zombies with indiscriminate abandon.
The big black helicopter that had been circling them since
before they jumped from the Beltway stopped almost directly over the Coast Guard boats and fired rockets into the
water, turning it into a raging lake of orange flames.

Through the glare of the spotlights and the flames and the
smoke, Eleanor could see the helicopter rocking back, its
nose pointed at the elevated roadway above them.

"Jim!" she shouted. "Turn us around. Get us out of here!"

But he was doing it already. The little wooden boat they
were in sucked down into the water as they turned, and then
rose on the crest of the wake wave as they accelerated.

Eleanor kept looking over her shoulder, and when the
rockets erupted from the helicopter, she threw Madison
down to the deck and covered her with her body. Shrieking
missiles thudded into the roadway above them, the explosions shaking the boat and deafening Eleanor's ears. Bits of
flaming concrete rained down into the water all around
them. Drifts of sparks swirled in the air. And though it lasted
only a moment, Eleanor could have sworn she heard the

flaming bodies screaming as they tumbled down from the
collapsing highway.

She pulled herself up onto her elbows.

Eleanor felt stunned by the concussive blast she'd just en-
dured, as though she were standing under a bell jar with the
world swirling all around her.

She turned Madison over and saw the fear and the blind
panic in her daughter's eyes. "Are you okay, Madison?" she
asked, unable to hear her own voice.

Madison nodded slowly.

Slowly, the silence in Eleanor's ears was replaced by a
painful ringing. She stood up, put her daughter on one of the
bench seats, and turned to look at the burning, groaning
Beltway as it collapsed into the water.

This must be how Lot's wife felt, she thought, *right before
she turned to a pillar of salt.*

And like Lot's wife, she found she was unable to turn
away from the destruction, the beautiful, horrific, world-
ending destruction, even as her husband called her name.

Half an hour passed.

They floated aimlessly through the decimated buildings
and the homes that listed in the water like wrecked boats
along a forgotten coast. Zombies staggered out of doorways
and slapped bloody hands on the fences, trying to reach
them. Eleanor sat ready in the bow of the boat, watching
them with the M-16 resting in her lap. She had a fully loaded
magazine in the breach, and three more in a pouch she wore
in a bandolier across her chest, but she knew those wouldn't
last long. If they got cornered, or caught in a stand-up fight,
she could burn through all four magazines in the blink of an
eye. So she watched the silhouettes separate from the darkness with a weary eye, determined to shoot only if they got
too close.

Behind her, Madison was crying softly. Over and over again, she kept muttering "Where are we gonna go? What's gonna happen to us?"

It was the paradox of parenting again, the question that had been hounding her since that first evening before Hurricane Hector, when the two of them had sat on the kitchen floor, laying by supplies. She both wanted to soothe her daughter's fear, hold her tight and comfort her, and at the same time slap the ever-loving shit out of her for making so much noise. Playing to her better nature, Eleanor tried to soothe her. But she couldn't answer Madison's questions, no matter how hard she tried. Madison was too frightened, too damaged by what she had seen, and mere words wouldn't compensate for that.

Years before, as a rookie patrol officer, Eleanor had responded to a family disturbance involving a married couple in their fifties. No sooner had she stepped through the door than the drunken husband started yelling at her, complaining of everything from his wife's addiction to heroin, to the bank foreclosing on his home, to the HPD's continuing efforts to frame his son for robbery. The man had asked her what he was supposed to do to fix his life, and Eleanor, who was stunned by the idea of a man twice her age asking her how to run his life, had said: "How the hell should I know? I'm twenty-five years old. What do I know about living?"

She was thirty-five now, a mother herself, a mother with a litany of troubles far beyond anything she could have imagined way back then, and yet she still didn't have any answers. Life, she realized, really was a junkyard tumbling down a staircase. Things happened without justification, without closure. There was no grand design, no pattern. None that she could see anyway. Every day, as Sheryl Crow so eloquently put it, was a winding road. She wished she could tell Madison that in a way that would save her the trouble of having to learn it herself, but she knew that was impossible. Like coming of age, it was something Madison would have to learn for herself. No one could do it for her.

Her mind was still chasing the rabbit around that same mental race track when they rounded a corner and glided up on Anthony Shaw, who was standing in the back of a small metal fishing boat, kicking the outboard motor as if it had just called his mother a dirty whore.

"Fucking piece of shit!" he roared at it, and kicked it again.

He yanked the pull cord and nothing happened.

"Goddamned fucking piece of shit!" he said, and gave it yet another kick. Then he stood up and ran his fingers through his hair. He dropped his hands down to his side and balled them into fists. He was standing that way, stiff with anger, when he seemed to sense a presence behind him.

Slowly, he turned around.

Eleanor was standing in the front of her boat, her M-16 leveled at him.

"Don't move," she said.

He just laughed at her.

"Jim, the light."

Their boat had a handheld spotlight mounted next to the motor. Jim fumbled with it, but managed to get the beam pointed at Anthony Shaw.

Anthony raised one hand to shield his eyes, but he said nothing.

In the glare of the spotlight's beam, Eleanor could see the two black duffel bags on the bench in front of Anthony.

"You stole that money, Officer Shaw."

"I told you. This is my family's life savings."

"You're a thief, Officer Shaw. You're a disgrace."

His smile slipped away. "What are gonna do, Sarge? You gonna arrest me? If so, how about you come on over here and try to put on the cuffs? I'd like to see you try."

Eleanor realized she didn't have an answer to that. What

was she going to do? Christ, she didn't even have a pair of cuffs with her. And she sure as hell wasn't about to get into another fistfight with him. She was pretty sure she wouldn't live through another round with Mr. SWAT.

So what then? What was she going to do?

He seemed to realize the answer before she did. She was going to do nothing. She was powerless, which meant that he controlled this situation. Eleanor had her husband and child with her. Anthony Shaw had only his rage and his money. She had the machine gun pointed at him, but he had the power.

And from the smile on his face, he seemed to know it, too.

He began to whistle. The sound was not musical, but shrill. Loud and shrill.

Eleanor saw movement out of the corner of her eye and glanced to the right. A zombie had stood up in the window of a home nearby, its eyes white and empty-looking against its mud-streaked face.

He whistled again, and the zombie responded with a desperate sounding moan, which was answered by other moans from the opposite side of the street.

"Stop it," she said.

He just smiled and went right on whistling, only louder now.

Oh no, she thought. *Officer Shaw, you crazy suicidal bastard.*

"I'm not gonna arrest you," she said, hoping to make him stop. "You know that. Not the way things are."

The smile left his face.

"Then why are you wasting my time, bitch?"

"Because I want to know."

He didn't respond. Instead he reared his head back and howled like a wolf in the night.

Eleanor could hear splashing all around them now, and she knew what that sound meant. She had seen the way the infected massed on verbal cues. It would only be a matter of time before every zombie in the area was swarming on their location.

"Stop that!" she said.

"Stop what?" he said. "What are you scared of? Her?"

He nodded to her right.

Eleanor didn't want to look. Anthony was smiling like a wicked child, and part of her knew that he was trying to trick her. How much more obvious could he be? She would glance to the side, then turn back to find him pointing a rifle at her. So she willed herself not to look, ignoring the splashing she heard over there.

His smile widened.

"Better tell your daughter to move out of the way. She's about to turn into zombie chow."

Eleanor flexed her finger over the trigger. She was stuck, and she knew it. She couldn't back down, and she couldn't shoot him. Not another cop. Not this way. He would do it to her in a heartbeat, but damn it, she couldn't. Not like this.

And then the splashing grew louder.

She felt the boat rocking as Madison moved to the port side.

"Mommy . . ."

And it was hearing her daughter calling her Mommy that did it. For the second time in just as many weeks she heard the helpless toddler calling through the voice of the girl. Eleanor turned, and saw a nearly naked woman with most of her face gone wading toward the boat. Her fingerless hands groped at the side of the boat.

Eleanor gasped.

"Mommy, shoot it!"

Eleanor turned the rifle on the woman zombie and fired a single round. It hit her in the forehead and laid her back into the water with hardly a splash.

A fast, simple death.

But there were more zombies behind her, coming into the street from the spaces between the apartment buildings. At first five, then nine, then a dozen more. They were everywhere.

She spun around, pointing her weapon at Anthony Shaw, but saw that he had beat her on the draw. He had his rifle pointed right at her, his finger tensed on the trigger. All he had to do was flinch, she realized, and she'd lose her entire family.

"Officer Shaw," she said, unable to keep the pleading tone from her voice.

"Shut up, bitch," he snapped. "Drop your weapon. Now! Put it down."

No way, she thought. *I do that and you execute me and my entire family.*

She swallowed hard, suddenly aware of the sweat popping out all over her body. She was terrified. Her bladder began to ache. Her legs were weak, her hands numb. But he just stood there, smiling through his rifles sights, coldly indifferent to her fear.

Off to her left, a spotlight beam came on.

Out of the corner of her eye, Eleanor could see it flickering between the buildings over there, catching the shrubs and balconies in silhouette and throwing their shadows across the water. It was coming from a flat-bottom boat.

And then a voice rang out.

"Anthony, is that you?"

"Yeah, Dad," Anthony answered, without taking his eyes off Eleanor. "Come on over."

Eleanor saw Anthony's eyes narrow, and she had just enough time to think *My God, he's gonna shoot*, when the boat started rocking. She teetered, thrown off balance, and as she fell backwards she saw Jim leaping forward, grabbing Madison around the waist, and jumping into the water.

Anthony started firing, and a line of bullets ripped through the hull where Eleanor had just been standing.

Eleanor rolled over onto her back. Cold salt water was bubbling up through the holes in the bottom of the boat. It was already two inches deep and climbing up the sides of her body. Without even aiming she stuck the barrel of her M-16 over the gunwale and fired a three-round burst. From the other boat, Anthony screamed, and Eleanor felt a savage, primal yell rising up within her.

"You bastard!" she screamed, and fired another burst.

Her second volley went wide, but it must have come close enough to scare him, for he dove over the side. When Eleanor heard the splash she sat up and tried to find him. A terrible vision of him swimming back under the boats and coming up next to Madison and Jim flashed through her mind, but she suppressed it. Instead, she made herself take a deep breath.

Slow down, girl, she thought. *Scan the water. Go slow.*

Half a dozen zombies were already in the water, attracted by the noise of the fight, and there were more coming through the gaps in the buildings, but they weren't close enough to be a threat yet. In the near distance, she could hear Captain Mark Shaw's boat accelerating around the line of buildings to her left. But there was no sign of Anthony Shaw. She looked everywhere, but the dark water showed no sign of him.

Then she saw his M-16 in the bow of his boat. There was blood on the stock, the shoulder strap caught on a cleat.

The zombies were moaning now, their noise surrounding her. The nearest one was almost to Anthony's boat, and she was running out of time. Another moment or two and she would have to start shooting or run away, and with Captain Shaw barreling down on them, they wouldn't get far.

Maybe I killed him, she thought.

But even as the thought started to seem possible, she saw him surface. He was moving along the far side of his boat, his hand inching toward his rifle.

"No you don't," she said, and fired at him.

She missed, but got close enough to force him back from the cover of the boat. He stood up, and for a moment, she had him framed squarely in her sights. He was bleeding from a nasty wound on his right shoulder, the arm hanging limply by his side. But it didn't seem to be causing him a lot of pain at the moment. To Eleanor, it looked as if he was debating with himself about reaching for his pistol. Would he have time to get off a shot? He was good enough to kill her with a single shot, but to do it he would have to draw his pistol across his body with his left hand.

There was rage in his eyes. She had him beat, and he knew it. He glanced to his right and saw a zombie just a few feet from him. He turned back to Eleanor and she could just hear him mutter, "Fucking bitch," before he turned and waded off toward a small, three-story apartment building on the other side of the street.

Things happened fast after that.

A few of the zombies were too close to ignore anymore. Eleanor shot three of them, then turned, and sighted in on a fourth. She pulled the trigger, but the gun was empty.

"Shit!" she said, and quickly ejected the magazine and slapped in another.

Captain Shaw's boat was up near the head of the block now. She could see the searchlight dancing through the trees, and knew he'd be on them soon.

"Jim, get Madison out of here!"

"What?"

"Jim, please, just do it! I'll hold him off, but you have to get her out of here."

"No way. I can't leave you here."

She pulled her pistol and jammed it into his hands.

"Get her out of here. Protect my baby. I've got to cover you guys. Shaw will kill us all if you don't get going now."

He seemed as if he was about to argue, but at that moment a zombie clawed its way over the gunwale of their sinking boat. Eleanor shot it in the face, blasting a spray of blood and bits of bone out across the water behind it.

"Go!" she yelled at him. "Go, Jim, please."

"I love you," he said, and grabbed Madison around the waist. She struggled against his grip, screaming not to leave her mother behind.

"I love you, too," Eleanor said. "Now get going."

She watched them slip away through a gap between a white concrete wall and an old gas station, then turned back to their boat. It was sinking fast now, its hull full of water. She waded over to it, grabbed Madison's backpack, and then moved over to Anthony Shaw's boat. It wasn't much for cover, but it was the best she had.

Captain Shaw was barreling down on her. She could see him up at the far end of the block, weaving between the roofs of submerged cars and trucks. She glanced over at the gas station, just to make sure Jim and Madison were out of sight, and saw more zombies entering the street.

Oh God, she thought. *Oh my God, this was a terrible idea. What the hell am I doing? Oh my God, he's gonna kill me.*

Then she looked down.

And saw the duffel bags.

Mark Shaw had watched the fight through a pair of night-vision goggles. Somehow, that lucky bitch had managed to get the jump on Anthony. Mark Shaw had no idea how that could have happened, but he'd been a cop long enough to know that if something could go wrong, it would go wrong . . . and it

sure as hell had gone wrong this time. He didn't know for
sure why they'd gotten into it with each other, but it wasn't
hard to guess. Somehow, she'd found out about the money,
and that meant they were in trouble.

But what was done was done. Anthony was hurt and
pinned down somewhere. Shaw's job now was to rescue Anthony and get them both out of here.

He raised the night-vision goggles one more time and
saw Eleanor hiding behind the bow of Anthony's boat, her
weapon aimed in his direction. The crazy bitch had even put
a backpack on. What the hell was she thinking?

He kept scanning the area, counting the zombies that
were pouring into the street from every direction. There
were at least sixteen of them. *Damn*, he thought, *she's in the
thick of it, isn't she?*

Shaw couldn't see the woman's husband or her kid, and
though he hated to leave loose ends, he figured that was
probably okay. From the number of zombies around their
position, he'd be surprised if they weren't dead. And that
would be just fine as far as he was concerned. The less
killing he had to do the better.

But Eleanor Norton, she had to go.

He traded the goggles for his searchlight, and gave the little outboard all the throttle it had.

Eleanor adjusted her grip on the M-16. Her hands were
wet and the gunmetal felt slick in her hands, like she couldn't
hold it right. Her fingers were tingling. Her face was flushed,
sweat beading on her forehead. Every breath hurt. Her mouth
had gone dry. First she felt hot, then cold. She kept her eyes
at the boat speeding toward her, but all she wanted to do was
lean over and vomit.

Oh Jesus, she thought. *Oh Jesus, I'm an idiot. I can't do
this. I can't beat him. Not Mark Shaw. The man practically*

invented SWAT. Her breaths were coming in shallow gasps now. *Dear God, please let me live through this. Help me. I want to hug my daughter again. I want to smother her face in kisses. Oh Jesus, please let me live.*

She raised the rifle. Sweat dripped in her eyes and she wiped it away with the back of her hand. Then she lowered her cheek to the stock and blinked until she had the boat centered in her sights. She was about to pull the trigger when Shaw hit his searchlight, blinding her with a glaring white light.

The next moment he was firing at her.

Anthony Shaw had commandeered a wooden-hulled boat, and when the bullets smacked into it, the air around Eleanor's head filled with splinters. A big one snapped loose with a whistling zing and cut her cheek just below her right eye. Gasping in pain, she recoiled from the side of the boat and touched her hand to her face.

It came away bloody.

She saw movement to her left and for a second thought it was Anthony Shaw coming back to help his father. But the ghastly apparition standing there was definitely not Anthony Shaw. One arm had been chewed off just below the elbow. Bits of tendon and raw strips of muscle showed through the bite marks on its cheeks. The eyes were milky white and hazy, but it tracked her well enough. She backed away, following the hull, and it came after her. There was another zombie behind her, a woman with a nasty black gash where her belly should have been. Eleanor shot them both, then ducked under the water just as Shaw fired another burst.

She crossed under the boat and came up on the other side, determined to give Shaw a taste of what he'd given her.

Eleanor raised the rifle and started firing.

The boat was moving from side to side, dodging through the exposed roofs of cars, but she wasn't aiming. She'd flipped the selector switch to fully automatic and was determined to burn through the entire magazine, the old pray-and-spray approach to target acquisition.

And she got lucky. Or at least she thought she did. The boat jogged suddenly to one side and smacked against the B pillar of the dark-colored passenger car with an audible thunk. The engine whined, then stalled, and Captain Shaw's boat began to drift toward the side of a building.

For a second, she thought she'd killed him. He was hunched over the motor, and seeing him that way, not moving, she let out a grunt of triumph.

"Yeah, you bastard, I got you! Ha!"

But the next instant he was standing up and yanking on the pull cord to restart the motor. It coughed, then roared to life.

"No," she said.

A voice in her head told her to run, and she did. She turned and half ran, half swam through a narrowing crowd of zombies. They reached for her, their gore-streaked hands clutching at the backpack she wore, but she managed to thread her way through them. She scrambled toward the far corner of a white cinder-block building and got around it just as bullets from Shaw's gun blasted a line of holes down the wall.

Just ahead was a long chain-link fence topped with razor wire, and beyond that was a small white church.

Mark Shaw cut the engine and let his boat glide into the street. He had his rifle ready and he was scanning the area just to make sure Eleanor Norton hadn't doubled back on him. He never would have suspected it, but the slippery little bitch put up a surprisingly good fight.

The funny thing was, though, that wasn't the Eleanor Norton he knew. The Eleanor Norton he knew was one of the new breed of kinder and gentler cops, the kind who

baked oatmeal raisin cookies for the men under her command and still met with all the victims' advocacy people
she'd dealt with back in her Sex Crimes days. She was more
like a den mother than a frontline police supervisor, and
frankly, he'd expected her to shrink up in a corner somewhere and beg for him to spare her life.

But the kitten, it seemed, had claws. She'd surprised him
going under the boat like she had, and she was evidently a
better shot than he'd given her credit for. That burst she'd
fired had knocked the throttle right out of his hand and
stalled the engine. Hitting a moving target like that in low
light and with zombies closing in all around you wasn't the
easiest thing in the world to do, and yet she had done it.

Shaw had underestimated her, and he imagined Anthony
had, too. That was the only explanation that made any sense.

"Anthony! Can you hear me?"

Several zombies were wading toward him, and at the
sound of his voice, they began to moan. He scanned the area
and counted thirty-one of them. There were more, it sounded
like, just beyond the line of buildings to his left.

"Anthony! Answer me, if you can."

There was a small apartment building to his left, the windows and doors blown away by one of the recent storms. He
thought he heard a faint voice coming from inside there
somewhere.

"Anthony, is that you?"

The voice came again, and this time he was sure. That
was Anthony in there, but his voice was distant, muffled.
When Anthony was fifteen, a kid from Friendswood High
School had slid into second base with his metal spikes up in
the air. He caught Anthony in the groin, and though he'd
been wearing a cup, the spikes had still managed to cut a
four-inch gash down the inside of Anthony's thigh. Listening
to the muffled voice inside that apartment building, Mark
Shaw was reminded of sitting in the stands that day all those

years ago, listening to the pain in his son's voice as he fought with the runner who had just cut him. His son was hurting. A father could tell these things.

"Hold on, Anthony. I'm coming."

He toggled the selector switch on his M-16 over to semi-auto and shot his way through the crowd of zombies. When he reached the door, he tied off the boat and went inside, lighting up the flooded building with the flashlight mounted to the barrel of his weapon.

"Anthony?"

"In here."

Shaw followed the voice down the hall and stopped in front of the door to 1-C. He tried to push the door open, but Anthony had it barricaded from the other side.

"Help me get this open, Anthony."

There was a slight pause, and then the sound of debris and furniture being pulled out of the way. Shaw pushed on it, and a moment later he had it opened. Anthony was standing there, a pistol in his left hand, his right arm hanging limp at his side.

"Did you get hit?"

"Yeah, I can't move it."

"You're losing a lot of blood there. Lean up against the wall there and let me look at it."

Shaw inspected his son's injured arm. The bullet had hit him high up, near the shoulder. Back in his SWAT days Shaw had been trained as a medic, and his first instinct was to check his son's breathing and his pulse. He seemed to be doing okay there, and that was good news. If he went into shock here, without any proper medical treatment, Shaw would never be able to save him. It would be hard enough just keeping the wound clean.

"Have you got any booze in the boat?" Shaw asked.

"What?"

"To sterilize it. We need to keep this clean."

"I don't know," Anthony answered. "I think maybe Brent had . . ." But he trailed off there. They hadn't spoken of what happened to Brent back at the EOC's boatyard, not in any sort of meaningful way, and Anthony seemed unwilling to bring it up now. Or maybe afraid to bring it up was more accurate.

"Brent had some? Vodka?"

"Yeah, I think."

"Come on," he said, and put Anthony's arm over his shoulder to support his weight. "Let's go check."

"Dad, I . . ."

"What is it, Anthony?"

They were moving into the hallway now. There was a zombie in the doorway at the far end of the hall and Mark Shaw dropped it with a single shot.

"She snuck up on me, Dad." Anthony said.

"What do you mean?"

"She found out about the money somehow and when she came up behind me . . . the bitch just shot me. No warning. I think she was trying to steal it."

Mark Shaw hesitated for a second, then continued. Had the boy forgotten that he'd lit them up with a searchlight right before the shots went off? Who did he think he was fooling? The only thing Shaw could think of was that he was covering for himself, the way he slinked off into this apartment building instead of staying in the fight.

Pride, he thought. *That's what it is, our goddamned stinking pride. Well, at least he comes by it honestly.*

"You're gonna be okay, son. Come on. Let's get you out of here."

Eleanor was aware of the smell as soon as she entered the church. She put the back of her hand over her mouth and nostrils, her face wrinkled up in disgust. Something was dead in here, and had been rotting for a while.

The church consisted of one small room, big enough to seat maybe a hundred people. It reminded her, briefly, of the little Methodist church her parents had brought her to when she was younger. But this one had been irreparably changed by the floods. The walls were mildewing plaster. They were literally melting, sagging and breaking apart in big wet chunks. Garbage and bits of seaweed and drifts of unnamable slag filled the spaces between the pews. Tree limbs were stuck in the rafters. And up near the altar, huddled together like a driftwood pile on the beach, were the bodies of some sixteen drowned souls.

A few of the bodies had been nibbled on by animals. One woman, down on her knees, her cheek resting against the back of a man in a filthy flannel shirt, was staring up at her with sightless dead eyes.

Eleanor found herself staring down into that woman's face, wondering who she was, what had brought her to die here, on this alter. What faith did she have? Did it offer her anything in those final moments? She wondered if the woman's faith could have answered Madison's questions back on the boat.

And then her reverie was broken by the rapid crack of gunfire coming from somewhere behind her. Captain Shaw was in the middle of all those zombies back there, and it wouldn't be long before he—and maybe his son, too—tracked her down.

It wouldn't be difficult. This little church stood on the edge of what must have been a wide, empty stretch of undeveloped land, for she hadn't seen any buildings beyond it. She would have to move if she wanted to live, if she wanted to find Jim and Madison.

She looked down at her red shirt and blue jeans and

wished she had worn something different. The red shirt, especially, was going to make her a sitting duck.

And then she looked down at the dead woman again, and an idea occurred to her. It was a terrible idea, a grotesque idea, but it just might work.

Quickly, she turned the dead woman over. Her face was purple on one side where the blood had pooled after death, but Eleanor steeled herself and started undressing the corpse. She could feel the dead woman's skin, and she gagged as she pulled the shirt off the body. Touching her was like poking the steaks through their cellophane shrouds at the supermarket, and she came very close to vomiting as the now naked dead woman dropped back down onto the pile of corpses.

She didn't give herself a chance to think about what came next.

She took off her shirt and slid it down over the dead woman. And then—God, she would rather walk into roll call wearing nothing but her bra and panties and her gun belt than do this—she put on the dead woman's shirt. She kept her eyes closed as she buttoned it up and then pushed the tails down into her jeans.

"I'm sorry," she said to the corpse as she slid her backpack onto the corpse and propped it up in the window.

And then she did something only her desire to see Jim and Madison again would have allowed her to do. She wedged herself down into the pile of corpses, covering herself with them, pushing from her mind the weight of all that dead flesh, and there she waited.

"Holy shit. Dad, look there!"

Mark Shaw stopped and followed the line of his son's finger. The only thing over there was a church, battered by the recent storms. He thought he saw a flash of red, but it was dark, and his eyes weren't what they once had been.

"Is that her?" he whispered.

"Yeah, that's her," Anthony said. "Same shirt, same hair."

"All right. I'm gonna put you down."

Slowly, he leaned his son against a lamppost, making sure that Anthony had his good arm around it for support before letting go. Then he raised his rifle and centered it on the dark spot above the red shirt. The dumb bitch wasn't even watching the obvious line of attack. Anybody who'd been through a basic weapons and tactics course would have found a better tactical position than that.

Mark Shaw raised the M-16 and centered Eleanor Norton's head in his sights.

Then he fired.

No hesitation.

He lit her up, and even he could see that the three-round burst he'd fired had taken most of her head clean off.

Eleanor heard the rattle of gunfire a moment before the dead woman's head splattered onto the water behind her. The body teetered and then collapsed, landing facedown in the water. Watching the body as it turned a lazy pirouette away from the window, Eleanor couldn't hold her stomach down any longer. She retched, vomiting all over a dead man's beard.

Her stomach was still heaving when she heard voices at the front of the church. Captain Shaw and his son entered the building and moved quickly to the altar. They stopped next to the dead woman wearing Eleanor's shirt and backpack and flipped her over.

The body rolled like a log in the water. There was very little left of the corpse's head above the jaw, just an open cavity with clumps of matted hair sticking to the back of the emptied skull.

"Damn," Anthony said. He turned away from the sight in disgust.

From her hiding spot under the pile of corpses, Eleanor watched Anthony Shaw closely. His right arm was dead by his side, the wound up by his shoulder obvious. She had drawn first blood. If nothing else, she had made the bastard pay for hitting her. And Jim, she reminded herself.

"What is it?" Captain Shaw said.

"Nothing, you just blew the shit out of her."

"Had to be done."

"Yeah," Anthony said. "But damn, that's a lot of damage."

From somewhere outside, Eleanor heard the sound of zombies moaning. She tried to identify the number of voices, but couldn't, and that only meant one thing. They were coming. Bunches of them.

Captain Shaw seemed to realize it, too. He started to move, then stopped to stare at the mound of bodies encasing Eleanor. Her eyes went wide and her pulse quickened. Had he heard something? Seen a flash of movement? She waited, cringing not only with disgust now, but fear as well.

But he didn't move toward the mound. Instead, he seemed to be looking through them, through her, as though wrestling with something.

"Idiots," he murmured.

"What's that?" Anthony asked.

"Nothing," he said. "Just thinking."

Anthony didn't answer at first. He watched his father like one who has lived with a powerful man for a long time and has learned when it is best to stand and wait in silence while the other wades in the tidal flow of his thoughts.

But then there was a noise from the entrance to the church and Anthony turned on it suddenly. Eleanor could only see dim shapes moving in the starlight that framed the doorway, but she could hear them moaning, and she could hear the irregular rhythm of their hands slapping at the water.

"Dad," Anthony said. There was an obvious note of alarm in his voice. "Dad, we need to get out of here."

Only then did Captain Mark Shaw turn from the corpses. He scanned the doorway, and then the windows along the sides of the church, and slid the M-16's sling off his shoulder.

"Okay," he said. "Get behind me, Anthony. Let's get out of here."

Eleanor found herself alone beneath the pile of corpses.

The Shaws had fought their way out of the church and then slipped away into the night, but the moaning remained. The zombies, Eleanor knew, were very close.

She waited, afraid to move out from beneath her hiding place among the corpses. Though the moaning had suddenly stopped, she knew from all the splashing that more zombies had entered the church. Working as quietly as possible, she wedged herself down deeper into the bottom of the corpse pile, and watched the narrow gap between the bodies.

Several zombies staggered past. She could see them bumping into pews and slapping absently at the water around their waists. Then one of the zombies stopped directly in front of Eleanor's line of sight and slowly turned its head in her direction. It had eaten something recently. She could tell it had made a kill right away from the clotted clumps of blood in its hair and the dark, ominous stains on its face and clothes. Mosquitoes swarmed around its face. She couldn't tell whether it was a man or a woman. Not even the thing's race was obvious, and it occurred to her that she was looking at the great leveler of humanity. At last, here was something that cleared the slate . . . not only of the mind, but of the body as well. All are equal before the zombie. And it wasn't beautiful. It was horrible in the most profound way imaginable. The essence was gone. Nothing but the shell remained . . . and in that, there was no beauty.

But the zombie was still staring into the pile of corpses.

Eleanor stared back at it, and she wondered what was behind those dead, vacant eyes.

Go away, she pleaded. *Please, go away.*

CHAPTER 19

Madison fought him all the way through the alley, kicking and screaming, beating against his back with her fists. She caught him in the kidneys once and he lurched forward, his knees buckling. He managed to carry her as far as the open courtyard behind the old gas station before his foot caught on something hard under the water and he pitched forward, face-planting into the water. Madison tumbled out of his arms and tried to scramble back to her mother.

"Madison, don't!" he said. Jim grabbed her by the waist and pulled her back.

"Let go of me! What the hell's wrong with you? We can't leave her."

He spun her around, and for a moment, the wild, bulging, unblinking intensity in her eyes frightened him. He'd never seen her so charged, so animated. It was as if she were giving off sparks.

But he held on.

"No," he said. "You stay here with me."

"We can't leave her back there." Big fat tears welled up at the corners of her eyes and ran down her cheeks. "She'll die back there."

"No, she won't."

"How do you know that? You can't be sure of that."

But he was sure. At that moment, with his daughter's shoulders still gripped tightly in his hands, he knew it. Jim wasn't exactly sure when the change in Eleanor had happened, but it had happened. Eleanor had become someone different, stronger than she had been before. She was in control. He could still see the confidence in her eyes and feel it coming off her like heat when she told him to take Madison out of the street. She would cover for them, she had said, and at that moment, he had believed it. His faith in her was as solid as his conviction that the sun would come up in the morning.

The change had taken place right in front of him, and yet it had been so subtle that he hadn't noticed it. He thought of her drowning the zombie outside of the Meadowlakes Business Park, of her taking charge of the Red Cross volunteers back at the Beltway, of her sitting in the bow of their little boat with the M-16 on her lap, of her telling him to protect their daughter as she held off two armed madmen and a city full of zombies, and suddenly he could see the through line. All the madness that had led them to this point made sense. All these years, Eleanor had been waiting for an obstacle big enough to stand in her way. And here it was, the catalyst. Her cocoon had ruptured, but what had flown free was not a butterfly, but a hawk . . . predatory, confident, ineffably beautiful. She was rising to the challenge.

She had only asked this one thing of him: protect their daughter.

Jim understood what he had to do. Now it was his turn to make good on his promise to Eleanor.

"Daddy . . . ?"

He tightened his grip on Madison's shoulders.

"Listen to me. Your mother is going to be fine. I know it. I can't tell you how I know it, but I do. I believe it. Right

down to my bones I believe it. She told us to get to safety.
We have to do that. She will find us."

Madison softened a little. He could feel the rigidity leaving her muscles. She nodded, and for Jim, the changing expression on her face was like watching a fire go out. Only a
steady calm remained. Had she also sensed the change in her
mother? He didn't think that she had seen it in the same way
as he, but she must have seen something. Why else would
she be yielding to him now?

"What do we do?" she asked.

Good question, he thought.

He looked around.

They were blocked on three sides by a chain-link fence
topped with razor wire. Beyond the fence, off to the left, was
a white, wooden building, dilapidated and sad-looking in the
dark, and he guessed it was a church. Just on the other side
of the fence was a large, rectangular building that might
have been an apartment or possibly an office building. He
couldn't really tell because of all the trash and tree limbs that
had accumulated in front of it. Looking farther down the
block he saw dark, barnlike shapes. No telling what they
were.

"We need to find a way to get over this fence," he said.

Shots rang out from somewhere behind him and he
turned. Madison had her back to him. In front of her, coming
down the narrow alley between the white cinder-block wall
and the gas station, were four zombies. Another staggered
out of the gas station. He could see two more inside, coming
toward the back door.

"Daddy!" Madison said.

She backed up, and Jim pulled her behind him.

He fired at the lead zombie coming down the narrow
alley, hitting it in the arm. The zombie staggered, but didn't
fall. Its arm dropped uselessly to its side, and yet it kept on
coming. He fired again and this time hit it in the chest. The

zombie took a few steps toward him and then sagged down into the water.

Jim turned to his right and saw the zombie that had come out of the gas station was almost on him. Its mangled hands reached for him. Looking into its dead eyes, its open, bloody mouth full of cracked teeth, Jim felt a shudder all the way down to his bones. He fired a hurried shot that hit the zombie in the hand and blasted off two of its fingers.

"Goddamn," he said, the bile rising up to the back of his mouth.

He fired again, and this time he got the zombie in the throat. The moan on its lips turned to a deep gurgling sucking sound, like a clogged drain

But, impossibly, it kept coming.

His third shot put it down.

"Daddy!"

More zombies were coming down the alley, clawing their way over the one he'd already killed. Five shots to put down two zombies, he thought. Christ, this isn't going to work.

"Madison, see if you can find a way through that fence."

"It's got razors on top of it!" she said.

"Just do it."

His hands shook. He tried to aim the gun, but the front sights were bobbing all over the place. He couldn't steady his hands. A voice in his head was screaming for him to shoot, but the trembling was spreading. His mouth went dry. First he was numb, then burning up. His breath was coming in fast, shallow gasps. When he did pull the trigger the bullet skipped harmlessly off the water near one zombie's hip before smacking into the side of the gas station.

Come on, he thought, *come on. Focus, Jim, get a grip.*

From just behind him he heard the musical jingling of the chain-link fence.

"Daddy, I found it!" Madison shouted. "This way."

When he looked over his shoulder he saw Madison slipping through the fence. A portion of it had come loose from the bottom of the fence pole and Madison was holding it open for him like a curtain.

"Come on, Daddy."

He rushed through the opening. It was low and narrow. She had made it through easily enough, but Jim was much bigger and it cut painful gashes into his back. But he got through, grabbed her hand, and together they waded over to the nearest building they could find.

"Where are we going?" she cried.

"In here," he said. He was thinking: *Get to higher ground. Or someplace we can barricade ourselves. Anything but remaining out in the open.*

They reached the building—it was an apartment building, he could see that now—and Jim started pulling trash and tree limbs away from the door. He glanced over his shoulder to make sure Madison was still right there with him. She was watching the narrow strip of water they had just covered. Zombies were pouring out of nearly every doorway and advancing through every gap between the buildings. Their moans were deafening.

"Daddy . . ."

"Help me with this," he said, and together they pulled a large tree limb from the apartment building's door.

Jim climbed up on top of a bed frame and kicked at the door until it flew open. He held the door open as far as it would go and peered inside. He could make out a long hallway running the length of the building. It was flooded, just like everything else, and the far end was lost in darkness, but it was better than out here.

"Okay," he said, "up you go."

Madison scrambled over the bed frame and dropped down into the hallway.

"There's something blocking the door on this side," she said.

"That's good. Here I come."

He squeezed through next to her, and together they pushed the door closed. A small refrigerator was just under the water, wedged into the corner made by the door and the wall. Jim pushed it against the door, knowing that it wouldn't hold the zombies back for more than a few seconds at best, and then turned to face the hallway.

He squinted into the darkness, wishing he had a flashlight. Something was dead in here. He could smell the rot mixed with an underlying note of mildew and sewage. Swallowing the lump in his throat he grabbed Madison's hand and led her into the darkness, the only sound a faint splashing as they waded through the water.

"Daddy, I don't like this."

"Shhh," he said, his own voice a stage whisper. "Check the walls. Try to find a door or a staircase. We've got to get to higher ground."

Behind them, the door exploded open. Madison screamed. Jim swung around. Dark silhouettes were filling the square of light at the end of the hallway. He could see them dropping down from the bed frame and into the water, spreading out to fill the hallway once they were through the doorway. He raised the pistol, but already there were more zombies inside the hallway than he had bullets.

"Run!" he said.

Madison took off in the opposite direction. Jim rushed off after her, but they had only made it a short distance when they heard the sound of wood crunching up ahead.

Madison stopped.

Jim came up next to her.

From the far end of the hall, they heard the sounds of hands slapping against the other side of the door. There was another crunch, and both father and daughter flinched.

"Daddy!"

Abruptly, the door caved in. The far end of the hallway

flooded with moonlight, and for just a moment, right before
the zombies started filling the hallway, they saw the stairs
leading up to the second floor. But there was no way they
could reach them. Already the zombies from the front end of
the building were moving past it, blocking it.

They were trapped.

"Daddy . . ."

Underwater, he thought. And then, with the same mental
breath: *Never work. They're jammed in shoulder to shoulder.*

"Daddy!"

The zombies were closing in on them. Jim could see a
sort of maddened frenzy in their ruined faces, their hands
outstretched and clutching for them. Their moaning sounded
like the starving pleading for food.

"Daddy!" Madison said. She was shouting to be heard
over the moaning.

There's nowhere to go, he thought. *Nowhere.*

The thought was answered by Eleanor's voice in his head:
You've got to protect our daughter. Please, keep her safe.

Then he looked up at the ceiling.

"Madison," he said, spinning her around to face him, "I
want you to climb up on my back."

"What?"

"Get on my back, arms around my neck. Come on, up."

He bent over and guided him onto his back. They had
done this a million times when she was a little girl, her holding on while he ran around the living room making horsey
sounds, but she was a lot older now . . . and so was he. He
prayed he could make this work.

"What are you doing?" she asked.

"Just hold on, baby. We're going up."

He put his hands on one wall, his feet on the other. As the
zombies closed in on them, he inched his way up the wall.

He didn't stop until Madison was mashed up against the
ceiling.

A moment later the zombies were right below him, their frantic, clutching hands swatting the air just inches from his face. He could feel their fingertips tugging at his shirt and his blue jeans. Water dripped from his clothes, hitting the horde below him in the eyes and in their open mouths, sending them into even wilder paroxysms of moaning.

Madison shrieked in his ears, her long hair spilling over the side of his face.

"Just hold on, baby," he said to her.

Just hold on.

CHAPTER 20

Turning from Eleanor Norton's dead body, Captain Mark Shaw surveyed the corpses piled up on the altar, and a growing sense of disgust rose up inside him.

Idiots, he thought. Shaw and his family had never gone to church, but even still, he had no objection to religion in and of itself. It wasn't a bad thing. Religion was, after all, just another word for duty. Perhaps some people needed to call duty by the name of God to make its yoke tolerable; he did not. Still, he understood religion. He could understand how a man could be prepared to lay down his life for God. Hadn't he been prepared to die in the performance of his duty, after all?

But being prepared for death and actively seeking it out were two very different things. The former required courage, the latter merely ignorance. There was no purpose in a death of the sort these people had apparently died, and that left him saddened and angry.

"Idiots," he muttered.

"What's that?" Anthony asked.

Shaw sighed deeply. "Nothing. Just thinking."

Anthony didn't respond, and Shaw was glad for that. He

loved Anthony. He was so incredibly proud of him. But the boy could be shallow and just as ignorant as the dead people on this altar. A father's love hadn't blinded him to that simple truth, and it was that reason he didn't want to hear the boy speak just now.

Zombies were entering the front door of the church behind him. Shaw could hear them back there, moaning, splashing around drunkenly, but he kept watching the pile of corpses, his mind turning toward Brent and the pointlessness of his death. Bitter rage flared up in him, unbidden and, for just a moment, uncontrollable. He closed his eyes and tried to force out the memory of Brent's screams, but they echoed on.

"Dad," Anthony said. There was an obvious note of alarm in his voice. "Dad, we need to get out of here."

Only then did Shaw turn from the corpses.

He scanned the doorway and the windows along the sides of the church, considering their possible ways out.

He slid the M-16 off his shoulder.

"Okay," he said. "Get behind me, Anthony. Let's get out of here."

He began to move and shoot. It was just like the standard rifleman drills in the FBI's Close Quarter Battle School, except that he was shooting at zombies instead of targets. Of course the waist-deep water kept the zombies from moving very fast, so they were practically standing still anyway. And they never flinched. They made no attempt to evade his rifle's sight line. They just kept coming, hands outstretched as if they were begging him for something. They might as well have been cardboard silhouettes.

He moved easily through the gathering crowd, pointing and shooting, measuring each shot before he took it. He felt absolutely calm and in control. There was no question about what would happen from here on out. They'd get the money, get back on his boat, and he would get what was left of his family out of this hellhole. Once his son was provided for, he would take whatever lumps he had coming in the court of public opinion. But his family would be provided for. That was all that counted.

"Anthony, you okay?" he asked over his shoulder.

Anthony was a few steps behind him, his pistol in his left hand. He had lost a lot of color from his face, but his eyes were still focused, still sharp.

"Yeah," Anthony answered.

"Breathing okay?"

Anthony started to speak, but the words came out as a cough. He closed his eyes and tried again. "A little short of breath," he said. "Can't really feel my fingers too good."

"Shit," Shaw said. "Okay, come on, let's pick it up."

Outside the church they stopped and scanned the area in front of them. There were more zombies than he had bullets to shoot trudging through the water toward the church, attracted by the sound of gunfire. Even more were coming in from the east. Briefly he thought of scaling the chain-link fence with the razor wire on top, but he knew that wouldn't work. Not with Anthony's arm all messed up.

That left one option . . . and it wasn't a good one.

Several shots rang out from the other side of the fence.

"Pistol shots," Anthony said.

"Yeah."

Shaw scanned the darkness up near the gas station, but all he could really see were the dim outlines of ruined buildings.

"I bet that's her husband and kid," Anthony said.

Shaw looked at his son and he realized he was probably right. Had Eleanor really lured him away so that her family could make a break for it? If so . . . Christ, he was impressed. He thought back over the few years they'd worked together and he never would have guessed she had it in her.

Well, he'd been wrong, simple as that.

"Mama bird," he said.

"What?"

"She was a mama bird," Shaw repeated. "A bird will fake a broken wing to lure a snake away from her nest. It's instinct."

"Yeah, she was no bird, though."

"No, she wasn't. It's instinct when an animal does it because an animal doesn't understand fear the way a person does. But Sergeant Norton was afraid and she did it anyway. That's not instinct, that's courage."

Anthony tried to grin, but only managed to get one corner of his pale lips to turn up. "Yeah, well, courage or not, she's still dead."

Shaw regarded him coldly. The boy's inability to understand the important things in life staggered him sometimes.

"Come on," he said. "We're going that way, through that copse of trees over there. Once we make it over the road we'll double back on the boat, get the money, and get out of here. It's the long way around, but it's the only option we've got."

"What about them, the husband and the little girl?"

"What do you mean? What about them?" Shaw asked.

"We can't let them live. They know about us."

"Listen," Shaw said, and paused. "You hear any more shots?"

"No."

"He was armed with a pistol, Anthony. Now look around you. We're surrounded by zombies. What do you think his chances are?"

Anthony didn't seem entirely convinced.

"Yeah, well, I still don't like it," he said.

"Anthony, your job is to do what you're fucking told. Got it? Now move. Let's get out of here while we still can."

Gradually, quiet returned to the church.

Eleanor listened.

The dead bodies on top of her were wet. Some were still in rigor mortis, their bodies stiff as furniture. In others, the muscles had relaxed. They were cold and pliable, and pressed up against her with a weight that she felt not only across her chest, but in her mind as well.

She wanted *out*.

She wanted out *right now!*

"Fuck it," she said.

She drew in two quick breaths through her mouth and pushed. The corpses sagged outward and away with an awful, almost liquid motion. Faces leered at her, the eyes utterly dead and yet accusatory. A woman's head rolled from one shoulder to the other, so that it landed faceup and directly in front of her, the mouth open in a silent groan.

Eleanor felt her stomach roll and then convulse as she dry heaved. There was nothing left in her to throw up.

"Oh Jesus," she muttered.

But she didn't stop pushing, and a moment later, she was out of the corpse pile, facing the flooded church. The bodies of dead zombies floated between the pews and there was a dense cluster of them by the front door. Only a few were still moving. One or two were even still moaning. But none of them was a threat. Not anymore. The Shaws had clearly done their work well getting out.

And from what she could see out the windows, there didn't appear to be that many outside the church, either. Had they followed the Shaws? The idea seemed reasonable enough. With Anthony wounded as bad as he was, they couldn't have moved all that fast. There would have been plenty of time for a crowd to gather and focus on the fleeing father and son.

"Lucky me," she muttered.

She crossed the altar to where her body double floated faceup in the water. The poor woman's face really had been blown clean off, and as she stood there over the corpse, looking down on it, the idea that she was looking at herself sent a shudder through her that went bone-deep.

"Thank you," she said, and with trembling fingers she worked the backpack's straps off the corpse and slid the pack onto her own back. With her foot she felt around the floor until she located her M-16. Then she reached under the water, pulled it up, and let the water drain out of the barrel before slipping out a side window.

No sense in going through more corpses, she figured, if she didn't have to.

Once outside she considered going over the chain-link fence with the razor wire, but the way the blades twinkled in the starlight made it pretty much a foregone conclusion.

So instead she followed the fence line up toward the street, figuring she would cross around the front of the gas station and retrace Jim and Madison's track down the narrow alleyway on the far side. The plan had seemed simple enough while she was thinking it, and it looked as if it was going to stay simple . . . right up until the moment she turned into the alley between the gas station and the cinder-block wall.

A group of zombies was huddled there, unable to push forward because of some obstruction and too unaware to turn around and go back the way they'd come.

Until they heard Eleanor behind them.

At that point, one of them turned around and began to utter a long, stuttering moan. The others followed suit, and within seconds, Eleanor found herself backing up toward the boats with at least fifteen zombies closing in on her.

She turned to the left and to the right and saw more emerging from the gaps between the buildings down the length of the street. They stared at her for a second, and then they too started her way.

"Shit," she muttered.

Just then she backed against the little green metal boat

Captain Shaw had used to catch up with her while she was still fighting with Anthony. The boat was empty, no rifles, no loose ammunition or magazines, but beyond it, coming from the far side of the street, were more zombies.

She threw her backpack and rifle into the boat and climbed in.

"Let's see if you start, you mother," she said, and pulled on the motor's rip cord. It coughed, sputtered, but failed to start.

From behind her, she heard a man's voice and she turned, her heart rising up into her throat for a second because she thought it might be Jim. But right away she could tell who it really was. Out beyond the narrowing ring of zombies, Captain Mark Shaw and his injured son were staring at her, their faces an almost comical mixture of rage and wounded pride and the utter shock of disbelief.

And, under different circumstances, she might have laughed. But for right now she was all business.

"Start, please," she said, and gave the rip cord another pull.

This time it fired up with a chain-driven rattle, belching clouds of oily black smoke. A zombie threw its arms over the side of the boat and Eleanor flinched away from the motor. But it only took a moment for her to regain control. She raised the butt of her rifle over the zombie's face and slammed it down onto the bridge of the thing's nose. It sagged back into the water and Eleanor landed hard on her knees, the boat rocking wildly. The motion caused her to fall backwards against the hull, where she stayed, eyes wide, her breaths coming in huge painful gulps.

In the distance, Captain Shaw was yelling something, but his voice was indistinct over the sound of so many zombies moaning.

Fingers clutched her hair, and she screamed and rolled in one quick motion. Three zombies were trying to get into the boat. Eleanor spun her rifle around and fired two bursts right into their faces.

No more time to lose, she thought.

She grabbed the throttle bar and dropped the motor's prop back down into the water. But no sooner had she got back on the seat than another zombie reached over the top of the motor, a swipe from its fingernails missing her nose by inches.

She didn't think about what she was doing. There was no time to. If she had, she might have died. She twisted the throttle's bicycle-type grip all the way open, throwing herself back down against the hull. The engine shuddered as the propeller cut into the zombie's crotch and belly. Eleanor could hear the engine straining as the blades cut into its midsection, and then, for a horrible moment, leveling out to the steady burring roar of a blender on frappe as the blades entered the guts inside, churning up everything they touched.

The zombie still had its arms outstretched, as if it had every intention of bear-hugging the motor, but it was jittering now like a man being electrocuted. His mouth was open and his cheeks were shaking, ropes of bloody spit flying out to either side. But the zombie never even blinked. Even as the motor finally burned itself out, dying with a sickening crunch that might have been metal unable to cut through any more bone, the zombie stared at Eleanor with a look that was both utterly vacant and insanely hungry.

But it too died, and shortly after the engine conked out, the zombie fell face-first onto the top of the motor, uttering a breathy sigh as it collapsed.

Eleanor, on her back in the bottom of the boat, looked up at the dead zombie, horrified by what she'd just done. Her hands were shaking, her heart beating a thousand miles an hour. This was a full-blown adrenaline dump she was experiencing, and all because of what she'd somehow managed to make herself do.

Zombies were closing in on her on all sides.

Behind her, the Shaws' voices were getting louder. But at that moment she didn't care about any of that. The only thing that seemed real was the memory echo of the throttle bucking in her hand as it cut into that zombie's guts and the blood that had splattered all over its face and the sickening crunch of metal on bone that had finally killed the engine and the zombie.

Those things were real.

But slowly, the adrenaline loosed its hold on her stomach and her muscles relaxed. She rose onto her knees and looked over the back of the boat . . . and all at once wished she hadn't. Blood was pooling out from the dead zombie like a spreading oil slick. Large pink and yellow chunks of its guts floated on the water. The zombie itself had been split open from the crotch up to the base of the sternum, a curling length of its spinal column jutting out behind it like a rat's tail. Eleanor gagged, but didn't dry heave this time. It was just too much to process right now.

She heard the shots that followed, but didn't realize the Shaws were shooting at her . . . at least, not at first. What she did realize was that the zombie that had been trying to climb into the boat while she had her back turned had just been perforated by rifle fire.

She heard a bullet strike the metal hull of the boat, and several others slam into the zombie that had luckily chosen the wrong moment to get between her and the Shaws. Eleanor watched the dead zombie slip off the gunwale and back into the water, a line of bullet holes down its back, and then looked up to see Captain Mark Shaw locking in his sights for another burst.

She hit the deck just as another three rounds struck the motor above her.

Oh Jesus, she thought. *Oh my God. What do I do? What do I do?*

Careful to keep her head down, she reached for her M-16

and pulled it in close to her chest. Then with her left hand she slipped one shoulder strap of the backpack over her arm.

"Please let this work," she whispered, and without pausing to consider what she was doing she stuck the M-16 over the bow of the boat and fired one-handed toward the Shaws. The next instant she rolled over the side of the boat and slid under the surface. There were zombies all around her, but as soon as she went under, she was lost to them. She kicked as hard as she could toward the edge of the street. Several times she bumped into zombies and felt their hands clutching at her back and at her legs, but she never stopped kicking. She swam until her lungs began to burn and the need for air was too great to ignore. Only then did she pop her head up and look around.

She had emerged just behind a female zombie. It turned toward her and lunged, but Eleanor was just out of the zombie's reach, and it fell face-first into the water. The woman popped right back up, spitting and swiping at the air with her diseased fingernails. Eleanor backed away, heading toward a small gap between an air-conditioner repair shop and a thrift store.

"Dad, over there!"

Eleanor spun around.

Captain Shaw and Anthony were almost on top of the boat now. *Christ, they'd covered a lot of distance*, she thought. *If I'd waited a second longer . . .*

She ran for the alley, expecting the air to fill with bullets at any second, but miraculously, that didn't happen. Eleanor rounded the corner, splashing and kicking as hard as she could, that voice inside her head, that voice that had grown more and more powerful since all this started, was screaming at her to go. *Run! Don't stop! Run with everything you've got!*

The alley was short. It opened onto a wide shallow sea that must have been a parking lot or a grassy courtyard before the floods. Ahead of her were three barnlike apartment buildings, white and dingy with steep sloping tiled roofs. An unbelievably huge crowd of zombies was pouring into the building on her left, their moaning so loud it seemed like a jet was passing overhead. More were coming from her right, attracted by the moaning. She was surrounded. Where was she going to go?

You gotta make up your mind, the voice in her head said. *Go. Go now!*

And so Eleanor ran.

Captain Shaw watched Eleanor slip into the alleyway with a dull rage that was becoming all too familiar. She had slipped through his fingers *again*. How the fuck did that happen? How was she even alive? He had killed her himself. He had blasted her brains out all over that fucking altar, all over those . . . those dead bodies.

A thought took shape in his mind. At first he refused to acknowledge it, but the more he tried to resist, the more sense it made.

After all, hadn't she done the mama bird thing once already?

What would stop her from doing it again?

"She switched her clothes with that dead woman I shot," he said.

Anthony turned to his father.

"You mean the one in the church?"

"Yeah."

Anthony seemed confused. Shaw watched his son thinking the problem through, and then suddenly the lights went on behind Anthony's eyes.

"You mean she . . ."

"Yeah, that's exactly what I mean."

"But how could she *do* that?" Anthony said. His face was

twisted up in a grimace as if he had smelled something bad. "I mean, under all those bodies . . ."

"It's called mental toughness, Anthony." Then, to himself, he muttered, "I just didn't think she had it in her."

He switched his rifle to semi-auto and started shooting zombies until the street was nearly clear. Then he went to his boat and examined the damage. Seeing what she'd done there, the way she'd nearly sliced the zombie in half with the propeller, all Shaw could do was stand in awe.

"Damn," he muttered. "She's a tough one all right."

Anthony was watching the alley where they'd last seen Eleanor.

"There's a lot of zombies over there," he said. "What do you want to do, Dad?"

Shaw stared at the gutted zombie for a long time without answering.

"What are we gonna do, Dad?"

"We're gonna find her, and when we catch her, we're gonna kill her."

Anthony nodded slowly.

"Okay," he said. "Okay."

"Good boy," Shaw said. "How's your arm doing?"

"It hurts like a son of a bitch. I can't feel my fingers."

"You feeling cold, short of breath?"

"A little, yeah."

"Okay, we need to hurry this up. Go over to your boat there and get the duffel bags. I'll carry them, but that means you're gonna have to do some of the shooting. You think you can manage that?"

Anthony stiffened. "Yes, sir."

Shaw nodded. "I hope so," he said.

The front door was blasted inward.

As Eleanor reached the apartment building's landing she

saw it hanging from its bottom hinge. Beyond the open doorway was a narrow hall that ran the length of the building. At the far end was another door, also blasted inward. She stopped in the entranceway and looked down. Smears of what was almost certainly blood covered the top half of the door. Bits of debris floated lazily on the water that flowed through the building's first floor.

The zombies, she realized, must have gone through every building out here, looking for survivors.

Looking for something to eat, she corrected herself.

And more would be coming soon.

She glanced back at the water she had just traversed. There was no sign of the Shaws, but at the moment they were only one of her worries. Eleanor had managed to make it most of the way to the building before the zombies pouring into the building next door spotted her, and once they did, they sent up the call. She watched in horrified dismay as they peeled away from the building they'd been trying to enter and stagger-stumbled toward her. Within seconds, they were closing on her from three sides, far too many for a stand-up fight. She had seen row upon row of them advancing on her position, an almost endless tapestry of psychotic and mangled faces, and she had run for the door.

She made it inside, and they followed, as she both knew and feared they would. For a moment it looked as if she might be able to wade down the hallway and go out the back door, but she very quickly saw that wasn't going to happen. Even before she reached the back door she saw a huge crowd, hundreds, maybe even thousands, emerging from the darkness south of the apartments.

"No," she said, shaking her head. "It's not fair. Damn it."

Zombies had already entered the front door, their moans echoing off the walls. Not knowing what else to do, she waded over to the stairs and climbed up to the second floor, where she turned and waited. She was thinking of the Meadowlakes Business Park, how the zombies had struggled with the stairs, and she hoped that would help her now.

She gripped the rifle tightly as the first moans reached the foot of the stairs.

This isn't going to work, the voice inside her head told her.

"Yes, it will," she snapped back.

She swallowed hard. Her waterlogged fingers felt cold and numb against the M-16's metal receiver. Her breathing was coming fast and shallow now.

It won't work, the voice said again. *Remember Bobby Hester, how you watched him climb the stairs. You've got to run. Go. Run!*

"It will work," she said. "It will."

But she didn't really believe it, and when the first zombies appeared at the foot of the stairs and started up, she surrendered to the voice inside her head and ran up the stairs as fast as she could make her legs go.

The stairs led all the way to the roof. She emerged onto a small rectangular platform dotted with pipe vents and fans, the floor ribbed with snakelike tar strips. Eleanor closed the door behind her and then turned around to look for someplace to hide.

But it was useless.

There was nothing up here big enough to hide behind. She had gone as high as she could go, and now, the zombies had treed her just as surely as bloodhounds driving a raccoon up a pine. She had nowhere else to go.

The moaning was growing louder, and with mounting terror she realized she could hear their footsteps trudging heavily up the stairs. She closed her eyes and prayed for something to take her away from all this, some helicopter to swoosh down out of nowhere and take her away. But when she opened her eyes again, the sky was as empty as it had been before she closed them.

In the distance, she could see towering columns of orange flame rising up into the night sky, filling it with a ghastly glow. There was gunfire, too, distant and muffled. And, faintly, rising up from the wreckage, the sounds of someone screaming.

We're dying, she thought. *Not just me, all of us. This city . . . it's dead.*

There was a dull thud against the roof's door and Eleanor flinched.

Already? Were they here already?

"All right then," she said, raising her rifle toward the door, "whenever you're ready."

"Anthony, move!" Shaw shouted.

Anthony grunted, half turned, and fired a reckless shot toward a female zombie just ahead of him. The zombie was crack-whore skinny, her clothes hanging off her emaciated frame in bloody tatters. Every inch of her skin was criss-crossed with cuts and scratches, as though she'd stumbled through a dense thicket of thorns. Her nose was gone. It looked as if it had been bitten off. There was nothing but a black, gummy hole there now, oozing infected blood. Her head hung forward, revealing a huge gash from the base of her hairline, down her forehead and across the orbit of her eye. She seemed so frail, so skeletal, that it was a wonder she was able to walk at all; but she did, and with every step she grew closer to Anthony.

"Shoot her or get out of the way, Anthony!"

"I'm trying," Anthony said, but Shaw was aware that his son's voice had changed. He was whining now, frustrated. Anthony had never been frustrated by anything in his life. Everything had always come so easily for him—athletics, girls, police work; but now the gunshot wound in his shoulder and the shock into which it was sending him were starting to cloud his head. He was missing easy shots, and with every miss, his frustration and his fear grew stronger.

"Focus, Anthony! Front sight on the target."

Shaw was yelling over his shoulder. He'd have shot the zombie for him if he'd been able, but they were surrounded, and he had plenty of his own problems to worry about.

They'd followed Eleanor back through the alley and come out on the wide stretch of water behind the apartment buildings just as she was running inside. In a flash, Shaw had realized what was happening. The infected were swarming the apartment building on his extreme left, but as soon as they noticed Eleanor blundering her way through the no-man's-land between the back of the thrift shop and the apartments, they went after her. He'd watched them pour into the building, and for a second, he'd allowed himself a rising sense of elation. They were gonna rip her to shreds . . . and that meant the zombies would do his job for him. He and Anthony could get the hell out of here.

And then Anthony had started shooting.

Shaw had spun around, ready to slap the shit out of the boy for blowing their cover, and stopped cold.

On their way back here they'd passed a darkened, empty doorway. Or at least it had seemed empty. But no sooner had they disturbed the water in front of the door than a steady stream of zombies burst out of it and went straight for Anthony. They were practically right on top of him from the start. Shooting his Glock left-handed he managed to put down six of them with perfect head shots, but it was a losing battle, and he was forced to run to his father's side for protection.

Shaw moved fast. He picked off the zombies nearest to Anthony and guided him into the open space between the buildings. It was the only place left to run.

Within seconds, they were surrounded.

Shaw and Anthony fell together back-to-back and started fighting for their lives.

"Keep your weapon up!" Shaw yelled at him. "Come on, Anthony! Stay with me, son."

But Anthony was fading fast. Between backward glances over his shoulder, Shaw could see that plain enough. Anthony's gun kept dipping to the water, as if it was way too heavy for him. His face was white as cheese. His breathing had become ragged, and underneath the raspy pull of his lungs, Shaw could hear the whimpers of frustration and fear.

Shaw still carried the duffel bags and the gas can, and he was about to toss them aside when a zombie erupted from the water and grabbed hold of Anthony's injured right arm.

Anthony let out a shrieking yell that Shaw felt down to his bones. He thrashed and kicked and tried to shake the zombie loose, but he was weak and all he managed to do was pitch over to one side and go under.

"Anthony, no!" Shaw cried.

Shaw spun around and shot Anthony's attacker in the face.

"Shit, where are you, Anthony?"

He jammed his free hand down into the water and groped around for Anthony.

The next instant his fingers closed on his son's shirt and Shaw yanked him up.

He stood Anthony up and saw that his eyes were drooping, but he was still breathing.

"Are you okay?" Shaw asked. "Did he bite you?"

But he already knew the answer. Even as he spoke, he could see the blood pouring down his son's shoulder, the shirt fabric ripped away to reveal a deep bite.

"Oh, Anthony," he said. He lost all control then. He tried to speak, but his throat was too tight to let the words out. Tears were streaming down his face. "Anthony, no."

"Daddy, I don't want to die. Please, don't leave me."

The words polarized something inside Shaw. He was still raging inside, still trembling with anger and denial and fear and love, and somehow, in all that mixed-up pain, he found the strength to talk.

"I've got you, Anthony. I won't leave you."

And with that he threw Anthony over his shoulder in a fireman's carry and ran toward the apartment building, firing his M-16 one-handed into the zombies closing in around them. Hands and faces danced in and out of view, but Shaw just ducked his head and ran. He felt the zombies clutching at him, pulling at him, but all of that was somehow secondary, a world away. All that mattered was getting his son somewhere safe and warm, providing for him, caring for him.

They entered the apartment's central hallway and were immediately thrown into darkness. He saw dim shapes midway down the hall, bumbling into each other as they attempted to mount the stairs, and he could hear the ones from outside splashing around behind him. He looked left, looked right, and saw a closed door a few feet down the hall.

Shaw set Anthony down next to the door and rammed it with his shoulder. It gave way on his second attempt, and he found himself inside the open doorway, looking at a decomposing corpse faceup on a mattress. He stared at it for a second, breathing hard. The skin on the corpse's face had turned black with rot, the chest and stomach bloated with the gases that accompany decomposition. Its hands were gnarled claws, and the tightening action of rigor had pulled them up in front of the chest in a posture that suggested the corpse was frozen while trying to push away some great weight.

Shaw let out a long, hissing breath of disgust. *So this is it,* he thought. *Last stand down here with the dead.*

And the dying.

Okay then. So be it.

He threw the duffel bags on top of the TV set at the foot of the bed, and then stepped back into the hallway, grabbed Anthony, and pulled him inside the room, leaning him up against the wall.

He closed the door and braced it with a dresser.

Then he crossed to the bed and with one quick motion dumped the mattress and the decaying corpse into the water, propping the mattress up so that it sandwiched the corpse against the wall.

No point in Anthony having to see that, he thought.

"Can you help me with this?" Shaw asked, getting into position to push the bed against the door.

He looked at his son. Anthony's face had turned so pale the blood vessels showed through the skin. His eyes were rimmed in red, his mouth hanging open. Anthony stared back at him, his expression a ghastly mixture of terror and blank incomprehension.

"It's okay, son. Just stand there."

He reached into the pouch he kept at his left hip and counted six more full magazines.

Damn it, he thought, *not nearly enough.*

But when he looked up at Anthony, his smile was steady.

"Don't you worry, son. Daddy's gonna take care of you."

CHAPTER 21

Eleanor backed away from the door. The zombies were banging on the other side, causing it to shake in the frame. Panicking, she looked around once again for something she could use as cover.

But there was nothing.

Get a grip, girl, she told herself. *Slow down. Focus. Think this through.*

"No," she said aloud. "No, I can't."

You can. You will. You have to, Eleanor. Get a grip.

The gun was a known quantity, something she could control. In the academy, her tactics instructors had taught her to slow down, analyze the situation. When things get out of hand, you get control of one thing, really focus, and everything else will start to fall in line.

Eleanor did that now.

She ejected the M-16's magazine and counted eleven rounds. She had those and one in the chamber and another full magazine in the back pocket of her jeans. But that was it. After that, she'd be reduced to using the rifle as a club.

How could she have made it through so much, she wondered, only to be reduced to this? It wasn't fair. She had fought a better fight than this. Hadn't she done everything a woman could possibly be expected to do?

The door shook with another hard hit, and this time, something cracked.

The wood was giving way. As she watched, a crack raced from just below the doorknob over to the bottom hinge. How many hands were pounding on that door, she wondered. Twelve, fourteen, more than that? It sounded as if the stairs beyond were full of the infected.

And then the door gave way.

It snapped off its hinges and fell from the door frame in two large pieces, and in the darkness beyond, Eleanor could see the faces of the damned. For a moment, they stared at her and her at them, and then they surged forward, a wave of teeth and fingernails.

She raised her rifle, the ghost ring sight centered on the lead zombie's chest . . . and then she lowered it. Inspiration struck. She stepped over the low wall of the air-conditioning platform and onto the steeply sloping roof. There was an uncertain moment, a deliriously acrophobic moment as her stomach rolled over, and she felt as if she might faint, and then she closed her eyes and forced herself to regain control. Then she opened her eyes and started crab-walking across the roof, the shingles rough as sandpaper beneath her fingers.

She moved toward the north corner of the building, passing beneath the air-conditioning platform, and chanced a look up. One of the zombies was lunging toward her. It went over the knee-high wall and tumbled forward, down the side of the roof and over the edge.

She watched it fall, arms and legs pinwheeling wildly in the air, and she let out a cry that was part terrified whimper, part triumphant yell.

Breathing hard, she looked back up at the air-conditioning platform.

More zombies were coming over the knee-high wall around the platform. Several of them lost their balance and went over the side of the roof. But others stayed on their feet and started toward her.

Moving in a crouch, Eleanor backed away. She had maybe thirty feet left of roof behind her, but she could already tell she was going to have to stand and fight. More and more of the zombies were making their way down the length of the roof.

She raised her rifle and fired at a female up near the roof peak.

The zombie collapsed and rolled down the side, taking six others with it.

"Yeah!" she screamed, shaking her rifle at the remaining zombies.

This is going to work, she thought. *It is really going to work.*

But there were still others she couldn't just bowl off the side. A fat, blond man in a blue T-shirt was closing on her. His jeans were soaked in blood, and with every shuffling step across the shingled roof, his tattered sneakers left dark smears of ichor. She stepped over the ridge and grabbed her gun by the barrel, holding it like a baseball bat.

She waited for him to step into range, and when he was close enough, she swung for his head. The blow knocked him down, but he grabbed for her at the same time, and the M-16's shoulder strap got caught up in his fingers.

The next instant, Eleanor was struggling to maintain her balance. The zombie was sliding down the roof sheeting, but it was pulling her with it, and try as she might, she just couldn't keep her feet. Eleanor pitched over forward, landed on her chin, and slid down the side of the roof. She saw the edge racing toward her, the yawning emptiness beyond it coming rapidly into view, and she clawed at the shingles for something to hold on to.

The next instant the zombie was tumbling over the side and falling free to the writhing carpet of clutching hands and upturned faces below. Eleanor followed after it, swinging her legs over the edge and catching herself on the eaves at the last possible instant.

She had only seen the ground below for a second, but that had been more than enough for her.

There were hundreds of zombies crowded in together down there, an infected bolus of hands and teeth and gore reaching up for her, their collective motion almost tidal.

Eleanor was delirious with panic. Her fingers were digging into the tar strip shingles, but it wasn't enough. She was slipping, inch by inch. Her legs pumped and kicked at the empty air. Her backpack and the M-16 seemed to weigh a ton. She would have jettisoned them if she'd had a hand free, but that couldn't happen now.

Her grip gave for just a second, and she slid four or five inches farther down, leaving only her nose and chin above the level of the roof.

A scream rose in her throat.

Above her, coming down the slope of the roof in a lurching, out-of-control trot was another zombie. This one was unable to control its descent and toppled over the edge, his fingers grazing the sleeve of her blouse as he went over top of her. But the others behind him were moving more slowly, and even in her panicked state, a part of her mind told her that at least one of those zombies would have enough control to attack her hands.

Then she caught a sound rising above all the others.

It was a scream. A young girl shrieking for help.

"Madison!" Eleanor yelled back. "Madison!"

In her mind Eleanor was absolutely certain that that sound was coming from her daughter, the way a mother will know the cry of her own hurt child above the din of dozens of others on a crowded playground.

Madison was down there somewhere. Alive. Alive but in trouble.

Eleanor kicked at the side of the building, praying for a ledge, a windowsill, anything she could use. What she found was a metal pipe. The toe of her sneaker raked across it. Frantic, she groped for it with her foot, trying to get a feel for where it was, and felt it curve upward, hugging the underside of the eaves.

Two more zombies sailed over top of her. She chanced a look down and saw them splash into the water, the zombie horde seeming to swallow them up whole.

Oh Jesus, she thought. *Oh sweet Jesus. Please make this work.*

Aware that she only had one chance to get this right, she reached under the eaves with her right hand and gripped the top of the pipe.

"Please," she said. "Oh please."

She let go of the roof and slid off the side, screaming as her weight dropped and her fingers nearly let go. But her grip did hold. Eleanor fell forward, smacking face-first into the wall. She brought her left hand up, slapping wildly at the pipe, and got her fingers around it. She pumped her feet against the wall until she got traction there and then was still. Her heart was pounding in her chest. A white hot pain shot up from her fingers to her shoulders, but she didn't care. She was deliriously happy just to be alive and she threw her head back and let out a yell that gave way first to laughter and then to tears.

Eleanor looked down and saw a window just below her left shoe. She could make it, she thought, as long as the pipe would continue to bear her weight. Working slowly, careful to keep as much weight as possible on her feet, she started to slide down.

When she reached the bottom ledge of the window she glanced inside.

The floor was a patchwork of puddles, dotted by glass blown in during the recent storms. Sodden furniture had turned gray from mildew. The front door had been knocked in, by zombies, she guessed, going room to room, looking for food, but there were no zombies in there now, and that was all that counted.

She climbed in through the window and sat down heavily on the ledge, exhausted down to the bone.

But she couldn't rest and she knew it.

Madison was out there. She couldn't hear her screams anymore, but she knew in her heart that her daughter was out there, somewhere, and that Madison needed her.

That was all it took for Eleanor.

The muscles in her arms and back ached. Standing up took a sheer act of will. But stand she did.

Eleanor turned and leaned out the window and looked down.

A blur of faces stared back up at her.

She felt suddenly sick, light-headed, and utterly empty of ideas. How was she going to get over there? And for that matter, what was she going to do if she did get over there? There were thousands of zombies down there, and all she had was a handful of bullets.

But she had to try.

From somewhere below she heard a man's voice yelling in defiant rage. The sound was followed by the chain-saw clatter of machine-gun fire.

Mark Shaw, she thought. *The fucking bastard's still alive, still fighting.*

She nearly spit on the floor in disgust, but then she stopped and thought about Captain Shaw . . . still alive, still fighting. He would fight, wouldn't he? To the very end. That was the kind of man he was.

Maybe she could use that.

She leaned back out the window and looked down. There

was a cinder-block wall down there that connected her building with the building from which she had heard Madison's screams. She could run across that. Maybe.

And maybe Captain Shaw could help her with the zombies.

She started to scream at the crowd. She yelled at the top of her lungs, waving at them, picking up trash from the floor and throwing it out the window at them.

"Up here, you fucking bastards! Come on. Come and get me!"

Her voice stirred them up, exactly as she hoped it would. Their moans rose from a dull roar to a maddened frenzy.

"That's it," she screamed, slapping the outside wall below her window. "That's it! Come on up. You want me? Come and take me!"

The crowd surged against the ground floor. They were pouring in through windows and circling around to the front of the building to enter the doorway there. But she could hear them in the hallway, too. The ones from the roof would be coming down. Probably already were. She was pretty sure she could hear them banging around out there on the stairs, searching for her.

And then she heard gunfire again. Coming hard, coming fast.

"That's it, Shaw," she muttered. "Chew 'em up."

She didn't give herself a chance to think about what came next. There was no way she could have, and still have had the nerve to go forward. She climbed out the window, one hand on the metal pipe, and swung herself out. Then she started down the pipe, blocking out the ravenous moaning below as best she could, thinking only of Madison.

As she went lower the sound of shooting grew louder. Shaw was, exactly as she expected, putting up one hell of a good fight. And it was driving the zombies into a frenzy. They were pouring into the building now.

"Come on," she said quietly, watching them. "Keep coming."

She dropped onto the wall and teetered there, her arms outstretched for balance. Zombies reached up for her, slapping the wall with their bloody palms, trying in vain to climb the slime-slick walls. She swallowed once and then turned all her focus on walking the wall.

One foot after the other, she thought. *One step at a time.*

She made it halfway across before one of the zombies managed to get a hand on her shoe. Eleanor wasn't sure how it had happened, whether it had jumped or simply scaled over the backs of the others, but the end result was the same. Its mangled hand clamped down over the toe of her sneaker and didn't let go. As the zombie tumbled back down into the water below, Eleanor pitched over. The pack shifted on her back. The M-16 slipped off her shoulder and she reached for it clumsily, barely regaining control of the weapon in time to prevent one of the zombies from grabbing it.

She was on her knees now, struggling to get back up. Faces swam below her, indistinct and hostile. The noise was tremendous. But she had her balance back, at least for the time being. Would it help, she wondered? The tendons in her ankles felt limp as wet spaghetti. Her legs were burning. Eleanor rose slowly, painfully, to her feet, straightened the pack and the weapon, and started walking again.

She rushed her final steps and actually lunged for the wall, catching the metal pipe that ran up the side of the building as if it was base in a game of tag. And maybe, she thought, in a way, it kind of was. She had made it across the courtyard. She was close now. Very close.

The window to her right led into a second-story efficiency apartment. Eleanor had to kick in the window to get inside, and once she did, she ran to the door and listened to the hallway outside. With so many voices moaning, screaming, it was hard to focus on exactly where they were coming from . . . behind her, below her, above . . . she couldn't tell.

Eleanor took a chance and opened the door a crack.

The hallway beyond was dark. She listened, and couldn't make out any footsteps. If this building was anything like the one she'd just left—and she didn't see why it wouldn't be; from the outside they appeared to be twins—there would be staircases at the front of the building and another in the back. She went out into the hallway and crossed to the stairs.

Looking down into the gloom below she could see zombies pushing against each other, trying to make their way back to the back of the building. At the same time she heard Madison screaming. She was very close.

"Madison!" she gasped.

Down below, several pairs of eyes turned toward her. They started up the stairs, a renewed hunger in their moaning, and soon a dozen or more were coming for her.

"Oh shit," she said, backing up.

She looked up. The stairwell twined up four stories, just like in the other building. There was room to retreat.

But when she looked back down the stairs, she realized that the number of her pursuers had grown. From an original dozen or so, a swarm had formed. They were pushing against each other, some falling onto their faces as the stronger ones behind them clambered over their backs in their rush to overtake her.

"That's it!" she screamed at them. "Come on up, you bastards! Come and get me."

She backed up the stairs, careful to keep just a few steps ahead of the lead zombie, calling out to them the whole time.

"Don't stop," she yelled. "Come on."

When she reached the third-floor landing she broke away from the stairs and sprinted down the central hallway to the back of the building. Here she had to be quick. She brought her M-16 up and worked her way quickly down the stairs, scanning every corner to make sure she wasn't stepping into a crowd of them.

She passed a dead and mostly eaten body on the second-floor landing, but no zombies, and she was thankful for that.

But then she jumped into the water at the ground floor and turned the corner.

And there, less than ten feet in front of her, was Jim . . . hanging from the ceiling . . . and Madison on his back.

Eleanor couldn't believe it. He had his hands on one wall, his feet against the opposite wall, his body like an arch over the floor, and below him, a swarm of zombies groped the air and tugged at his shirt.

"Leave him alone," she said, her voice just a notch above a whisper.

The zombies turned toward her. One by one their hands dropped from the air, and they came for her.

Eleanor felt something click inside her. Some important part of her was coming into focus and everything seemed to slow down. She saw every face in that zombie crowd, and as she raised her rifle and started firing, she felt utterly calm and completely in control. The zombies went down one by one, and when the last empty cartridge shell flew from the weapon's breach, the water was choked with bodies. Nothing moved but the water. It lapped against the walls and rocked the dead bodies gently.

They were alone now.

Eleanor looked up at her husband, at the ashen, sweat-soaked expression on his face, and said, "Jim?"

He dropped from the ceiling then. He and Madison landed in the water with a dull splash.

Madison let out a startled cry that was silenced by the water.

Eleanor ran forward and scooped her up and squeezed her so hard Madison began to choke.

"Mom," she gasped.

"Oh baby," Eleanor said. "Oh my sweet baby."

She held Madison at arm's length then, barely believing that she was holding her again. Madison's dirty face was lined by tear tracks. The whites of her eyes stood out with startling clarity.

"Mom, I was so scared."

"I know, baby. Are you okay? Did they hurt you?"

Madison could only shake her head no, and then she started to cry. Eleanor pulled her close and hugged her and thought there was no way under the sun she was going to let that little girl go again.

Until her gaze met Jim's.

Eleanor had seen exhaustion before. She'd seen it as a girl in the faces of the rescue workers during Hurricanes Rita and Ike. She'd seen it in the faces of her fellow cops after the Westheimer riots five years ago. And she had seen it in the eyes of the refugees who waited up on the Beltway for their turn to go through the military's checkpoint. But she had never seen exhaustion like she did in her husband's eyes. The man had been pushed to his very limits, and yet he continued to hold on. She could only imagine what it must have been like, supporting himself and Madison both up on the walls. How long had been like that, twenty-five or thirty minutes?

"Oh, Jim," she said, and she let Madison go and reached for him.

He staggered forward and collapsed against her. She took his weight by throwing her arms around him.

"Jim, you did it. I can't believe it. You saved our daughter. Thank you."

He grunted, but didn't embrace her. She backed away slightly and looked at him.

"Jim?"

The muscles in his upper arms felt hard as concrete.

"Jim, are you okay?"

"I can't feel my arms," he said.

She laughed at that, laughed hard, and when at long last she got it under control she threw her arms around his neck and kissed his cheek.

"Come on," she said, looking first at Jim, then at Madison. "Let's get out of here."

CHAPTER 22

The door caved inward. Mark Shaw's gaze snapped toward it, M-16 at the ready. Hands were reaching through the narrow gap, pressing on the door, shaking it. The zombies had managed to open it maybe three inches, but the bed frame and the dresser were holding, for now, and Shaw lowered his weapon.

Anthony was still standing in the same place, swaying drunkenly, a soul-sick look in his eyes.

Shaw took the pistol from Anthony's hand and walked around the bed frame so he could see out the gap. A zombie was trying to jam his face through the opening, the lips pulled back in a grin of bloody teeth, and right before Shaw shot him in the face he had a flash of Jack Nicholson in *The Shining*, jamming his head through the door he'd just hacked with a hatchet, taunting Shelley Duvall with an insanely shrill, "Heeeere's Johnny!"

Shaw's first shot killed the zombie, but there were too many bodies pressing up against it from behind, and though the corpse sagged downward, it didn't fall.

Shaw had just enough room to see over the dead zombie.

Working slowly, taking each shot in its turn, he emptied the remainder of the magazine into the crowd.

Let the corpses pile up, he thought. *The fuckers'll have to climb their way over. Maybe it'll slow them up a little.*

When the gun was empty he tossed it aside. There was no point in holding on to a weapon that didn't have any bullets. And it wasn't like they were going to get out of this alive. Shaw realized with an eerie calm that he'd already resigned himself to that fate. The only question was how long he could hold out.

But that wasn't the only question, was it?

There was Anthony to think about, too. Shaw licked his dry and cracked lips, then looked at his youngest son, his wonderfully gifted child.

Anthony was doing badly.

Besides a distinctly circular swaying, he was pale, so very pale. His lips had lost their color. His eyes were red-rimmed and they had a glazed, unfocused look, as if he were high on dope and close to passing out. Beads of sweat rolled down his cheeks.

Shaw thought: *What about you, son? When the time comes, will I be able to do it for you, like I did for Brent?* But with the same mental breath he answered his own question: *Yes, you will. You have to. There is a duty to perform, and you will do it. Just like you've always done. Just like you tried to teach to your sons. Maybe Anthony won't understand why you have to do it. Maybe he'll spend his last few lucid moments pleading for you to save his life instead of taking it, for as gifted as he was, Anthony was never the one to make the hard decisions. He never understood that mercy could be savage, or that sometimes a father's love could hurt. He never understood.*

The zombies continued to pound on the door. Shaw could hear the wood snapping. It wouldn't be long now, two or three minutes at the most. Soon, there would be some hard fighting, some Davy Crockett-at-the-Alamo hard fighting.

Shaw let his gaze slide from the door back to Anthony.

"I'm sorry," he said.

Anthony's milky eyes turned on Shaw's, and then seemed to slip out of focus again.

"I could have handled this better, I know," Shaw said. "You trusted me to do the right thing, and I thought I was doing the right thing. But sometimes it's hard, you know? It's hard to always know what the right thing is. When you're a dad you just kind of go with your gut most of the time and hope that dumb luck will see you through it. Most of the time it does, and when it does it feels so good, but . . ."

Shaw trailed off. He was rambling, not making any sense, and he knew it. Anthony was just staring off into space, as if he was empty inside. None of this was getting through.

You're talking to yourself, Shaw thought.

"Yeah, maybe," he muttered.

He fingered the edge of the dresser, his mind turning back over the years.

"You don't remember this," he said to Anthony, "but when you and Brent were kids you had this bedroom furniture set that your mom insisted we get for you. 'They're growing boys,' she said. 'They need real furniture.' "

He laughed to himself.

"I still remember it. The Easton Collection, in honey pine. Easton, like the baseball bat, you know? I was a detective at the time, making shit for a paycheck, and that furniture cost a ton of money. But your mom said you guys had to have it, and she begged me to buy it. What could I do? I mean, it was for my boys, you know? Only the best. I'd do anything for you guys."

He looked at Anthony, but there was nothing there. The boy had no time left. He'd probably go before the door did.

Shaw sighed.

"I worked God knows how many hours of overtime to get the money to pay for that furniture. I must have done a dozen twenty-hour shifts, maybe more than that. But I did it. We got the money and bought you guys the furniture. 'Course the first thing you did was color it with crayons. I remember you threw Brent into the bedside table about a month after I bought it and broke the lamp. God, you guys were horrible to each other. But it didn't matter, you know? All the work, all the extra hours. It didn't even matter that you wrote all over it. I'd never been so proud in my life, just knowing that I had provided for you, that I had done my job as your dad. There's a power in that feeling that makes it all worth it. That's what I wanted to do here, with this money. I wanted that feeling all over again. I wanted to know that I had provided for you."

Anthony stirred then.

Shaw looked at him hopefully. "Anthony? Do you understand that? You don't . . . hate me, do you? I promise you, I didn't want this to happen."

"Can I see the money?" Anthony said. His voice was slurred, the words coming out in a dreamy monotone.

"Sure," Shaw said. "Yeah, of course."

Shaw turned back to the mattress, where he'd stowed the two duffel bags. He unzipped one of the bags and looked inside.

"What the . . ." he said.

He stared at the contents, blinking rapidly, not at all sure what was going on. He turned the bag over on the mattress and what tumbled out made no sense at all. Plastic trash bags. Duct tape. Dust masks. Glow sticks. Candles. Chemical water purifiers. It was a classic survival kit, the kind the folks from FEMA had lectured his unit to prepare for their families at home.

And then it hit him.

Eleanor Norton, he thought. *That fucking bitch. She did*

this. She beat me. How the fuck did that happen? How did that *fucking happen?*

He turned to Anthony, a stack of napkins in his hand, and had no idea what to say.

"Anthony, I . . ."

Anthony held out his hand. "I want to hold it," he said.

Shaw looked down at the napkins.

"Anthony, this . . ."

But then he understood, and he tore the band that held the napkins together and he stuffed the loose napkins into Anthony's groping hand.

He closed Anthony's fingers around the paper.

"You got it?"

"Yeah," Anthony said. There was a dreamy sort of distance in his voice and in his eyes. "It's nice," he said. "God, it's nice. I never thought I'd hold so much. I never thought . . ."

He trailed off.

Shaw watched him carefully, studying his eyes, the tremor in his lips.

"Anthony?"

"Dad, I wanted to . . . to say. . . . I wanted to . . ." He raised his hand slowly, and the paper napkins tumbled from his fingers and floated down to the water around his hips. Tears were streaming down Shaw's face now. "I wanted you to know that I . . . I love . . . I . . ." Anthony trailed off again, as though he were deep in thought, considering exactly the right way to say what was weighing on his mind, and while he was lost in thought, the change happened.

The last spark of intelligence left his eyes. The essence of who he was, who he had been, was gone.

His left arm came up slowly. His mouth fell open and a moan rose up from his throat.

Shaw watched the change, weeping, then raised his rifle.

"I love you, too, Anthony. God help me, I love you with all my heart."

And then he fired.

The bullet snapped Anthony's head back and he sagged down into the water.

Shaw crossed the room quickly and scooped Anthony up in his arms. He pulled him back over to the mattress and threw his arms around him and rocked him gently.

"I love you," he said, kissing the top of Anthony's head. "I love you, Anthony."

Shaw threw back his head and yelled at the top of his lungs. There was so much inside him, so much rage and love and fear and bitter, bitter loss, and it came out of him in a flood he couldn't have controlled for all the world.

His high, lonely cry was met by renewed moaning from out in the hallway.

The door burst open, the top half coming loose from the hinges and falling over the top of the bed frame.

Shaw was ready for them. As they scrambled over the top of the bed frame, he was waiting with the M-16 trained on the doorway.

"Come on, you bastards!"

He started to fire, and he didn't stop shooting, not until they pulled him down into screaming oblivion.

CHAPTER 23

It was a little after 3 A.M. when Eleanor and Jim and Madison slipped away from the apartment building and began their solitary trek toward the city walls. In the distance they could hear gunfire and helicopters and indistinct sounds that might have been screams. And, closer, coming from all around them, the moans of the infected.

There were survivors, too. Not many, but a few. They walked silently on, bound for God knew where. They didn't hail the Nortons, and the Nortons didn't wave or call out to them. It was as if they all existed under glass bell jars, visible to each other, but worlds and worlds apart.

It made Eleanor feel sad and small and very tired.

To the south, the sky was a hazy orange. The oil refineries were still burning, and the breeze carried the smell of ash and the sea, and under that, the deep, worn-in stench of chemicals and death. If this didn't qualify as hell, Eleanor wasn't sure what would.

"We have to find a boat," Jim said. "I don't think I can walk much farther."

Eleanor, her hair in damp clumps around her face, her eyes heavy with exhaustion, knew exactly how he felt. She wasn't far from falling over herself. Only Madison seemed to have any stomach left for a long walk. There was a sort of electric buzz around her. The girl couldn't stand still. Her eyes darted everywhere. She flinched at the slightest sound. Eleanor watched her and knew the poor thing was in for a crash when the adrenaline wore off. She just hoped it wouldn't happen too soon.

"I guess," Eleanor said, "we head toward the wall and hope that we can find something. A lot of boats got left there."

"How far you suppose it is?"

She shrugged. "An hour's walk maybe. I don't know."

His shoulders sagged visibly. In the faint starlight he looked ten years younger, his hair darker, his chin more defined. And that was it, she realized. He did look younger. The exhaustion, the resignation, had given him a boy's look. And yet one that seemed to hold the world at arm's length. She wondered if her own expression was equally as youthful.

No such luck, sister, she thought. *It doesn't happen for women that way. The men get younger looking, the women just get exhausted. You probably look exactly like you feel, like you've been run over by a truck.*

They trudged on.

In the distance Eleanor could see a street lined with the ruins of shops. Beyond that was the Beltway. Even from this far out she could tell that great lengths of it had collapsed and fallen into the water. Around them, the neighborhood had become a nightmare of burned buildings. Whole blocks seemed to have caught fire. In places, nothing remained but a few blackened poles sticking up from the water. Burned debris floated past them.

"Did those helicopters do all this?" Madison asked.

"I think so."

"Why?"

"To push people back from the fence, I would imagine. My guess is they're going to put up some kind of wall around the city, at least for the time being."

"But what about all the people?" Madison asked. "What about the ones who aren't infected?"

Eleanor sighed. "I suppose they'll be locked in with the zombies," she said.

"Oh my God," Madison said, cupping a hand over her mouth. "That's . . . isn't that against the law or something? How can they do that?"

"These are desperate times," Eleanor said. "People do desperate things."

Madison didn't respond to that. At first Eleanor thought it was another of Madison's angst-filled teenage moments, where everything about the world of adults seemed stupid and unkind, but then she realized that Madison was crying.

"Hey," she said, and put an arm around her. "Hey, you're okay."

"They're gonna lock us in here," Madison said.

Her untidy brown hair had developed a kink above her forehead. Eleanor touched her daughter's hair and tried to smooth it down, but the hair wouldn't cooperate.

"We're gonna find a way out," Eleanor said. "I promise you. I'm gonna take care of you."

About a mile farther on they found a boat.

Jim noticed it first.

They were walking next to a line of shrubs that had somehow escaped the rockets and the fires that had destroyed everything else around here. Eleanor was watching Jim. He had stumbled twice in just a few minutes, and he seemed to be having some trouble breathing. He put a hand to his chest and rubbed there absently, the way a man will do when he's felt a hitch in his heart beat that he hopes is nothing.

"Jim, you holding up okay?"

"Yeah, I just—" he said, and that was when they heard the sound of tree limbs scraping up against a metal boat hull.

They all stopped.

"You hear that?" he asked her, suddenly perking up.

She nodded. "It sounds like it's coming from over there."

Over there was on the other side of the line of shrubs. Jim didn't hesitate. He ducked into the shrubs and disappeared.

"Jim, wait!"

There was a long pause, and then Jim's voice rose over the shrubs. "It's okay," he said. "You two come on through."

Eleanor glanced at Madison and Madison shrugged. "After you, Mom."

"Thanks."

Eleanor stepped through the shrubs nervously. The branches were scraggly enough that she was able to hold them out of the way for Madison, revealing a small silver boat with its prow jammed into the canopy of a fallen tree. Eleanor peeked around Jim's shoulder and saw a dead man sitting in the boat. His head had lolled back over his shoulders, but Eleanor could still see the blackened flesh on one side of his face. His clothes too were burned.

"Eww," Madison said. "What happened to him?"

"Must have gotten caught in the explosions over by the Beltway," Jim said.

"But how did he get all the way over here?"

"Who knows?" Jim said. "Maybe he got injured over there and died while he was trying to get away."

"Maybe he drifted over here," Eleanor offered.

"Yeah," Jim said. "Could be. Here, help me move him off the boat."

Eleanor and Jim grabbed the dead man by the back of his shirt and pulled him down into the water. Then they pulled the boat from the tree canopy and gave it a quick once-over.

"Looks like it'll work," he said.

"Yeah. Madison, you ready?"

Madison glanced at the dead man floating face up in the water, swallowed, and then got in. Eleanor followed, then Jim last. He tried to pull the starter cord on the boat's outboard, but he couldn't make it work.

"Eleanor, can you . . ."

"Huh?"

"My arms," he said lamely. He looked mortified. "I can't. They hurt too bad."

She understood then.

"Oh, yeah. Sure."

They switched places, and Eleanor got the motor started and guided them away from the line of shrubs and toward the Beltway.

They were facing due east, and the coming dawn had lit the sky in tones of pink and gray. Ahead of them, the Beltway and the buildings around it looked like London in those grainy old black-and-white movies from the Second World War. Everywhere she looked, Eleanor saw skeletal ruins crumbling into the water. Some were little more than a single wall. Everything had been touched by fire. Gray concrete dust still hung in the air, moving slowly, like smoke on the water.

The water was thick with charred bodies. A few, horribly, still moved, and some of them could even raise a blackened hand and moan.

The Beltway itself was a jumbled mess. Large pieces of concrete jutted up from the water at odd angles, and in the screen of dust they resembled the prows of ships sinking into the ocean.

A helicopter flew overheard, very close.

Eleanor had already cut the motor a good distance back, rowing them to this point. She didn't want the motor's noise to attract soldiers—or worse, more zombies—and she thought that decision might save them now. The helicopters almost certainly had heat-sensing equipment, so they would pick them up for sure, but if the boat was just drifting, maybe they wouldn't appear any different than the other bodies in the water and in the derelict boats. After all, most of them had been badly burned. Heat signatures would be everywhere.

"Get your head down," she said to Madison. "Everybody stay still."

"Mom . . ."

"Shhh," Eleanor said. "We're okay. Just stay still. It'll be gone in a second."

The helicopter glided slowly overhead. The pilot didn't appear to be looking for anything in particular, just cruising, and Eleanor watched the aircraft glide away until the red taillights were far in the distance.

"I think we're okay," she said at last.

"No," Jim said. "Eleanor, we can't do it this way. As soon as they realize that we're not a derelict, they'll fire on us. We didn't come all this way to die now."

"No," she said, "you're right."

"So what do we do?"

Eleanor smiled. Twenty-four hours earlier, she would have answered Jim's question with an "I don't know." But now, things had changed. She had changed. And she knew exactly what they needed to do.

"Hang on," she said. "We're doubling back."

The first fingers of daylight were spreading over the flooded ruins when she finally found what she was looking for.

"Okay," she said in a whisper, "you two wait for me here."

"Eleanor, I . . ."

"Hey, it'll be okay. Jim, I can do this."

He looked at her then, and the expression on his face was one she didn't quite recognize.

"What is it?"

"It's you," he said. "You've changed."

She started to object, to ask him what that was supposed to mean, but he stopped her.

"No," he said. "No, no. It's a good thing. I mean . . . oh hell. Eleanor, we've been married fifteen years, and I never knew this woman was inside of you. It's like you've blossomed. . . . You've . . . you're like Superwoman. Or Wonder Woman, or whatever the hell she's called. But you *have* changed. All I'm trying to say is I like it. I like this."

She was blushing to the roots of her hair.

"I don't really . . ." she started to say, but trailed off.

He leaned forward and kissed her then. "Just be careful, okay? Please."

She nodded.

Jesus, she thought, mentally kicking herself, *are you crying? Stop being such a girl.*

Eleanor mopped the tears from her eyes with the back of her hand. Then she handed Jim her backpack.

"You two get going," she said.

"I love you, Mom," said Madison.

"I love you, too, baby. Go with your dad, okay? We'll be out of here before you know it."

Madison hugged her. Eleanor didn't want to let go, but she knew this had to get done. They were running out of darkness.

"Go on," she said, guiding Madison toward Jim.

Jim took Madison by the shoulders and together they climbed out of the boat and swam silently over to a pile of broken concrete not far from a hole in the chain-link fence the military had set up. Two National Guardsmen were standing sentry duty by the hole. They were sitting in a small white fishing boat, drinking coffee from Starbucks cups, looking tired and bored. From the shelter of a bent-over street sign, Eleanor watched Jim and Madison glide into position, so that they were less than thirty feet from the sentries.

Good, she thought. *Good job, Jim.*

Then she turned the boat away and paddled a good distance off. Looking back to the east, she faced the spreading dawn. The horizon was lit with red and copper and gold, the flooded landscape below it a tapestry of shadow and murky light. Years later, when she thought back to this time, to leaving Houston, this is how she would remember it—the crumbling walls dappled with red sunlight, the water towers standing like mute giants over the rubble and the burned bodies, the demolished Beltway. She was tempted to turn back to the south and get one final look at the rest of the city that had been her home her entire life, but something told her not to, that looking back was somehow the wrong thing to do.

It certainly hadn't worked for Lot's wife.

It was the second time in as many days she had thought of the story of Lot's wife, and she couldn't help but chuckle now at the idea of a woman turning into a pillar of salt. But while she could laugh at the image, she could not laugh at the sense behind the story. For wasn't there a certain undeniable truth in it? Didn't it tally with Eleanor's own situation, just a little? There was nothing behind Eleanor but the ghost of a city—the end of one life, and the beginning of another, but much more uncertain, life. And maybe that was why Lot's wife turned into a pillar of salt. Maybe she couldn't reconcile the palaces of her memory with the ruins of her reality.

Maybe.

But there was no more time for idle thoughts and stories. She scanned the ruins to the east, looking for a target. There were burnt corpses all around her. She pulled one of them into the boat and positioned it next to her.

"You ready?" she said to the dead body. "Well, good. At least one of us is."

And then she twisted the throttle all the way open, turning the little boat on a collision course with the military. She pulled the rifle's sling over her shoulder and threw one leg over the gunwale.

"See you around," she said.

Then she jumped over the side.

From his hiding place, Jim watched the little boat accelerate through a debris field of wrecked trucks and garbage and toppled street signs. There was a body hunched over the motor. He projected the line of the boat's course and figured it would hit about six hundred yards north of their position.

That is, if the military didn't blow it out of the water long before that.

In fact, he was already seeing movement around the quarantine wall. A pair of helicopters was sprinting that way, their noses dipped toward the water in an attitude that made them look fiercely determined.

Boats were scrambling outside the wall as well. He could see four of them powering up, turning that way.

Then he looked back at the hole. The two sentries were still sitting in their boat, drinking their coffee, their weapons leaning against their seats, only now they were craning their necks toward the little boat, watching it speed to its imminent destruction.

Jim wished he could make some sense out of the voices coming from their radios, but it just sounded like a garbled mess to him, the same as Eleanor's police radio had back when she was still a patrol officer.

They didn't seem too concerned, though.

"Daddy . . . ?"

Madison was looking at him. *Poor thing is terrified*, he thought. *Well, that makes two of us.*

"It's okay," he said. "Your mother's gonna be along here any second."

"Are you sure this is going to work?"

No, he wanted to say.

Instead he smiled and squeezed Madison to him. "Your mother knows what she's doing," he said.

And to himself he added, *Please let that be true.*

Eleanor rose slowly from the water. She was behind a pile of concrete beams, watching the National Guardsmen through a gap in the rubble.

Definitely weekend soldiers, she thought.

The two men were in their mid-thirties, both a little over-weight, both more interested in complaining about their assignment than in watching their surroundings. And that was just as well. She had swum hard and fast to get here before the little motorboat reached the wall. If these two had managed to keep their heads out of their asses they would have surely heard her coming.

Oh well, she thought. You snooze, you lose.

She stepped around the cement pile with her weapon up and ready.

"Hey, hey!" one of the men said. Their coffee cups went flying as the two men reached clumsily for their weapons.

"Don't do it, guys," Eleanor said. "Hands where I can see them."

From somewhere off to her right, Eleanor heard the sound of guns firing and she figured the little boat and its corpse captain had just been reduced to floating splinters.

She didn't break her concentration, though.

"Fellas, I don't want to kill you. Nobody else needs to

die. Just keep those hands up where I can see them. Go on now. That's it. Keep 'em up."

"Who the fuck are you?" one of them said. The name plate on his uniform said GLADRY.

"Does it really matter, Mr. Gladry? You and Mr. Unwin there need to step out of the boat and onto the roof of that pickup there."

Gladry just stared at her.

"Move!" she said.

"Fuck you, lady. We're not going anywhere."

Eleanor swallowed, flexed her finger on the trigger. Jesus, she didn't want to do this. She did not want to kill these guys.

But just then, from beside her, she heard Jim's voice. "You heard the lady," he said. "You boys need to move it."

Eleanor glanced at him. She was going to tell him he was crazy, order him back behind cover, remind him she had this under control, but that all changed when she saw him. He was standing there, water dripping off him, her pistol in his hands and pointed at the two National Guardsmen.

And then he winked at her.

The bastard actually winked at her. She would have laughed if she weren't so damn terrified.

But evidently it was enough for the one named Unwin, because he stepped over the side and onto the roof of the pickup next to their boat.

Gladry tried to reach for his radio, which was resting inside a cup holder next to the driver's seat, but Eleanor stopped him.

"No," she said sharply. "Leave the radios, leave the weapons."

The soldier nodded, raised his hands in a gesture of surrender, and followed Unwin onto the pickup.

"You can't do this," Gladry said to Eleanor.

Without taking her weapon off them, Eleanor gave a hand sign for Jim and Madison to climb into the boat the soldiers had just left. The two soldiers watched them get onboard. Their faces were taut with suppressed tension. A vein in Gladry's forehead seemed to pulse.

"You're wrong about that, Gladry. I'm getting my family out of here, and I can, and I will, do anything to make that happen."

Then Jim lowered his hand toward her and Eleanor took it, and he swung her up into the boat. She picked up their radios and inspected the display. It was a Motorola, same as the one the HPD used, but with a slightly different channel system.

She tossed both radios into the water.

"Hey!" Gladry said.

Jim looked at the ripples where the radio had just sunk below the surface, and then to Eleanor.

"They can track those," she said. She motioned at the pistol in Jim's hand. "Cover them for a second."

She ejected the magazines from each of the soldiers' rifles and cleared the chambers. Then she tossed the rifles into the flooded cab of the pickup the two men were standing on.

"What did you do that for?" Unwin said.

"Just because I want my family to live doesn't mean I want you to die," Eleanor answered. She tossed their magazines into the flooded bed of the truck. "You can get those back once we're out of sight. Deal?"

"Fuck you," Gladry said. His face was turning beet red now.

"I'll take that as a yes." She turned to Jim and pointed at a line of buildings off to the left. "Take us out slowly, around that block over there. Don't go too fast. I don't want to attract any attention."

"Okay," Jim said, and they moved out.

They were able to follow Highway 290 for about twenty minutes before the water got too shallow for the boat. After that, they ditched it and started walking. It didn't take long before they started hearing the sounds of cars in the distance.

"Eleanor," Jim said, "you think we can stop soon? I don't think I can walk anymore."

It was the heat and the humidity. It was getting to her, too.

"Yeah, I guess," she said. "Cypress is just up the road a ways. Maybe we can find a truck stop and get something to eat."

He just shook his head.

"What?" she asked.

"I don't have my wallet with me. Everything was lost when I lost my backpack. Do you have yours in your backpack there?"

"No," she said.

"Yeah, well, we're pretty much screwed then." He kicked at a pebble on the ground. "Do you at least have any water?"

"No."

"Nothing? No juice boxes, nothing?"

"I dumped all that stuff," she said.

"You dumped it?"

She nodded.

He looked at her then. "What is it? Why are you smiling? If you dumped our supplies, what's in there?"

She took her backpack off and laid it at his feet.

"Open it," she said.

A baffled grin was starting to appear at the corners of his mouth. "What are you up to?" he said as he unzipped the pack.

Then he looked inside, and the smile slid off his face. He reached in, and pulled out a cellophane-wrapped brick of hundred-dollar bills.

"What the . . . ?" he said. "There's . . . there's like forty of these things in here."

"I know," she said. She tried to hold in the giggles, but couldn't quite manage it.

"That's like . . . how much . . . how much is this?" he said, stammering.

She shrugged.

"I think it's about seven million dollars."

Eleanor glanced at Madison. The girl's eyes were wide open and bright.

"Seven million dollars," Jim said. His voice was hushed, reverent.

"About that," Eleanor said. "What do you think? You're the insurance man in this family. Is that enough for us to start our lives over?"

He threw the brick of money into the backpack, and as he sat there on the side of the road, he began to laugh. It was the deep, glorious sound of unfettered joy, the kind of laughter she hadn't heard from him in years. The next instant Madison joined him, and to Eleanor, their laughter sounded like freedom.